traitor

j.f.r. coates

j.f.r. coates

Text copyright 2019

Cover by Ilya Zyor

www.artstation.com/ilyar

Traitor

978-1-922061-69-0

Print Version

J.F.R. Coates

Queensland, Australia

a note from the author

Reborn has gone under extensive rewrites since its initial release in 2015. If you read Reborn before November 2019, then large parts of this book will not make sense to you. Please contact me for information on how to get the updated version of Reborn.

J.F.R. Coates

acknowledgements

This book wouldn't be the same without some very important people who have helped me out in various ways.

My husband is, as always, such a huge support to my writing career, and I wouldn't be able to do what I do without him.

To my family and friends, who have offered their support to me, whether as readers, editors, or cheerleaders. Thank you for all the help!

To fellow writer and friend, Shane Jason Taylor, for your help in crafting Traitor into the story it is. May your red pen never run dry.

To my backers on Patreon. Thank you for your financial support and making my writing a more viable option for the future. Your enthusiasm for my books is a genuine joy to see, and you do more than you realise.

And finally to you, the reader. Thank you for picking up this book and reading it. I truly hope you enjoy it.

J.F.R. Coates

about the author

J.F.R. Coates was born and raised in picturesque Somerset, England, but she moved out to Brisbane, Australia as a teenager. She grew up reading from a young age, starting with Enid Blyton's *The Famous Five* and *Secret Seven*, before finding her calling with J.R.R. Tolkien's *The Hobbit*. Speculative Fiction has gripped her ever since, and now she calls amongst her favourite authors Maggie Furey, Phillip Pullman, and Robin Hobb.

She still lives in Brisbane, where she lives with her husband and – as seems ubiquitous for authors – her two cats.

You can follow her on Bluesky at @jfrcoates.bsky.social, or Facebook at /jfrcoates.

She also has a Patreon, which allows for sneak-previews of what's to come, as well as additional stories that fit in around her novels. All support is always gratefully received. https://www.patreon.com/jfrcoates

J.F.R. Coates

chapter one

The twin stars of Alpha Centauri were still small on the viewscreens of the *Harvester*, but they dominated the attention of everyone on the bridge. Those on the crew who had never visited the Sirius System would never have seen a binary system before. Even Rhys had only seen Sirius and the Pup a few times, and he sat back in his seat in wonder.

To the human-turned-starat captain, it wasn't so much the sight of the stars themselves that filled him with such awe, but what they represented. This was the culmination of both the most amazing and wretched month of Rhys's life. A month ago he would never have imagined he would be drifting in Centauran space, minutes after broadcasting a message of surrender. A month ago he had been human, seething at the loss of his best friend who had chosen to defect from the empire. That had triggered a chain of events that had robbed him of his humanity. Everything he had thought stable and secure in his life had been taken from him, and he was left with almost nothing but a broken body and the loyalty of his crew.

That loyalty had already cost Rhys dearly. His first officer should be standing by his side, but there was no one there. Edgar Scott had given his life for Rhys to escape the clutches of the Vatican in his frantic escape from Terra. Trying to hold back a fresh wave of tears as the thoughts of his first officer's sacrifice threatened to overwhelm him, Rhys looked up to the viewscreens. He blinked away his tears and flicked his ears, then turned to the sensory officers.

"Uh, Miss Pool. Mr Dewson. Why do we have ships approaching and no call?"

"Nothing on the scanners," Pool replied. She didn't look up, but Dewson did.

"Shit," Dewson said simply. He tapped Pool on the shoulder, who finally looked up from her equipment. She blanched, and looked between her monitor and the viewscreens as though unable to believe what the visual cameras were telling her.

A dozen ships approached. They slowly fanned out to spread around the *Harvester*, blocking off any escape route. Rhys had never heard of any ship cloaking itself so completely that it didn't show up on scanners, especially at such close range, but he knew Dewson and Pool wouldn't have missed them on their sensors. Though the ship had taken damage in their escape from Terra, Rhys had been told that had been repaired. The realspace sensors hadn't been impacted by the damage anyway.

Rhys's tail twitched as he rose to his feet. He leaned most of his weight onto his left foot, with his right still unable to take much pressure before pain flared in his leg. He held his weakened arms close to his chest, trying his best not to move them too much. His heart hammered loudly as he waited for a message to come through from the ships. There was a temptation in his mind to ask his weapons officer to raise the shields, but he also knew that would be a bad idea. He didn't want to do anything that might provoke the Centauran ships into aggression. He glanced across to Deborah Simms, but she had turned away from her terminal, hands rested on her lap. The weapons officer wasn't about to do anything stupid without orders.

Finally, the communications officer raised his hand to indicate that someone was in communication with the ship. He held his other hand to his ear and nodded a few times as a nervous buzz of conversation rippled around the bridge. Everyone fell silent as McDonald spun around in his chair to look up at Rhys. "Fleet-Admiral Bosler has requested to speak with you directly."

"Put them through," Rhys said. He stiffened his back and tried to draw himself up to a greater height, but he didn't have much to work with.

The viewscreens flickered, and the image of a human woman in an unfamiliar military uniform emerged above the view of the surrounding ships. Her eyebrow lifted. "I am Fleet-Admiral Bosler of the Centauran Defence Fleet. May I ask who I am speaking to?"

Rhys limped forward so he could be clearly seen. His shoulder twitched as he instinctively started to salute, but he kept his arm by his side. "I am Captain Rhys Griffiths, formerly of Terra."

"I was unaware TIE had changed their policy on starats," the fleet-admiral said. "How did you come by a Terran warship?"

"They haven't, Fleet-Admiral," Rhys replied. He straightened his back, trying to hide the wince of pain as he put too much weight on his leg. "I was once human, and a respected captain of the Terran fleet. Since becoming a starat, my situation changed drastically and rapidly, and I come to Alpha Centauri now because there is no home left for me on Terra."

"Become a...? Interesting," Fleet-Admiral Bosler said. She scratched her nose as she turned her head to one side, clearly listening in on an unheard conversation at her end. She turned back to face Rhys, some of her black hair falling across her eyes. She quickly swept it to the side. "It's not for me to decide whether you have the right to stay here or not. It is only for me to escort you to Centaura. We ask that you surrender yourself to my ship, the *Shield of Justice,* for further questioning. We will dispatch a crew to pilot your ship. Will you comply?"

Rhys nodded. "I will, yes."

"That's good. It makes things much easier. Stand by for further instructions. And remember, any sign of aggression and we will open fire. You will not survive." Leaving her threat hanging in the air, she terminated the contact and her image disappeared from view. The ring of ships around the *Harvester* provided the perfect credibility to her words. Rhys had no doubt that they would be destroyed before they could even fire a single shot.

Rhys sunk back down into his chair. He glanced around the bridge, and he could sense the relief that was spreading through his crew. He was apprehensive about leaving them all behind, but he knew also that he didn't have much choice in the matter. It would be his first time on board a CGP ship, the *Terrestrial Dawn* aside. He didn't really count his brief detainment on the *Dawn*, as that had been a ship that had just defected from the empire. These ships had been built on Centaura. He wondered how different they were.

Rhys looked around his bridge. In his absence he would need someone to take command, but the chain was broken without his first officer. Scott had only been first officer for such a short period of time after his predecessor had been removed from the ship in disgrace. There hadn't been time for Rhys to even consider someone else to step up if necessary. Thankfully, some had stepped up out of necessity. With Scott killed, and Rhys in an induced coma in the medical ward, there had been no one of official authority to guide the ship during the six days through subspace.

"Mr Chekolin, you'll have the bridge," Rhys said, addressing the ship's pilot. "You'll co-operate with their every demand. I don't expect I'll be able to return to the *Harvester* before descending to the planet, so I entrust you to dock her safely. Don't do anything rash, and we'll all be together again on the surface. Good luck."

"Aye, Captain," Chekolin said. He saluted his captain, and the rest of the crew followed suit. Only McDonald didn't address Rhys, but his head was bowed as he was in conversation with someone on the *Shield of Justice*.

Rhys rose to his feet and took a few steps closer to the screens at the front of the bridge. He couldn't take his eyes away from the binary stars. This far out in the system, they were both distant and small. Even the closer of the two was barely a quarter of the size of Sol from Terra. But they were still beautiful. Rhys couldn't wait to get closer to them, and to see the twin stars in the sky from the surface of Centaura.

"Captain?" McDonald said. The communications officer raised his hand to get Rhys's attention. "They're sending a shuttle across. They ask that you be ready to board it once it docks with the *Harvester*."

Rhys nodded and spun around on his toes. His heart started to hammer in his chest again. His tail flicked back and forth as he made a few unsteady steps. The ache in his right leg was more noticeable all of a sudden. He bit his lip and glanced up at the ship's pilot. "She's all yours, Sub-Lieutenant Chekolin. Look after her."

"Will do, Captain. She's in safe hands. Good luck yourself," Chekolin replied. The pilot walked with Rhys for a few steps, but the pilot stopped and turned around next to Scott's former station.

The crew saluted Rhys as he left the bridge. He hurried back down through the ship as quickly as his injured hip allowed. The ship was starting to noticeably cool now that they were able to vent some of the excess heat. Without most of the services crew, the ship still felt eerily quiet. Almost half of those needed to smoothly run the ship had been left behind on Terra, as they had refused to follow their captain into exile from the empire. Rhys didn't blame any of them. He couldn't blame them. Because of him, they would have lost everything. Their homes, their families, and their old lives. He could only be grateful for those who had decided to follow him.

Rhys knew he couldn't delay in getting down to the shuttle bay. He wanted to be there before the shuttles arrived, so the CGP could have no doubt that he was following their requests. His leg protested the quick pace though, and he grimaced as he limped on. He tried to hold onto the wall for support, but almost fell over entirely as he leaned to his right, his arm useless to use for support. He couldn't place any pressure on his hand without his entire arm flaring up in pain. He was glad no one saw him, and he forced himself to stop for a moment to regain his composure.

Rhys was surprised by who met him at the shuttle bay. He had expected his services commander to be one of the first to refuse to remain on the *Harvester*, but Simon Briggs stood by the sealed airlocks. The human turned as he heard Rhys's footsteps on the metal floor.

"Captain," Briggs grunted, looking almost embarrassed to be seen there. "The shuttles are about five minutes away."

Rhys slowly approached Briggs, his head tilted to one side and one ear crooked. Since his transformation, his relations with the services commander had been strained, especially as Rhys had foisted several more starats into his service. "I didn't expect to see you here."

Briggs shrugged his shoulders and turned away again. "Better than staying behind, wasn't it?"

"For me, maybe. I would have thought you would have wanted to stay behind. That you wouldn't want to work on my ship," Rhys said. He flicked his tail as he stood by the service commander's side. The two looked out through the empty airlock. In the distance Rhys could just about see the approaching shuttle.

"You're still my captain," Briggs said gruffly. He stood with his hands behind his back, and didn't once look down at Rhys. "I'm not like Cooper. I don't... I try not to be."

Rhys kept his silence. Briggs had certainly been guilty of abusing his starat workers before, and Rhys, through his neglect, had allowed it to happen. Rhys chose not to bring this up. If Briggs was attempting to apologise for his past behaviour, then Rhys didn't want to discourage him from it.

"I did what you asked, Captain," Briggs continued after a few moments of awkward silence. "I spoke with them. Didn't know they could speak, other than following orders."

Rhys twitched his muzzle. "Truth be told, nor did I. That's why I don't blame you for anything you did under my command. It would be hypocritical of me to blame you, or to accept any apologies from you."

"I've already apologised to them both, Captain," Briggs said. He half-turned away from Rhys, keeping one eye on the shuttle bay. "I don't know if my apology has been accepted, but I have done what I could."

"That's all I can ask, Commander Briggs," Rhys said. He stood a few paces behind the services commander, hands resting limply by his sides. There wasn't much more that could be said between them. Rhys was glad for the seemingly genuine contrition from Briggs. It was too late now for grudges and ill-will to be spread through the crew.

Right on time, Briggs announced the Centauran shuttle was docking to the ship. The services commander focused on making sure it was properly connected before he went to open the airlock. Metal banged against metal, and air hissed as it vented into the airlocks as ship and shuttle joined together.

Eight humans and two starats were inside the shuttle. Rhys noticed they were all armed, and that the humans were all shorter than normal. They barely stood taller than the pair of starats. One human stepped forward ahead of the others and extended his right hand to Rhys. The starat hesitated before offering his in return, and he couldn't help the whimper of pain that came with the human squeezing around his hand. The human withdrew his hand, his face reddening slightly, as though he had only just noticed the bandages wrapped around Rhys's hands.

"I'm Captain Griffiths of the *Harvester*," Rhys said. His hand trembled as it dropped back down to his side, and his voice was tight with pain "I trust everything is as planned."

"Commodore Brent here," the human replied. He gestured for his companions to come forward from the shuttle. "So far, yes. Everything seems normal. You're to take the shuttle back. Fleet-Admiral Bosler will be expecting you. She's quite looking forward to it, in fact."

Rhys nodded and stepped to one side so everyone could emerge from the small shuttle. The two starats took a good look at him as they passed him, but didn't say anything. He was slightly unnerved by their attention. "Commander Briggs can see you up to the bridge. Sub-Lieutenant Chekolin knows you're coming and will be expecting your arrival."

"Once we've seen you off, then we shall follow your commander," Commodore Brent said. He gestured into the shuttle with one hand, his other returning to rest just above his pistol.

Rhys quickly moved into the shuttle, not wanting to give the commodore any chance of using the pistol. He wasn't alone in there. A third starat was waiting inside for him. Her fur was pure white, and her pale, pink eyes seemed to gaze unseeing until they locked on to him. "Take a seat, please," she said. Her voice was breathy, ephemeral. He quickly obeyed, and the airlock sealed closed behind them. The shuttle felt strangely heavy. The air pulled down painfully on his arms, and each movement took that little bit more effort. Gravity pulled stronger at his body than he had ever felt before.

The albino starat moved to the front of the shuttle. She pressed a few buttons on a control panel and spoke into a microphone. "I have him. Departing now."

Rhys could hear the shuttle detach from the *Harvester*, before the gentle rumble of its engines started to carry him away from his ship. The albino starat didn't appear to be piloting the shuttle at all, so Rhys could only assume that it was following an automated path between the two ships. The starat stayed to the front of the shuttle, and Rhys wasn't sure if he was meant to stay away from her. After a couple of minutes waiting in silence, he slowly rose from his seat. He had to fight the oppressive weighty feeling that pushed him down to the floor. The other starat was sat in the front row of seats, her eyes closed and head bowed.

"I'm Captain Rhys Griffiths," he said, hoping to introduce himself to the albino. He realised a moment later that she probably knew exactly who he was already. She was on a mission to collect him, after all.

The starat looked up sharply. "Snow," she said simply. She made no indication whether Rhys was permitted to approach closer or not, and he could only assume she had stated her name. It certainly suited her pale fur colour.

"Nice to meet you, Snow. May I sit here?" Rhys asked, gesturing down to the seat next to the albino. His hand bumped against the seat, jarring his elbow and sending thumps of pain through his arm.

Snow stared up at Rhys with unblinking eyes that seemed to stare right through him. She nodded. "You may."

Rhys sat down by her side, and she immediately darted out to grab hold of Rhys's hand in hers. She ignored his cry of pain as she pulled his palm up to her muzzle and sniffed deeply, before slowly moving along until she reached his elbow. Though alarmed, Rhys didn't pull his hand back, not until he felt her tongue against his fur. He recoiled then and held his arm close to his chest as he leaned away from the albino.

"You have an interesting scent," Snow said, seemingly unaware of the discomfort she had caused. "More like a human than a starat. Most unusual."

Rhys pinned his ears down as he looked across to the other starat. "You know about that? Were you with the Fleet-Admiral?"

Snow shrugged her shoulder. "Know? I don't know. I don't know what I'm supposed to know. I smell human on you. Not on your fur or on your clothes, but on the essence of your very self."

"What does that mean?" Rhys asked. He tilted his head to the side and frowned, suddenly wondering if it would have been better had he stayed in his seat at the back of the shuttle.

The albino starat smiled. "You wouldn't understand if I told you."

Rhys leaned back in his seat and dropped his arms down onto his lap, wincing as even the light weight of his hand hurt his injured hip. He knew he wasn't going to get any answers from the albino starat, so he decided to just drop back into silence until they reached the *Shield of Justice.* He wasn't afforded the opportunity, as Snow reached across to gently brush her fingers against his right arm. "This was a recent injury, wasn't it?"

Rhys pulled his arm out of Snow's reach. He half-turned away from her and cradled his right arm close to his chest. He hunched forward and curled his tail up over his lap. "Very recent, yes," he said quietly.

"I might be able to help with that. If you get past Fleet-Admiral Bosler, then I will seek you out," she said. She placed a hand on Rhys's shoulder, but he shrugged her away. "No one should suffer with limitations of the body like that. Trust me. I of all people know the suffering that brings."

Rhys scoffed, but then he looked back at her. He looked into her pale pink eyes. They didn't move at all, with no small movements as they adjusted and focused on their surroundings. They were completely still. He flicked his ears. "You're blind, aren't you?"

"I see more than you do," she said. She smiled and placed a finger on her lips. "Hush now. We're about to dock with the *Shield*."

"Already?" Rhys asked in surprise. He hadn't expected the journey across to be over so quickly. But sure enough, after only a few moments he felt the rumble of the engines as they slowed the shuttle down. A loud bang followed shortly afterwards, jolting the entire shuttle. Snow didn't move at all, though Rhys almost fell out of his seat. A few rattles and clanks followed, before silence fell on the shuttle again.

Snow was first to her feet. Rhys watched as she walked, trying to find a hint of her blindness, but she walked unerringly. She even stopped by the airlock door and turned to look right at Rhys with her sightless eyes. "Are you coming? The shuttle isn't going back to your ship."

Rhys moved as quickly as his aching leg could carry him. He reached Snow's side just as the airlock opened up again. Instead of the dark interior of his ship, the doors opened out onto a bright, open hall. A semi-circle of further airlocks all faced a flat wall, in front of which stood a dozen officers and officials of the CGP. Again, Rhys was struck by how short the humans were. They were, on average, only about a dozen centimetres taller than the four starats present amongst their number. Like inside the shuttle, Rhys felt like he was being pressed down to the floor by a heavy weight resting on his shoulders.

In the middle of the crowd, Rhys recognised Fleet-Admiral Bosler. He didn't know what was expected of him, whether he should step forward ahead of Snow and introduce himself. Before he could properly decide, the fleet-admiral moved forward herself. "Captain Griffiths," she said. She spread her arms wide. "Welcome to the *Shield of Justice*. You will be under my personal guard until we reach Centaura, where you will be handed over to Major-General Ulrich for debriefing. She deals with all military refugees from Terra."

Rhys nodded and flicked the tip of his tail. He wanted to ask about Aaron Lee, but he decided to save those questions for a more appropriate time. "It's a pleasure to meet you, Fleet-Admiral," he said instead. "I certainly hope to make a good impression."

"We shall see. Come with me then," Fleet-Admiral Bosler said. She waited for Rhys to come up by her side, before turning on her heel. No one tried to cuff him or restrain him in any way, though the men either side of the fleet-admiral closed in to block off any attempt of escape. Not that Rhys had anywhere to run to. He tried not to limp too prominently as he followed after the fleet-admiral.

Beyond the shuttle bay was a mazy network of corridors to Rhys. They were all clean and bright, so much more so than the *Harvester*. They were wider than any corridor or passageway on every empire ship he had been on, though the ceilings appeared lower. Everything felt spacious, like he wasn't actually on a spaceship, though the soft rumble of the engines told him otherwise. The engines grew louder as the ship began to manoeuvre in preparation for the jump to Centaura.

It wasn't long before Rhys was left alone with Fleet-Admiral Bosler. They climbed a flight of stairs which led up to a single doorway, which the fleet-admiral opened with a touch of her hand on a scanner. The door opened up onto a wide balcony. The first thing that grabbed Rhys's attention was the view. Beyond the edge of the balcony were wide screens that showed off the binary stars.

Cautiously, Rhys limped forward ahead of the fleet-admiral. She said nothing to warn him, so he moved all the way forward to the railings that ran around the edge of the balcony. Below him, Rhys realised was the main bridge of the ship. Already he could see the crew was hard at work, but to Rhys's surprise the view of the binary stars drifted out of view as the ship slowly spun around.

"I thought we were going to Centaura," Rhys said uncertainly. He glanced back at Fleet-Admiral Bosler, who had pulled the door closed behind her. She approached the balcony railing and pointed towards a small red spot in the middle of the screens as they stopped rotating. The star was barely bigger than those providing the expansive backdrop of the galaxy, but as Rhys focused on it he realised it was much closer.

"Centaura orbits Proxima Centauri, not Toliman or Rigil," the fleet-admiral said in explanation. She smirked as she looked down to Rhys. "Has the empire forgotten that? Interesting."

"I..." Rhys paused, all confidence taken out of him by that simple declaration. "I can't recall Proxima Centauri ever being mentioned. We only ever mention Alpha Centauri."

"I wonder..." Fleet-Admiral Bosler said, but she didn't clarify any further. Instead she just smiled as she looked down at the bridge, before barking down a couple of orders. "Prepare the jump drives. Launch when locked on."

The ship's engines whined loudly as it made the jump into subspace. The screens flashed to the familiar white, but after a few moments something different happened. Specks of red and black streaked across what was usually an endless plain of unchanging white. At first Rhys thought they were entirely random, but then he realised there was a pattern to them, and they were coalescing into a more regular formation. The specks and streaks whirled around the ship with small tendrils reaching out. Eyes appeared to gaze from the void. He got the impression of something living out there, but that was impossible. There was nothing in subspace.

"Deal with it, Snow." Fleet-Admiral Bosler's voice rung out through the bridge. It snapped Rhys's attention back from the mysterious patterns for just a moment. He looked down to the bridge to see the albino starat standing with her hands outstretched towards the front of the ship. When Rhys looked up again, the distortions were gone. The screens were all white again.

The fur on the back of Rhys's neck was raised. He had jumped hundreds of times in his ship, but never had he seen anything like that before. He didn't know what to make of it, but he felt uncomfortable asking the fleet-admiral about it. He felt like that would display more of his ignorance. It was a situation he hadn't felt in a long time about military matters. He had been confused about his new starat body and the realisation that they were far more than barely-thinking slaves, but on the bridge of a ship he should be his element. He didn't like not knowing something that seemed like common knowledge to everyone else, but it was even worse to draw attention to his ignorance.

Instead, Rhys just stood beside the railings. He wanted to grip onto it for support, but his hands hurt just thinking about trying to squeeze his fingers around the cold metal. He realised he was breathing quickly, and he tried to control that again. His thoughts kept snapping back to those eyes though. Nothing lived in subspace, he tried to remind himself of that. Nothing could live there. It was an empty void. It was emptier than even the vacuum of space.

Abruptly, the screens flickered from white to black. At first, Rhys was worried it was that strange entity again, before he realised they were back in realspace. His ears flicked as he glanced down at the bridge, worried they had been forced to jump back into realspace early, but there didn't appear to be any concern on the bridge below. He then realised what should have been obvious to begin with. Proxima Centauri loomed large on the screens. The star was deep red, a much darker shade than Sol. The star looked large on the screens, but the view wasn't magnified at all. Rhys could tell they were fairly close to the star.

Somehow, they were already there. Rhys knew that journey would have taken over an hour in an empire ship. It should have, at least. The entourage of supporting ships all appeared on the screens around the *Shield of Justice*, and the *Harvester* was amongst them. He knew Chekolin had never piloted the ship so quickly before. Travelling so fast through subspace was too dangerous. Countless ships had been lost before they had found a safe speed to travel through the white void.

Almost lost in the surprise, Rhys noticed a planet orbiting close to the red dwarf. Like the star it partnered, the planet appeared red in colour. Even from their great distance, Rhys could see small pinpricks of light on the dark side.

They had reached Centaura.

chapter two

Centaura appeared to be a large planet. From afar it had a red tinge to the surface, but closer up Rhys could see that there were bright blue oceans on the surface too. There wasn't much green on the surface, though there were some areas to the far north that were a deep, vibrant emerald. There were two major landmasses, separated north to south. Around the equator was a single, unbroken ocean with only a few small islands to break up the endless expanse of blue.

Above the planet was a massive satellite that reminded Rhys of the Star Hub around Terra. It gleamed in the light of Proxima Centauri as it hung above the north pole. As they got closer, Rhys noticed a second, smaller satellite above the northern continent, and then a few more, dotted around between the two continents. He could just about make out a thin tendril running between the planet and each of the smaller satellites. Rhys could only assume they were space elevators that connected them with the planet's surface.

The *Shield of Justice* docked smoothly at the first satellite Rhys had seen, which was the largest of them all. It looked almost as big as the Star Hub. Fleet-Admiral Bosler didn't speak once as her crew worked. From what Rhys could see from his vantage point above the bridge, she didn't need to. Her crew were incredibly efficient, working in tandem together without the need of someone to co-ordinate their actions. Rhys knew his crew were capable of the same, but it was beautiful to watch nevertheless.

Once the ship's engines were powered down, Fleet-Admiral Bosler led Rhys back out from the bridge. He was quickly taken out through the airlocks that connected the ship to the great satellite. Memories of the Star Hub came to the fore again. Clean, crisp corridors curved out of sight in both directions, with massive windows providing a brilliant view of the planet below. Rhys wanted to stop and look, but the fleet-admiral gave him no opportunity to do so. She hurried him on, leading him counter-clockwise around the ring.

As they descended deeper into the satellite, Rhys noticed that there were three more humans following just behind them. He wasn't surprised. He expected to be treated with distrust, but having an armed guard made him feel nervous. His tail puffed up a little, despite his best efforts to control his worry.

Finally, they reached what appeared to be a central hub for the satellite; a massive circular room with the words Network Central written in massive letters around the top of the wall. Unlike the Star Hub, it seemed to be solely dedicated for military use, as Rhys couldn't see any civilians present. Four wide corridors branched off from the great hall. The ceiling was constructed of a transparent material that looked a little thicker and sturdier than glass, letting the dim light of Proxima Centauri in, and giving a clear view of the galaxy above. Between each of the corridors were numerous doors that led to the shuttles, leading both to the surface and the other satellites that orbited Centaura.

The fleet-admiral had a short conversation with a starat behind one of the desks. A shiver had passed through Rhys's spine when he first saw that starat. She wasn't a slave, or a servant. She was an employee. A worker. Rhys wanted to talk to her, but the fleet-admiral directed Rhys to follow her towards the shuttle bay.

They boarded the first shuttle in the bay, with Rhys boarding before the fleet-admiral and the armed guards. The starat was the only one who took a seat, not trusting his leg to support his weight, and he didn't want to try and keep himself upright should he fall. Instinct would bring out his arms to grab onto something, and he knew the pain would be almost unbearable.

"We'll just be a couple of minutes from the Caledonia Station and the elevator down to the city below," the fleet-admiral said. She leaned on the back of the seats in front of Rhys, looking down at the starat with interest. "I'm fascinated to learn more about you, Captain

Griffiths. Even if I won't be directly involved with your integration into Centaura, I will still be keeping an eye on your progress."

"I'm flattered, Fleet-Admiral," Rhys replied. He couldn't meet her eye, and he looked down at his tail, draped across his lap. "I hope I can live up to your expectations."

"I have no doubt you will," Fleet-Admiral Bosler replied with a nod of her head. "You will be a great asset to Centaura, I'm sure."

Rhys simply nodded and kept his silence. He didn't yet know how he would feel serving for Centaura. As much as he knew he was no longer welcome in the empire, it was still his home. He was still Terran in his heart, and he didn't know how long it would take for that to change, if it ever would. If he were ordered to open fire on Terran ships, he didn't yet know if he would be able to carry out such a command without hesitation. He looked down at his bandaged hands. If he were ordered to open fire on Cardinal Erik, then he would have no such moral dilemma.

As the fleet-admiral had promised, the shuttle docked at the second satellite just a few minutes later. Once again they disembarked into a network of wide, open corridors that curved around the central hub of the satellite. This time, instead of delving deeper into the middle of the satellite, they dropped down a few levels to sink to the lowest depths, closest to the planet below.

The corridors were busy. Humans and starats alike walked past as they travelled between the space elevator and the shuttles that took them to the various other satellites. There was a mixture of both civilian and military, but it wasn't long before the fleet-admiral led them through a checkpoint into a secure area that was only for those in the Centauran military. A single flight of stairs sunk down to the lowest point of the satellite beyond the checkpoint, and Rhys soon found himself in a wide, glass-walled room. Two other similar rooms could be seen on either side. Directly in front of them were six doors that led to the shafts of the space elevator.

"This is where we leave you, Captain Griffiths. I am due back at Central for a debrief with my captains," Fleet-Admiral Bosler said. She stepped back to fall into line with the pair of armed guards. "Major-General Ulrich is already waiting for you on the surface."

Rhys wasn't sure whether he was meant to salute. He hesitated a few moments, before providing a quick one. Tensing his elbow so much sent a spasm through his arm, and he quickly lowered it back to his side. The door opened behind him, and he stepped back into the enclosed pod. He tried not to think about the significant drop that was about to follow.

"Until next time, Captain Griffiths. Good luck," the fleet-admiral said. She surprised the starat by quickly saluting him, before the doors closed and sealed Rhys away inside the pod.

There was room for at least a dozen people inside the pod, but Rhys was the only one present. There was only one small window in the elevator, through which Rhys could just about make out some of the infrastructure of the elevator shaft, with a brief glance at the dark sky beyond that. His stomach lurched as the pod began to descend, and through the window he could see the rapid acceleration of the pod as it fell to Centaura. He looked away from the window as a sudden sense of vertigo struck him. It was rare he got to actually see the planet approaching at such an incredible speed, and it unnerved him greatly. Reminded him of some old nightmares he would rather forget.

The entire trip down to the surface took nearly ten minutes. Rhys tried to ignore everything that was happening outside the window, but occasionally his eyes were drawn to the changing colours. For a while everything was red as the pod heated up, and the elevator shook slightly as it descended into the atmosphere, but then everything turned a dark, almost black, blue. Gradually the colour lightened from almost black to a deep twilight azure. Clouds whipped by, before the elevator started to gradually slow. It shuddered and then came to a halt as the view of the sky disappeared. His legs felt heavy and the air weighed down onto his shoulders. He had to lean against the wall for a moment to feel confident in his balance.

The doors hissed open, and Rhys limped out to find himself in a huge room that reminded him somewhat of a warehouse. He was up on a raised platform, where the other elevator doors opened up. Down below was a large, open floor with barriers that zigzagged across the room. It would usually have been an area where people would queue to use the elevator, but for now it was empty.

One starat and two humans were waiting for Rhys. The starat stepped forward and offered her right hand for Rhys. He tentatively returned the gesture, but she barely touched his bandaged hand as she shook it. She wore a uniform similar to the fleet-admiral, but like most starats in the empire she forwent the use of shoes. "Welcome to

Centaura, Captain Griffiths," she said. "I'm Major-General Ulrich. It's a pleasure to finally meet you."

Rhys tried to hide his surprise, but something must have shown as the starat laughed. "You're not in the empire anymore, Captain Griffiths," she said. She gestured for Rhys to start walking. She stayed by his side as one of the guards moved on in front. "You'll find things happen very differently here."

Rhys breathed out slowly. "I can already see that, ma'am," he said in a small voice. He had not been a starat for very long, but he knew that there were very few humans in the empire who would ever tolerate a starat of rank in the military. Only a handful of starats were more than simple slaves, but here was a major-general. Already he could feel some vindication in his choice to flee Terra, if only for the benefit of the starats on his ship.

"Of course we have already heard about you," Major-General Ulrich said. Her tail flicked up a little. "Though you aren't quite what we expected. We didn't believe the reports when they first came through."

Rhys's ears perked up as he looked across to the other starat. "You knew about me? How?"

Major-General Ulrich smirked. "We've had our eyes on you for a long time, Captain Griffiths. Longer than you may have expected."

Rhys didn't have a response to that. He wanted to question it, to find out why they had been watching him, but he didn't want to press them so soon. If anything, he felt a little dizzy that he had been spoken about this far away from home. What they could have seen in him, he wasn't sure. Before the incident with the teleporter he had never once entertained the idea of defection. He had been willing to sever his oldest friendship over the matter with Aaron, and had reconciled the fact they would never see each other again. He wasn't sure he wanted to know the answer to his worried thoughts. He fell into silence as they walked a little further, before the major-general directed him into a small room. The door was closed behind them, and the two guards waited outside.

In the middle of the room was a single table, with a chair on each side. A pair of cups and a pitcher of water were the only things on the table. Major-General Ulrich sat down on one side and gestured for Rhys to take the other seat. He was glad for the seat. The heavier gravity was hurting his already weakened leg. The other starat clasped her hands together and leaned forward to rest her elbows on the table. "So, Captain Griffiths. Tell me your story."

***

Rhys didn't know how long he talked for. He told the major-general everything that had happened to him since his transformation in the teleporters. He held nothing back, detailing just why he had come to be forced to leave the empire. He paused only a couple of times to take a drink of water, his hands trembling as he gripped onto his cup between both palms. All the while, the starat opposite just sat still and nodded occasionally, but never interrupted him, though she did wince when he got to the part about his torture at the hands of Cardinal Erik. She asked to see the wounds to his hands, and she looked slightly nauseous as she looked at his declawed fingertips.

Once he was finally finished, the major-general leaned back in her chair. "That does match our information on you," she said with a nod. She kept her eyes away from his hands. "I am glad you didn't choose to lie. It would have made things uncomfortable for you."

Rhys's ears flicked. "Just how recent is that information, and how did you come by it?"

"We knew you have been held in Mount Cotton, and we knew that you intended to flee to Centaura. We had that information as soon as it happened, though our latest report did not include your injuries. As for our source, they will make themselves known to you. They have our permission to reveal themselves whenever they choose," Major-General Ulrich said.

Rhys's head buzzed with dozens of questions, but he held his tongue. There were forces at work here that went way over his head, and that thought worried and confused him. He was used to knowing exactly what was going on all around. He'd had the trust of Admiral Garter to know more than perhaps his rank would normally have allowed, but here he was powerless and without any channels of information.

"Now," Major-General Ulrich said. She tapped her fingers on the edge of the table. "I believe you are being honest. Our source has already confirmed everything you have said, and they are willing to vouch for you. However, that doesn't mean we can totally trust you yet. You come from a state that purports to be our enemy. Terra has delusions of superiority when it comes to their relationship with us, but even so, we can't have you gallivant around alone and with the same rank and access you would normally be accustomed to. However, I do believe you should be allowed the opportunity to prove yourself."

"That's all I can ask for," Rhys said. Internally he was relieved, but he tried not to let too much of that show. He couldn't stop his tail swishing beneath the table though.

"At the request of our source, you will be granted asylum on Centaura," Major-General Ulrich continued. She pulled open a small drawer beneath the table that Rhys hadn't noticed earlier. She pulled out a small tablet and slid it across to Rhys. "After a period of three months you will be permitted to apply for the Stellar Guard. Should you succeed, you will be returned to your ship. Your crew will be offered the same opportunity."

"And if I don't succeed in my application?" Rhys asked, needing to know what the price of failure was. He glanced down at the tablet, but it was switched off. He left it on the table for now.

"Then you will be free to pursue a civilian life on Centaura, but you will be barred from leaving the planet," the starat warned. "Beyond that though, you will be free as a civilian of Centaura. So long as you follow our rules."

Rhys nodded. "Then I must say, that is a most fair offer, Major-General. I understand I probably didn't have any choice in the matter, but I accept your generous terms."

The starat flashed a quick smile. "You always had a choice. You could set everything down right now and choose to live a life amongst our civilians, but I don't think you're that kind of starat, are you?" She rose to her feet as Rhys shook his head. He quickly stood as well. He tried to pick up the tablet, but even that weight was too much for him to hold, and he couldn't pinch his fingers tight enough to get a grip on it. The major-general pulled out a canvas bag from beneath the table and took the tablet from Rhys, before slipping the bag over his shoulder. "That's for you to keep. It will have plenty of information for you, about Centaura and how things are done here."

"I thank you again, that will be most useful," Rhys said. He felt a little awkward as she adjusted the bag so it hung comfortably over his shoulder.

"We already have accommodation arranged for you and your crew, though this should only be a temporary measure," the major-general explained. She guided Rhys from the small room, knocking on the door first to warn the guards they were emerging. "It will be up to you to find something more permanent when you're settled. Some suggestions and advice on where to look are pre-loaded on the tablet."

"Again, you're too generous," Rhys replied. He was glad for the offer though, as he had been unsure what he was going to do in terms of accommodation while he and his crew settled on Centaura.

Major-General Ulrich laughed. "We offer this to all refugees from Terra. Don't worry, Captain Griffiths. We aren't giving you any more than we would otherwise offer." She led him down a small corridor, further away from the elevators. To Rhys it felt like they were delving deeper into the building as it got a little darker, but to his surprise they came up to some windows that looked outside. It was gloomy and dark, little brighter than twilight on Terra.

A familiar face was waiting for them. The albino starat, Snow, was standing by the windows. She was turned to face out through the windows, but Rhys wasn't sure how much she saw. Her ears twisted slightly as they approached. "So Captain Griffiths passed the test," she said quietly, still facing towards the windows.

Rhys looked behind her, quickly taking in the view beyond. They were high up on a plateau. Beyond the nearby rocky lip, Rhys could see the lights of a nearby city. Hanging in the sky above the city was Proxima Centauri, though whether in early evening or late morning, Rhys couldn't be sure. It didn't produce much light, leaving the landscape in an eerie twilight.

"What are you doing here, Snow?" Major-General Ulrich said. The starat held her hands out to stop the two guards by her sides.

The albino finally turned around. She smiled at the major-general. "I'm to take the captain from here. You may leave him in my care." She beckoned for Rhys to join her, but he remained behind Major-General Ulrich. He wasn't sure who he was meant to take command from, so he stayed with the starat he believed held higher authority.

"On whose orders?" Major-General Ulrich demanded. Her tail whipped up as she stared down the albino, though Rhys had to wonder how futile that was considering the albino's apparent blindness.

"From Amy," Snow replied. She picked at her claws, not even looking in the direction of the major-general with her sightless eyes.

Though no rank was given, Rhys could tell the major-general took orders from this other person, as she immediately stood down. All traces of aggression disappeared from Major-General Ulrich's body, and she stepped aside to leave Rhys with a clear path through to the albino. "Very well," she said tersely. "I trust you'll take him through to his accommodation at Appletree afterwards?"

"Of course. We'll see him safely home, don't worry," Snow replied. She held her hand out for Rhys, who warily stepped forward.

"Don't go too hard on him straight away," the major-general said. She sounded nervous, but she didn't address Rhys at all.

Snow held her hand up to her chest. "On my honour. His body and mind will be safe with us," she said.

Major-General Ulrich snorted, but didn't say anything to contradict the albino. "Very well," she said, before turning to Rhys. "You will get further instructions and information at a later time. I won't be your only contact within the military, but I will be overseeing your integration on Centaura. Your only restrictions on movement are to military facilities – without my explicit permission – or to interplanetary travel facilities. Otherwise, your movement will not be limited. Any questions, Captain?"

"None at all, thank you," Rhys replied. He had many questions, but he wasn't yet sure if Major-General Ulrich was the right person to ask. He didn't want to appear like he didn't know what was going on. Especially not to a superior officer.

"Then I shall leave you in Snow's hands. Good luck, Captain Griffiths," Major-General Ulrich said. She spun on her toes and started to head back the way she had come, with the two human guards following right behind. For a moment, Rhys felt like going after them, but he stayed where he was with the albino by his side. She watched the three leave. At least, she faced in their direction. Rhys still wasn't sure if she could see or not.

The albino waited until the major-general had disappeared back into the dark corridors before she turned to Rhys. "Now that we're free of all the nonsense of the military, it's time to take you to who is really running this show. Come with me."

"You're with the government?" Rhys asked, unsure who else she could be referring to.

Snow laughed. "Them? They only think they know what's going on. No, I'm taking you to someone even better than them," the starat replied. She placed her hand on Rhys's shoulder and gave him a small push to start walking. "I'm taking you to Amy."

***

The base of the space elevator was embedded deep within the middle of a mountain, with the plateau it opened out onto overlooking the nearby city of Caledonia, the capital of Centaura. That was all the information Snow was willing to give, and she fell silent after they got into a driverless car. The albino starat had given the vehicle a destination address, then leaned back in her seat and closed her eyes, hands resting behind her head.

Rhys was not too displeased by the silent company. It allowed him the opportunity to look out the window as the car followed the winding road down the side of the mountain. He was tempted to pull out the tablet in his bag to start learning about what he was seeing, but his wrists and elbows ached when he started to move his arms. Instead he kept his focus on what was going by outside the car. The city gleamed bright in the soft light of Proxima Centauri. Surrounding the city were rows upon rows of greenhouses that stretched as far as Rhys could see. After they merged onto a wide highway, Rhys saw nothing but the greenhouses for over ten minutes before they finally gave way to the suburbs that surrounded Caledonia.

Small sparks of light above attracted his attention. He squinted his eyes and looked up into the deep blue sky, pressing his cheek against the car window to better see. Tendrils of light snaked across the sky. For a moment he was reminded of the mysterious colours he had seen in subspace, but these sparks followed a strict, orderly pattern in a web of even squares. He couldn't see where they originated from, or how far they spread. He wanted to ask Snow about them, but he didn't know if she would be able to see them.

Rhys leaned back into his seat and looked forward again. They were getting closer to the city now, so close that the tall skyscrapers of Caledonia were starting to touch Proxima Centauri. The star loomed so large in the sky, yet provided so little light. Even so, Rhys couldn't look up at it, but he did notice a pinprick of light not far to the right of the giant red disc. It looked like a normal star, but then he realised that it was actually two, and that they appeared much closer than any star would normally be. That had to be the binary Alpha Centauri system.

Closer to the surface, Rhys noticed the lattice of sparks and light suddenly flare brighter. It pulsed out from above city and extended out in a great web that travelled beyond the distant horizon. Rhys frowned and glanced across to his companion. Snow's fur had raised slightly, especially around her neck.

"Prox is restless today. That's the fourth flare in the last couple of hours," the albino said quietly, without looking up.

Rhys only just heard her, and he leaned forward to catch anything else she may have said, but Snow fell back into silence. "Prox? The star?" Rhys asked, but Snow didn't answer. He sunk back into his seat and looked up to the electrical lattice in the sky. "Oh. It's a shield, isn't it? Electromagnetic, I'd say."

Snow still kept her silence, but Rhys was sure he was right. Now that he had associated it with flares from Proxima Centauri, he recognised it clearly now. It was an electromagnetic shield that dissipated the energy from the red dwarf's flares and activity. The planet had to have its own magnetic field, but clearly it wasn't enough to keep life secure and safe on the planet's surface. He wondered how it had been created. As far as he knew, there was no such technology available in the empire, or else they would have long ago colonised Mercury. He had to wonder what other surprises Centaura had for him.

The great highway gradually thinned out as several roads branched off, leading into the various districts of the city. Their destination appeared to be right in Caledonia's heart, and Rhys watched out the windows with interest. The streets were packed, and thousands of pedestrians walked on the wide footpaths beneath the thin shadows of the buildings. There were more humans than starats, but the ratio looked much closer than it had ever done on Terra. What was more, the starats appeared to be workers like the humans, and not subordinates. Starats in business suits looked strange to Rhys, but he was happy to see it. Once again, Rhys was struck by how short the humans appeared to be.

On the footpaths was disorganised chaos, but the roads themselves were smooth and orderly. Every vehicle Rhys could see was driverless, and they followed set tracks in the roads. Rhys noticed different coloured lights in each lane, and it didn't take him long to work out what each meant. Green allowed the car to accelerate, amber to slow them down, and red to stop entirely. It was an electronic dance of colour and movement, and it all worked with incredible precision. Rhys had never seen anything quite like it.

As he was admiring the incredible display, their car turned off the main road and down a ramp into an underground carpark. The artificial lighting was brighter than the natural light from Proxima Centauri, and for a moment it dazzled Rhys's eyes. The car parked up in one of the empty bays, and Snow embarrassed Rhys by helping him open the door when he fumbled with the latch a few times. She kept her hand on his shoulder as she led him back outside.

The first thing that struck Rhys was the warmth. Despite the poor light, the air was hot and sticky, reminding him of the temperature in Australia. Almost immediately he could feel sweat plastering his fur to his clothes. His tail twitched in distress, ears pinned down to the top of his head. He could barely walk beneath the heavy air, and his leg ached with every step. His ribs felt like they were about to crack again as he breathed in.

"Just a short walk," Snow said. She tugged on his shoulder and pulled him out amongst the crowd. He was almost knocked from his feet as a human bumped into him, only able to stay upright because of Snow's hand on his body. The human grunted out a quick apology, but was soon lost in the maelstrom of bodies.

The albino didn't seem to suffer at all in the crowd. She was easily able to sidestep through the crowd, walking with a confidence that belied her sightless eyes. She never stumbled or seemed to lose her way, and once again Rhys had to doubt his initial impression that the albino was blind. She confidently led him to the steps of one of the tallest buildings in the city. A name ran down the side of the building in massive red lettering. Jennings.

Snow opened the wide glass doors at the top of the stairs, letting out a blast of air-conditioning that chilled Rhys's fur. She held the door open for him, and he hurried inside, glad to be out of the heat so soon. Inside was a wide open lobby with a small reception right in the middle of the room. A balcony ran around the room close to the cavernous ceiling.

Three receptionists were sat behind their desk in the middle of the room; two starats and one human. Both starats were taking calls, but the human was free and he held up his hand as Snow pulled the door closed behind Rhys.

Rhys shivered as he walked across the lobby. The air was cold, and he felt the stares of a few people as he walked up with Snow. He hunched his back and held his bandaged arms close to his chest. He felt like his injuries were attracting some attention, and he wasn't sure he liked all the eyes on him. He was still used to humans glaring at him in hatred. He was self-aware of the clack his claws made on the smooth tiled floor. Even though Snow and every other starat around were making the same noise, he felt like his thundered around the room.

"Is this him?" The human looked over the two starats with interest as he tapped a pen against the desk.

Snow nodded and gave Rhys a little push forward, so he was standing slightly in front of her. "Is she ready to see him?" the albino asked.

"Soon. She's just finishing up another meeting," the human replied. He let the pen fall from his fingers with a clatter as he checked something up on his computer. "I wasn't expecting him to be needing so much work."

"Nor was I," Snow said testily. Her hand fell away from Rhys's shoulder.

Rhys's ears folded slightly as the tip of his tail twitched. "Are you talking about me?"

Snow waved her hand to brush Rhys's protests aside. "He's worse than I thought he would be, but we'll fix him up just fine."

"What do you mean by that?" Rhys asked, slightly alarmed. He wasn't sure if he liked being talked about as though he wasn't there.

"Has he shown any abilities yet?" the human asked, still speaking as though Rhys couldn't hear them.

"Not yet, but I can sense they're there, just waiting to be unlocked," Snow said. Again, she placed her hand on Rhys's shoulder and gave him a little push. A small flare of pain shot down his arm, but he hid the grimace quickly. "Should we wait down here, or can we go up already?"

"Head on up. I'm sure you don't need anyone to show you the way," the human said after a brief pause to check his computer.

"I know the way, thank you John."

Tightening her grip on Rhys's shoulder, Snow pushed him around the reception area in the middle of the massive foyer. She pushed him towards a row of elevators along the back wall, which were all separated by some potted plants, the likes of which Rhys had never seen before. They were vaguely reminiscent of ferns, but their oily red leaves were unlike any Terran plant. Rhys wanted to stop and look at them for a moment, but Snow bundled him into a waiting elevator.

Snow pressed a button to take the elevator up to one of the highest floors in the building. The elevator started to move with a sudden jolt that had Rhys leaning against the wall for balance. His hand knocked against the metallic wall, making him wince in pain. He regained his footing as he got used to the slight swaying of the elevator as it rose.

"So, who exactly is it we're seeing?" Rhys asked, trying to break the silence with Snow once more.

Rhys was surprised when the albino actually answered. Partially. "Her name is Amy," Snow replied. She flicked her tail and turned around to face Rhys. "What she does, she can explain better. What she is though, is your key to a good life on Centaura."

"I thought I had already been offered that through the military. Why is Amy any better than what they can give me?" Rhys asked in surprise.

Snow laughed. "They're offering what they can. Simple. Basic. It's a living, if that's what you want." She grinned at Rhys, her unseeing eyes staring right at his. "What Amy is offering, is to pull back the veil and teach you things you didn't even realise you never knew."

Rhys frowned and gently scratched an itch on his thigh. The pressure on his soft fingertips made him clench his jaw. Without any claws to protect them, everything felt tender and sore. He shifted his hand, instead rubbing against the itch with the heel of his palm, but that didn't do much to make it go away. He swished his tail and tried to ignore it as the elevator shuddered to a halt.

The doors opened to a small foyer. The room was lined on the two side walls with couches and small tables. On the opposite wall was a large double door with a small desk just to the side. A single starat was behind the desk, and he hurried out to meet them.

"Oh, is this him?" the starat asked, his voice bright and eager. He looked strange in a formal suit. The bright tie he wore didn't match the suit at all.

"This is him," Snow replied. "Is she ready yet?"

"Not yet," the starat replied with a shake of his head. "She's seeing another new recruit. Take a seat though and help yourself to the tea and biscuits. Or would you perhaps prefer a coffee?"

Rhys shook his head as his ears curled up. "No, thank you. Tea will be fine," he said. He started to move towards the couches, but paused and looked back to the starat. "Why is everyone expecting me? How do you all know who I am?"

The starat held a hand to his chest. "Don't worry, it's nothing sinister, I promise you that. I'll let Amy explain everything though. That's more her area. I'm Mortimer, by the way. If you do need anything, just give me a yell."

Mortimer retreated back to his small desk, leaving Rhys to make his way to the couch and sit down. Snow crunched loudly on some of the biscuits that filled a plate on the table, but Rhys didn't reach for any. His arms ached too much to even move them. He felt almost like crying in frustration. He didn't know how he was going to be able to manage anything when he could barely use his arms at all. Most of his muscle had been eaten away by the poison he had been forced to endure by Cardinal Erik, and Doctor Sparks had given him little assurance that it could be rejuvenated. He didn't know how he would cope with that. He stared down at his skeletal, clawless fingers and sighed.

Rhys squeaked in surprise as he felt a hand on the back of his shoulder, tearing his mind away from his dark thoughts. He looked back to see Snow had shuffled across to sit right next to him. She wiped at his eyes, which Rhys was alarmed to realise were wet.

"She'll fix you," the albino said quietly. She held a biscuit up to his muzzle, practically forcing it between his lips before he opened his mouth to bite down on it. The albino starat smiled. "And then I'll make you better."

Rhys quickly swallowed the biscuit and leaned back as far as he could. "I beg your pardon?" He licked a few of the crumbs from his lips.

"We can fix you," Snow repeated. She moved away from Rhys again, sitting on the far end of the couch with her feet up. She grinned again. "All your hurts and aches. Your weaknesses. They can all be gone."

Rhys leaned back into the soft cushions of the couch and looked down at his arms. They were little more than bones wrapped in skin that had yet to regrow any fur. "How?" he asked the albino. He shook his head slightly. "More importantly, why? Why would she help someone she's never met before? What does she want in return?"

Snow waved her hand in his direction. "Don't worry about the why for now," she said. "As for the how? Amy's been pouring money and research into cybernetics and limb restoration tech for years now. She's the only person on this planet with the resources and the contacts to give you what you need, when you need them."

"You didn't say what she wanted in return," Rhys said tersely.

"She will ask for less than anyone else would ask for," Snow said. She reached back and snapped her fingers. Seemingly in response to her actions, the large double doors behind Mortimer's desk opened.

Rhys didn't look towards the doors. Questions still swirled around his head. Snow's answers had only given him more to ponder, but he looked up just in time to see a familiar face disappear behind the elevator doors at the far end of the room.

"Aaron?" he asked in confusion, his voice little more than a strangled whisper. He jumped from his seat, but the doors were already closed, and human was gone.

A small corner of Rhys's mind was sure he'd imagined it, but his legs shook as he sunk back down onto the couch. His tail had puffed up as his heart thudded loudly in his chest. He was sure it had been Aaron. He would always know that face, but in the very brief moment their eyes had locked, there had been no recognition in his best friend's eyes. Aaron wouldn't know him anymore.

Rhys felt like he had been punched in the gut, before his whole body went numb. He barely even noticed as Snow tugged on his arm.

He swayed on his feet as the albino pulled him up off the couch, before she patted him across the muzzle. "You can speak to him later," she said quietly. She pulled him on the arm again to lead him on. In a daze, Rhys followed after Snow and Mortimer through the double doors.

A single starat waited for them. She stood with her arms folded behind her back, facing out towards the many windows that let in as much light as the weak Proxima Centauri could manage. From the window was a view of the entire city. Towering skyscrapers dominated most of the close terrain, but beyond the small buildings of the suburbs stretched out almost to the horizon. The twinkling of light on a river was just about visible to the distant left, as were the mountains and the space elevator in the opposite direction.

The starat was dressed in a simple t-shirt and running shorts. As she turned around, Rhys noticed her ear was pierced with a diamond stud. Her coffee coloured fur was brushed pristine. She spread her arms wide and smiled warmly. "Welcome to Centaura, Rhys. I do hope Snow has been a good companion." Her ears flicked, and the corners of her mouth twitched in amusement. "Please, take a seat and get comfortable. I'm sure you have plenty of questions, but let me explain things first, alright?"

Rhys nodded as he was guided to one of the seats in front of Amy's desk. The chairs were clearly designed for starats, as they had large holes in the back for a tail to slip through without being crushed or trapped in some way. Rhys settled down in it and realised just how uncomfortable he had been sitting down since his transformation, with the compromises he'd had to make for his tail.

Snow sat down by his side as Amy took the seat on the other side of the desk. She leaned forward and clasped her hands together, elbows resting on the desk. "How familiar are you with our history? Even Terra can't have forgotten the early days of the Centaura colonies."

Rhys frowned and scratched at his leg with his foot. "I know Centaura was settled peacefully at first, but then they demanded their freedom from the empire and started attacking trade routes," Rhys said, but he was stopped by a raised hand from Amy. Both she and Snow shared a quick laugh with each other.

"Is that the story they're telling?" Snow muttered beneath her breath. "Bastards."

"That's not quite what happened," Amy said, hiding a smirk beneath her hand. "It's true that Centaura was settled peacefully, but the young colonies were refused permission to gather their own resources. Instead they were required to purchase goods and food from Terran sources at massive costs. It took a few years, but the Centauran colonies believed this to be unfair, and started to ignore those orders and began local industries and farmlands."

"That simple act started a war," Snow added. She growled softly beneath her breath and clenched her fists together. "Terra sent dozens of ships to land massive armies on Centaura. They outnumbered the colonists five to one. It would have been slaughter."

"But there was one thing Terra didn't consider," Amy continued. "That Centaura would allow starats to fight by their side. Suddenly the fight was not so one-sided, and with the help of their starat allies, the Centauran humans were able to push back the Terrans. Since then, no Terran army has been able to get close to our planet. And not a single trade route was attacked."

Rhys sat in silence as he tried to digest that. It completely contradicted all he had ever been told about the origin of the war that had plagued Terra for almost two centuries. He had never once doubted the story he had been told, but hearing a contradictory tale from two starats suddenly threw a new light on everything. He shuddered and looked up at Amy. It sounded so real. So plausible. He couldn't help but believe it. "What else was a lie?"

"Almost everything the empire is built on is a lie," Amy said. She gestured a lot as she spoke, and Rhys had to stop focusing on her hands a few times. "It structures itself around two things: the war with Centaura, and the morality and divine truth of the Vatican. Both of these are lies. What do you know about Veritas?"

"He was the son of God, reborn on Terra," Rhys replied. He had learned all about Veritas when he was younger, almost before he learned how to read and write. Everyone in the empire learned it. The words spilled from his tongue with ease. It was a doctrine that had been told to him countless times. "He was martyred just after Centaura was settled, but his death set about a wave of renewed religious belief, as well as the near total eradication of all other dissenting religions. It was his death that brought the Vatican back to a position of power, after centuries of eroded respect."

"It was a con. A deceit," Amy replied. Even though Rhys knew there was no one from the Vatican around, his still let out a little squeak of fear, his eyes flicking around the room just to make sure. He had known people to be taken away to the Vatican vaults for much less. If the starat noticed his reaction, she didn't comment on it. "We have records that show the man known as Veritas was actually called Matteo Birghitti, and that he was a carpenter in Rome. Fitting, I suppose, given his alleged predecessor. But still a fraud. He was paid a fortune by the Vatican, and after they faked his death he lived a life of luxury and anonymity in Geneva. It was all an elaborate lie by a desperate religious order trying to regain relevance in an increasingly scientific world. It worked on Terra, but on Centaura the renewed fervour never got a strong grip."

Rhys swallowed. His throat felt dry suddenly. "If it was so easy to work out, why didn't more people on Terra protest?"

"They did," Amy said tersely. "Unfortunately, enough people wanted to believe, and they ignored the evidence that contradicted this belief. It was bloody. There were thousands who died. Soon it became a crime of blasphemy to doubt the Vatican, and as the empire gave them more and more power, it soon became dangerous to speak out. They've had two centuries to consolidate that power now. Two centuries to repeat the lie so often that now I think even they have forgotten it's not true."

Rhys shook his head and looked beyond Amy. He stared at the building opposite, looking at the reflection of Proxima Centauri rippling against the glass. "What does this have to do with me?"

"We know a lot about the empire. We have spies throughout the two systems, but getting detailed and accurate knowledge out is difficult," Amy said. She clasped her hands together again. "Even harder is getting a real imperial insight into that knowledge. We don't know how someone from the empire would really react, and to that end we've been recruiting a few imperial refugees. As both a starat and captain, you offer an even greater insight."

"I haven't been a starat for long," Rhys reminded them.

"No, but the experience would still have opened your mind to how starats are treated there. There are few in the Terran military who can claim that," Amy replied. She reached out and placed her hand on his arm. "You can offer us more than you know. And in exchange, we will fix the damage the Vatican did to you. We will make you better than before."

Rhys sighed and bowed his head. "What are you even trying to do?"

"Make life for starats better," Snow said. She put her hand on top of Amy's. "You want that, don't you, Rhys?"

"I do," Rhys whispered. He didn't know what he was getting into, but he knew that he needed to help starats in the empire. He had vowed to improve conditions for them, however he could. If Amy and Snow were working toward that, then he needed to offer his help if he could give it.

Amy beamed widely. "Then the Starat Freedom Union is for you. Let's get you measured up for your new arms. Trust me, Rhys. These will be better than what you had before."

"New arms?" Rhys yelped in surprise. He hugged his arms close to his chest and whimpered slightly in pain. "What do you mean, new arms?"

Amy leaned forward and gently took hold of Rhys's hands, taking care around his clawless fingers. "These are no hands to do hard work with. They have been crippled and ruined, and can't be made whole again," she said, looking up into Rhys's eyes. "But we can remake them so they are better than they ever were. Our cybernetics are better than anything you could have dreamt of in the empire."

Rhys pinned his ears down. "I'm... not sure I am comfortable with that," he said uncertainly. He pulled his hand away from Amy's, tucking them close to his chest. "You can't do anything with what I already have?"

Amy twitched her muzzle and glanced to Snow. She scratched behind her ear and sighed. "No. I can see already there is nothing to be done with them. They are damaged beyond repair, and I doubt the muscle will ever recover. Should you keep them as they are, then they will forever be weak."

"Never recover?" Rhys asked, a shudder passing down his spine and into his tail.

Amy shook her head. "It's not the first time I've seen this particular torture method. I doubt it will be the last either," she said, before tapping her claws against her desk and pursing her lips. "I understand you may be apprehensive about this. That is only natural. But what we are offering you is a wonderful opportunity. Both for you to continue your service in the military, and to better your quality of life with arms that could actually do something."

Snow grinned and turned her sightless eyes towards Rhys. "It's not like you've had those arms long, is it, Captain Griffiths? Hardly any time to grow attached to them."

Rhys pursed his lips and stared down at his hands. The albino was right. They hadn't been part of him for very long, but even through all the bandages that wound around them, they still looked like his. He had grown used to this starat body, accepted that it was his own. He didn't want to change that again.

"We can give you some time to consider it, but we can't wait too long," Amy explained. She sat back down behind her desk and clasped her hands together. Rhys couldn't help but get the impression he had disappointed her. "We have plans in place that could involve you, but for that we would need you to be strong and capable, which you currently are not."

"What kind of plans?" Rhys asked, his ears flicking up in curiosity

Amy waved his question away. "Right now, they are not plans we trust you with knowing. The Union requires a little secrecy in order to keep its missions secure and our operatives safe. There are ears and eyes everywhere, even here, who would see us fail. When the time comes, we will let you know what we intend to do."

Rhys nodded his head. He was disappointed, but not too surprised by the answer from the other starat. He was a stranger here, and they couldn't know if he could be trusted. He knew he would have to build that trust, especially if they were offering him a way to help improve life for starats back in the empire. He didn't know how they could possess the influence for that, but Amy appeared to have plenty of power on Centaura.

"No matter which choice you make today, we will be in regular contact with you," Amy said. She held one hand out towards the albino starat. "Snow will be assigned to your crew as a minder, so I will always have a way to speak with you. She will be helping you integrate into Centauran life, as well as preparing you for the work I have ahead for you, and perhaps some of your crew too."

Rhys glanced up. He tried to rest his hands on Amy's desk, but he dropped them down to his sides after a few moments. "If you're willing to offer the same thing to my crew, then there's one who needs some help more than me. He lost a leg, and has been suffering with an inadequate replacement ever since. I promised I would find a way to help him."

"Snow will evaluate everyone. If he will be of assistance to us, then we will offer him the same that we have offered you," Amy said.

Rhys nodded his head again. The tip of his tail quivered. There was a part of him that wanted to just accept Amy's offer right away, but he couldn't be sure that she was right. There had to be some hope that he would be able to recover the use of his hands again, so he didn't want to go through something so drastic right away. He needed time. He hadn't had the chance yet to properly speak to Doctor Sparks about his chances, and he didn't yet know if the military could offer him something similar. There was so much new information being given to him that he was feeling overwhelmed. He didn't want to make any important decisions in that mindset.

"I will give you some time to think about it," Amy said. She rose back up to her feet and rested her hands behind her back. Her long, thick tail curled around her right leg. "Snow can take you to your accommodation, and she will keep her eyes on you."

Rhys looked across to Snow, who had her back to them as she stood facing the windows. He bit back a comment about her not being able to see, still not fully convinced that was the case. She didn't seem to use her eyes to navigate around, but she moved with total confidence. Rhys didn't know how she did it, and didn't expect an answer should he ask. He turned back to Amy.

"Thank you so much for this opportunity, and I will think hard about your offer," he said. Out of instinct, he held out his hand to shake hers. He immediately regretted the decision, but the other starat was gentle as she held hers out. Even the gentle touch sent a spike of pain through his wrist.

"You could be a great help to Centaura, Captain Griffiths, if you stay with us. There will be other powers looking to get their claws on you, but stay by my side and you'll do well," Amy said. A steely glint had entered her eye, but she didn't elaborate on who else she thought might try to use Rhys. He knew to keep his mouth shut for the moment and just nod.

The starat gestured for Rhys to go back through to the main office. Amy and Snow followed right behind him. Amy called for Mortimer to come in, and immediately opened the double doors and poked his head through. "Snow and Rhys are all finished here," Amy said to her assistant. "If you could show them out and see if Stephen is ready for that meeting."

Mortimer bowed. "Of course. Rhys, why don't you follow me?" the starat said. He held out the tray of biscuits to them. "Are you sure I can't convince you to have another one?"

This time Rhys did take one of the biscuits, though it hurt his fingers to even hold it. He tried to keep the pain from his body language as he turned to face Amy one last time.

"Thank you again. William will most appreciate your kindness. And for what you offer me, I'll have to think on it. But I thank you for the offer. I don't know how I would repay you," he said. He bowed his head towards her before she returned back into her office.

Amy smiled and nodded her head back, but it was Snow who answered. "You'll repay us more than you could ever know. You'll end this, once and for all."

chapter three

Snow took Rhys back out of the city. For a while, Rhys thought they were heading back towards the space elevator, but they turned off the main highway before they reached the wide band of hydroponics farms that surrounded Caledonia. They descended into a maze of suburbia, but their automated vehicle never once got lost. Rhys was surprised at how many people walked, emerging from a significant number of public transport hubs. Again, about half were starats.

There wasn't much difference that Rhys could see in the architecture of the houses compared to those back on Terra. But for the eerie twilight and the occasional flash of light from the electromagnetic net above, he could well have been on the outskirts of any empire city. He glanced up to the sky, where a few stars were visible. He wondered if any of them was Sol. He had never felt so far away from home and what was familiar, but he didn't go quite so far as to regret his decision. He had already seen advantages here for starats, and he had been given opportunities to settle as well.

Rhys's attention came back down to the surface when he noticed the low-set houses were broken up by an area of five-story apartment blocks. These larger buildings were separated from the rest of the suburb by a gated wall that ran around the entire complex. It appeared that these were their destination. The car pulled over to an empty spot on the side of the road opposite the front gate, and Snow instructed Rhys to get out. Once again, Rhys was struck by the sudden heat of the evening air, and he twitched his muzzle and tail in disgust.

Snow swept her hand across to the cul-de-sac of apartments. "There are blocks like these throughout the city. They're owned by the military, and are used for temporary accommodation for military refugees," the albino starat explained. "One block for each crew. One has been set aside for the *Harvester*, so you're all still together. And me. You get to deal with me as well." She grinned widely, before waving her hand for Rhys to follow.

The albino opened the gate with a passcard, before leading Rhys across to the third apartment block on the right of the narrow street. The road was lined with plants, and a small garden grew between each building. The tallest plants looked like some kind of tree. Woody stalks gave way to wide, red leaves. They reminded Rhys of palm trees, but for the curious, tendril-like appendages on the edge of the leaves. The tendrils drifted in the gentle wind that did little to dispel the cloying heat.

Another swipe of Snow's passcard opened the front doors to the apartment. Rhys was glad to get back out of the warm air outside, and when he stepped into the building he was struck at how similar to a hotel lobby the ground floor was. But for the two starats, no one was present, but there was a closed cafe to their left, and an unmanned help desk to the right. Rhys flicked his tail and approached the desk. There was a pile of leaflets stacked to one side of the counter, but the rest was completely empty. He picked up one of the leaflets, noticing that it listed some of the tourist attractions around Centaura. He tucked it into the bag that still hung from his shoulder.

Rhys limped after Snow as she crossed the lobby floor. She led him up one flight of stairs, and Rhys gingerly held his hand on the banister as he ascended behind the other starat. The stairs led onto a narrow corridor that stretched out on both directions, but it was the door directly opposite that Snow wanted. She used a different passcard to open the door.

Inside were three rooms that only increased Rhys's impression of a hotel. The first room was a little sitting room with an attached kitchenette, and that led through to the bedroom and the bathroom. The bed looked wide enough for four starats to sleep on, and a quick glance into the bathroom revealed a plethora of towels and two hair dryers stacked by the sink. It was simple, but Rhys knew he would be comfortable in those rooms.

"I trust this meets your satisfaction," Snow said. She wandered ahead of Rhys, running her hand around the wall as she walked through the bedroom. She occasionally paused to hold her hand to her twitching muzzle.

"It does, yeah," Rhys said. He crouched down in the kitchen, opening the fridge in the kitchenette. A few basic supplies were already in there, as well as a bottle of wine. "This is all for me?"

Snow turned to face him. "This is all yours. Your crew all have something like this each, though the wine is a little something extra. Your last privilege as captain, before you're a civilian for three months," Snow said. She grinned and swished her tail. "Everyone will start arriving when they get through security vetting. Should take them another few hours as we have less information on them, and we rushed you through to meet Amy."

"And she said you'll be staying with us?" Rhys asked. He hadn't considered the fact that he would be effectively a civilian until he applied to be a part of the Centauran military.

"I'll be two doors down. Close at hand in case you need any help."

Rhys was glad of someone to help them ease into all the different changes on Centaura, but he wasn't sure he enjoyed the prospect of having Snow so close by all the time. He tried to ignore her blank stare as he found himself unnecessarily interested by the kettle in the kitchenette. His mind burned with so many questions, but he couldn't work out what to ask first. His thoughts kept drifting back to Amy, and to the earlier chance sighting of Aaron.

Overwhelmed with so many thoughts in his head all competing for attention, Rhys turned away from the kettle and slowly slunk towards the bed. He sat down on the soft mattress and put his bag down by his side. He pulled out the tablet, before tossing it on top of the bag. He stared at the switched off screen. His face reflected in the dark surface. For just a moment he expected to see his old, human self there. He didn't know what had brought on that expectation. It had been a long time since he had even thought about his human face. He was comfortable in his starat body now, so much so that he was scared of accepted the artificial augments Amy was offering him. Cold metal and carbon fibre would hold none of the warmth of flesh. He didn't want to be human again. He just wanted to be as he was now, but without pain any time he tried to move his hands.

Then there was Aaron. Rhys still couldn't be sure if it really had been his friend in Amy's office. He knew Aaron had to be around somewhere, but he had not been expecting to run into him so soon. That was a meeting he both longed for and dreaded. To look into Aaron's eyes and see no recognition…

Snow perched on the edge of the bed. "It is natural to have so many worries right now, Rhys," she said. She reached out with one hand, almost resting it on Rhys's knee before he shuffled further away. Her hand fell to the mattress and remained there. "That human we saw, Aaron Lee. You were close to him, weren't you? Would you like me to arrange a meeting?"

Rhys blinked in surprise. "No, thank you," he said uncertainly. He started to move for his tablet again, before looking up at the albino starat. "How do you do that?"

"Do what?" Snow asked, her usual grin on her face.

"You always seem to know what I'm thinking. I've never known anyone who can do that. Not even Aaron could, and he knew me best," Rhys said quickly. He knew that the CGP had been spying on him, gleaning information on his actions, but no amount of research could have accounted for the knowledge Snow seemed to have on him.

Snow shrugged her shoulders. "I look and I see. It's not that hard, when you know how. So. Aaron. Are you sure you don't want me to talk to him?"

Rhys shook his head. He doubted he was going to get any better answer out of the albino. "No, thank you. Just tell me where I will be likely to find him. I'll go see him on my own time," he said. He knew he would have to go soon, but he wanted to be the one to decide when it happened.

"A good choice," Snow replied. "I am sure there is a lot Aaron Lee no longer knows about you."

Rhys looked down at his body. His tail was draped across his lap, and he slowly stroked it with his skeletal fingers. "Just a few things, yeah," he said quietly. He honestly had no idea how his friend would react to the news that he was no longer human. He could only hope that Aaron of all people would accept it. After all, Aaron had had a starat on the bridge of his ship. It wasn't like Aaron could ever be another Captain Favre, who had never attempted to disguise his disgust at the new starat.

Snow's ears twitched, and she looked up sharply towards the door. Rhys felt a prickle of fear run down his spine and into his tail. His fur fluffed up as the albino jumped from the bed and stalked across the room. He didn't know what the starat had heard, but she seemed perturbed by it. He got to his feet and tentatively followed after her, catching sight of the door the moment she opened it.

There was no threat beyond, but a familiar human looking in. Doctor Sparks held up his hand and waved. "I was told I would find you here, Captain. May I come in?"

Snow stood in front of the doctor, not allowing him to take a step forward. She took hold of his hand and held it to her muzzle for a few seconds. "I don't know you."

"It's alright Snow, I know him," Rhys said quickly, trying to ease the mind of the albino.

Snow sniffed at Doctor Sparks's hand again, but she stepped aside after a moment to allow the doctor to come through into Rhys's room.

"You got through quickly," Rhys said. He stepped back and fell back onto his bed. He tried clenching his fingers a few times, but couldn't tighten them much before they started to hurt too much. "Snow said you'd all be a few hours still. Is everyone else here?"

"Ah, no, not yet," Doctor Sparks said. He pushed the door closed behind him and scratched behind his neck. "I didn't need any clearance as I, well. I already have it."

Rhys's eyes narrowed, then opened wide as he realised the true meaning of the doctor's words. "You? You're the..." Rhys trailed off for a moment. Given what he had done, it wouldn't sound right to accuse Doctor Sparks of being a traitor against the empire. He finished the sentence lamely. "Source? Major-General Ulrich said there was a source of information on me. That's you?"

Doctor Sparks sucked in his breath, then exhaled slowly. He leaned against the wall. "I've been an agent for Centaura for just over five years. I've been feeding them information about the empire and, more specifically, anyone who could be a future asset for Centaura to exploit."

"That's how long you've been on my crew, isn't it?" Rhys asked. The hint of a growl emerged in his voice. A tingle of electricity ran up his left arm. "Was this… was this all planned?"

"Getting you to Centaura was the long term goal, yes," Doctor Sparks said, but he held up his hands to stop Rhys's outburst before it happened. "The incident with the teleporter was not. I just want to make that clear. That was a complete accident, but it did give an opportunity to exploit. I had hoped you would follow Aaron without much nudging, but that proved to be an incorrect assumption."

Rhys sunk back on his bed as he tried to process all of that. He rubbed his right arm as an insidious thought delved into the back of his mind. Slowly it wormed its way forward. Coldness spread through his limbs. "You spoke with Aaron before he came to Ceres?"

"Before, yeah. Haven't been able to since as he doesn't have the clearance to directly speak with anyone in the empire, but he shouldn't be far away," the doctor said, but his words faltered as Rhys's tail twitched. The starat's hands clenched, despite the cracks his weak tendons and joints made, and his ears folded in fury.

"You…" Rhys gasped. He felt faint as everything he was accused of at Mount Cotton came rushing back to him. He held up his arms and snarled. His hand was still clenched in a tight fist, even through the agony it was causing him. He felt like his muscles and tendons were on the verge of breaking completely. Doctor Sparks recoiled. "They did this to me because of you. They knew someone was sending messages between the *Harvester* and the *Dawn*, and they thought it was me."

"That's not possible," Doctor Sparks said. He backed away from Rhys, only to bump against the wall. "We were careful. They were untraceable."

"Well they had them anyway," Rhys snarled. He weakened his clenched fists and cradled his quivering hands close to his chest. "It should have been you they questioned, but they refused to listen to me. I told them it was someone else, but they thought I was lying. Because I'm a starat."

"Captain, I'm sorry," Doctor Sparks said. His words sounded dull and hollow to Rhys's ears.

Snow interjected before Rhys could reply. "You are not there anymore, Captain Griffiths. No one will ever ignore you because you are a starat again." The albino sat down on the bed beside Rhys and she gently held his hands in hers, her touch soft enough that she didn't hurt him. "Those burdens are no longer for you to bear. We are treated with respect and equality here. You've seen that already."

Rhys hissed and turned his face away from both Snow and the doctor. He pulled his hands away from the albino and wiped his eyes with them, shamed to realise there were a few tears there. His tail thumped against the mattress. "I know you didn't mean it," he said. He sighed and looked up at the doctor. "And I know I never experienced it my whole life, but you will never know what it was like to be a starat there."

"No, I won't," Doctor Sparks said with a shake of his head. "But like this one said, you aren't in the empire anymore. You won't be mistreated. They can help you in ways that were never possible on Terra. I can make it better, I promise you."

"How can you make it better?" Rhys said. His voice felt a little hoarse, and he struggled to clear his throat.

Doctor Sparks grimaced and scratched the back of his head. "I admit, I don't yet know, Captain. But I promise you, I will do all I can to repair the damage that cardinal did to you. Given that it was my actions that led you there... I can only say sorry and hope that fixing your arms will make up for it."

Rhys flicked his ears. "Snow said they can't be fixed."

"Are you a doctor, Snow?" Doctor Sparks asked, turning his gaze towards the albino starat for a moment.

Snow shook her head and smiled. "I am not. I specialise in cybernetics and a few other exotic fields of research. But by all means; use your surgeon's knives on him. I'll be waiting to repair what you have broken further."

Doctor Spark frowned slightly. "If you say they can't be cured, then I guess that's your opinion. But I want to look over him first, alright? He's my captain, and it was my stuff up that got him like this."

Snow scoffed, but she didn't say anything.

Rhys pinned his ears down and looked away. "I know you didn't intend for any of this," he said quietly. "If you can fix it, great. But even if you can't, your apology is still accepted."

"Thank you, Captain. I truly did not mean for any of this to happen as it did. All I knew was that Centaura were interested in bringing you out here, and then… shit just happened," Doctor Sparks said. The human put his hands on his hips and sighed. "I've got an interview at the hospital soon. I'll see if I can fit you in for an appointment soon. Sound good?"

Rhys nodded. "Sounds good, yeah."

The doctor held out his hand for a moment, before dropping it back down. "Won't shake your hand just yet," he said with a nervous chuckle. "But I promise you, Captain. I will get this sorted. I'd better be off though."

"I'll see you later then," Rhys replied. He forced a smile to his face, but he was still disturbed by the doctor's revelations that he had unwittingly been behind Rhys's torture. He followed the doctor to the corridor and waved goodbye, before closing the door behind him. He turned to find Snow standing right next to him.

"I shall leave you alone as well," Snow said. She held out a passcard and waited for Rhys to take it from her. "Keep this on you. It will let you through the front gate, and into your room should you leave. Aaron Lee is living in the apartments directly opposite. Same room number as you. I don't expect him to be back home for another ten hours though, so don't go until then."

"Thank you," Rhys said. His ears curled up slightly as a flutter of fear passed through his body at that information.

"The doctor can't save your arms. Only Amy can," the albino said as she opened the door. She didn't look back as she stepped outside. "I would hate to see you in more pain because of your doctor friend."

The door closed before Rhys could reply. With a sigh, he turned back into his apartment. He had been given so much to think about, he didn't know where to begin in order to start breaking it all down. Rhys slipped out of his clothes and hung them up in his empty wardrobe, before collapsing onto his belly on the bed. The soft light of Proxima Centauri bathed over his fur as he stretched out his limbs.

Three months of civilian life loomed over Rhys. It had been years since he had been off active duty for so long. He'd received three months of compassionate leave almost fifteen years previously, but since then had almost worked without break, with only a few holidays with Aaron amongst it all. Already he was getting nervous just thinking about it.

He rolled over onto his back, flicking his tail out of the way, as he reached for the tablet by his side. He supposed he may as well use the spare time he had wisely and learn more about Centaura. There was certainly going to be a lot of information to take in. He switched the tablet on and got to work.

***

It had been just over a month since Rhys had last spoken with Aaron, but so much had happened in that time. How could he possibly hope to explain everything that had happened since that meeting in orbit above Ceres? Rhys knew he couldn't put it off though, but as he waited outside Aaron's apartment, he couldn't pull up the courage needed to knock on the door. He could hear someone inside, but he just leaned against the opposite wall, almost paralysed with fear.

To make matters worse, Rhys had slept poorly. He had waited for Prox to set before attempting to sleep, but he hadn't realised the red dwarf lingered in the sky for so long. It still hadn't reached the horizon, almost fourteen hours after he had first touched down to the surface of Centaura. As far as he could tell, clocks were still run to a Terran-style time of roughly twenty-four hours days, but these were not linked to the spin of Centaura around Prox. It wouldn't take him long to adjust, but it had thrown him off to begin with.

His brief sojourn outside had been an unpleasant one. The temperature had increased further, and fewer people had appeared on the streets. He was glad of the powerful climate controls inside all the buildings, as he didn't feel like he had just stepped out of the shower just by walking around. At least he had been able to change to civilian clothes that didn't feel like they trapped heat against his fur. A delivery of some of his belongings from the *Harvester* had interrupted what little sleep he'd managed. He had yet to see anyone else from his crew, but he had heard the activity in the apartment block to know they had arrived.

A door opened and closed. Rhys's ears flicked up at the sound, but he didn't look up. The door wasn't Aaron's, so it wasn't any of his concern. Footsteps approached and stopped just in front of him.

"Can I help you?"

Rhys looked up at the vaguely-familiar voice. A human woman stood in front of him, and it took a few moments for him to recognise her as Aaron's first officer, Lieutenant Carter. She had been the one to escort him through the *Dawn* when Rhys had been accidentally captured in Aaron's brief raid on Ceres. Naturally, she didn't recognise him. She wasn't dressed in military gear, instead favouring a simple shirt and a short skirt.

"That's Captain Lee's apartment, isn't it?" he asked, pointing towards the opposite door.

"Yeah, were you waiting for him?" Carter asked. Before Rhys could give an answer, she had already knocked on the door. Rhys froze in alarm as he heard a muffled reply from his friend. Carter spoke a little louder to talk to Aaron through the door, though Rhys couldn't make out the responses. "Did you know you've got a starat out here waiting for you? Yeah, he's just out here. Not sure." She flashed a smile at Rhys as she addressed the starat again. "He'll be out in a moment."

"Thanks," Rhys said in a strangled whisper. It had been taken out of his hands, but deep down he thought that was for the best. He couldn't back down now.

"Anything else I can do for you?" Carter asked.

Rhys shook his head. "No, that was all, thank you."

"Then I'll leave you be. If he doesn't come out in a couple of minutes, just knock on the door again," Carter said. She took a couple of steps towards the stairs that led to the ground floor, before pausing again. "Who are you, anyway?"

"Just an old friend," Rhys replied. That answer seemed to appease Carter, as she just nodded her head and descended down the stairs. For a moment, he almost felt like following after her, but before he could move anywhere the door opened and Aaron stepped out. He was dressed in a smart shirt that looked similar to his military uniform, but it was still one of the few times Rhys had seen his old friend in civilian clothes.

"Hi, you were waiting for me?" Aaron asked. There was no recognition in Aaron's face at all, and that hurt Rhys. He had been expecting it, but it still made him falter.

"Can we talk in private?" Rhys asked quietly.

Aaron stepped to one side and gestured to Rhys, welcoming him into the apartment. Rhys barely looked up at his friend as he walked past. Inside the apartment looked almost identical to Rhys's rooms, with just a few personal effects providing the differences. A couple of pictures were hung up on the wall, and Rhys felt like he was punched in the stomach as he recognised one of himself with Aaron. It had been while they had enjoyed some shore leave in New Zealand nearly ten years earlier.

"Are you alright? Did you want to take a seat?" Aaron asked as he closed the door behind them. Rhys gratefully sat down on the offered sofa, while Aaron sat down opposite him next to the dining table. The human frowned slightly as he looked down at Rhys, hands clasped in his lap. "You look scared. Is something the matter?"

Rhys shook his head and took a deep breath. "I'm in the apartments across the road. We got here yesterday," he said, trying to keep his vice from trembling.

"Refugees from Terra?" Aaron asked. He leaned back and smiled. "Welcome to Centaura, I guess. We've only been here about a month, but it's been... quite the change. What ship did you come on?"

Rhys looked up at Aaron and stared him right in the eye. "The *Harvester*."

Aaron leapt to his feet like an electric current had passed through his chair. He stumbled back, almost falling over before he caught his balance with an outstretched hand against the wall. "Rhys is here? Where?" He didn't even wait for an answer before he made for the door, but Rhys quickly jumped up as well and tried to position himself between Aaron and the exit.

"Wait, Aaron. You need to listen to me first," he said. His tail trembled and his ears were flat against his head, but he puffed up his chest and tried to make himself look as big as possible, but in front of his old friend he felt so small.

Thankfully, Aaron didn't try to force his way past. Instead the human took a step back as his face tightened with fear. "What's happened to Rhys?"

Rhys leaned back against the door. His tail tucked up between his legs. "There was an… incident with some teleporters. The ones on Ceres are utter shit, and, well. It did something that wasn't meant to be possible."

"Where is this is going?" Aaron asked. His voice wasn't unkind, but it sounded impatient. He shook his head and sunk down into the seat Rhys had just vacated.

"The teleporter lost my genetic information, Aaron," Rhys said. He almost couldn't force the words out, but once they started the others came easier. "It gave me the body of a starat. You won't find Rhys over the road, because he's right here, Aaron. I'm him."

Aaron had gone still, and Rhys fell silent to let the human process what he had just been told. "You say you're Rhys," he said after a long pause. He spoke slowly, each word carefully considered. "Even though you look nothing like him. Sound nothing like him. I'm sorry, but how am I meant to believe that?"

Rhys pointed to the picture of Aaron and him on the wall. "It's been a month since I last saw that face. I used to see it all the time, but now it's like looking at a stranger," he said, before clenching his jaw. He turned aside from the smiling human face. "We had that photo taken outside Christchurch. We'd gone skiing, but you spent most of the trip with your new girlfriend. Jenny Taylor was her name, I think. You met her on the first day of that trip. Whatever happened to her? I don't think you mentioned her since."

"Jenny Taylor…" Aaron muttered. His eyes darkened as he lowered his head. "She thought it would be funny to punch a starat until he fell to the ground. Then she kicked him a few times. I was so ashamed by the incident I never spoke to her again. And I never mentioned her to anyone. No one but Rhys."

"Shit, you never told me about the starat," Rhys said, appalled. He sat down on the sofa next to Aaron. His tail draped across his lap, and he gripped the hand rest as tightly as he could before it started to hurt.

"I didn't," Aaron said. Rhys couldn't be sure whether Aaron believed him yet, but at least he wasn't denouncing him. Rhys kept staring down at his lap.

"Why not?" Rhys asked, before he answered his own question with a sigh. "Because I would never have cared. I didn't care about starats at all, but that was why you left, wasn't it? I should have known. There was a starat on your crew, when I last saw you."

"He..." Aaron started to say, but his voice choked up in a sob. The human placed a hand on Rhys's shoulder. "It really is you, isn't it?"

"It's really me, yeah. This is me now," Rhys said. He was then surprised as Aaron pulled him into a tight embrace. His feet left the floor, but thankfully Aaron's arms slipped beneath his, so they weren't pinned to his body.

"I can't believe it," Aaron said. He squeezed Rhys in his arms, his head resting on the starat's shoulder. He laughed loudly as he pulled back, the doubt fading from his eyes and replaced by sheer wonder and delight. "I never thought I'd see you again. I dreamed that you'd follow me, but I never thought you actually would."

Rhys's ears perked up and he shook his head. "I don't think I would have done so, if this didn't happen," he said, gesturing down to his body. "I still barely believe it, really. Everything all happened so fast, but now I'm here and I think I made the right choice."

"Caledonia is an interesting city, and Centaura is beyond anything I could have imagined. I think you'll like it here," Aaron said. There was a slight tightness to his smile that disappeared so quickly Rhys wasn't sure if he imagined it. He then laughed, the humour chasing away the momentary concern. "I won't lie, this is not how I imagined I'd see you, even in my wildest dreams. You're a starat, I just can't believe it."

"Trust me, nor can I," Rhys replied with a chuckle. He rubbed the side of his muzzle and flicked his ears up, feeling almost bashful as Aaron looked over him. "It was difficult to adjust, and I still get confused sometimes, but I'm getting there. Really made me think hard about how I'd been treating starats too."

"You took your time there," Aaron said, laughing softly. "I was never comfortable talking about it though, not even with you. I was always worried what the Vatican would say about it, but here... they really don't have any influence on Centaura at all. You'll be amazed how much they hold the empire back, and not just about starats. Your arms, for example. You can get that fixed up. I know some people who can help you."

Rhys flicked his ears, head tilted slightly to the side. "I've already spoken to Amy Jennings. I'm considering her offer. I... saw you there, briefly, but I was too scared to say anything."

"I... I didn't see you, I'm sorry," Aaron replied with a shake of his head.

"Wouldn't have done you any good. You wouldn't have known it was me anyway," Rhys laughed in reply.

"Very true," Aaron muttered. "So were the arms part of the teleporter incident too?"

Rhys shook his head and gripped hold of his tail as tightly as he could. "No, that was afterwards." His ears pinned back as he looked up at Aaron, holding out his hands so the human could see the extent of the damage to them. "Let's just say there was a lot of resistance to a starat serving as captain. I was handed over to the Vatican, and I was very lucky to get away. It could have been so much worse, but once I was rescued I knew I couldn't stay in the empire. We fled as soon as possible, with everyone who was still loyal to me. Except for one, who I lost." He bowed his head and closed his eyes for a moment.

Aaron grimaced. "I'm sorry, Rhys."

"He was a good man. A great one. More than I realised, most of the time," Rhys said. His throat felt like it was closing up, and he found himself leaning into Aaron's arms. "He died to save me from a worse fate."

"We'll remember him, Rhys," Aaron said. He patted Rhys on the back of the head. "I'm sorry you had to go through all of that. Makes my escape feel like a clean break. But trust me, it will be better for you here."

Rhys sniffed and took a deep breath to clear his throat and mind again. He nodded weakly. "I'm sure it will be. You're here, after all."

Aaron got up from the sofa and crouched down in front of the fridge in the kitchenette. He pulled out a bottle of chilled white wine and held it out for Rhys. "I'd been saving this one for a special occasion, and I don't think anything is more special than this. I know it's still early, but do you want a glass?"

"I'd never turn down a drink with you," Rhys said with a weak smile. As Aaron pulled out a couple of glasses, Rhys inspected the bottle with interest. It was a Terran wine, from a vineyard Rhys didn't recognise. To have brought it so far must have made it a special bottle. He was glad Aaron still felt highly enough of him to share such a bottle with him. He poured a generous portion for each of them, and they tapped their glasses together.

"To a prosperous future," Rhys toasted. He could barely lift the filled glass up.

Aaron held his glass up and gazed just above Rhys's head. "To a free future."

***

Rhys's head was buzzing as he made his way back across the road. In part it was from the wine, but he was also thrilled that he had been able to talk to Aaron again. It had felt so natural, so normal. It was like they hadn't been apart. So much had changed between them since their last friendly meeting on Mars, but despite all of that they had been able to laugh and drink together as though everything was as it had always been.

Rhys couldn't recall a time where he had been so filled with genuine happiness, and he couldn't keep the smile off his face as he pushed open the doors into the apartment block he now called home. This time, the lobby area was a little busier, with a few of his crew sitting down by the small cafe, which was now open. A group of around a dozen from the services crew sat together with coffee as they chatted amongst each other. None of them looked up to see Rhys, but he paused for a moment to just stand and watch. He was too far away for even his sensitive ears to hear exactly what was being said, but he was glad to see that they all appeared comfortable. They had all chosen to join him on Centaura, and he couldn't see any regrets amongst them.

After a few moments, he moved on. He wanted to read up more on Centaura, fascinated by the history and the structure of the planet. There had been interesting titbits of information that suggested that Amy and Snow had been telling the truth when it came to the history of the great war between Centaura and Terra. At first, it had made

Rhys's stomach uncomfortable with the idea that he had been living a lie, but it had quickly descended into a morbid fascination to know more.

Rhys wasn't given that opportunity though, as there were starats waiting for him at the top of the stairs. He didn't have the chance to brace himself before he was knocked off his feet by an excited Twitch, who wrapped his arms around Rhys and barrelled him to the floor.

"Hi, Captain Rhys! Did you miss me? Oh, I didn't hurt you did I? How are the arms?"

"Of course I missed you, Twitch," Rhys said with a laugh. He slowly pushed the starat off him so he could clamber back up to his feet. He winced slightly as the impact had jarred his sore hip, but it was nothing he couldn't walk off again. He held out his arms to show Twitch he hadn't damaged them any further than they already had been. "They're as well as they can be. I was taken to meet this starat in the city though. She's offered to give me two new arms, if I wanted them."

"New ones?" Twitch said with a gasp. "You mean you'll become a robot? That's so cool!"

The other starat waiting for Rhys cleared his throat and stepped forward. "And what about me?" William asked.

Rhys flashed a small smile towards the other starat. "I asked her. She said she needs to evaluate you first, to see if you can help her. She didn't say what it means, but if you pass her test, she will give you a new leg."

William blinked in surprise. He bowed his head, seemingly trying to hide the smile on his muzzle and tears in his eyes. "Thank you, Captain Rhys," he said in a strained voice. "I really do appreciate that."

"I hope it works out for you," Rhys replied. He reached out to gently place his hand on William's shoulder, unable to provide any more pressure than just a delicate touch. "I still don't know what to do with mine."

"Why haven't you accepted her offer yet?" the starat replied, his ears flicking curiously as he looked down at Rhys's damaged arms.

Rhys sighed and dropped his hands down to his side. He turned away and shook his head. "I don't know. I think I'm scared about it. About becoming something different, again."

"I know why you might be scared, Captain Rhys. But at least you have the choice," William said, placing his arm around Rhys's waist. Twitch sidled up to Rhys's other side, also leaning against the starat.

Rhys sighed and closed his eyes. He felt comfortable, at least. Despite all his aches and pains, he knew he had friends who were willing to help him through the tough choices. They were friends and adopted family now, as they went through a time of turmoil together. But for Doctor Sparks, no one really knew anything about Centaura. They would have to learn together.

"Have you seen the sun?" Twitch asked, cutting into Rhys's thoughts as the starat slowly took Rhys's hand back again. "Though I suppose it's not the sun, is it? Not Sol? It's a different star, and it looks so big. It's weird, isn't it? Why are all the trees red too? Aren't they meant to be green like they were on Terra? We never had any trees on Ceres, so I don't know what's normal." Twitch's questions spilled from his mouth too quickly for Rhys to answer each one, so he just let the starat empty his curiosity first.

By the time Twitch had finished, Rhys had entirely forgotten what the first question had been. He laughed and shook his head. "Has he been like this the entire time?" he asked William. The other starat sighed and rolled his eyes, giving Rhys the answer he needed.

"You should have seen him when he realised he was being given a bank account," William said.

Twitch whooped in delight, squeezing Rhys tightly in an embrace. "I'd forgotten about that. They gave me a bank account. I can have money of my own," the starat said, his words spilling over into each other. "Though they were saying lots of stuff is free anyway, so I won't be needing the money for much, but I would still have it. It's so exciting. I've never had any money before."

Rhys wriggled his way out of Twitch's tight embrace, wheezing slightly as he struggled to regain his breath. He was always amazed at Twitch's strength, especially when it came to giving hugs. "That's great," he said weakly, having to lean against the wall for a moment. He rubbed his ribs and grimaced.

"Hey Captain Rhys, can we see your room? It's probably really fancy because you're the captain, isn't it?" Twitch asked. He tugged at Rhys's hand and pulled him away from the wall, though he quickly relented from Rhys's whimpers of pain. Rhys didn't have much choice but allow himself to be led across the corridor. He swiped his card to open the door, and Twitch bounded inside. Rhys and William followed behind. Twitch's ears sunk as he looked around the series of rooms. "Oh. It's all the same. Who do you have next to you? I have William one side, and Leandro on the other."

Rhys felt cold suddenly. "I don't know," he replied. He sunk down on the couch and tucked his tail up close to his legs. "It would probably have been Scott."

Twitch's face fell. He dropped to his knees in front of Rhys. He held Rhys's hand in his own and squeezed as tight as he could. "I miss him."

"Yeah, me too."

"He did his duty," William added. He sat down beside the other starats, his leg held stiffly out in front of him. "I know it makes it no easier to accept, but that's war, isn't it?"

"It's war, yeah," Rhys said quietly. He closed his eyes and gently touched his hands to his cheeks. "And the life of a starat too, wasn't it? Always afraid your friends are going to be taken away or killed."

Twitch placed his hand on Rhys's knee. "That's just what we were used to. Never made it easy."

Rhys's muzzle flicked into a brief, sad smile. "At least we got you out. It's a start."

"But not where it finishes," William added, the touch of a warning growl coming into his voice.

Rhys raised up his hands. "I know. It won't finish here. I don't yet know which will be the best option to take, but either through Amy Jennings or through the military, I will ensure that we still fight for everyone we left behind."

"I know you will, Captain Rhys," Twitch said brightly. He pulled himself up onto the couch with Rhys and William. He leaned against Rhys and gently stroked the captain's shoulder. "Won't he, William?"

On Rhys's other side, William sighed. "I have more faith in you now than I did before, I'll give you that, Captain." He paused for a moment and frowned. "I don't know if you'll listen to my advice, but I think you should go and see what this Amy person is offering. Snow spoke to me earlier, and I like what she said, though she didn't mention anything about my leg. I got the impression she was evaluating me."

"Though she is very creepy," Twitch added.

"She's holding something back, I agree," William said with a nod of his head. "But all the same, she's offering something real and tangible here. Has anyone else offered you that?"

"Not yet. Everything is a few months away at least if I stick around and wait for the military," Rhys admitted. He tapped his foot against the floor. "It wouldn't hurt to see what she has to say, at least. And she is doing you a big favour with your leg."

"And your arms, if you let her," William said.

Rhys spread out his bandaged hands. "I don't know there. I'll wait until Doctor Sparks has told me there's no saving them as they are."

Twitch drummed his fingers against Rhys's thigh, making him wince in pain as Twitch's fingers came down on his injured leg. "Ooh, sorry Captain Rhys," Twitch said, pinning his ears down as he grinned nervously up at the captain. "Did you know Doctor Sparks was a spy?"

"Not until yesterday," Rhys replied with a grimace. "Some of the things I was accused of in Mount Cotton suddenly made a lot more sense. I wasn't being held just because I was a starat. There actually had been a real threat against the empire."

"More than just a starat captain?" Twitch asked with a giggle. He clapped his hands together and grinned. "A few more days and the entire empire would have collapsed from such a travesty."

"If only," William said wistfully. The starat leaned back and smiled as he idly toyed with his prosthetic leg. "Still, Captain Rhys. I think you should at least hear what this Amy has to offer you. Sounds like it's more than anyone else at the moment."

Rhys flicked his ears. "You think I should?" he asked the two starats by his side. He had already reached for his tablet, which he had left on the coffee table just within reach. He pulled it closer, tensing in pain as he did so.

"I think so, Captain," William said.

"Me too," Twitch added.

Rhys took a deep breath and nodded. "Alright then. I'll let Snow know. I'll meet with Amy again and hear what she has to say." He switched on the tablet and prepared to make the call, but before he could do so it chimed with an incoming notification. A message from Snow was waiting for him.

"Good choice. I'll see you tomorrow morning. Sleep well."

A shiver ran down Rhys's spine and tail as the albino once again displayed some eerily prophetic powers that he simply couldn't explain. He glanced to the two starats either side of him. "I wish she's stop doing that," he muttered quietly. Neither William nor Twitch disagreed with him.

chapter four

The sun had finally set. Rhys had woken up to a nearly-complete darkness outside, though there was still a significant orange glow on the western horizon. He was used to waking up with the setting of the nearest star. Life on Ceres had often involved waking up with the setting sun, as the small dwarf planet spun almost twice as fast as Terra. Here was the opposite. Centaura spun so slowly that each day was significantly longer than those Rhys was used to. Now that he was aware of the mammoth days, he knew not to try and stay awake while Prox was in the sky.

Of course, Proxima Centauri was so weak that it didn't make too much difference to how bright it was. Instead of a soft twilight, everything was reduced to complete darkness. Few stars were visible in the sky, drowned out by the light pollution from Caledonia. The Alpha Centauri binary stars were by far the brightest. Rhys still didn't even know where to look to find Sol.

Rhys had spent most of his morning trying to recover from another poor night's sleep by lounging around his room. He had his tablet switched on, trying to learn more about Centaura, but he couldn't properly focus. He wasn't yet sure why he had been sleeping so poorly. He had travelled around the Sol System enough to quickly adapt to new sleep cycles that the slow movement of Prox shouldn't have been an issue.

Rhys could only hope that he wouldn't come to regret his decision to meet up with Amy and Snow again. He knew what they were offering: a potential way back into service, quicker than he could achieve with the Centauran military. He didn't know if he could sit on his hands for the several months Major-General Ulrich was suggesting he wait.

Snow had sent through a message when she intended to pick Rhys up, and though that time was nearing, Rhys hadn't moved out of bed except to quickly make himself a cup of tea. He was still sitting up in bed when he heard someone knock at the door, precise to the second when Snow said she'd be there. After rubbing his eyes and stifling a yawn, Rhys finished getting dressed. He struggled to get his tail through the right hole in his trousers, and he was still fumbling with the button by the time he opened the door.

As he had expected, it was Snow waiting for him outside. She had changed from her military-style uniform. Instead she wore a plain white shirt and running shorts. She flashed a quick smile. "Ready to learn about the Starat Freedom Union?"

"About as ready as I'll ever be, I suppose," Rhys replied. He pulled the door to his apartment closed behind him. Twitch, William, and Leandro were waiting a little further down the corridor. The grey-furred starat had been invited to join them by Snow. They weren't waiting for anyone else, and Snow led the group of starats outside the estate, where an automated car was ready to transport them away.

At first, Rhys had thought they were going back to the Jennings offices again, but instead Snow took them through the city and out the other side. Twitch spent most of his time excitedly pointing out anything that was different to Ceres, which was almost everything. He squealed in delight as the shields above the city flared bright as they absorbed radiation from Proxima Centauri.

The far side of the city was much the same as the area around Appletree, with a wide ring of suburbs eventually giving way to hydroponics farms. However, this time the farms didn't seemingly go on forever, as they were cut off by a wide river not too far beyond the outer reaches of the city. A towering bridge carried the highway over the torrents below. The highway continued on, winding between the low hills in the distance, but they turned off onto a small side road not long after the bridge reached the far side of the river.

At the end of the road was a small network of buildings. A large warehouse was the biggest of the six, while the other five all appeared to be homes, though as Rhys got a closer look he realised one of them looked more like a shop.

As they got out of the car, Rhys noticed the air was much cooler without Proxima Centauri in the sky, though the heat hadn't completely dissipated yet. Snow led them towards the large warehouse. William stayed up by the albino's side as he limped along, while Leandro and Twitch hung back with Rhys. The albino hadn't clarified any further about where they were or what was planned for them. Rhys's tail flicked nervously as they approached the looming warehouse.

The front door of the warehouse led into a small reception area. Windows inside showed off a factory floor beyond, which appeared to take up most of the space inside the building. Rhys couldn't tell what was being produced, but there was certainly activity in there.

The factory floor wasn't their destination though, as Snow led them through to a different room. A few tables were scattered around the room, with chairs circled around them all. A projector hung from the ceiling, pointing towards the blank wall on the far side of the room. Rhys was immediately put in the mind of a classroom. They also weren't the only ones present.

Four other starats were already in the room, as were two humans. Rhys flicked his ears in surprise as he saw Aaron chatting with a starat with almost pure black fur. Rhys tried to get Aaron's attention, but he was too focused on the conversation with the black-furred starat, who seemed vaguely familiar to Rhys. He couldn't place where he had seen the starat before. The starat had a strange headband that was visible through his fur. It was dark and matte in colour, almost perfectly blending in beneath his fur.

Rhys settled for sitting at the same table as Aaron, with Twitch and Leandro sitting by his sides. William took a seat with Snow at the front of the room, both still in conversation with each other. They muttered quietly as they spoke, so much so that Rhys couldn't make our any of their words.

"This all seems unusual," Leandro said quietly. The grey-furred starat leaned forward in his seat, resting his hands across the table. His ear had folded in a little as he looked around the room and those who had been gathered together.

Before Rhys could answer, the door closed behind them. Rhys looked back, and his eyes widened as he recognised Amy. He placed his hand on Leandro's. "That's her. She offered to replace my arms, and give William a better leg."

Amy smiled at Rhys as she walked past. She didn't stop until she reached the front of the room, before she spun on her toes to face everyone. All conversation immediately died at her presence.

"Welcome to my home and workshop. I've spoken to most of you in person, but for those few who haven't met me, I'm Amy Jennings," the starat said. She looked around the room, and her eyes lingered on Rhys and Twitch for a few moments. "You are all here because I believe you have got what it takes to help us. Either Snow or I see potential in you, in some capacity."

"What is it you do?" Rhys asked. All eyes turned to him. Amy smiled.

"I'm glad you asked that, Captain Griffiths. We have many goals, but fundamental to our cause is seeing that no starats suffer under imperial rule on Terra. You're all here from the empire. You don't need me to tell you how bad it gets for starats over there," Amy replied. She looked around the room as all attention returned to her. "What we do is not officially endorsed by the Centauran government. They are aware of us and our goals, and they give us enough liberties without treading on our tails all the time."

Aaron drummed his fingers against the table. "If this isn't permitted by the government, will it have any impact on our asylum claims?" he asked. "I've been here a month now, nearly. I'd hate to be arrested or sent back to Terra because I got involved with some fringe organisation."

Amy held out both her hands, palms extended to the group. "I swear to you all now, being involved with me will not hinder your asylum in any way. However, if anyone is uncomfortable with that fact, then you may leave now. No hard feelings."

No one moved. Rhys's eyes flicked towards the door for a moment, but he stayed firmly on his chair. His tail curled around the leg as he rested his arms on the table.

Amy clapped her hands together. "Wonderful. That means we can continue with our plans," she said. Her smile grew a little wider. "We'll be splitting off into two different groups soon, as some of you will be staying with me, and others going with Snow. What we will be learning here are things you will never have known on Terra.

Forbidden knowledge. Banned knowledge. The stuff that would have gotten you killed in our old lives. Isn't that exciting?"

Rhys wasn't sure if he agreed with exciting. A chill did run down his spine as he looked up at the starat. Her teeth were bared in a savage grin.

Amy wasn't finished. After giving her words a few moments to sink in, she continued. "I know some of you, especially most of the starats, will never have had any formal military training. Some of you will be learning how to shoot and how to act in combat situations. The rest of you will be with Snow for some more interesting lessons. All of you will be attempting to unlearn many of the lies taught to you by the Empire."

"Just how do you propose on doing any this?" the starat by Aaron's side asked. "It's all wonderful and grand ideas, but how do you think we can make a difference from all the way out here?"

Amy flicked her ears as she looked across to the starat. "The Starat Freedom Union has been infiltrating the empire for decades now. This has been over thirty years of my life's work, but never have I felt this good, this positive about what we're doing. Never before have we had two captains from the empire defect at the same time, and both over starat rights," she replied. She gestured her hand towards Aaron and Rhys, but the starat glanced across to the other human in the room, who was sat back with pursed lips and a permanent frown on his face.

"You're never going to change their minds," the starat by Aaron's side muttered darkly. He folded his arms across his chest and leaned back into his seat.

"Maybe not. Nick, wasn't it?" Amy said. The starat nodded to confirm her assumption. "Maybe not, but now I believe we have the resources to fully push for change within the empire."

Rhys lifted up his hand to get Amy's attention. "Why is this something the Centauran government doesn't want to get involved in?" he asked, when she pointed towards him.

Amy twitched her muzzle as she looked down to Snow for a moment. "Unlike Terra, Centaura doesn't look upon our... disagreement as an active war. Instead, our government views Terra as an annoyance, but not one that needs an active response. It's very much a case of 'out of sight, out of mind' for them."

Rhys tilted his head to the side. "Not at war? What about all the Centauran ships in the Sol and Sirius systems?"

"Propaganda from the Vatican and your government, mostly," Amy said with a shrug of his shoulders. "Sometimes there are Centauran ships in Terran territory. Sometimes those are even military ships. But they aren't there for war."

Rhys looked across to Aaron, but he couldn't tell whether or not his friend was as stunned by that information as he was. He hadn't been involved in many battles with Centauran ships, but he had always been convinced by the real threat they had portrayed. He didn't understand how it could be a Vatican ruse. He knew they controlled almost everything through the empire, but this would be something he was sure even they could not be capable of.

Amy had already moved on, and Rhys shook his head to try and clear his thoughts so he could focus on her again.

"There will of course be lots of training you'll need to go through," Amy said. She paced back and forth in front of the tables. "Some of you have been picked for your tactical skills or the knowledge you bring, or simply the sheer determination you have. Others Snow picked out because she believes you show aptitude for skills not yet understood by the empire."

She paused and placed her hands on the back of a chair as she stopped her pacing. "I trust you to know that any information discussed amongst our organisation does not spread beyond it. We are a military organisation, albeit not an official one. I don't want any of our plans leaked to our enemies," she warned, before she pointed to a door at the far side of the room. "Now. Rhys, Nick, Twitch, and Leandro. You will all follow Snow through there. Everyone else will remain with me."

Rhys nervously rose to his feet with the other starats called upon. Rhys waved his hand in Aaron's direction as he turned to leave, and the human waved back, but didn't say anything. He had whispered something in Nick's ear as the other starat had started to rise.

The second room was almost identical to the first, though it had a couple of windows that looked out onto the factory floor. Snow stood in front of these windows, facing towards the floor, as the starats behind her sat down. She didn't turn around before she started to speak. "Who can tell me what subspace is?"

Rhys was about to answer, but Nick spoke before he could open his mouth. "It's the dimension through which ships travel in order to reach faster-than-light speeds. Not much is known about it, but it is known that gravity in real space appears to thicken the divide between the two, making it tougher to cross in or out close to a major gravity well larger than, say, a small dwarf planet."

Twitch leaned in close to Rhys and whispered in his ear. "Oh I am so glad I didn't answer. That is not what I was going to say," he said with a small giggle. He abruptly fell silent as Snow finally turned around. Her sightless eyes fixed on Nick.

"Correct, but only for the fundamentals," Snow said. She spoke slowly as she stood with her hands clasped behind her back. "It is certainly true that the Terran Empire knows little about subspace beyond what you explained, but the truth is that we, and the Vatican, know a lot more about it. The Vatican chooses to suppress this information. We, however, share it. We use it."

Rhys scratched his muzzle and leaned forward. "Are you saying there are other ways to use subspace?"

"More than you could possibly imagine," Snow said. She held out her hand and snapped her fingers. A pen appeared between her fingers, and she twirled it around them. "The power over matter and energy is at our fingertips. All you need to do is learn how to control it."

Rhys rose slowly from his chair. By his side, Twitch squeaked in excitement and clapped his hands. The other two starats had both stood up as well, staring at the pen in Snow's hand. "Magic and cheap tricks?" Rhys asked sceptically. He was sure it had to be sleight of hand, but Snow's sleeves were too short to hide anything in.

Snow smiled and tossed the pen towards Rhys. He caught it clumsily as his arm jarred painfully. "Isn't it an old Terran expression: 'Anything sufficiently unknown is indistinguishable from magic'?" she asked.

Rhys turned the pen over between his fingers. "I've never heard of that before," he mumbled. The pen felt real in his hands. It was solid, but somehow Snow had been able to conjure it from nothing. There had to be some trick behind it, but he couldn't see how it had been done. Even as he held it, with another snap of Snow's fingers, the pen was gone. One moment it was there, but the next, with a flash of heat and burst of cinnamon scent, his fingers grasped nothing but air.

"The fuck," he whispered quietly, staring down at his now empty fingers.

Snow grinned widely as she held the pen in her hand again. The same pen. Rhys could see the little red band of tape around the lid. "All matter and energy in realspace is intrinsically linked to subspace," she explained. Again the pen twirled between her fingers, and Rhys watched it closely in case it vanished once more. "Amongst humans, it is a rare ability to be able to manipulate this connection, but for starats it is much easier. No one knows why. It's probably an accidental result of our artificial creation."

"And we can all do this?" Leandro asked. The old starat had leaned forward, his ear curled in. "I have never come across anyone in the empire who can do this, and I have lived a long time. Seen many places. I do not mean to doubt you, but I have experienced more than most imperial starats."

"It is unlikely to be an ability that is stumbled upon," Snow said. She turned her pale eyes towards Leandro. "In the empire, knowledge of this ability is suppressed by the Vatican. They imprison or kill anyone who shows an aptitude for it. They use this very same ability to track down those who can use it, so I am not surprised you have not heard of this ability before. There are none in the empire who can wield it and have survived."

Twitch raised his hand, a wide smile across his muzzle. "And we're all to learn how to do this?"

Snow nodded. "I hope to teach you, yes. With luck, you will all become psykers under my tutelage."

"Cool!" Twitch said, clapping his hands together. He bounced in his seat, tail swishing back and forth in his excitement. "When do we start?"

"We start right now, but don't expect to be achieving anything for quite some time," Snow said in warning. "It is a difficult skill to learn, let alone master. I would be surprised if any of you can even sense subspace within the first few lessons."

Twitch snickered to himself, but he didn't share his thoughts this time, though Rhys was still fairly confident he knew just what the starat was thinking of. Snow flicked her ear as she turned her head to look down at Twitch for a moment, but she otherwise didn't react to the laughter. Instead, she tucked the pen into her pocket.

"Matter manipulation, sometimes call telekinesis, will be your first goal. I hope to have you all moving small objects with nothing more than subspace control soon after you first learn to touch across," Snow said. She looked sightlessly around the small group of starats. "I expect you all to master the basics within months. To do what I can do though, that will be years of study. Not all of you will succeed. I hope at least one of you will."

Rhys felt a prickle of unease run down his spine. "And just what is it you can do?"

"Exist fully in neither one nor the other. I am always aware of subspace and realspace simultaneously," Snow explained. She clicked her fingers and a spark of golden energy flared to life, burning brightly for a few seconds before fading away again. "I am a psyker, with the power of subspace at my control. Or, if you prefer to use a different term, a magician. Soon you all will be."

"That's so cool," Twitch squeaked. He squirmed in his seat as he snapped his fingers a few times. Nothing happened, but the beaming grin on his muzzle didn't fade.

"I want you all to mimic my pose here. Hands out, palms up. Eyes closed," Snow instructed. She held her arms out in front of her, palms flat and facing the ceiling. She smirked as she looked around the room at the four starats watching her. "Yes, you will look ridiculous. That will happen a lot in my lessons. Get used to it."

Rhys glanced to his side to see Twitch immediately obeying the albino. He still had the same giddy smile on his face as he held his hands out in front of him. Rhys's eyes slid away from the starat and down at his hand. He rubbed his fingers together, then tensed them. He didn't know if his ruined hands would have a negative effect on his ability to do... whatever it had been Snow had done. If it was even a real thing. He sighed and stretched his arms out, trying to stop his hands from shaking so much. He didn't know what he was expecting, but he might as well give it a try.

***

Snow had been right to give her warning that she didn't expect anyone to make any progress. Their first lesson was little more than holding out their hands with their eyes closed and listening to Snow talk about what subspace was and the potential that was contained within it. Through it, they would eventually learn to manipulate matter and energy within realspace. Even after Snow broke down the link between subspace and realspace, Rhys wasn't sure he truly believed it. Everything still sounded like magic to him.

His head hurt just thinking about it. Every time he closed his eyes he felt like he could see the shadows of subspace, but it was just a trick of his eyes flashing afterimages against the inside of his eyelids. They reminded him of the entities he had seen on the *Shield of Justice*. He had meant to ask Snow about those on the way back from Amy's factory, but the albino had not joined them on their return back to Appletree Estates.

Rhys lay back on his bed with his eyes closed, hands resting on his forehead as he tried to suppress a headache. In the background he could hear Twitch babbling about the lesson with David, but he was doing his best to ignore the conversation. The quiet murmur of William's conversation with Richard in the next room was more reserved, but Rhys could still hear the excitement in William's voice. He still didn't know what the other group had discussed while Snow had instructed them in subspace manipulation, but for now he simply didn't want to ask.

Instead of the voices around him, Rhys tried to focus on the sounds and smells of the meal Leandro and Steph were cooking. The aroma of fish and spices teased at his nose, as did the sizzle of meat in the pan. The kitchenette in the other room was small, but Leandro had declared it satisfactory for what he wanted to make. Rhys had briefly wondered where they had acquired the ingredients from, but Twitch had been vociferous in letting everyone know he had spent his own money for the first time.

Rhys just let the sounds wash over him as he thought over everything Snow had said once more, trying to find something in there that made sense to his mind. He couldn't think of anything. He'd never had any experience with it before, and he'd never even heard of those abilities. He had a hard time even believing that Snow's trick with the pen was anything more than that: a trick. So many of his beliefs had already been overturned, but this one he refused to accept so easily. Learning that the empire had been built on a series of lies was one thing. This was the fundamental nature of reality. He had thought he'd had a good grip on reality.

Rhys must have briefly dozed off, as he was suddenly woken by someone shaking his foot. He squinted his eyes open to see Steph at the foot of his bed. "Come and get some food," she said. The sounds of conversation had migrated into the other room.

After rubbing his muzzle, Rhys slowly sat up. His head was pounding with a fierce headache, and he wanted to just sleep it off, but the smell of fried fish in the other room was tantalising enough to spur him into movement.

Rhys felt almost like he was drunk as he lurched into the other room, having to rest his hand against the wall for support to stop his spinning head from pitching him down to the floor. He carefully slid into an empty chair and held his head in his hand.

"Is everything alright, Captain Rhys?" Leandro asked. He passed a couple of plates around the table. Steaming fish was delicately placed over a bed of vegetables and rice. It smelt beautiful to Rhys's nose.

"Just a headache. All that stuff earlier, and the stronger gravity. It's getting to me a bit," Rhys replied. He closed his eyes and leaned back, just letting the steam fill his nose for a moment. A chair scraped against the floor, and a few moments later a strong hand squeezed around his. He felt something press against his palm. He opened his eyes again to see David standing over him. In his hand was a couple of white pills. He flashed a quick smile of thanks to the larger starat.

"Food is the cure to most ailments, I have found. Eat up, Captain Rhys," Leandro said. The grey-furred starat finishing serving up the meals for everyone as they crowded around the small table. There wasn't much room, and Steph's arm kept bumping into Rhys's ribs, but no one else seemed to mind the lack of space. As Leandro sat down between Twitch and Richard, the old starat started to smile. "Though you would not know the story of the governor in Toledo. Everyone in Mount Cotton loved that story."

An awkward silence fell on the table for a moment. Most of the starats had left people behind when they had fled Terra.

It was Richard who broke the silence. "Why don't you tell us the story? It must be nice to have a new audience."

Leandro's ear tucked down as he looked around the small group. "I am afraid it's not quite so grand as some of my other stories. I was still a kit, still in my home city even, just south of Madrid. My family were owned by the governor of the region. It was where I learned how to cook." The old starat cut up a piece of fish and held it up in the air on the end of the fork. "This very meal in fact, was the first one I learned."

Leandro took a bite of the fish, and that motion seemed to break the little spell around the table. The starats, who had been holding back from eating, all started to tuck into their meal. Rhys struggled to hold onto his cutlery probably, though he nudged aside Steph's offers to cut the food up for him. The first mouthful was like an explosion of flavour in his mouth. The fish had been coated in a layer of herbs and spices, which complemented the bed of vegetables and rice perfectly. For most of his life, Rhys had lived on military rations, which were rarely plentiful or full of flavour.

"Then, one night it was my first time cooking the governor's meal by myself. Everything was going quite well," Leandro continued, speaking slowly between mouthfuls. "At least, until they started to eat the fish. It was then that I realised I had put a bit too much chilli into the mixture. It was meant to be one small chilli for the entire meal."

"How much did you use?" Steph asked through a mouthful of fish. There had been no such risk of Leandro using too much chilli this time, as there was a perfect amount of spice to the fish.

"I used three," Leandro said. He grinned bashfully. "Per plate. I have never seen any human go so red since. I think the governor's son could not eat anything for a couple of days afterwards, it burned his mouth so much."

Steph held a hand over her mouth to disguise her snort of laughter, and she quickly mopped up some of the rice she spilled. "Were you punished for it?"

Leandro's smiling demeanour flickered and faded. When his smile returned, it was weak and sorrowful. He brushed one hand over the small stub of his ruined ear. "Sadly, yes. The governor's son... I can not remember his name, it was so long ago, but he had quite the cruel streak. He took my ear as punishment."

"Shit," Rhys muttered, alarmed at how rapidly the tale turned from a light-hearted affair to something dark and cruel.

Leandro shrugged his shoulders. "That was what it means to be owned property, Captain Rhys. I am sure everyone around this table has a similar story to tell."

"My leg, for starters," William said with a grunt.

Rhys pinned his ears down as he looked around at the starats.

Steph swallowed a mouthful of fish. "I have a burn mark on my back where some human children tried to brand me."

"My old master broke my wrist," David said. "I had to treat it myself, but I wasn't given any time off work for it to heal. I was sold on because I was no longer productive, but that did lead me to Normandy, where I met Twitch."

"I broke my ankle because I was pushed down some stairs," Twitch said, somehow making it sound like a positive experience. His voice was still bright and bubbly as he mimed with his fork to show something rolling down a flight of stairs. Rice and vegetables splattered against the table. He bounced on his seat and grinned to Leandro. "This fish is delicious."

"I lost a tooth after Cooper punched me in one of his rages," Richard added. He held a hand up to his muzzle. "Thankfully it wasn't a front tooth, but it still irritates me occasionally."

"And look at you, Captain Rhys," Twitch said brightly. He reached across the table to gently stroke Rhys's hand. Twitch's claw lightly touched on the scars on Rhys's palms, before gently tracing up his bony finger. "You've only been a starat for a month or so and you've got the worst injuries out of all of us, except for William."

Rhys flattened his ears and pulled his hand away from Twitch. "It's not a competition I'm happy to have taken part in. It's not a competition any of us should have been a part of," he said quietly. He stared down at the half-eaten meal in front of him, his appetite suddenly gone. "How could this have happened? Some of it was on my ship. I... I failed you."

"And you paid for that," William said with a low growl. He put his fork down and looked across the table. "You have the chance now to fix it. To make things better. You've already brought us here, and for that we're all grateful. But that can't be all of it."

"It is why Amy chose us," Leandro said. His appetite had not been impacted by the conversation, and he still spoke around mouthfuls of food. "She knows we're motivated to change things. We all are."

"You gave us the opportunity to fight and to make a difference," William said. He picked his fork up again and jabbed it into his food. He growled softly. "Only a coward wouldn't take that opportunity when it's given to them, and I know I'm no coward. None of us are. But for you to join us, you need to fix your hands. Are you a coward, Captain Rhys?"

"I am not a coward. You know that," Rhys growled back. He clenched his hand around his fork, doing his best to hide his grimace of pain. "For all the mistakes I made as a human, you all know that I would do anything for us now. I would have died with Cardinal Erik, rather than betray who I am now."

"I hope it never comes to that again. We aren't asking you to die for us," Richard said, placing his hand on William's to calm the other starat. "We'll all be joining you tomorrow. Snow has given us permission to come with you and learn how to fight."

"We're all fighters," William said. He swept his hand around the table, spilling a few grains of rice with the movement. "All of us are, even if we aren't soldiers. We know the right thing to do."

"And I'm a fighter with you. I'm just cautious. The right goal doesn't justify every means to get there," Rhys warned. His knife clattered to the floor as he lost grip on it, but he didn't go to retrieve it. He swore beneath his breath. "Amy sounds dangerous. I don't know how she plans to free starats in the empire yet, and until I do I can't completely trust her."

Rhys looked around the table, meeting the eyes of every starat there. None of them said a word. None of them needed to. They had already made their case. Rhys knew how bad their lives had been in the empire, and what they had left behind. Rhys had tasted their suffering directly, but they had experienced it their whole lives. They had something good on Centaura, a life of comfort and peace, but they were not willing to settle for that. They wanted to fight for the starats they had left behind.

"You've given us a wonderful opportunity," William said, some of his anger relenting again. "With or without you, we will do this. I hope that you'll be with us, and that you'll have some shiny, new arms to use."

Rhys sighed softly. His hand shook as he lifted his fork up, taking a small mouthful of fish and rice. He slowly chewed and swallowed. "I haven't heard back from Doctor Sparks yet. I won't make a decision on my arms until then." He put his fork down and gently rubbed the back of his skeletal hand. "But as for the rest? I'll be right there by your side the entire time. I will fight. We will win."

chapter five

Rhys was surprised by a summons back to the space elevator for a meeting with Major-General Ulrich. He had not been told what the meeting was about, and a shiver of worry ran down his tail. Unexpected meetings with superior officers had rarely been the bringer of good news in the past.

His head still prickled with a headache after a second lesson with Snow the previous day. He had spent much of that lesson trying to remain as still as possible while he reached for the impossible. He had made no progress at all, and he still wasn't even sure what he was meant to be trying to find. If anything, he was glad of a day away from the factory and Snow's eerie stare. The albino had not been present as Rhys made his way out into the cool darkness that had finally come in after the sticky heat of the long Centauran day. Instead, he had been instructed to make his own way up to the elevator on the outskirts of the city. A car had been sent to pick him up, but there had been no driver inside.

The way back to the space elevator was a nervous one. Rhys couldn't sit still for long, and he could never get his tail comfortable. Though there had been an assurance from Amy that associating with her would not hinder his request to stay on Centaura, he had to worry about the timing. He feared there was a connection. He knew right away that if he was told to stay away from Amy, then he would have no choice but to do so. She offered a way to get back at the empire quicker than the Stellar Guard seemed willing to provide, but that could not come at the risk of his future on Centaura.

Rhys was greeted by a starat at the main gate of the elevator facility. He was quickly cleared for entry and sent through with an escort to meet the major-general. She was deep inside the facility, well away from the windows that looked out over the city. He was led to a small office and asked to take a seat inside. It was not the same office that he had first met the major-general.

He didn't have long to wait before the door opened again. He rose as Major-General Ulrich entered. She came in alone, and she gestured for Rhys to sit as she took her seat on the other side of the desk. She placed a tablet down between them, but left it switched off for the moment.

"Welcome back, Captain Griffiths. I trust you're settling in nicely?" the major-general said. She tapped her fingers together. Her ears and tail betrayed nothing of her thoughts.

"Very well, thank you Major-General. We have been treated very nicely," Rhys replied. He kept his tail tucked beneath his chair and tried to stop his aching hands from tapping against the table.

"How are the hands treating you?" Major-General Ulrich asked. She nodded down to Rhys's arms as he rested them on the table between them.

"No improvement, Major-General. I have received an offer to fix them, but I'm not sure yet whether I'm willing to accept it or not," Rhys replied. He rubbed his fingers together. The sharp stabbing pains where his claws been had receded slightly, instead just leaving him to deal with a constant ache that radiated through his fingers and wrists.

"Yes, we have noticed you have developed an affiliation with Amy Jennings and her organisation," Major-General Ulrich said. She clasped her hands together and peered forward.

"I was told that wouldn't be an issue," Rhys said warily. A flick of his ear betrayed a momentary alarm.

"It is not," the major-general replied. She looked towards the door for a moment, before her eyes flicked up to the corner of the room, near the ceiling. Rhys had noticed a camera up there when he walked in, but he didn't turn around to look up. "Some might say knowing my cousin may enhance your prospects."

"She's your...?" Rhys started to say, but he was silenced by a raised hand from the major-general. He quickly shut his mouth.

"She is, but knowing her comes at a cost. She is incredibly ambitious, and she will stop at nothing to see her plans come through," Major-General Ulrich said. She frowned and rubbed the side of her muzzle. "I don't have any advice to give you, as I don't know what she has offered you, and frankly, I don't want to know. Just be careful that you know what you're getting into with her."

"I will be," Rhys said. A shiver ran down his tail. "Thank you for the warning, Major-General."

Major-General Ulrich smiled again. She switched on the tablet between them and flicked through a few screens. She then spun the device around on the table so Rhys could properly see the display. It was a collection of resignation letters. "A few of your crew have requested to be stood down from duty. As their captain, we will need your approval to ensure they can be fully integrated into Centauran society."

Rhys was saddened to hear that some of his crew weren't going to be staying on. He flicked through the names. Most of them were in the services crew, but he was somewhat surprised to see that Commander Briggs was not in their number. Two from his operations crew would be resigning. James Sutherland, the cadet sensory officer, and Donald Mathers the cadet pilot. Rhys added his electronic signature to the resignation forms, though he couldn't produce anything like his usual signature thanks to the pains in his fingers. He pushed the tablet back across to Major-General Ulrich.

"They will still be permitted to remain at Appletree," the major-general said. She flicked through the forms to make sure Rhys had signed them all, before switching the screen off again. "After that though, they will no longer be considered your crew. They will be civilians. Though you won't have been approved for service in the Stellar Guard, you are still military."

Rhys nodded his head. He got the impression that he had been summoned for much more than accepting some of his crew's resignation. That information could have been sent to him at the estate.

"For now though, we have a mission for you."

Rhys's ears perked up. He tilted his head to one side. "A mission, ma'am?" He paused and frowned. "May I speak freely?"

Major-General Ulrich nodded. "You may. Now, and for as long as you're in this office."

Rhys tapped his finger against the table once. A sharp pain stabbed through his hand, and he pulled his hand down to rest on his lap. "I thought it would be months before I got tasked with any mission."

"That is correct. Think of this as a supervised training mission in enemy territory," the major-general said. She flicked through a few screens on her tablet again, before turning it to show Rhys a visual of the Pluto system. "We need to test the loyalty of you and your crew. We need to know that you're willing to fight for us, and for that we have arranged a small raid on a quiet, out of the way base. It will give you the chance to show us that you are committed to our cause in a place that away from the empire's firepower."

Rhys took hold of the tablet. He had never visited Pluto before, but it was instantly recognisable. The view of the visual showed Charon looming just behind the dwarf planet, and a few pinpricks of light betrayed the presence of some of the other, smaller, moons. "And what's the target? I've never heard of anything strategically valuable on Pluto," he asked. He glanced up to see the major-general watching him closely. Her hands were steepled together beneath her muzzle.

"Pluto is not the target. Charon is," the major-general said. She held out her hand to take back the tablet, but she only had it for a few seconds before she gave it back. The focus had changed to the largest moon of Pluto, and the small cluster of buildings on its surface. "There is a prison on Charon, reserved for those prisoners the empire would prefer to forget about, and those the Vatican doesn't care about. It is not a pleasant place."

"I'm assuming there are people there you want to get out, major-general?"

The major-general nodded and smiled. "Precisely. Some of our spies end up there if they're not careful enough," she said. She spread her hands out. "The raid will leave tomorrow. We will be using your ship, and your crew. This will be supplemented by myself and two dozen soldiers. Are there any problems with this, Captain?"

Rhys frowned. "My ship will be a known defector."

"There were unused transponder codes in the data cache of your ship. A new identity can be placed on it in a moment. I think it deserves a new name anyway," the major-general said. She smiled wryly. "The *Harvester*? Really? How crass."

Rhys bowed his head and stared down at his hands. He had never thought about the name of his ship before. That had merely been the identity it had always had, since before he had taken up command of the vessel. Rhys's tail curled around the chair leg as he looked back up at the major-general.

"If it's safe to use my ship, then I will be happy to lead it to Charon," he said. His hands stayed resting on his hips as he fought the urge to stroke his tail.

Major-General Ulrich smiled and rose to her feet. Rhys was quick to stand up after her. "I'm happy to hear it," she said. She took the tablet back from Rhys, but she didn't show him to the door or dismiss him right away. "You will return here tomorrow. A transport will be sent for you and your crew. I'll send through exact times on your tablet."

"I understand, Major-General. I'll make sure everyone is prepared," Rhys said. He saluted the starat as she opened the door.

The major-general placed a hand on his shoulder to stop him from leaving. "One last thing. I have an exception request for a few of the starats. William won't be required to go through assessment until he's got his new leg," she said. She flicked her tail, and her ears folded in slightly as she frowned. "I also have a request from Amy that she keep hold of Twitch and David. She did not give reasons why."

Rhys flicked his ears. He wondered what Amy needed of Twitch and David, but he didn't try to question the order from the major-general. He nodded his head. "I'll see to it, major-general."

"Until then, you're dismissed Captain Griffiths. I'll see you tomorrow."

Rhys saluted Major-General Ulrich once more, before he turned on his toes and left her office. He managed to keep the smile from his face, but he couldn't stop his tail wagging in delight. He had not expected to return to active duty for a few months still. Even if it was only a training exercise, it would still be active service. Despite knowing that he would be going up against the empire, he was still looking forward to it.

***

Rhys was the first from his crew to be waiting for the transport. He sat alone in the lobby of the apartment block and smoothed down his pristine uniform once more. It felt strange to be wearing the insignia of TIE on his breast, but he had nothing else to wear for military duty. He rested his hands either side of his fresh cup of tea, though he was barely able to lift the steaming cup. The warmth helped to soothe some of the pain in his fingers.

His silent vigil didn't last long. Footsteps thundered down the stairs, and a starat leaped out into the middle of the lobby with a single jump. Twitch almost fell over, but he was able to maintain his balance as he spun around on his toes. He punched the air above his head and crowed out in victory. "I won, hah! Oh, hi Captain Rhys. I didn't see you there."

The loser of the seemingly one-sided race was David. He came down the stairs at a much slower pace. Twitch skipped around the larger starat as they approached Rhys. David took a seat opposite him, but Twitch remained standing as he bounced around the pair.

"Did you give him coffee or something?" Rhys asked. His brow raised as he watched the starat.

David raised his hands in protest. "I didn't give it him. He found it himself."

"I pity Amy then, if she's got to handle him like this," Rhys said with a laugh.

Twitch finally came to a rest and perched himself on David's lap. The larger starat ruffled Twitch's headfur. "She's not handling me," Twitch protested. He stuck his tongue out at Rhys. "I'm not that kind of starat."

David raised his brow, but he didn't say anything to contradict his partner. Rhys quickly tried to steer the conversation in a different direction.

"Do you know why you're seeing Amy?" he asked David.

The larger starat shrugged his shoulders. "I'm not sure yet. I don't know why it's important enough to pull us away from your ship."

"We'd much rather be going up there with you," Twitch said brightly. He pointed up to the ceiling. Then he frowned and pointed towards the floor. "Or is Terra that way. Whichever way it is! I'd rather be there."

"Must be something important. Even Major-General Ulrich didn't know what it was about," Rhys said. His smile was tinged with a little sadness. He would be away for just over a week, but he knew he would still miss Twitch in that time. He also worried for him and David. They were two starats in a wholly new environment, and almost everyone they knew would be leaving them alone. He could only hope they would be well looked after. At least they would also have William to keep them company.

"Maybe we're being sent on a super-secret mission," Twitch said. He bounced a little where he sat on David's leg. His feet swung back and forth a few centimetres from the floor.

"I doubt that," David laughed. He ruffled Twitch's head again and held the other starat close. "Maybe it's to do with that weird subspace stuff you were telling me about."

Twitch stuck his tongue out again, this time in disgust. "Ugh, I hope not. That stuff is freaky."

Rhys's ear twitched. "I was expecting another joke there," he said quietly.

Twitch grinned widely. "I thought about it, but I can't just make the same joke every time. You'll be expecting it then. Gotta keep you on your toes," he said with a giggle.

Rhys just groaned and gently held his head in his hands. He was saved by the arrival of more of his crew. Leandro emerged from the elevator, along with Chekolin and Riley. The two humans saluted their captain, but Leandro slunk up quietly and stood nervously by Rhys's side. "May I talk with you privately, Captain?"

Rhys excused himself from Twitch and David. He thought about bringing his cup of tea with him, but his wrists protested the heavy cup, so he left that behind. Leandro didn't take him far; just to the far side of the lobby. It was far enough away that even the starats wouldn't be able to overhear them.

"They are sending us to Charon," the grey-furred starat said quietly. He didn't meet Rhys's eye as he stared down at the floor.

"If you'd rather stay behind…"

"No!" Leandro looked up sharply. His ears pinned back. "Sorry, Captain. No. I do not wish to be left behind. The exact opposite. Do you know who is imprisoned there?"

Rhys shook his head. "I don't know. I haven't been given the list from the major-general yet."

"Can you guess who might be there?" Leandro asked. His voice descended back down into a strained whisper. "Someone hidden on a desolate rock, waiting for lights in the sky to rescue him?"

Rhys suddenly understood. Leandro had told him that story back on Terra. "The Silver Fox," he said simply.

"I owe him everything," Leandro said quietly. The grey-furred starat smiled weakly and placed his hand on Rhys's shoulder. "Please. I can not go to Charon and not try to free him."

"I will do everything I can."

Leandro pulled Rhys into a hug, taking care not to squeeze around his arms. There were tears in the older starat's eyes. "Thank you, Captain. I know it is going to be dangerous out there, but I have to at least try."

"I understand. He was important to you, wasn't he?"

"More than you could ever imagine, Captain Rhys," Leandro said. His hand dropped down to his side and he bowed his head. "I had always hoped for this chance."

"We'll get him out," Rhys said. He patted Leandro on the shoulder once, only to wince and clench his teeth as he sent a sharp stab of pain all the way up his arm. He took a deep breath to compose himself and slowly unclenched his fingers.

Leandro took a step back from Rhys. "You are in no fit state for combat, Captain Rhys." There was worry in the older starat's eyes.

Rhys shook his head. "No. But I have my orders. I'll do this as best I can. I've got a good crew to help me through."

"We will have your back, Captain. Does not mean I am not worried too," Leandro said. He glanced over Rhys's shoulder. There was a bit more noise coming from the far side of the lobby as more of Rhys's crew made their way down.

Rhys tried to keep his worry from showing. He turned around so he didn't have to look towards Leandro. The tip of his tail kept curling up as he looked around the lobby. Everyone on his operations crew was present, but for the two who had resigned. He caught the eye of Briggs, who gave him a thumbs up to let the starat know everyone from his part of the crew was there. A quick glance out of the front doors confirmed that the transport had just arrived.

Rhys nearly clapped his hands together to attract attention, but he stopped himself just in time. Instead he settled for a quick shout. Conversation stopped instantly. All the humans came to attention. A couple of the starats followed suit, though they didn't look sure where to put their hands or tails.

"From today we're soldiers of the CGP, of Centaura," Rhys said. He clasped his hands behind his back so his crew couldn't see how much his fingers shook. "We're going to show them we can still fight, even if it's for a different cause. You've all made your choice to stay with me, so let's go and prove that Centaura can trust us. Let's move out."

The crew saluted Rhys, and at his gesture they filtered out into the dark night and to the transport that waited for them. Rhys lingered a few moments longer, until he was the last one in the lobby with Leandro, Twitch, and David. Leandro placed his hand on Rhys's shoulder for a moment, before he, too, went outside.

Twitch appeared to have calmed down slightly, though his foot still shook as he remained perched on David's lap. Rhys slowly approached.

"I'm going to miss you, Captain Rhys," Twitch said sombrely. He hopped up off David's lap and pulled Rhys into a hug.

Rhys gently rested his hand against Twitch's back. "You be safe here, alright? Don't go getting into any trouble."

"I'll try to keep him safe, Captain Rhys," David said. He laughed, but there was worry there too.

Twitch broke off the hug and scampered back to David. His tail was drooped between his legs, and Rhys noticed the starat try to surreptitiously dry his eyes with the back of his hand. Rhys raised his arm in farewell.

"I'll see you in a week," he said. The two starats waved back. Rhys turned on his toes and pushed the door open, and he stepped out into the cool night air. He took a deep breath and composed himself. He was back in military duty, even if it was just for one short mission. He needed to make sure he was in the right frame of mind. His future career depended on it.

***

The journey back to the elevator went smoothly. Rhys stayed by himself at the front of the transport, and no one approached him for a conversation. His ears occasionally picked up snippets of talk amongst his crew, but he mostly kept his eyes closed and head bowed. He knew combat was still several days away, but he wanted to get into the right mindset as soon as possible. He had to be ready for anything. This would be the first time he would be the aggressor in any combat situation. Every time before, he had been defending the empire from alleged CGP attacks in the Terran system. It would be a whole new experience for him, and he would need to pull on knowledge that had only been learned in theory.

Major-General Ulrich had not been present at the base of the space elevator, but there had been someone to greet them. The human guided them through the facility and up to the elevator itself. The ascent to Network Central excited some of the starats. Some of the humans joined in the excitement, as it was not often they got the chance to experience a space elevator. On Terra, everything was usually shuttles or teleporters.

A short shuttle ride from Network Central followed. The *Harvester* wasn't docked at the main satellite over the Centauran north pole. Instead, Rhys recognised the first satellite he had come to with Fleet-Admiral Bosler. He was surprised to see her waiting outside his ship, with Major-General Ulrich by her side. The other human with them was an even bigger surprise. Aaron was with them.

Rhys saluted his two superior officers. For the moment, he tried to ignore Aaron. They waved him down, and the crew behind him.

"Everyone on board and in positions. We have two hours before authorised launch," the fleet-admiral said. She held her hand out to Rhys. "Captain Griffiths, if you could remain out here for a moment."

Rhys half-turned. "Mr Chekolin, you have the bridge until I board," he ordered. The pilot saluted him, before he began to lead the crew into the ship. The airlocks were locked open, creating a simple corridor into the ship. Rhys couldn't wait to get back on board. It had only been five days since he had arrived on Centaura, but already that felt like a lifetime. He resisted the urge to follow his crew on board, instead waiting by the two superior officers.

"We understand you're missing a first officer," Fleet-Admiral Bosler said. She gestured towards Aaron. "Captain Lee here has volunteered his time to fill in that position for this mission."

This time, Rhys did flash a quick smile to Aaron, who returned with one of his own. "Most appreciated, Fleet-Admiral. I've known Captain Lee for most of my life, but we've never worked together. It will be great to have that opportunity."

Fleet-Admiral Bosler nodded. "I expect you'll be working more with the major-general, with Captain Lee running the ship enroute. There is a lot to prepare, and I am eager to see the results of your exercise."

"Understood, Fleet-Admiral," Rhys said. The excitement that he would be working with Aaron wasn't tempered by the thought that he was effectively handing his ship over to his friend for a while.

"I will brief you fully on what I expect on flight and when we reach Charon before launch. Captain Lee will oversee that procedure," Major-General Ulrich said. She looked up to the human by her side, who towered over both starats and the Centauran human. "In fact, why don't you get acquainted with the crew, Captain Lee."

Aaron saluted the starat. "Can do, ma'am. See you on board shortly," he said. He turned on his heel slightly to salute the human. "And thank you, Ma'am, for trusting me with this opportunity. I won't let you down."

"Thank you, Captain Lee," Fleet-Admiral Bosler said in dismissal of the other human. Aaron ducked inside the airlock and soon disappeared inside the *Harvester*. The fleet-admiral turned back to Rhys. "Major-General Ulrich will be monitoring you and your crew. She will report back to me, and her judgement will be used in your assessment. Just remember, Captain Griffiths. This is a once-off mission to assess your loyalty and ability. Once this mission is complete, don't expect any further deployments with the Stellar Guard for at least three months, should your application be successful."

"I understand, Fleet-Admiral," Rhys replied quickly. "I'm just glad for the opportunity. Like Captain Lee, I won't let you down."

"Major-General Ulrich will be the judge of that, Captain," the fleet-admiral said. She held her hand out to the side. "Safe flight, Captain Griffiths. I look forward to seeing the report on your return. With any luck, you'll be successful, and your acceptance here will only be a formality."

"I hope so too, Fleet-Admiral," Rhys said. Understanding that he was dismissed, he saluted the human and turned into the airlock. The major-general followed right behind him. The airlock closed once they stepped into the *Harvester*.

Rhys paused for a moment and took a deep breath. The ship smelled as it always did. The air was slightly recycled, though still mostly fresh as the ship was still docked. A few loud clunks and rattles ran through the ship as all the systems were powered on one-by-one.

"If we could go to the briefing room," the major-general said. "I have a few things to show you, and to get you prepared for the mission."

"Understood, Major-General. Just this way," Rhys said. It was not a long walk to the briefing room, which was kept close to the bridge. Acting through habit alone, Rhys almost walked right onto the bridge before he stopped himself. Thankfully, he didn't have to double back on himself. He led the major-general through to the briefing room, just down the corridor and next to the mess hall. The major-general walked alongside Rhys the entire way, seeming to know exactly where she was going.

The briefing room was tightly packed with chairs, all facing one desk opposite the door. It had been where Rhys had first stood in front of his crew as a starat, and that memory sent a shiver down his tail. He still remembered the terror that had almost paralysed him, and the sheer relief when his crew had pledged their continued loyalty to him, despite his tail and fur.

There was a package on the table. Rhys glanced across to the major-general, who still walked by his side. The other starat approached the table and took the only chair against it. For a moment, Rhys thought about pulling up another chair, but the thought of moving a chair with his hands made him grimace. He remained standing.

Major-General Ulrich opened the package. Inside was a set of gloves, similar to those on a space suit. The arms of the gloves seemed to be extended out much longer than they needed to be, and they thickened out around the wrists. The fingers looked like they were made of a different material, with strands of metal reinforcing the structure. The other starat held one up for Rhys to see.

"These will help you overcome the weakness in your hands," the starat explained. She held the opening of the glove out, encouraging Rhys to place his hand inside. A little daunted, Rhys still did as was expected, though he did hiss in pain as the soft inner lining of the glove pressed down on his wounded arms. The major-general didn't stop until the glove was on completely.

Rhys tried moving his fingers, but he found them to be locked in position. With his free hand, he traced over the glove. He was surprised to find that his hand was resting in the wrist of the glove.

"What are these, ma'am?" Rhys asked.

"Power gloves," the major-general replied. She held the second glove out. "They're used when someone has limited or weakened movement in their hands. They can take a little getting used to, so I'll ask that you use our few days of flight to familiarise yourself with them."

Rhys couldn't help the small whimper of pain as his left hand was enclosed within the power glove. They didn't weigh much, but he could still feel their weight pull down uncomfortably on his wrists. At least the padding inside was soft enough that they didn't rub on his flesh.

The major-general leaned in close and flicked a couple of switches on the wrists of the gloves. A tingle of electricity shot up Rhys's arms, and this time the glove responded to the small movements of his fingers.

Major-General Ulrich placed her hands on the gloves. "Now, be careful. The gloves enhance your movement. A small movement with your fingers will result in a larger one from the glove. That's why it can be tough to get used to them. You'll need a lot of practice."

Rhys tried moving his hands. The other starat had been right. Even just a simple twitch of his fingers provided a sharp jerk from the glove. It tapped against the table a few times. "Thank you for these, Major-General. I was worried about going into the field with my hands," he admitted. He was glad for something to help bolster his limited strength, even if it did need some getting used to.

"They will be yours just for this mission, but we can look into getting some for you permanently should you be successful," Major-General Ulrich said. She pushed aside the now-empty package and pulled out her tablet. She placed it on the table between them. "For now though, we are going to start discussing what will happen on Charon."

"We're freeing captives, is that right, ma'am?" Rhys asked. He tried not to let himself get too distracted by the power gloves, but he did keep twitching his fingers to get used to the sensitivity.

The major-general clasped her hands together and leaned forward. "We are. I already have a strategy and list of captives I want to free, but I'm not going to tell you what my plan is," she said with a soft smile. She pointed a finger to Rhys. "I will be giving you all the information you need. Maps. Diagrams. Detailed information on every prisoner held on Charon. Then, a day before we reach the dwarf planet, you will tell me what you plan on doing and who you think should be rescued. If I like your plan, we'll go with that. If I don't, then I will run the mission and I'll get to see how good you are at following orders."

"I'm guessing releasing everyone isn't an option?" Rhys asked.

Major-General Ulrich shook her head. "Notwithstanding the logistics of getting a prison population of around one hundred back onto your ship, but most of them would still pledge loyalty to the empire, despite being imprisoned by them. They would not make good recruits for us. We'll be looking at three prisoners to free. Four at the most."

Rhys hooked his foot against a chair and dragged it closer to the table. He took a seat and gently pulled the tablet to him. Aware of the eyes of Major-General Ulrich on him, he started to read. He wanted to know everything about Charon. Who defended it. Who was imprisoned inside. He wanted to prove that he was a good leader. The promise he had made to Leandro also hung close to the front of his mind. He had a lot of work to do.

chapter six

Saying goodbye to Captain Rhys was one of the strangest things Twitch had ever done. It felt bizarre knowing the former-human would be leaving him for so long. In the short time since he had first had that fateful encounter with Captain Rhys, they had only been separated the once, and that had not been planned. Twitch was still proud of his involvement in helping Captain Rhys escape from his imprisonment at the hands of Cardinal Erik.

Seeing the transport leave was a different feeling though. Not only was it taking Captain Rhys away, but also all the other friends he had made in such a short time. Both starat and human. He was left behind with only David and William for company. He hadn't seen Doctor Anthony on the transport, so he didn't know if the *Harvester's* doctor had remained.

Twitch's hand was still raised in farewell, though the transport had been out of sight for several minutes. David placed a hand on his shoulder. "We should go back inside," he said.

Twitch slowly dropped his hand. "Yeah, I guess so," he said quietly. He didn't want to think about how he was going to be missing all of his best friends, though he did at least still have the most important person in his life. If he had been told David would also be going with Captain Rhys, then he would have found a way onto that ship, no matter what it took.

A small noise by his feet distracted Twitch for a moment. He looked down to see a small furred creature wind its way between his legs. He gasped in delight and crouched down to run his hand over its back. The small creature let out a little chirruping noise.

"Oh, look how cute it is," Twitch squealed in delight. He beamed up to David. "Is it an alien? I wonder what they call it?"

Twitch picked up the little creature and held it close to his muzzle. It squirmed in his grip a little, then lashed out with claws that raked along the starat's arm. Twitch dropped the creature in surprise. It landed on all four feet and darted away into the undergrowth.

"I think they call it a cat," David said with a laugh. "They're from Terra."

"Ow!" Twitch held his hand over his arm, where the vicious creature had attacked him. "A cat? I've heard about those. Don't they own humans?"

David pried Twitch's fingers away. There was a little blood on his fur, but the cuts weren't deep. They just stung a lot, especially as David felt around the wound. "It certainly seems like it, sometimes," David said. He smiled and kissed Twitch's hand. "You'll be fine. I've got some antiseptic cream in our room, just in case he had something on his claws."

Twitch nodded and leaned into his partner. "Will you have to bandage me up like Captain Rhys?"

"I don't think so, no," David replied. He stuck his tongue out at Twitch. "It's just a small scratch."

"Fine, I don't get to be dramatic," Twitch replied with an over-exaggerated sigh. "You never let me do anything fun."

David laughed again and swatted Twitch gently across the ears. "Oh sure I don't," he said, but anything else he had to say was interrupted by a starat coming out from the apartment block.

Snow walked as she always did. Her head was held high, and her eyes didn't move at all as she walked confidently, seemingly not needing vision at all to know where she was putting her feet. She didn't stumble once, and even gracefully sidestepped a bump in the pavement that Twitch's foot had caught a couple of times already. Twitch had always been slightly unnerved by her. Her body had no scent.

Twitch's ears pinned back as she approached. "I'd have thought you would have been going with Captain Rhys," he said, trying to hide his discomfort in a bright smile. Then he remembered that she couldn't see him anyway. His smile wavered slightly.

"I have other business to attend to here," Snow replied in her usual soft voice. She bowed her head towards the two and extended her hand to Twitch. "Business that also involves you both. Would you care to come with me?"

Twitch nervously took hold of Snow's hand. He looked up to David, but he just shrugged his shoulders and followed after them. To Twitch's surprise, she only led them back up the stairs again and into the apartment building. It felt eerie and quiet inside with the ship's crew present.

"Go see to your arm, then meet me back down here," the albino said. She flashed a toothy smile to Twitch. "I know you'll be excited about what we have to show you."

Twitch raised his brow, but he let himself get pulled away from Snow. He followed David towards the elevator. He didn't look back towards Snow, and David's hand remained firm against his back as they hurried along. David didn't say anything until the elevator doors closed.

"There's something strange about her," David said quietly.

The elevator lurched as it started to rise up to their floor. "There's a lot strange about her," Twitch replied wryly. He wrinkled his nose. "Captain Rhys seems to trust her though. He's a good judge of character."

"How do we know that, though?"

"Well he trusts me, doesn't he?" Twitch asked, beaming from ear to ear.

"I don't think that's a point in his favour," David said, smirking as he lightly bumped hips with his partner.

"You wound me," Twitch said. He held his hands to his chest for a moment. "Oh no wait, that was the cat."

The elevator chimed as the doors opened. David put his arm around Twitch again and gave him a gentle nudge. "Come on you. Let's get you patched up, and then we can see what the creepy Snow wants."

Twitch leaned into David as they walked down the corridor. The door into their room was faulty, and it took a couple of attempts to push it open. It had been an issue ever since they had first moved in, and no one had yet been around to fix it. Twitch had been worried at first, but David had reminded him that no one would be able to gain access to the building who wasn't already in Captain Rhys's crew, or one of the other newly arrived refugees from Terra. At the moment, that only appeared to be one other ship, captained by one of Captain Rhys's old friends.

David took a few moments to search through the barely-organised contents of the room. Twitch's little corner of belongings had been neatly tidied, but David had been less disciplined in how he had discarded his stuff. They didn't have too much to call their own, and most of it was strewn out across the floor. Clothes had been scattered around, and a couple of rolls of bandages fell from a cabinet as David opened it. He found what he was looking for though. In his hand was a small tube of antiseptic cream.

"This will keep the cut from being infected, and will help it heal faster," David said. He held the well-used tube carefully. He squeezed out a little of the white cream and rubbed it over Twitch's arm, making sure it didn't all stick to his fur. It stung Twitch a little, but he kept still as his partner worked. David sighed and looked down at the tube when he was done. "I brought this over from Ceres. Maybe I should have left it for everyone back home. This was all we had there. Here… we have so much more."

Twitch placed his hand on David's arm. He leaned in close and kissed David on the side of his muzzle. "They'll be fine. Probably held a party when they realised I was leaving," he said. He grinned and gently pried David's fingers away from the small tube of cream. "They'll all be getting along just fine without us, I promise."

"I hope you're right," David said. He tried to smile, but Twitch could recognise the sadness still in his partner's eyes. David just wasn't as good at hiding it as he was.

Twitch shivered as he cleared his mind. His tail perked up and he kissed David's hand. "We'd best not keep Snow waiting."

"I'm right behind you."

***

Their destination was back to the factory in the outskirts of the city. Twitch had spent most of the journey through Caledonia staring out the windows. He squealed in delight every time the shield sparked into life. It was less common at night, without Prox in the sky. The sparks were less intense, and they always seemed to originate from somewhere beyond the western horizon. They arced across the sky still, like nothing Twitch had ever seen before. He had seen lightning just once before: a ferocious storm had ripped through Sydney while he had been there. The sparks across the shield reminded him of that storm, but without the terrifying wind and rain to go with it.

But for the silent crackle of lights against the shield, the night was otherwise clear. There were no clouds to obscure the stars that were visible through the light haze from the city. The constellations Twitch had become familiar with on Ceres were not present. It was a totally unfamiliar map of stars above him.

The small complex of buildings by the river appeared to be empty. Twitch had never seen anyone else there, other than Amy and Snow, and the small group who humans and starats she had inducted into her Union. There weren't even any signs around the buildings to identify what the place was called. Twitch had heard Captain Rhys call the place 'the factory', and that was what Twitch had decided to call it as well.

Snow didn't take them through to the usual rooms near the river. Instead she led them into the massive warehouse and the factory floor beyond. Everything was quiet and still inside the cavernous room. All around the walls were machines with a purpose that even eluded Twitch's mind. There were conveyor belts between most of them, so he knew it was some sort of production line. His attention was soon drawn to the middle of the room.

Kept apart from everything else was another imposing structure of metal and carbon fibre. It stood three times his height, and it was just as wide and deep. Snow approached it. She placed her hand on it as she turned around.

"You know what this is?" she asked Twitch.

"It's a Denitchev Drive, isn't it?" Twitch replied breathily. He had never seen one fully before. They had always been embedded deep inside the ships he had worked on. He recognised the tell-tale particle emitters on the corners of the massive device. Normally, they would be hooked up to a series of pipes that would feed the particles through to every part of the ship's hull. These were left open to the surrounding air.

Snow's mouth twitched in a brief smile. "It is, yes. Are you familiar with how they work?"

Twitch nodded eagerly. He hurried up to Snow's side, leaving a bemused David standing a few paces back.

"This would connect through to the ship's engines," Twitch said, placing his hand on a massive input valve just within his reach, partway up one of the flat sides of the Drive. He grinned to Snow. "Put simply, ionic particles go in, Denitchev particles come out."

"And it needs the ionic particles?" Snow asked. She leaned in as close to the input valve as she could reach, though it was still over her head.

Twitch nodded again. "Yeah. It reacts to the Denitchev crystals. They get stripped down and converted to the particles, which then react to electricity to make the jump into subspace," he said quickly. His tail swished behind him as he looked up over the massive Drive. It was a model he wasn't familiar with, but he could easily make out all the different parts. There weren't too many different ways to make a Denitchev Drive.

"How good are you at fixing them?" Snow asked. She took a step back from Twitch as he started to circle around the Drive.

Twitch poked his head out from the back of the Drive. His smile stretched across his muzzle. "Fix them? Depends what's wrong with them, and what parts are available. I've been able to bash together a fix for pretty much anything though."

"Then how would you like to repair this one? It came from a ship that got decommissioned a few weeks ago. It's just been sitting here since then," Snow said. She tapped her hand against the side of it. "The Drive broke in the ship's final flight. They were lucky they weren't too far out from Centaura."

"What's it doing here then?" David asked, cutting in before Twitch could say anything. "If it was decommissioned, shouldn't it have been scrapped? Or are things done differently here?"

Snow turned to David. Her sightless eyes fixed on him for a moment. He stood his ground and stared back at her. "They normally are," she said slowly. "This one was held aside for Amy though. She has an interest in seeing how they work."

Twitch pinned his ears back as he looked up at the Drive. "I mean, I can get it working, but it's not like we can just fire it up anywhere," he said nervously. "It won't work without the ionic emissions, and even if we did, any electricity and everything could be ripped into subspace. Especially without any shields around it."

Snow placed her hand over her chest. "Don't worry, Twitch. I can assure you, Amy will not do anything unsafely. She already has plans on how to keep things safe. You can go over all her plans if you like, just to make sure."

Twitch thought about it for a moment. David looked uncertain, but he grinned and nodded his head. "Sure, I can do that for you then. Give me a little bit to look over this and see what needs fixing, and I can give you a list of parts I need."

"Then I shall leave you be for now. I would recommend not touching anything else around here," Snow said. She swept her arm around in an arc, gesturing to the machines around the walls of the factory. "But if you need me, I will be in the office by the entrance."

"I'll give you a shout if I need anything," Twitch replied. He looked up to the Drive again. Some of the parts he would need to look at were on the top, well out of reach. Most starats would ask for a ladder, but Twitch was not like most starats. As Snow started to walk away, he jumped up onto the side of the Drive. There were small handholds here and there, and he was able to quickly clamber up until he was sitting atop the massive device. There were a few more emitters on the top, which was a feature Twitch hadn't seen before. He could also see the port that was used to fill the Drive with Denitchev crystals.

Twitch called down to David. "Do you think you could find some tools? Definitely need a drill at least."

There wasn't an immediate reply from David, but Twitch knew his partner had heard him. While he waited for his tools, Twitch started to explore around the Drive so he could familiarise himself with the different features of this particular model. He recognised almost everything. The emitters and the ports were pretty standard. The crystal housings appeared to be larger than those on TIE ships. An identification number was etched into the metal near the side of the Drive. Most of the number looked like it had been scraped away, but Twitch could just about make out one word. *Victory*. He could only assume that was the name of the ship. Or part of it, at least.

Twitch scampered around the top of the Drive. He tested a few of the seams that would allow him access to the deeper workings of the machine, but these were all sealed closed. Without any tools, he would have no chance of opening them up. He couldn't stop the grin on his muzzle. This would be a fun experience. It would be his first time working on a Denitchev Drive on the ground, and not in the tight, claustrophobic confines of a spaceship.

David's head emerged above the side of the Drive. He had found a ladder and had perched it against the side of the machine. In one hand he carried a small toolkit. He handed it up to Twitch, but his face looked trouble enough to cause Twitch's smile fade slightly.

"Everything alright?" Twitch asked. He crouched down in front of David, who rested his arms on the side of the Drive.

"I don't know. This all seems a bit strange," David said hesitantly. He gently touched one of the emitters close to him. "Why is this more important than us going with Captain Rhys? Why does Amy need a Denitchev Drive? It's hardly something she can just bolt to her car or anything like that. It's specialised. It's for a spaceship."

Twitch rubbed his muzzle. "It's a bit strange, yeah. Could just be curiosity though," he said. He didn't want to think too hard about why Snow and Amy wanted him to do this. He was just excited about the prospect of having something to fix again. He had always enjoyed that work on Ceres. It had been one of the few things that had allowed him to keep the smile on his face.

David grimaced and pinned his ears back. "I'm sure it's nothing to worry about," he said, though Twitch could see that he wasn't convinced by that. "I'm just saying we need to be careful. This is a new place. We don't know how it works yet. We need to be careful."

"I know," Twitch said. He sat down on the edge of the Drive with his legs dangling down. His tail gently thumped behind him. "We have a chance here though. We can forget what happened to us on Ceres. All that bad shit, all the time. Here's going to be good for us, I can feel it."

David smiled weakly. "You always try to think positive, aren't you?"

"We both know what the alternative is," Twitch said. His voice was strained, and he turned from David to clear his throat and to wipe his eyes with the back of his hand. Emotions threatened to bubble to the surface. Emotions he had been able to keep at bay since before he had met Captain Rhys and his life had suddenly changed for the better. He didn't want them to come back again.

"Well, we'll just need to be careful," David said again. He sighed softly. "You get to work there. I'll only be in your way. Never did understand this stuff like you do."

"Nah, you fix people. I fix machines," Twitch said. He stuck his tongue out at David, who grinned back at him before disappearing back down the ladder.

With some tools now available to him, Twitch was able to properly get to work. The smile returned to his face. He was back in his element now.

***

Though he worked for several hours, Twitch made no progress on fixing the Denitchev Drive. He hadn't expected to be able to do so. There were no logs on what was wrong with it, and Snow had been unable to provide any more information. Twitch couldn't work out whether she was testing him, or whether she genuinely didn't know the answers. By the time he finished for the day, he had gotten familiar with the Drive, but had not been able to get started on working out why it had failed. Snow had not seemed concerned by his lack of progress. She didn't even ask how well he had been doing.

Twitch felt exhausted as he made his way back to Appletree with David. The constant darkness was having an effect on him. The Terran days had been long enough. The current night had gone on for many times longer than a Cerian night, and still Prox was nowhere near lighting up the eastern horizon. Twitch longed for daylight, for what little of it they got.

Snow did not join them on the way back. She had claimed she had work to do, and had only walked as far as the car they had arrived in. She had set the navigation to return them to Appletree, then assured them both that the car would return to her once it had set them off at their destination. Twitch had been dubious, but almost as soon as they had stepped out and closed the door, the car started to move again. He watched it go in amazement. He had never seen anything quite like it before.

Twitch turned away as the car disappeared around a corner in the road. It was only then that he realised there was a starat waiting by the gates of the apartment complex. Twitch had never seen him before. The starat bounced on his toes as he waited for someone. As Twitch watched, the starat pressed a button that was meant to open an intercom system to someone in one of the apartments. There didn't seem to be any answer, and the starat's ears drooped.

"Can we help you?" David called out.

The starat jumped in surprise. He wore a formal suit and tie, which had been perfectly tailored to his body. Like all starats, he didn't wear any shoes, and his tail was left uncovered. His fur was dark, almost as deep in colour as David's. "I'm sorry, I didn't see you," the starat said. He hurried across the street and offered his hand to David. "I'm looking for Captain Griffiths."

"He's not here at the moment," Twitch said. He shook hands with the starat after David, only realising as he gripped hold of the starat's hand that his were still covered in grease and oil from the Denitchev Drive. He grimaced in apology as the other starat wiped his hand on his tail.

"Do you know when he'll be back?"

"Another week, at least," David said.

The starat hissed in displeasure. "Ah, that is a pity." He then composed himself again and straightened his back. "But where are my manners? I have not introduced myself. I'm Maxwell. I work for Minister Bakir. She was hoping to arrange a meeting with Captain Griffiths soon. How well do you know the captain?"

"We're on his crew," David said. He placed his hand on Twitch's shoulder before he could start speaking. "We'd normally still be with him, but we had some work down here that needed our attention."

Maxwell tapped his fingers against his muzzle. "And you came from Terra with Captain Griffiths?" he asked, but he didn't wait for an answer before asking a new question. "Would you care to meet the minister instead? I would hate to go back to her without any news at all."

"Oh, we can do that," Twitch said. It sounded exciting, getting to meet a minister. He didn't know why they would want to see him, and he hoped he wouldn't be a disappointment compared to Captain Rhys, but he was still willing to go.

David sounded more reserved, but still he appeared to have the same concerns. "Would she really want to see us? We're no-one special. Just a couple of starats who followed Captain Rhys here."

"You're starats fresh from Terra. You could really offer a good perspective for her," Maxwell said. He smiled nervously and twisted his tail in his hands.

"We can do it, can't we David?" Twitch said, grinning widely. He bounced on his toes, already feeling excited for the meeting. He had never met a minister before. He didn't know what exactly a minister was, but they sounded important.

David sighed and relented. "Alright, we can."

Maxwell's face lit up in a smile. "Oh, that's wonderful. I'll let Minister Bakir know. Would two days from now suit you? I can be here to collect you."

"Sure, we can do that," Twitch said. Snow hadn't told them they were expected back at the factory the next few days, so as far as Twitch knew they would be free to wander where they pleased. He was slightly disappointed that he would possibly be delayed from working on the Drive again, but this sounded fun and new.

Maxwell rested a hand on his chest. "I'm glad. David, was it? And…"

"Twitch!"

"Well, David and Twitch, it's been lovely to meet you. How about we say 11. Would that work for you?" Maxwell said. He flicked out his wrist and, to Twitch's surprise, slid across a small patch of fur to reveal a small computer screen. Twitch watched with wide eyes as Maxwell tapped on the screen with the claws of his other hand. The starat didn't seem to notice Twitch's rapt attention, even as he looked up again.

"Works for us," David said, filling in the silence Twitch had created.

"Wonderful," Maxwell said brightly. His tail flicked as he closed up the small panel on his wrist. "I won't hold you up any further today. Until next time then."

The augmented starat held out his hand to David again. After a moment of hesitation, he shook Twitch's hand again. It was the same hand he had opened up, but Twitch didn't feel anything strange or unusual about it. The hand felt like a normal hand. Twitch was almost disappointed. He had thought it would feel like metal or something, and he just hadn't been paying enough attention the first time.

David opened the gate to the apartment complex as Twitch watched Maxwell leave. It wasn't until the starat disappeared from view that Twitch finally followed after David. He scampered after his partner. "Did you see that? His arm! That was so cool," he squeaked in delight.

"It was hard not to see," David said with a laugh. He wrapped his arm around Twitch, not seeming to care about the grime and grease on his partner's fur.

"Do you think he's like a robot and can shoot lasers out of his hands?" Twitch said. They walked up to the apartment block, which still looked strange without many lights on. It felt deserted.

David shook his head and light flicked Twitch across the nose. "I doubt that one."

Twitch stuck his tongue out. "Well that's boring then. Why have robot arms if they don't have lasers?"

"Not everything needs lasers," David said. He pinned his ears back as he looked down at Twitch. They stepped inside the apartment block. The air inside was cool against Twitch's fur.

"Where's the fun in that?" Twitch retorted.

David just sighed and shook his head again. "Come on. Let's get you cleaned up. If we're going to see this Minister Bakir, then we'll want to look decent at least."

"It's two days away," Twitch protested.

"And you're covered in so much dirt it will take you that long to clean out," David replied. He ruffled Twitch's head, and his hand came away stained with grime. He held the dirty hand out as evidence.

"What if I get called back to see Snow tomorrow? I'll only get dirty again," Twitch said. He didn't think he'd picked up so much dirt inside the Denitchev Drive, but as he looked back he realised he was leaving a footprint of oil from his right foot. There were dark splotches all through his fur, especially around his hands.

"Then you get clean again tomorrow after all of that," David said. The two waited for the elevator to come down to the ground level. "This minister sounds important. We'll want to make a good impression."

Twitch nodded and swished his tail. He didn't know who Minister Bakir was, or why she could possibly have any interest in him. But knowing that she would be interested in him made him feel important. It wasn't often that had ever happened. It had never happened before he had met Captain Rhys.

That fateful meeting at the teleporters had changed Twitch's life. Despite the occasional dark whisper at the back of his mind, everything had changed for the better. He wondered if he could use this meeting with Minister Bakir to help give Captain Rhys something back. Of course, he had already given Captain Rhys a massive upgrade on the body he possessed, but there had to be something more than turning the former human into a starat. He owed it to Captain Rhys.

Grinning to himself, Twitch followed after David. He was excited for the future. He let the feeling wash over him. He wasn't used to the feeling, and he would revel in it while it was still something new.

chapter seuen

The next day followed the same pattern for Twitch. He was summoned by Snow to see her back at the factory, and he spent several hours trying to discover what was wrong with the Denitchev Drive. This time, he was by himself. David had remained back at Appletree, preferring instead to study some of the material he had been given by Doctor Anthony. David wanted to get a proper knowledge of medicine and healing, rather than trying to piece together a cure for starats' injuries and illnesses with archaic and outdated knowledge. It was all gibberish to Twitch, as much so as anything mechanical was nonsense to David.

By the end of the day, Twitch had been able to strip down the Denitchev Drive so he could see all the individual components strewn out across the floor of the factory. Everything was meticulously organised, so he would know exactly how to put it all back together again. He had still been unable to determine just why it had failed.

Snow had reacted dismissively to the news that Twitch would be meeting with Minister Bakir. She had simply told him that she expected him back the following day. Twitch had felt a prickle of discomfort as he had left the factory that day, but all was quickly forgotten by the time he returned to Appletree and the excitement of the following day had begun to build.

When the following morning eventually arrived, Twitch was out of bed long before the alarms went off. He had barely slept, but he quietly made himself a coffee and forced himself to sit still and watch out the window. Everything was still dark. There was no sunrise to watch, but he still liked the view. They were close enough to the city centre that he could see the glow of the massive skyscrapers reaching up towards the electromagnetic shield that protected the surface.

David woke up almost an hour after Twitch. He didn't comment on the coffee Twitch was drinking, only going to make one for himself. The two had sat in comfortable silence, slowly getting ready for the day ahead. It still felt strange to Twitch. He wasn't used to having time to himself, to do nothing more than sit around and think about things. Life on Ceres had been busy and frantic, with very few occasions to just settle. It wasn't just the caffeine in his system that made him twitchy. He almost needed to feel busy, or else he was somehow wasting time.

Twitch was almost impatient by the time they finally left their small apartment. The never-ending night was starting to cool even more. The air was crisp outside, and David had to go back in to get something warmer to wear. Twitch remained outside, bouncing on his toes as he kept moving in order to stay warm.

Maxwell arrived right when he said he would. David had just returned in a thicker coat, carrying a second one for Twitch, who refused to wear it just yet. Instead, he hurried towards the gates, waving in greeting to the other starat. Once again, Maxwell was dressed formally in a suit and tie that looked much better on humans. Twitch hoped he was never expected to wear something so stifling.

The other starat looked relieved as Twitch and David approached. "Oh good, you're here," he squeaked quietly. "I was worried you wouldn't come."

"Why wouldn't we?" David asked. One ear had curled down, and his tail flicked to the side in confusion.

Maxwell's ears pinned back. "Oh, I just thought you might have spoken to… never mind. Nothing to worry about now," he said. He tried to push a smile onto his muzzle, but it just came out as an uncomfortable grimace. "Shall we just move on? The minister has a busy day, and I don't want to be late."

"Of course, lead on," David said. He made sure the gate closed behind them, before the three starats made their way to the waiting car. It was much larger than any of the other cars Twitch had been in since arriving on Centaura. There still wasn't a driver, but there was enough room for nearly a dozen to fit into the back, though there were only enough seats for four. There was no one else in the car, and as soon as the door closed behind them, it started to move.

Maxwell stayed quiet as the car made its way towards the main highways. Twitch was fine with that, as he got to look out the windows again and admire the view. David tried to talk to the starat a few times, but he was met with just a few awkward short answers, usually just saying that Minister Bakir would explain everything. David soon gave up and looked out the opposite window to Twitch. Silence fell between them all.

***

Their destination was a large, circular building in the very centre of Caledonia. It wasn't as tall as the skyscrapers around it, but it had a much larger footprint on the ground and took up two blocks of the neatly organised city grid. A small park surrounded it, filled with the bizarre red trees and plants that had attracted Twitch's attention from the moment he had first seen them. Several massive flagpoles rose up in front of the building, though the flags at their tops hung limply without any wind to keep them aloft. Twitch recognised none of the flags.

Though Twitch wanted the opportunity to explore the park and see all the different native plants, Maxwell didn't give him the opportunity to do so. As soon as they got out of the car, they were guided towards the large front doors. The doors were open wide, but there were six security guards close by. All were human.

Maxwell was let inside without any delay. A couple of the humans stared at Twitch and David, but nothing was said to them as they hurried after the other starat. A wide hall opened out before them. The walls were decorated with carved wood, and a couple of ornate chandeliers hung down from the ceiling.

"What is this place?" Twitch asked in awe.

"Parliament," Maxwell replied, speaking over his shoulder. He walked right past the reception desk in the middle of the hall. Twitch and David both hurried up to stay by his side, in case anyone questioned why they were there.

At the far end of the hall, two sets of stairs rose up to a balcony level. Maxwell led them to the stairs on the right. The balcony stretched out either side of the hall into a corridor that slowly arced around in a circle. The augmented starat seemed to know exactly where he was going, and he led the two starats down the corridor.

Several doors lined the wall on their right, on the outside of the gently circling corridor. On the inside there was nothing but a wall with portraits of various humans. By the time they reached the sixth picture, Twitch realised that there was a plaque underneath each one. They had been the presidents of Centaura.

"These have been your leaders?" Twitch asked Maxwell.

The augmented starat didn't break his stride. "They were, yes."

Twitch flicked his tail. "And Minister Bakir is now?"

Maxwell let out a little laugh. "Not yet, no. She's the Minister for Terran Information and Immigration."

"Oh," Twitch said. He wasn't sure if he was meant to understand what that meant. He looked back at the portraits. A pattern quickly emerged. "They're all human."

This time Maxwell did pause. He half-turned to look back to Twitch. His jaw clenched. "They are, yes. We hope to change that in the future, but..." He trailed off and sighed.

"I thought here was meant to be good for starats," David said. A little worry crept into his voice as he moved out of the way of a couple of humans coming in the opposite direction. They both bowed their heads in thanks.

"Oh, it is," Maxwell said quickly. "Don't get me wrong, things are good here. But that doesn't mean things can't be better. That's what Minister Bakir is trying to do, but sometimes it's... ah, you'll see."

Twitch felt a small flutter of fear run through his chest. He didn't know what Maxwell was insinuating, but he didn't like the sound of it. He knew things weren't as bad as in the empire. He wasn't property. He was a free person here. No one could take that away from him. He didn't know what would happen if someone tried. It took a touch from David on his shoulder to get Twitch walking again, but there were dark thoughts gathering in the back of his mind. His smile flickered and faded, but it snapped back into place the moment Maxwell started to look back.

"Well we'd better see Minister Bakir and see what we can do," Twitch said brightly. He managed to keep the strain out of his voice.

He'd had so many years of experience of it, the deception came naturally to him.

Maxwell came to a stop outside one of the doors on the outside of the curving corridor. "This is her office just here. Wait a moment and let me see if she's ready for you." He opened the door and slipped inside, closing it behind him. A couple of muffled voices drifted through, but Twitch couldn't make out what was said.

Twitch used the brief respite from Maxwell to mentally recompose himself. He closed his eyes and leaned back against the wall and tried to chase away the dark thoughts that had been building. He focused on the Denitchev Drive. He mentally mapped out everything he had done on it. He knew where he had put every piece and what each part did. His muzzle wrinkled. There was something he was missing. Something obvious that hadn't jumped out at him. His eyes moved rapidly behind his eyelids as he mentally scanned the factory floor. He felt like the answer was right there, just beyond his grasp.

A door opened, and Twitch's mental map vanished. His ears perked up. He picked up the scent of two starats other than David, one that he recognised as Maxwell. The scent seemed strangely muted from the second one, though not as extreme as Snow's complete lack of aroma. He opened his eyes to see David looking down at him. A familiar expression was on his partner's face. It was subtle; just a raised brow and cocked ear, but it told Twitch that David was there for him, no matter what. If he needed some space, then David would take him somewhere else. If he needed someone to talk to, or a shoulder to lean on, then David was there.

Twitch responded with a small shake of his head. He would be fine. He had everything under control again, and the smile returned to his muzzle as he turned to face Maxwell, who had leaned out of the partially-opened door.

"Minister Bakir is ready for you. Would you care to come in?" Maxwell said. He pushed the door open a little wider and stepped to the side.

Beyond the door was a small office. It was cramped inside, with a few chairs surrounding a neat and tidy desk in the middle of the room. Either side of the windows at the back of the room was a couple of metallic cabinets. It took Twitch a moment to recognise them as databanks. His eyes then drifted down to the person sat behind the desk. There was not a human there, as he had expected. Instead a starat with dappled brown and black fur looked up at him with green eyes. She gestured to the empty seats in front of her desk.

Twitch quickly sat down. The chairs were designed for starat tails; something which he had been delighted to learn about since coming to Centaura.

"So you must be David and Twitch," Minister Bakir said. Her voice was gravelly and deep, much more so than any other starat Twitch had heard. "I do apologise that it has taken me so long to meet you. I have been exceptionally busy recently, and I don't usually involve myself with military defections. That is the area of the Minister of Defence. But you… you are different. It is not often starats are included on the crew from defectors."

"I'd have thought that would have been reasonably common," Twitch asked with a frown. He would have thought that most humans who came to Centaura did so at least in part because starats meant more to them than possessions and slaves.

"Sadly not, I'm afraid. We have to steal some starats away from defectors so they can be freed from service," the minister explained. She looked over the two starats sat in front of her. "But your captain is most unlike any who have ever come here. It is a shame that he was not able to make it here, but I do look forward to meeting him. How did a starat progress so far in the empire of all places?"

"Oh, he used to be human," Twitch said. He grinned at the minister's look of shock. "He used a teleporter after me. Things went a bit wrong, and he came out looking just like me."

A look of distaste spread across the minister's face. "One of the better outcomes for using those unstable machines," she said, the hint of a growl beneath her words. She quickly composed herself. "But if Captain Griffiths was once human, then perhaps he is not the person I need to speak to. Perhaps it is you both, after all."

"What do you need to know?" David asked warily. Beneath the desk, his hand found Twitch's and squeezed gently. A warning to be careful with what they said.

The minister didn't answer right away. Instead she looked towards Maxwell and nodded her head slightly. The other starat returned the nod and moved across to stand in front of the door. The screen on his augmented wrist was visible again, and he watched it intently.

"I am the Minister for Terran Information and Immigration," Minister Bakir said. She relaxed back in her seat slightly, but Twitch could see in her ears that she was straining her senses. "It is a useless position. A token effort by the government to make it look like there are starats in high places. It is a ruse to make things seem like they are progressing normally."

Twitch felt that little flutter of fear and worry in his chest again, but he quickly pushed it down. His hand squeezed tighter around David's.

"That's definitely worrying," David said uncertainly. His fingers squeezed back around Twitch's hand. "But I'm not sure why you're telling us this."

Minister Bakir tapped her fingers against her desk. "You're new here," she said after a few moments. "No one knows who you are or where your loyalties lie. I would like to offer you an attractive proposition to make sure those loyalties lie with me."

"Our loyalty is with Captain Rhys," Twitch said immediately. He looked up to David. "Isn't that right?"

David nodded. "We owe him for our freedom. We won't act against him."

Minister Bakir held one hand up. "Of course, I understand that, but Captain Griffiths has no standing on Centaura. If he wants to make a change, either here or back in the empire, then he needs people with knowledge and power here. People like me."

David twitched his muzzle. His hand moved away from Twitch's as he leaned forward. "And what would you expect us to do?" he asked. He leaned forward, lifting up off his chair slightly. "We were slaves in the empire, but we aren't idiots. I know enough about politics to know that a politician doesn't offer something for nothing. What do you want out of us?"

Minister Bakir let out a small laugh. She smiled. "You're not naïve, I can see. That's good. I would have been cautious had you accepted my offer without thinking," she said. She lowered her hand, gesturing for David to settle back down in his seat. Twitch heard Maxwell's shoulders thump against the door as he leaned back as well. "I'm offering you a job. To be my eyes and ears throughout parliament, and Caledonia itself. In return, you will get a house – better than anything you can get on universal income, a strong salary, and the ability to be a force for change."

Twitch squeaked in surprise, but he kept his mouth firmly closed. He sat on his hands to stop them playing with his tail or tapping on the desk.

"That sounds like you want us to be spies or something like that," David said. He frowned and shook his head. "I'm a medic. Twitch is a mechanic. We're not exactly trained for anything like that. I wouldn't know where to begin."

"A spy? No, nothing quite so formal," Minister Bakir said. She rose to her feet and turned to pull a thin sheet of a transparent material from the databanks behind her. She placed it down on the desk and pressed a button on the side. A holographic image immediately sprung into life. It was nothing like the grainy and unconvincing holographic projectors that TIE occasionally used. The image of a human looked completely real. He moved and gestured as he talked, but there was no sound.

Minister Bakir gestured down to the projected human. "This is President Shawn. He was elected three years ago, and while he appears to be popular in the polls, I have noticed a few alarming trends under his rule. I need to know if these are real, or if I'm just chasing shadows. I need you to go places where I or Maxwell will be recognised. I need fresh eyes to see things I am used to seeing."

This time David didn't speak. His tail curled around the back of his chair as he stared down at his lap. Twitch knew his partner didn't know what to say. He looked up at the minister. He could see a fire in her eyes, but also a worry. Her ears were perked right up, and she was trying and failing to hide little jerky movements every time there was a noise from beyond her small office. She was scared about something. She was scared about someone hearing the conversation. That wasn't something Twitch wanted to be involved in.

"We can't do that," Twitch said. He shivered as a tingle ran right down his spine and tail. His eyes caught the minister's, and the disappointment she showed sent an uncomfortable feeling through his stomach. He grimaced and felt himself relent a little. "At least, not until Captain Griffiths is back. I want to talk to him about this first."

The smile partially returned to Minister Bakir's muzzle. She exchanged a quick look with Maxwell, before she nodded once. "Very well. I can allow that. My information has it that he will return from Charon in around one week. I will give you until his return to make a decision, but please don't delay too long. I doubt there will be many willing to give you this sort of opportunity so soon after your arrival."

Twitch thought about mentioning Amy and Snow, who had seemed to offer Captain Rhys a lot already, but he held his tongue. He wasn't sure whether he should mention her to Minister Bakir, and David also kept his silence about them.

"I will tell you this, though," Minister Bakir continued. She switched off the hologram of the president. "There has not been a starat slave on Centaura for two centuries. No matter what I might say about how things could be better here, they are not what they are like in the empire. What little duties my role entails involve learning about the atrocities committed by Terra on starats. It sickens me, and I will do anything I can to fix the situation there. But before I can do that, I must clear out my own house. I need to know what's going on here, and only then can I start looking back to Terra."

"I don't know how Terra can be saved," David said in a quiet whisper. He kept staring down at his lap. His hands were clasped together. "Everything is so ingrained. Even some starats believe we deserve what humans do to us."

"All the more reason why I need help in understanding what it's really like over there," Minister Bakir said. She placed her hands down on her desk. "I can only imagine what it was like, and even then, I doubt I even come close. I need Terran starats. When I have enough, I can go to President Shawn with an actionable plan."

"We just can't commit to something like that now," David said softly.

Minister Bakir nodded. "I understand that. Think about the offer. Talk things over with your captain. Do you have a tablet?" She waited for David to pull his tablet out from his pocket. She held a small transparent sheet from her databanks against David's tablet, which beeped a couple of times. "You have my contact details now. Send me a message when you're ready to meet again."

Twitch slowly stood up. He extended out his hand for the minister to take. "We will, thank you," he said. A nervous smile spread across his muzzle. He knew what the minister was asking of them. It was something he wanted done, but Twitch knew he couldn't possibly be the starat to do it. He was a mechanic. He fixed machines. David fixed people. Neither of them could fix societies.

Minister Bakir inclined her head. "Until next time then. Thank you both for coming to see me. Maxwell will be able to show you out."

The door opened behind them. Twitch lingered for a moment longer as David stepped out into the curved corridor. He looked towards the minister as she turned her back on them. She slotted the datasheet back into the storage bank next to the window. Twitch knew she had offered them a great opportunity, but the cost was surely too much. This wasn't something they could do. With his head bowed, Twitch followed David and Maxwell out of the minister's office.

There was a lot to think about.

***

Maxwell left David and Twitch at the front of the parliament building. He had offered to take them all the way back to Appletree, but David had suggested that they use the opportunity to have a look around Caledonia, as they hadn't had the chance to see the city properly yet. Maxwell had enthusiastically supported the idea, and he had given them a list of recommended places to visit. He had excused himself from joining them though, as he had other matters to attend to.

Twitch had waved farewell to the starat, only realising after Maxwell had gone that he had never had the chance to ask the other starat about the augmentations. An opportunity had been missed, but Twitch tried to ignore his disappointment. He was daunted but excited about what was to come. He had never walked around a city before. He had never been anywhere with buildings that were quite so big. He had seen Sydney and Brisbane from a distance on Terra, but he had not walked between the towering skyscrapers. In Caledonia, they were so tall that he could barely see the darkened sky.

Twitch had never seen so many people in the same place before. They crowded close on the narrow pavements. Humans and starats alike walked together. The starats didn't cower and jump away from the humans in their desperation to avoid bumping into them, though

Twitch's instincts almost kicked in several times. He kept wanting to hide in the shadows beneath the buildings, but David's hand always held onto his.

The noise was almost overwhelming. People were talking all around them, and Twitch's ears kept trying to listen in on it all. The whine of electric motors on the roads were barely audible. His nose was likewise struggling to keep up with the assault of scents. The smell of humans and starats all melded into one, and competed with the smells of food, bitumen, metal, and many others that Twitch couldn't identify.

A short walk away from the parliament buildings was a large pedestrian open mall. Here, the crowds were a little thinner as there was more room to walk, though the number of people around them was even greater. Twitch kept pressed close to David, not wanting to lose his partner in the crowd. David's ears were perked up, and he kept on looking around. It was a brave tactic, as it meant he wasn't always focused on what was directly in front of him. Twitch had to nudge him a few times to stop him from walking into someone.

On either side of the wide walkway were rows of countless shops and restaurants. They were all open, with streams of people walking in and out of almost all of them. Twitch had been to the commercial centre on Ceres a few times, but that was utterly miniscule to what he saw now. There had been half a dozen small shops where people living on Ceres could get all they needed. Here, there was choice. There were options. It almost paralysed Twitch's mind to see how vast the single mall was. He imagined he could walk for hours and still not see everything.

Small side alleys branched off from the main mall strip. Some of these seemed to go through to the other roads that ran parallel to the mall, but most ended at the back of the buildings that faced onto the next street. The alleys were almost deserted, with very few people passing through them. David led them on a weaving path through the mall, moving from one side to the other and fighting through the crowds.

David's hand tightened around his. "I think someone is following us," he whispered. Twitch could barely hear his partner over the noise around them, but his eyes widened in panic. He started to turn, but David hissed in warning and tugged him along. "Don't look. Eyes forward. Stay with me."

"Do you know they're after us?" Twitch asked, keeping his voice just as quiet. He longed to look back, but he kept his head facing forward. "There's so many people here. They could be after anyone."

"They've followed us all the way from parliament. Always about ten metres behind us. Always looking right at me anytime I look back," David replied. His hand squeezed a little tighter. "The train station isn't too far away, I don't think. We need to get home, quickly."

Twitch squeaked in worry as David started to pick up his pace. He didn't run, but he walked briskly through the crowd. They angled towards the left side of the mall. The fur on the back of Twitch's neck prickled as he desperately tried not to look back. For a split second he gave in. He looked back to see three humans just a few metres behind them, all standing at least a head taller than almost anyone else, looking right at him. He locked eyes with one of them, before he quickly turned his head away again.

"We should run," Twitch squeaked.

"Not yet," David replied. Twitch could feel the tension in his partner's body. The tightness of the grip around his hand wasn't just protectiveness. It was panic and worry too. His tail was stiff, and every step was jerky and awkward. Twitch felt just the same.

A few more seconds passed by. They walked past one of many clothing stores. They advertised tail warmers for starats in the wide windows. On the other side of the store was one of the narrow alleys that led through to the adjacent street.

"Down there," David said. "Run. Now!"

Twitch didn't need to be told twice. He broke into a sprint the same time as David. Behind him, he could hear a human shout. He didn't know if it was their pursuers. He didn't want to wait to find out.

"Shit!" David swore. Twitch quickly saw why. This wasn't an alley that led directly through to the next street. Instead it forked and ran adjacent to the mall before it reached the next road, behind the shops. They couldn't turn back. Twitch could already hear footsteps after them.

David turned right. Twitch followed after him.

The back alley was lined with bins and rubbish, as well as the occasional pallet of stock that hadn't yet been pulled inside the back entries of the stores. Twitch chanced a quick glance back. The three humans were close behind. They didn't appear to have any weapons on them.

He couldn't see another way out of the back alley. It stretched on almost as far as he could see, and it ran perfectly straight. Unlike the pristine mall, it was dark and dirty down the back-alley. There wasn't much light to see by.

The humans behind didn't even try to shout or call out to them. They just chased. They slowly closed in, no matter how fast Twitch tried to run. David stayed just a couple of paces ahead.

Twitch's heart thudded. His chest felt tight as he struggled to keep breathing. His throat and thighs burned. He couldn't stop.

Suddenly, David turned right again. Another small alley opened up. It had been almost completely obscured by a couple of bins pulled partially across the narrow opening. Twitch almost stumbled as he tried to turn, and he felt a sharp twinge run up his left ankle as one of his old injuries complained from the exertion. He managed to stay upright, but he fell just that little bit further behind David, and closer to the chasing humans.

David disappeared into the crowd of noise at the end of the alley. Twitch tried to follow, but he was accidentally caught by a stray arm. Thrown off balance, he lost his footing and rolled down to the concrete ground. He grazed his elbow and knee as he fell, but he was back to his feet almost before the offer of apology came from the human who had hit him by mistake.

"It's fine, it's fine," Twitch quickly squeaked. He barely paid any attention to the human as he looked around to see where David had gone. He couldn't see him. His eyes flicked back to the concerned human. "Which way to the train station?"

"Northern end of the mall. You can't miss it," the human said. He pointed. "That way."

"Thanks," Twitch gasped. His legs protested the movement, but he started to walk again. There wasn't enough room to run.

Though he knew where to go, he felt lost without David by his side. His head spun, and his arm hurt from where he had fallen. He just wanted to get back home.

There was a central reservation in the middle of the mall. A few native trees grew in small stone squares. Rows of benches provided somewhere for weary shoppers to sit and rest. An empty bench provided Twitch with a vantage point. He stood on it and looked around the crowded area. He couldn't see David anywhere. Instead he saw his pursuers. One of them was behind him. Two had circled around ahead. All three of them had seen him. Another three in the crowd further north were looking at him.

"Ah fuck," Twitch muttered. He quickly jumped down again, hoping to hide himself amongst the crowd. He knew he couldn't go on ahead. He didn't know how many more there were chasing him. He had to be unexpected.

He couldn't go north. Instead he ran east. He slipped between the packs of people slowly meandering through the mall. He headed right towards the shops on the far side, and he was lucky to find an alley almost right in front of him. He hurried down into the dark shadows, hoping he hadn't been seen. He was not that lucky. He heard someone shout.

The alley Twitch had dived down didn't pass through to the next street either. Twitch turned to his left at the first chance he got, making sure that he was still going north. His ankle hurt with every step, and he couldn't maintain his pace for long. He knew he couldn't outrun them. His eyes darted around the alley, trying to find somewhere to hide. A quick glance back confirmed the humans hadn't turned the corner yet. He didn't have long. Only seconds.

He dived into the first bin he came across, and quickly pulled the lid down on top of him. He made sure it didn't slam shut and give away where he had gone. Only a small slither of dim light made its way around the lid. Twitch clamped his hands over his muzzle, partly to muffle the sound of his breathing, but also to mask the stench of the rubbish.

The footsteps of the chasing humans faltered and stopped.

"Shit, I was sure he came this way," one of them said.

"Probably for the best. Too many potential witnesses here," a second added.

A shadow passed across Twitch's face as one of the humans stood between the bin and the nearest light. For a brief moment, the starat caught sight of a glint of gold at the human's wrist, which was all he could see. On his cuff, he had a small gold badge of two crossed swords.

Another human leaned on the bin. Twitch could hear fingers drumming against the lid.

"Did you manage to ID them at least?"

"Nothing, no. Don't know if they're new here or just not in the system."

"Shit," the first human said. "You two, stay in the area and keep searching in case they're still around. The rest of you, head back to the minister and keep watch on her. If they're important, they'll show up again."

"Aye, sir."

Slowly, the humans seemed to leave. Their footsteps receded away, but still Twitch didn't dare move. He didn't take his hand from his muzzle as he waited. He had to be sure that there weren't any humans nearby at all. His ears strained for any sound, but all he could hear was the slightly muffled rumble of the crowd on the mall.

Twitch waited a few more minutes. Nothing seemed to move outside his hiding place. He gently pushed up the lid a couple of centimetres. No one shouted out. No sounds of any sudden movement. The lid moved up a little more, and Twitch peered out. Up and down the alley was empty. They had gone.

He quickly slipped out and shook off the worst of the rubbish. He knew his fur was going to stink for days, but it was better than being caught. He shuddered to think what those humans had wanted him for.

Taking care of his hurt ankle, Twitch slowly limped up the alley. His ears and eyes were strained for any sudden movement, but everything was still and quiet. A door slammed somewhere close by, which made Twitch leap into the air in fear. Nothing happened. No one started running.

Letting out a whimper of fear, Twitch carried on heading north. Every time he passed a small alley he made sure that he hadn't gone beyond the mall, but each time he could see the light and crowds as busy as ever. Finally, the alley came to an end. Another road ran perpendicular to the alley and the mall, and on the far side was the train station. He couldn't see any of the humans who had been chasing him, but Twitch still made sure he stayed to the shadows as much as possible as he stepped out of the alley.

The road had six lanes of traffic all heading in the same direction. Small green lights dotted between the various lanes, and a cluster of humans and starats all gathered together on either side of the road. Twitch slunk in amongst them. A few starats wrinkled their noses as he approached, though none of the humans appeared to notice him.

The lights on the road blinked to amber, and then to red. The flow of cars came to a halt and a gap opened up between them. If there was a signal for the pedestrians to start walking, then Twitch missed it. He was jostled into crossing the road by a group of humans behind him. Towards the train station and safety. He hurried across the road. He found a sheltered corner to hide in.

Twitch reached into his pockets to find his transport passcard. His fingers instead closed around his tablet. He had forgotten all about it. He still wasn't used to having things he could call his own, especially something as valuable as the tablet. It was everything he could have ever wanted. Information. Communication. Navigation. A green light blinked, letting him know he had notifications. He had two dozen. All from David. All in the last five minutes. He grimaced. His tablet had been set to silent when he had used its torch feature as he had dismantled the Denitchev Drive.

His hands shook as he called David back. His partner answered instantly. "Twitch?"

"I'm here… I'm safe," Twitch said. His voice was as shaky as his hands.

"Where are you? I'm so sorry, I didn't know I lost you."

"I'm at the train station. Just outside the main gates."

"I'm… I'm just inside. Stay there." David sounded a little out of breath, and through the speakers Twitch could hear his partner running. Just a few seconds later, he could hear David calling out his name. A few seconds after that, David had Twitch wrapped up in his arms. "I'm so sorry. I didn't know you were gone until too late."

"It's alright, it was my fault for falling back," Twitch said, speaking right into David's shoulder. He felt tears spring to his eyes.

"No, I should have made sure you were with me." David broke the hug. His cheeks were sodden wet. He had been crying for more than the last few seconds. "I'm sorry. I'm so sorry."

Twitch stretched up to kiss David. "I'm fine, it's not your fault. But we should go inside, in case they're still out there."

David sniffled and nodded. He let himself be guided by Twitch back inside the station. The ticket guard gave them an odd look as they swiped the cards, but no one stopped them. Signs to all the different platforms hung down from the tall ceiling. Normally Twitch would have been excited to see the station and the mag-trains at the many platforms, but instead all he felt was terror. It felt like there was almost as many people inside the station as there had been on the mall. Though his eyes were still wide and searching, he couldn't see any sign of the pursuing humans.

"They were watching over the minister. That was why they were chasing us," Twitch said. His heart was starting to slow down again, but his tail was still tucked in between his legs.

"The minister?" David asked. His arm was wrapped tight around Twitch as they walked. "Then she's too dangerous for us. We can't accept her offer, no matter what."

Twitch shook his head. He had already been thinking the same thing. "I just want to go home."

"Me too," David said. He leaned down to kiss Twitch on the top of the head. "Come on, our train is this way. I'm not going to let go of your hand until we're home, alright?"

"I love you."

"Love you too."

chapter eight

Rhys had barely set foot on the bridge of the *Harvester* in the four days it had taken to return to the outskirts of the Sol System. He had spent most of the time either in his quarters, or in the briefing room with either Major-General Ulrich or Aaron. It had been nice being in the less oppressive artificial gravity on his ship, even after just a few days on Centaura. The major-general and her soldiers had complained a little about the lesser gravity, but it hadn't been long before they had become used to it.

The *Harvester* had come out of subspace a little way inside the orbit of Pluto to vent heat, and also to maintain the correct angle of approach they wanted. They were a long way from the sensory range of Pluto. This far out into the Sol System there was nothing to detect them. Only Neptune occasionally got close enough to Pluto to matter, and that was on the opposite side of Sol.

Rhys would have liked to have been on the bridge for the return to realspace, but instead he had been in the briefing room as he tried to work out the final details for his plan to liberate the prisoners from the Charon prison. Everything was almost in place. He just had to convince the major-general which prisoners they should focus on.

"I definitely think we should free Maggie Grey," Rhys said. He looked up from the screen resting on the table. Major-General Ulrich sat opposite him, as she had done for most of the last four days spent in the small room.

"Why do you say that?" the other starat said. She gave nothing of her thoughts away. There wasn't even a twitch from an ear.

"She was working on Mars when she was taken. She was there for several years," Rhys said. He glanced back down to the notes he had been given. A lot of information had been redacted, but there was still enough for him to understand the basics of what she had been doing. "She wasn't able to get any meaningful messages out to Centaura for almost two years before her capture. I can only imagine the information she must have learned in that time."

Major-General Ulrich nodded her head, but Rhys wasn't sure if that was approval of his choice, or just acknowledging his explanation. Either way, Rhys continued.

"I think the second should be Pierre Beaumont. He spent some time on the factories on Luna. He'll know what Terra is capable of, and all the latest technology they're starting to develop," he said. He carefully pressed down on the screen of his tablet to swipe across to a new page. He had mostly gotten used to the power gloves, but he was still a little clumsy with them for delicate tasks. Anything was preferable to the pains in his hands whenever he tried to hold something.

"Both good choices," Major Ulrich said, nodding once more. "Anyone else?"

Rhys flicked his ears. "The Silver Fox."

Major-General Ulrich reacted this time. She blinked and leaned back in her chair, trying to portray nonchalance, but her ears had perked right up. "An interesting choice. Why him?"

"He's been a thorn in the empire's side for decades. He's a skilled pilot and has a good mind for strategy. He's an enemy to the empire," Rhys said. He didn't want to mention Leandro, or his own loose connection to the Silver Fox. It had been his former first officer who had betrayed the pilot and allowed him to be captured.

"The enemy of our enemy isn't necessarily our friend," Major-General Ulrich said cautiously.

"True, but he has fought against the empire his whole life. There are few who have ever come close to his successes against our… against imperial ships," Rhys said. He was glad he had never been deployed against the Silver Fox, for it had been a hopeless task for many years. "Plus I know he has a love of starats. He may not agree with everything Centaura stands for, but I know he will not be opposed to us."

The major-general clasped her hands together beneath her chin. "I will admit, I did not think of the Silver Fox at all. He presents an interesting target. I had also targeted Maggie and Pierre, but tell me, why didn't you think James Lancaster was a good target?"

"His last detailed update was just two weeks before his capture," Rhys said. He rubbed his muzzle. The power glove still felt stiff and strange to the touch. "You said we could realistically expect to recover up to four people. I couldn't see anyone else on the prisoner list who would be beneficial for us, but given Lancaster wouldn't have much new information… he shouldn't be a primary target, but if we have the opportunity, we can move for him too. The other three should be higher priority."

Major-General Ulrich smiled. "My thoughts exactly, Captain Griffiths. The thought of the Silver Fox interests me, and I'm willing to add him to our targets. Maggie and Pierre will be our primary goals though. They are the most important two to retrieve. I wish we could take more, but we're already close to capacity as it is."

"I understand, ma'am," Rhys said. A smile came to his muzzle, and a small weight was removed from his shoulders. He was worried his justifications wouldn't please the major-general, but it appeared that he had judged everything correctly. It wasn't long now before they would start putting that plan into action. Already the ship was starting to feel cooler as all the excess heat that had been building up was vented out into space. The approach to Pluto wasn't far away.

***

Rhys had only briefly stopped by the bridge to ensure that Aaron was completely up to date with the plan. It felt strange, not being present when all the communication with Charon and Pluto was meant to happen, but it was decided that as Rhys was needed on the surface, Aaron would maintain his position on the bridge. Aaron had wished Rhys good luck and tried to act calmly, but Rhys could see the tension on the bridge. Everyone was nervous. This was their first time acting against the empire. Rhys doubted his ears would perk up until the mission was over. He knew exactly how everyone was feeling.

The crew had been split roughly in two. Half would remain on the *Harvester*, while the remainder would descend to the surface in one of the shuttles. There would be four empty seats in the shuttle for the prisoners they planned to release.

Rhys made his way down to the armoury ahead of schedule. He wasn't the first to arrive. Leandro was already there. Rhys had made sure the grey-furred starat was on the ground team. He had been a pirate once. Rhys knew that Leandro would be able to handle himself.

Leandro had already put on his combat suit. They had been provided by Centaura, and they were a significant upgrade on the old suits they had replaced. They were tough enough to provide some protection against gunfire and they were designed that they would maintain a vacuum seal around the body, even if the outer layer was punctured. Rhys didn't expect to need the vacuum protection inside the prison, but he would be glad of the armour should their plan go awry.

"Are you ready for this?" Rhys asked the older starat. He winced as he slowly slid off the power gloves so he could start suiting up. His hands felt as frail and weak as ever, probably not helped by the fact he had barely used them at all over the previous four days.

"Will we be getting him, Captain Rhys?" Leandro asked. His voice shook. He held his helmet tightly in both hands.

"We will," Rhys said simply. He didn't need to tell Leandro about the priority of the four prisoners they were targeting. All that mattered was that Leandro knew there was a chance they would be able to rescue the Silver Fox.

Leandro sighed and closed his eyes. He leaned back against the row of lockers behind him. "Thank you."

Rhys smiled back at the grey-furred starat, but he didn't say anything. He focused instead on trying to suit up without hurting his hands too much. It was a difficult proposition, but he had been able to get most of it on by the time others from the ground crew started to arrive. Most of the number was made up of the major-general's soldiers. They numbered two dozen, and they would be complemented by three more from the *Harvester's* services crew. They had been volunteered by Commander Briggs as the most suitable for a ground assault.

The arms of Rhys's suit had been specially designed to fit back into the power gloves. With a little help from Leandro, he was soon prepared to leave. He left his helmet off for the moment. He squeezed his right hand tight, activating the bullet shield embedded in the wrist. It snapped out into place correctly, and he slotted it back into place again after the test was complete.

Major-General Ulrich was the last to arrive. She was already suited up to lead the twenty-nine humans and starats to the shuttles.

"Please ensure your oxygen tanks are full and your weapons have ammunition," the major-general said. She stood in the doorway to the armoury and looked around the squad. "We don't expect to need oxygen, but this is Charon. If anything goes wrong, we're a long way from any help. Helmets on. Cameras on."

"Cameras, major-general?" Rhys asked with a flick of his ear.

"Centauran policy, captain," the major-general replied. She tapped the visor of her helmet. "Everyone has a camera attached to their helmet. Everything we do is recorded on the ship's data core. I've already had yours hooked up, thanks to Commander Briggs."

Rhys twitched his muzzle. "I didn't realise you did anything like that, ma'am."

"Just for combat missions. Makes for good training and debriefing," Major-General Ulrich said. She looked around the rest of the squad. "Now, come on. We're almost in launch range of the shuttles. Charon will be expecting us."

Rhys fumbled a little with his helmet, but he was able to get it securely attached before he needed to ask Leandro for help. As soon as it clicked into place, an electronic HUD flickered into life on the inside of his visor. It displayed his heart rate, oxygen reserves, and exterior environment information. A small red icon in the top right corner indicated it was recording his visuals. The name Ulrich flashed up on the top left as the major-general started speaking. Her voice came through the helmet's speakers crisply and clearly.

"Alright everyone, move out. We're taking Shuttle 4 for this."

There was only a short walk between the armoury and the shuttle bay. Rhys followed directly behind the major-general, with the rest of the squad just behind him. The ship gave a few shudders around them as it slowed down on the approach to Charon. Using some of the transponder codes gleaned from the ship's data core, they were disguised as a Terran ship travelling to Charon with the excuse of transferring prisoners. Rhys didn't know whether the lie had been believed, but Aaron hadn't contacted him to say they had been uncovered. Their scans had revealed no Terran ships near the dwarf planet. The closest warships would be based at Uranus. It would be a journey of several hours for any ship to reach them. Even if Pluto called out for help immediately, they should still have enough time to do what was needed and get away before reinforcements arrived.

The airlocks were opened, and the squad filtered through into the shuttle. Slate-grey walls enclosed around them. The shuttle would be cramped, but there were enough seats for everyone in the narrow rows that took up most of the room inside. There were no screens to the outside, but the shuttle was entirely automated anyway. Rhys was glad no one would be able to see the worry etched into his face as he sat down in the front row.

Another starat sat down next to him. With their tinted visors, it was difficult to tell who it was. Leandro's name flashed up on his HUD.

"These suits are really good fits," the starat said. His hands patted down on his legs. "I've never had one that had somewhere to put my tail, and my ears aren't being crushed either."

"That sounds uncomfortable," Rhys said with a grimace. The helmet pinched down on his ears slightly, but it wasn't painful.

"You have no idea," Leandro laughed. "I spent most of three months stuck in a suit with my tail wedged down with my leg. I told you that story once. It ended with the Silver Fox. It feels only right that today will end with him too."

Before Rhys could answer, the private communication channel was cut as Aaron overrode it. He spoke directly to everyone on an open channel. "Right, Charon have given us permission to approach. They sound sceptical, so be careful," he said. A small click sounded in Rhys's ear as the channel changed from open to private. Aaron's voice continued. "Be on your guard down there, Rhys. You're trying to impress them, but you don't need to take any risks."

Rhys smiled in the privacy of his helmet. "I'll be fine, Aaron. You just worry about looking after my ship. I don't want anything out of place when I get back."

"So... I shouldn't have eaten the biscuits down the side of your chair?"

"Aaron, those have been there since Ceres."

Aaron laughed. "Still tasted just fine."

"I can't tell if you're being serious or not," Rhys replied. He shook his head.

"Guess you'll have to find out when you get back, won't you? Just ten seconds until you launch. Good luck, Rhys."

"Good luck, Aaron."

The channel between them terminated. Rhys was left alone in his helmet once more. He closed his eyes and prepared himself for the shuttle launch. He only had a few seconds to wait before he felt the familiar press of Gs on his chest. The shuttle had dampeners to limit the effects of g-force, but there was still a noticeable push back into his seat.

Rhys tried to control his breathing as the shuttle raced away from the *Harvester*. He knew it wouldn't be long before they were safely docked at the Charon prison, but any journey in a shuttle always unnerved him. It threatened to bring back unpleasant memories. He was glad he wasn't using a teleporter though.

Rhys ran through the plan once more in his mind. Everything relied on them making it down to the surface. Once there, he was sure they would have the firepower to overrun the defences of the prison, especially if they were able to prevent any alarms being sent down to Pluto. They had aerial support from Aaron, who would be able to position the *Harvester* to protect them from any attacks from the ground. In theory, everything should work just fine, but Rhys knew never to trust theory. He had to be ready to think fast if needed. The major-general had given him authority to command the squad. She would only overrule him in dire situations. Rhys hoped it would never come to that, for it would be a poor example of his leadership.

The shuttle soon docked on the dwarf planet's largest moon. Metal clanked as the airlocks connected. Rhys rose to his feet and set his comms to link in to everyone. "You all know what we're here for. They might be hostile out there, but hopefully they haven't seen through the ruse yet. Stay prepared, but do not open fire unless fired upon, or you hear mine or Major-General Ulrich's order. Remember, the codeword is 'khan'. If you hear that, under any circumstance, that means we are in a hostile situation and you have full authority to shoot to kill. Good luck out there."

Rhys knew he didn't need to go over his plan again. Everyone had been briefed on exactly what was expected of them. They knew the dangers that potentially faced them on the other side of the airlocks.

The doors slid open. Beyond them was a small, empty corridor with a dozen airlocks sealed closed. At one end of the corridor was a window that looked down to the red surface of Pluto. For a fraction of a moment, Rhys thought the sight looked eerily like Mars. He turned his head the other way. A closed door blocked off the other end of the corridor, but it opened before he reached it. His hand twitched towards the pistol on his hip as a human stepped into the doorway. They were armed too, but their weapon was still at their hip as well.

Rhys switched his comms onto open broadcast, so his voice was emitted from the speakers just beneath his jaw. "We're here for prisoner transfer to the Vatican vaults," he said. He straightened his shoulders and looked up to the human who stood in their way.

"I heard nothing about that," the guard said warily. He stepped back, but not far enough to clear the doorway.

"Urgent summons. Comes right from His Holiness, I was told," Rhys said. He knew what he had planned to say to convince the guards. He wanted this done smoothly and without any shots fired.

The human guard glanced back. A couple of other humans were stood not far behind him. They were stood behind a desk backed onto the far wall of what appeared to be a reception area. One of them shrugged. The first guard turned back. His mouth was open slightly. His hand relaxed from his side. Then he paused and frowned. Confusion quickly turned to anger. "Is this some kind of joke?" he spat. His hand started to move to his hip again. "Starats trying to order me around?"

Rhys switched off his open broadcast. "Shit," he said quickly, before opening a comms channel with his crew. "Code khan. Hostile situation."

Rhys hadn't even moved by the time several gunshots rang out around him. The guard in front of him likewise had no time to react before he was gunned down. Before he hit the ground several of Rhys's crew had moved forward. They fired quickly, and the other two behind the desk had been neutralised.

A starat jumped behind the desk. Leandro's voice soon reached Rhys's ears. "Alarms were activated. Pluto has been notified."

Rhys swore again in the silence of his helmet. He had hoped they would be able to avoid that. It meant plans needed altering. Now they would need to take care of the prison guards, as well as the barracks on Pluto. He quickly barked out orders. "Gamma team. Bunker down here and secure a perimeter. Reinforcements from Pluto will come by the space elevator. Defend it until we return."

Rhys slowly spun around on the spot. The elevator doors were just beyond an airlock next to the shuttle bay. Any reinforcements would be forced to filter through slowly. Three further doors opened off from the reception. A black door was behind the desk, though Leandro had already tried to open it. Locked firmly, even with the passcard he had taken from one of the fallen guards. That left two further doors at opposite ends of the room, both branching off into different corridors. Rhys knew where the prisoners were located. Two in each direction.

"Beta team. Your targets are Beaumont and Lancaster. Alpha team, with me. We take the Silver Fox and Grey. Stay alert and move out. Gamma team, keep me updated on your position."

The crew immediately split apart into the three groups. They had already been assigned which team they were a part of. Within twenty seconds everyone was prepared and ready to move again. The gamma team were already using the furnishings around the reception to erect crude defences to overlook the space elevator, whilst also not neglecting the other points of entry from the corridors. A shiver ran down Rhys's tail. He was glad he wasn't required to stay back there. He hurried to the head of the alpha team. His pistol was gripped tightly in the synthetic fingers of his power gloves. Inside the safety of his suit, his real fingers struggled to stop shaking.

There were no doors leading off the corridor. It was a long, white passage that ran for nearly a kilometre along the surface of Charon. It linked two separate buildings, and it provided small windows that looked out over the barren surface of the moon. Pluto loomed angry and red over the horizon.

"Quick thinking there, Captain Griffiths." Major-General Ulrich's voice reached Rhys's ear across a private channel.

"I should have realised they'd never believe us the moment they saw some of us are starats," Rhys said quietly. It was a mistake, and one he should have prepared around.

"If it makes you feel better, captain, I didn't think of it either," the major-general replied. "We both knew it was going to come to a fight sooner or later. No matter what, we were going to have to fight our way back out."

Rhys was only slightly buoyed by the thought the major-general hadn't considered the same problem, but she had an excuse. She had not grown up in the empire, where starats were never treated with respect. He had known that. He should have seen it coming.

A set of locked doors impeded their progress at the end of the corridor. The control panel beside the door flashed red. "Cutters come forward," Rhys commanded, adding a physical gesture to his spoken command.

Two humans approached the door. Together, they used an arc cutter to slowly slice through the door. Sparks flew as the heated blade cut through metal around the lock. It seemed to go so slowly, and Rhys tapped his foot nervously as he watched.

With a loud crash that echoed through the corridor, a large chunk of metal fell from the door. The cutters quickly stepped back, and Rhys moved forward with three others to cover them with the bullet shields. Without the lock to hold it in place, the door slowly swung open.

Rhys's HUD warned him that the air was cold and thin beyond the doors, though it was still at a breathable level. He tucked his tail close between his legs as he scanned around the room beyond. Gone were the pristine white walls. These were dark grey concrete. Small patches of damp were visible here and there, slightly white with frost.

"Be on alert for any guards," Rhys said, speaking across an open alpha channel. "There should be a dozen stationed in this wing."

As if to emphasise his point, a cloud of dust erupted from the concrete behind them as a single shot missed its target. Rhys reacted quickly. He crouched to the ground and tracked where the shot had come from. He saw movement on the far side of the room, and he quickly raised his pistol and fired twice. The first shot hit the guard in the chest. The second struck the concrete wall behind where he had been crouched. He had fallen to the floor and didn't move again.

Rhys suppressed the familiar sensation of sickness in his stomach. No matter what he did, he always felt that nausea in combat. In many ways, he didn't want to lose it. It meant he still cared. He still had respect for the lives he was taking. He allowed himself half a moment to feel that guilt, before he forced it from his mind.

A small voice spoke in Rhys's ear as the gamma group leader contacted him. "We're prepared here, Captain. Elevator is coming this way. Expected arrival in one minute."

"Understood, lieutenant," Rhys replied. He kept his eyes scanning around the room as he followed two humans and one of the starats across to the corridor that branched off at the far side of the room. "Keep me updated. Let me know if you need reinforcements."

"Wilco, Captain."

The line cut out. Three of Rhys's soldiers hurried forward to the next corridor. They fired a couple of shots, and Rhys heard a body crumple to the ground. Two down. There were ten more, somewhere. They had probably found a more defensible position further in, where they kept the inmates.

Rhys moved forward slowly as he retook the lead position. The wide corridor was plunged into darkness as the lights were cut to the facility. Immediately, Rhys's visor switched to low light mode. Everything took on an eerie green tone as his visor artificially lit up the corridor and the open room beyond. He could see a few doors ahead, leading to the various cells. His visor also picked up movement as the guards tried to get into position.

It took Rhys just three shots. Two of them hit his targets, and those two guards didn't get back up. The defence force returned fire, but they were just as hindered by the darkness as Rhys's assaulting crew. Rhys also knew from experience that the low light vision was worse on the Terran equipment. Without realising it, the defending guards had handed Rhys an advantage.

Squeezing his right hand, the bullet shield snapped into place. He could still see through the transparent screen, even in the low light, but was tough enough to protect his body from any enemy fire. Holding his right arm up so the shield protected his head, and with his left hand he took aim with his pistol.

His right arm shuddered as the bullet shield caught the brunt of several shots. Another clipped against his leg, but the shot didn't cause any damage. He emptied his pistol's cartridge before he fell back behind the second line to reload.

The human in front of Rhys fell to the floor, leaving him exposed. He crouched down to keep as much of his body behind the bullet shield as he frantically tried to reload. In the darkness, it was harder to control the precise movement of his power gloves. Without the ability to feel his fingertips, he needed to see the motion to act with precision.

It took longer than Rhys would have liked, but he was soon able to step forward and take the place of the fallen human. But for their bullet shields, they didn't have much cover, but they were still able to advance forward. The imperial guards were starting to fall back. One dropped his weapon and fled. Before Rhys could react to them, they had already fallen with a bullet to the back of the head.

A couple more of his soldiers fell back as stray bullets snuck between the shields, but it took only a minute more before everything fell quiet again. The guards had been neutralised.

Rhys took a deep breath and gestured for some of his soldiers to move forward and ensure there were no more threats. He turned to see Major-General Ulrich crouched beside one of the fallen. "Two injuries," she said, seeming to notice Rhys's attention. "And one fatality."

Rhys closed his eyes for a moment. It always felt worse when the deaths were on his side, but he knew that there was nothing he could do. This was war. Everyone present knew what they were risking. "Can you arrange someone to look after the wounded," Rhys requested. He had been given authority over the major-general for the mission, but he still didn't feel comfortable giving her a direct order.

The major-general nodded her head. "I'll see to it myself. You focus on our targets."

Rhys quickly looked around. Though he couldn't see much, he could still just about make out the identification numbers on the cells either side of them. He knew exactly which numbers he needed to look for. He barked out orders to his team. "You two, guard the way back. You two, the way forward. I don't want anyone sneaking up on us. I want the door to Maggie Grey's cell opened up in the next two minutes. Understood?"

A mixture of "Yes, Captain" and silent salutes rippled around the assault team. Everyone got to work in their assigned roles. Rhys stayed in the middle of it all and set his HUD to contact the other two team leaders.

"Gamma and beta come in. Status update."

"Beta here. Defence neutralised and primary target acquired. Secondary target in two minutes."

"Gamma here. Situation under control, though we are expecting enemy reinforcements on Elevator Two and Three."

Rhys allowed himself a small smile. "Good work, both of you. We're moving on our primary now. Beta, fall back and reinforce gamma when you have your secondary target."

"Wilco, Captain."

They were a little behind the other group. Rhys knew that he needed to speed things up a little. He pulled aside three from the group clustered around Maggie Grey's door. They were already working on opening the door to her cell, with the arc cutter slicing around the secure lock.

Rhys made sure Leandro was one of the ones he pulled away from Maggie's door. "Come with me. We're moving on our secondary target. Bring the cutters as soon as you're done here."

Rhys could see the tension in Leandro's shoulders as he moved across the cell block, checking every number for the right door. The Silver Fox was being kept a little further down, beyond the bodies of the guards who had died trying to protect the facility. Rhys tried not to look down at them.

Leandro stood in front of the door once they found it. He remained almost perfectly still. Rhys stood beside him. His hands touched against Leandro, as they waited for the arc cutter to finish with Grey's cell. They didn't take long, and they quickly hurried across the cell block to begin work on the second door. Metal screeched as sparks erupted from the door, but Leandro didn't move even as the sparks washed over his suit.

"Are you alright?" Rhys asked Leandro, trying to pull the older starat away from the door.

"I am just trying to think what to say," Leandro said. He laughed weakly as they spoke on a private channel. "All these years waiting for this moment, and I do not even know what to say."

"Would you like us to open it?" Rhys asked. He held out his hand, but Leandro shook his head.

"No, it has to be me."

Rhys could feel Leandro's hand shaking, and he took a step back to allow the other starat the space to open the door. This was the moment Leandro had been waiting for. He wasn't going to take that away for him.

The lock fell away. At a gesture from Rhys, the two cutters stood back. The door opened. Inside was a small cell with a toilet and a bed, and barely enough room to stand. A single flickering bulb swung from the ceiling, but all was as dark inside the cell as outside. A gaunt, aging human sat on the bed, pressed up against the far wall. What little hair he had left was white and wispy as it clung to his scalp around his ears.

"Who is that? Little loud today, aren't you?" the human barked. "Why are the lights out?"

Leandro shook as he slowly removed his helmet. "Emile... it is me," he whispered quietly. His helmet fell to the floor with a clunk as he took a couple of shaky steps forward.

Rhys switched his helmet's torch on. Leandro was bathed in light.

The Silver Fox stared. "Leandro?" he asked hoarsely. "Is that really you?"

Leandro crouched down in front of the bed. His hands lightly rested on the Silver Fox's shoulders, before he pulled the frail human into an embrace. "It is me, it really is me. I am here. I wanted to save you, like you did to me all those years ago."

"Oh, my love, it's really you. You're here," the Silver Fox said. Tears flowed from his eyes as he leaned into the starat. "I'm so sorry I could never find you again. I looked and I looked for so long."

Rhys was distracted by a call in his ear from Major-General Ulrich. "We have Grey, but she needs medical attention. We need to make a move quickly. Are you almost done?"

"Almost done," Rhys replied, before switching to open broadcast. "Leandro, we need to go."

Leandro sniffed as he turned his head. "Understood, Captain Rhys." He let go of the Silver Fox for just a brief moment to reattach his helmet, before he helped the human up out of his bed. The Silver Fox could barely walk, but with Leandro's support he was able to take his first steps out of the cell. Rhys wondered how long he had been trapped in there.

Though Leandro was loathe to let the Silver Fox go, the rescued prisoner was transferred to the two humans who had come with them. They were able to carry the Silver Fox between them much quicker than the human was able to walk.

Rhys called through to his other team leaders. "We have both targets and are making our way back. Any movement from the elevators?"

"We're reinforcing now," the beta leader responded. Her voice sounded strained, and Rhys could hear the muffled sounds of gunfire echoing through her speaker. "We released an additional prisoner, a starat, by mistake. I've lost track of him though. He fled as we began reinforcements."

There wasn't any response from the gamma leader, but Rhys didn't need one. He knew he would be busy trying to fend off the guards from Pluto. There had been no communication from Aaron above them, so he knew there wasn't any threat from any unexpected ships arriving. All the same, Rhys wanted to hurry back. He quickly caught up to the rest of the alpha team as they began to make their way back to the reception.

Maggie Grey was also being carried. She looked worse than the Silver Fox. She was just as frail as he was, but she had several cuts running down her arms and legs. Rhys shuddered. He recognised the style of cuts, and the growing infections around the wounds. They had been administered to him as well, at the hands of Cardinal Erik.

"Hurry," he said quietly. He didn't even know if he had broadcast the command to his crew, or whether he had spoken it just to himself. He didn't want to be reminded of his torture from the Vatican. He was unsure if it was a Vatican tactic that had spread to Charon, or whether there was someone from the church present on the small moon. He had no desire to run into a cardinal.

Rhys re-engaged his shield as he hurried ahead of the two carried prisoners. The group split into two. Those who remained behind to guard the prisoners, and those who were capable of reinforcing the gamma team. Rhys led them all, and he burst through the doors at the end of the long corridor with his shield raised.

The doors to the elevators were barricaded by the guards from Pluto. Surrounding them was the gamma team, with a few from the beta team to add to those who had fallen. Rhys took a couple of shots before anyone could react to his presence.

"Beta team, can you get your objectives to the shuttle safely?" Rhys called out. He slid down to rest behind the makeshift shelter that had been built from upturned furniture. The holes that had already been ripped through them proved it wasn't much protection, and he made sure to wedge his shield between himself and the humans by the elevator.

"Already secure, Captain," came the quick reply. "We have the assets and the wounded back here."

"Any sign of the additional starat?"

"None, Captain. Sorry. He's vanished completely."

Rhys sucked in his breath and quickly glanced over the top of the furnishings. "Major-General, we'll provide cover. Get Grey and the Silver Fox back to the shuttle. Then we fall back."

"Understood, Captain. We'll be through in five seconds."

Rhys counted to two seconds. "All up. Open fire and protect the assets," he called out. He was the first to emerge from beneath the barricades. He raised his shield and fired his pistol. He didn't target anyone in particular. He simply fired and hoped to cause enough confusion amongst the imperial ranks that they couldn't return fire.

A few shots bounced off his shield, but none reached his body. A primal snarl threatened to burst from his muzzle, but he bit down on his tongue and kept quiet.

Out of the corner of his eye, Rhys could see movement approaching the shuttle bay. At his command, the gamma and beta teams began to move back from the barricades. They had nothing but their firepower and shields for defence now as they slowly paced back. The front row crouched low, with those behind remaining upright. Between them all, their shields made almost a complete wall to shelter behind.

Those to the sides of the wall peeled off to the side and behind. They quickly filtered through the airlocks as the imperial guards started to emerge from the elevator.

Rhys was the last one left. His shield cracked from the force of several bullets striking it at once. He fired his pistol one last time before he stepped back into the airlock. The doors sealed shut, and he fell backwards into the shuttle. The engines were already firing.

Rhys patched himself up to the *Harvester*. "We're on our way back, Captain Lee," Rhys called out. "Be alert for possible ground to air missiles."

"We're watching out for you, Captain. Ready to receive." It wasn't Aaron who responded, but Jermaine McDonald, the *Harvester's* communications officer. "Docking will commence in two minutes."

The broken shield didn't collapse into its housing, leaving Rhys to clumsily work around it as he removed his helmet. Still lying on his back, he propped himself up on his elbows as he looked around the shuttle. Almost everyone else had been seated. The major-general crouched down by his side.

"All four targets acquired," she said softly. "Loss of one life, with six wounded. One serious."

Rhys pinned his ears down. "It could have gone smoother," he said.

"But it could have gone so much worse, Captain Griffiths," the major-general said. She held out her hand for Rhys to take. "I couldn't have asked much more of you there. You demonstrated your ability to fight for us, and you didn't hold back when you could have. On that regard, you can consider this a pass."

A small smile started to spread across Rhys's muzzle. He had passed the first test given to him. One step closer to returning to the fight, but this time he would be fighting for starats.

All he had to do now was find some way to permanently fix his hands.

chapter nine

Twitch had spent most of the last week locked up in Snow and Amy's factory. David had been with him most of the time. They hadn't felt safe at home, without the protection of Captain Rhys and his crew around. There had been no further attacks. They hadn't seen anyone acting strangely around them – not at Appletree or at the factory, but still Twitch felt like he was being constantly watched. The fur on the back of his neck prickled constantly.

They hadn't told anyone about what had happened in Caledonia. Not even Snow or Amy knew about the incident. They had agreed not to tell anyone, for fear that the humans were still spying on them.

Twitch had tried to distract himself with the Denitchev Drive. He had finally got it working a couple of days after the incident in Caledonia when he had found a few snapped wires deep inside the Drive. It had been a simple fix in the end, which surprised Twitch. He doubted a Drive would have been scrapped for such minor damage. He had asked Snow where it had been retrieved from, but she had not answered his questions. Instead she had charged Twitch with improving the Drive. She wanted him to make it as efficient as possible. He didn't know why she would have wanted such a thing, but he had not questioned her, as he knew he would get no answer.

Most of Twitch's attention had been focused on the ionic reaction chamber and the particle emitters. He had always known they were the most inefficient parts of the Drives, but most of that was an acceptable loss. The Drives didn't need to be overly efficient in how far they could spread the Denitchev particles, as they only needed to cover a single spaceship.

Twitch was buried halfway inside the opened Drive. He was attempting to rearrange some of the parts so he could install an enlarged ionic chamber to allow for more crystals to react inside the Drive at once. In theory, it should create a more powerful flow of particles that could be projected at a greater range. It required him to be upside down inside the Drive with just his knees bent over the side to support him. A thick visor covered his eyes as he sliced through metal with his particle cutter.

Through all the noise he was making, Twitch only just heard someone knocking on a door. He ignored it. David was out on the factory floor somewhere, studying some of the medical journals Doctor Anthony had given him.

A few minutes passed without any interference from anyone. By then, Twitch had cut the hole he needed, and his head was starting to feel a little heavy from being upside down for so long. He switched off the particle cutter and attached it to the straps around his wrists. Using the handholds he had installed, he was able to haul himself out of the Drive. He lifted his visor and rubbed his muzzle, smearing grease and strands of shaved metal through his fur. He looked down from his perch on top of the Drive, expecting only to see David. He was surprised to see him talking to Amy.

Amy waved as she looked up to Twitch. "Didn't want to disturb you," she called out. She approached the side of the Drive as Twitch clambered down it. "How are things going with it?"

Twitch was surprised to see Amy. It had been the first time he had seen her on the factory floor. Usually Snow had been the one to question him about the Drive. He shrugged his shoulders. "Well, I think. I'm working on enlarging the crystal input system and upgrading the ion pumps to…" he said, before pausing. He grimaced and looked across to Amy, expecting to see a blank expression on her face. He was disappointed that he was right. He sighed softly. "Making it emit more Denitchev particles. If you want a bigger area for the Drive to cover, you need more particles to cover that area. Then it's just adding more emitters to cover it."

"And does it work?" Amy asked. She looked up to the top of the Drive.

"When I finish putting it all back together again, yeah," Twitch said. He flashed a nervous smile. "Just have to fill it with crystals and put ionic emissions through it."

Amy placed her hand on the side of the Drive. When she moved it, the fur on her fingers was covered in a fine black powder. She rubbed her fingers together, a look of distaste on her muzzle. "And how big do you expect those changes will make the effect radius?"

Twitch grimaced. "Hard to tell without testing," he said. He clicked his tongue and twisted his muzzle. "I'd say, with the changes I've made, probably a fifty percent increase?"

Amy didn't reply right away. She slowly circled around the Drive, giving Twitch a brief moment alone with David. His partner looked worried. His ears were curled down, and his tail was tucked between his legs. Twitch could only exchange a quick glance with David before Amy re-emerged from the other side of the Drive.

"How big could you make it?" she asked.

The nervous smile remained on Twitch's muzzle. "How big can you make a shield?" he replied. He slapped the side of the Drive. "You'd need a shit tonne of crystals – official term – and a very powerful ionic drive, but in theory… there's no limit to it. The more fuel it has, the more particles it makes. The more particles, the bigger the area it can reach, so long as you have enough emitters."

Amy grinned and clapped her hands together. "Good, that's what I like to hear," she said. She pulled Twitch close and held her arm over his shoulder. "But that's not the real reason why I came here today. You can head home early today. I got word that Captain Griffiths is docking at Network Central in half an hour. I'm sure you'll want to be back home to meet him."

Twitch brightened up immediately as his worries were shoved to the back of his mind. "Captain Rhys is back?" He broke away from contact with Amy, leaving a few smudges of grease on her clothes. He bounced on his toes as he grabbed hold of David's hand. "Do you have everything? We should go back now."

"Yeah, just give me a sec," David said. He pulled back and quickly retreated to where he had been studying. He scooped up all of his books and tablet, before he stuffed them all into his bag.

"Do tell Captain Griffiths that I pass on my best regards," Amy said. She ran a finger over the gold bracelet around her wrist, and she didn't look up to meet Twitch's eye. "I am most interested to hear how his mission went."

"You're not coming too?" Twitch asked. He scuffed his foot against the concrete floor. "Is Snow?"

Amy laughed and shook her head. The diamond stud in her ear glinted in the lights above. "No. We both have important work that needs doing. It will just be you two, though I do expect you back here tomorrow to finish assembling the Drive. And Captain Griffiths too, as Snow is eager to continue her subspace lessons."

"I'll be sure to pass on the message for you," Twitch said. He nodded a couple of times, before sidling away from Amy to stand beside David again. His tail kept trying to wrap around his leg.

Amy had turned to face the Drive. Her tail was arched up and slowly swished from side to side. She didn't say anything to them. She barely even seemed to notice they were still there. She didn't react as Twitch followed David out of the factory. A prickle ran down Twitch's spine. He glanced back, but there was no one behind him. No one followed them. He shuddered and tried to forget the eerie sensation. He was going to be scared enough returning to the largely unprotected Appletree estate without imagining eyes watching him from behind.

***

Appletree looked no different to usual. Everything was still and quiet, with barely a breeze in the air. Prox shone down weakly from almost directly above. It was early afternoon, and the temperature had been gradually creeping up ever since Prox had breached the horizon four days earlier. Twitch hurried inside with David right behind him. No one had been waiting around on the road, but he didn't want to take any chances.

The front lobby was almost completely empty. Only William was present. He was sat down at the small café close to the elevators. He had his back to the front doors as he read something on his tablet, but he turned his head as they closed. He raised his hand in greeting. "Barely seen you around at all since the captain left," he said as Twitch and David cautiously approached.

"Just been busy," Twitch said. He grinned widely and showed off the black streaks in his fur where he had wiped his oily and greasy hands. "Rebuilding a Denitchev Drive for Amy."

William flicked his ear up. "For Amy? Why does she need one of those?" he asked. He swung around on his chair and gently rested his legs down on the ground. His left foot hit the floor with a rough clunk.

"She hasn't told us," David said. He took a seat opposite William.

Twitch remained standing. He looked down briefly at the metallic travesty of a foot that stuck out from the bottom of William's trousers. "Why won't you let me look at that? I can make you something better."

A smile spread across William's muzzle. His ears perked up, and his tailtip twitched. "I'm getting a new one," he said brightly. "Amy said it should be ready in the next couple of days."

Twitch squeaked and clapped his hands in delight. "Oh, that's awesome. So, you'll be a little bit like a robot, will you?" he said, the words all spilling out together. "Will I still be able to look at it? I might be able to make it better."

William's brow lowered. His eyes flicked across to David. "I, uh... we'll see," he stammered. He rested his hands in his lap. "I'll have to thank Captain Rhys for it, when he gets back. For all his faults, he did... he did arrange with Amy to get this done for me."

Twitch's grin stretched wider. "Well he's almost here," he said, bouncing on his toes as he spoke. "That's why we're back here, so we can be ready for when he's here. He should be up at Network Central already."

"Huh, I didn't know he was due back today. Would have been nice to show him my new leg when he got back," William said. He picked up his cup of coffee and carefully lapped at the hot liquid. He wrinkled his nose. "I suppose you'll be getting cleaned up before he gets back?"

Twitch nodded eagerly. "Yeah. It's pretty messy work, but I like it," he said. He glanced to David, who was watching the doors. "We should probably go up though. Let me know when you get the leg. I really want to see it!"

William curled his tail in nervously. "I'll definitely let you know."

Twitch squeaked in delight. Every tooth was on display as he grinned widely, and his ears were perked right up. He waved goodbye to William as he bounded towards the elevators. David followed behind a little slower.

Though Twitch was still worried about being so vulnerable in Appletree, the knowledge that Captain Rhys was so close gave him a little confidence. That, and the excitement for William helped distract his mind a little. He wondered how the leg would work, and if the other starat would ever give him the chance to tinker around with it. He had never had the chance to play around with a cybernetic limb before. They were so rare in the empire, and those who possessed them hardly ever came to backwaters like Ceres. It would be exciting.

The door to their apartment still hadn't been properly fixed, though Twitch had been able to liberate some scrap metal from Amy's factory. With it, he had been able to fashion a crude lock to wrap around the handle of the door and attach to the frame. It didn't do much to secure the room, but it did give them both a little peace of mind. Twitch secured the door behind them, before stripping out of his dirty clothes. He hurried into the shower, eager to feel clean once again. He couldn't wait to hear the stories of what Captain Rhys had been doing.

***

Captain Rhys was one of the last people back. Twitch had been happy to see Richard and Steph when they returned, but he was disappointed to hear that they had never had the chance to leave the *Harvester* at all. They hadn't had the opportunity to see the surface of Charon, which they were both grateful for. Neither had ever held a gun before, so they were not enthralled by the idea of going into a combat mission.

Twitch said little about what he and David had been up to. He didn't want to worry any of the starats that they had been chased through the streets of the city. He didn't even want to mention the minister and her offer, for the fear that any other starat who knew about it could be targeted by the same humans.

Finally, Captain Rhys arrived. He had Leandro and an unfamiliar human with him. Twitch squeaked in delight and leapt up from his conversation with Richard and Steph. He hurried across the lobby and surprised the captain with a tackled hug. Captain Rhys only just managed to stay on his feet, though he kept his arms well out of the way.

Twitch grinned and swished his tail as he looked to his mirror image. "Missed you, Captain Rhys!"

"Missed you too, Twitch," Captain Rhys replied. He took a step back away from Twitch and slowly lowered his arms. His fingers were still struck by the occasional spasm, and they looked no healthier than when he had left for his mission. Twitch's ears curled down a little as he looked at them. "Did you get up to much while I was gone? Didn't you have some important work to do for Amy?"

Twitch flicked his ears back up and nodded vigorously, trying to hide his concern for Captain Rhys's arms away again. "I did, yes! She had me fixing a Denitchev Drive, and then upgrading it. I had a lot of fun."

"A Denitchev Drive? That's interesting. Why would she need one of those?" Captain Rhys mused. He turned to Leandro, who had remained by his side. Twitch's eyes followed the captain's gaze, before drifting across to the elderly human who leaned into the grey starat's side. The captain noticed where his attention had moved to. "This will be a treat for you."

The strange human smiled at Twitch. He held his hand out for the starat. "You must be Twitch," he said. His voice sounded hoarse and strained. "I've heard a lot about you. My name is Emile, but you may know me better as the Silver Fox."

Twitch had rarely found himself speechless before. Only when he had first met Captain Rhys as a starat had he been truly lost for words, but this was almost as shocking. His mouth hung open as his ears folded back. He had heard stories of the Silver Fox since he had been a small kit. He had never expected to meet the human. "Silver Fox?" he whispered quietly as the awed fog that had permeated his mind started to clear. "That is so cool! Do you still have your sword?"

The human laughed. At Captain Rhys's insistence, they started to move towards the little café and one of the empty tables there. "No, I'm afraid not," the Silver Fox said with a sad shake of his head. "When I was captured, that was one of the first things they took."

"Aww, I would have liked to see that," Twitch pouted. He sighed dramatically as the Silver Fox sat down with Leandro. Twitch took a seat opposite them, and he was glad when Captain Rhys took the seat next to him. "Is it true you had a starat on your crew?"

This time it was Leandro who laughed. The Silver Fox turned his head to the grey starat and smiled. "He did," Leandro said. He tapped his chest. "Emile didn't rescue me and abandon me at the first opportunity. I stayed with him for ten years before I was lost."

"I should never have sent Giles to look for you," the Silver Fox said with a weary sigh. "I should have gone myself."

Captain Rhys slumped against the table. His ears folded flat against his head. Twitch rested a hand on his back, but the captain barely reacted. "If I'd have known what Cooper had done…"

The Silver Fox held up a hand. "I told you already. You could not have known, Captain Griffiths. I was an outlaw, and your old first officer was quietly lauded as a hero, I'm sure. There was a long time that I hoped for revenge on him, but now I just want to live what I have left of my life." He smiled, and his old, weary face was transformed into radiant happiness. "I may not have long left, but every second out of that cell is a blessing I could never have hoped for. To have Leandro by my side is all I could ever ask."

Twitch looked between the Silver Fox and Leandro. He recognised the look in the grey starat's eyes. It was the exact same look David had whenever they looked at each other. Leandro's attention was solely on the human next to him. Twitch's legs swung beneath his chair as he looked at the couple happily. There was no sadness at all in Leandro's eyes. There was only happiness and adoration.

Twitch gently touched tails with Captain Rhys. This time the captain did react. He glanced up and across. A pained grimace was on his face, and his ears were curled in. Twitch's eyes flicked down to the captain's arms. "Are you getting those fixed like William's?"

Captain Rhys shook his head. "I don't know yet. I still want to see what my options are first," he said. As he spoke, he tried to clench his hand into a fist, but he could barely bend his fingers before he whimpered in pain and stopped. Twitch wanted to reach out and cup his hands around Captain Rhys's, but he held himself back. He knew that would only hurt the captain more.

"William is getting his leg soon," Twitch said, trying to press home the point. He kept the excited smile on his muzzle, but deep down he was worried. He was scared for Captain Rhys. Humans had already chased him through the streets. What if they chased down the captain too? If he was still injured, then he may not be able to fight them off. His ears threatened to curl in, but he managed to keep them perked up. "How about you see how much William likes his leg, then you can decide on your arms?"

Captain Rhys sighed. "I'll consider it, alright?"

Twitch knew that was likely all he was going to get out of the captain. He giggled and nodded. "Alright, Captain Rhys! Maybe you should get them in red so someone can tell us apart."

That brought a smile out from Captain Rhys. "Always thinking positive, aren't you, Twitch?"

The dark thoughts at the back of Twitch's mind laughed bitterly. None of that showed on Twitch's body. He beamed brightly as his tail swished high. "Gotta be somebody who does that."

Twitch was happy. He had all his friends back safe. Their presence made him feel safe, but there was a worry that had seeded deep within his mind. There was the thought that he needed to be made safe. He got the feeling he had scratched beneath the surface of the veneer of safety on Centaura. Both Amy and Minister Bakir had facilitated that. They were somehow integral to the dangers that lurked beneath the surface. It was only with Captain Rhys that he was truly safe.

Twitch wanted to feel safe all the time.

chapter ten

Nick held out his hand to stop Rhys walking past him. Snow had wasted no time in summoning Rhys back to the factory for more lessons about subspace. He had been back on Centaura for less than twenty-four hours. Both Twitch and Leandro had been excused from the second lesson, leaving Rhys alone with just Snow and Nick. Twitch had come with Rhys, but the other starat had disappeared off to work on the Dentichev Drive he had been upgrading. Rhys had caught a glimpse of the work Twitch had been doing, but it all looked to be a mess of parts to him.

As the second lesson had been so long after their first, Snow had not expected any progress to be made. She had not been surprised. Rhys had only managed to bring himself to the verge of a headache, and Nick had not said a word about his progress. Snow had already left, and Rhys had been about to follow after her. He turned around to face Nick, and quailed under the fierce gaze he was met with.

"So, you're Captain Rhys Griffiths of the *Harvester*?" Nick asked.

"I am, yeah," Rhys replied. He looked over the quivering starat, and something clicked within his memory. His eyes widened slightly. "Oh, I remember you."

Nick took a step back, and for a moment his anger faded. "So miracles do happen," he muttered beneath his breath.

"You were the navigator on the *Dawn* over Ceres," Rhys said, confident he had the starat placed.

Nick's lip came up in a snarl as the fury came back. "Guess I was wrong. You're still the same human who doesn't give a fuck about us."

Rhys took a step back, bumping against the wall. His tail tucked up between his legs, and his ears pinned down flat against his skull. "What's that supposed to mean?"

"You don't care about us. You never have and you never will," Nick said, jabbing his finger into Rhys's chest. Rhys tried to parry the finger away, but Nick's claw still dug into his skin. "You only care about yourself. That's what all of this is about. Making the best of a bad situation."

"That's not true. I just fought for Centaura. I killed for them. And I did that because I want to help starats," Rhys replied quickly. He tried to grab hold of Nick's hand to push it away, but the starat was too quick and his arms were too weak. "I swear to you, this is not just a bad situation for me. I know the sins of my past can't be forgotten, but I do truly, genuinely care now."

Nick snarled. "Humans don't change." He jabbed Rhys once more in the ribs, before turning to walk away.

"Captain Lee changed," Rhys said to the starat's retreating back.

Nick stopped mid stride. His shoulders trembled and his tail thrashed from side to side. He whirled around with blazing fury in his eyes, but when he spoke his voice was surprisingly soft. "Aaron? You think Aaron changed? He didn't change, and nor have you."

"I have changed. I swear to you," Rhys said, the touch of a growl coming into his voice. "The human I had been was a result of society and how starats are perceived. Was it wrong? Yes. But I'm not that person anymore."

Nick advanced on Rhys. "Yes, I was on that bridge with Aaron. Yes, you looked at me for a brief moment. You noticed me because I was somewhere where I shouldn't be," the starat spat. He grabbed hold of Rhys's arm and pushed him against the wall, ignoring the gasp of pain Rhys made. "You saw me, but you didn't know me. You didn't recognise me, and you still don't. You look at me as though I was a stranger. So no, you haven't changed, and I know you never will."

"I don't understand," Rhys whispered. He didn't struggle or resist as the starat kept his hand pinned against Rhys's left arm.

"You think you were the only brother Aaron had growing up? That you were the only one he cared about?" Nick growled. He released Rhys and took a step back to sit on the edge of the table. "We hung out all the time as kits. The three of us. But you never had eyes for me. Ignored me all the time. If ever you spoke of me, it was to ask Aaron why that starat was here. And he would always respond, 'because he likes being around me'."

"I..."

"No, don't speak. You don't get to speak now. This is my turn," Nick snarled. His voice started to crack with emotion. "Aaron and I agreed to keep up the pretence. I was just some dumb servant who clung to its master. We wanted to tell you, but we were scared that if you knew, you'd run off home and tell your parents, and I would be taken away. I'd never seen Aaron again."

Nick trailed off and took in a few deep breaths to compose himself again, but Rhys didn't dare fill the silence with his voice. He barely even moved. It felt like he had been punched in the stomach.

"There were times I tried to convince Aaron to tell you. I thought it would be better than living the constant lie, but he never wanted to. He never trusted you. He. Didn't. Trust. You," Nick said, jabbing Rhys in the chest with each word. "That ate Aaron up inside. He couldn't trust one of his best friends with such a big secret about himself. You don't care. But Aaron has always cared. He didn't change, and nor have you."

"I... I didn't know, I'm sorry."

Nick snarled again. "No you're not sorry. Like I said, humans don't change. If you wanted to apologise and sound genuine, you should have done it thirty-five years ago."

With one last jab in Rhys's ribs, the starat spun around on his toes and stalked out of the room. Rhys was left alone, and he slowly dropped down to his haunches as he felt tears starting to well in his eyes. He held his hands over his brow. The revelations sickened him, showing in fierce light the human he had once been. He had already known he had never particularly cared about starats, but he couldn't have possibly realised it sunk to the depths of ignoring that Aaron had been childhood friends with one.

He knew he didn't have to prove anything to starats like Nick. He was never going to be liked by all starats, but this wasn't just some starat who disliked him because he had been human. This was personal, and that cut Rhys deep.

Rhys wiped his eyes dry and rested his head back against the wall. Alone in the classroom, he just let himself sink into his thoughts. He would never be able to forget his past, and he didn't expect starats to do the same. One day though, he hoped they would forgive him for it.

***

Rhys didn't join the others, instead choosing to sit alone in the classroom with just his thoughts for company. He tried to convince himself it was because he simply wanted to be alone for a while, and not because he wanted to avoid Nick. Ultimately though, it was the starat that dominated most of his thoughts. Rhys strained his memory, trying to remember the starat in their childhood, but he kept drawing blanks. Every childhood memory he had with Aaron was just of the two of them. He didn't doubt the starat's claims. The conviction in Nick's words was enough to convince Rhys that they were true.

He was found, half an hour later, by Amy. The starat opened the door and poked her head in. She flicked her ear when her eyes caught Rhys, sat down behind the rows of desks. "Thought I'd find you here," she said. He closed the door behind her and approached Rhys. She perched on the edge of the closest desk. "Nick said he didn't want you to keep up with the program. Said your heart isn't in it."

Rhys growled softly beneath his breath and clenched his fist, but he didn't say anything. He got the impression Amy hadn't finished talking.

"You don't have to prove anything to him," the starat continued after a small pause. "You don't even have to prove anything to me. Only Snow's opinion matters as to whether you stay here. She is a good judge of character and I have never known her to be wrong. Don't be the exception."

Rhys sighed and shook his head. His hand slowly unclenched as he stared down at his feet. "I do care, I really do. No matter what Nick may think," he said quietly. He twitched his muzzle and thumped his head back gently against the wall. "I know I fucked up pretty bad when I was human. But I'm not that person anymore. I shouldn't keep being judged as that person."

Amy held up her hand. "I know that. Keep proving that to Snow and you'll have nothing to worry about," she replied. She reached out to take hold of Rhys's hand, and she hauled him up to his feet again. She held onto his arms for a few moments afterwards, looking into Rhys's eyes as he struggled not to whimper in pain. "Have you decided what you're doing with these yet?"

"Not yet," Rhys said, shaking his head. He leaned back against the wall and sighed. "William tried to convince me to do it, but I'm scared I won't feel like me anymore. I've always been told that the flesh we are given from birth is sacred and sacrosanct. I know it's nonsense that I'm clinging to that, given how long I've had this body, but it still feels like me."

"I can't pretend to understand that," Amy said with a shake of her head. She let go of his arms as she slid off the side of the desk she had been perched on. "But you will need to make a decision soon. It will take a while to get you measured to a good set, and then we have to make them and arrange the surgery. Then you will need to adapt to them. And through all of this, we need you learning more about what we're doing. We need your skills. Those you already know, and those you are learning."

"But I don't know anything about what you're doing," Rhys snapped, before sighing and holding his hand against his muzzle. "Sorry. I just don't like not knowing what's going on. I know what you plan on doing, but I don't know how you want to go about it."

Amy patted Rhys on the shoulder. "Come on outside with me. We can talk privately."

Rhys flicked his ears in curiosity as he followed Amy out the classroom. He could hear the sounds of the other starats together in one of the nearby rooms, but Amy led him directly outside. The air was sticky and warm again, despite the cool wind that blew down from the northern mountains. Rhys felt the wind blow through his fur, but it didn't do much to dispel the heat in his body.

"How far would you be willing to go?" Amy asked. She didn't look back as she walked around the side of the large warehouse, and for a moment Rhys didn't even realise she was speaking to him.

"What do you mean?"

"How far would you go?" Amy repeated. This time she looked back, though she didn't break her stride. "What order would you not follow?"

Rhys didn't answer at first. It was a complicated question, and required a lot of thought first. He had rarely had the need to question his superior's orders before, and as such had never needed to test his morals against an unethical order. But, knowing what he did now, he had to wonder if there were any instances in his past that his current self would come to regret.

Amy asked another question before Rhys had chance to sort through his thoughts. "Would you follow an order to destroy a ship which contained lives you had deemed innocent?"

Rhys blinked and flicked his ears back in surprise. He had not been expecting that. "Is that an order that's likely to be made?"

"Answer the question please," Amy replied tersely.

"I..." Rhys sucked in his breath and looked away from the starat. She had led him to the banks of the great river. A few creatures that reminded Rhys vaguely of crocodiles prowled on the opposite shore. "I have carried out orders in the past that targeted lives that were, in hindsight, probably innocent. I cannot say in any certainty that I would be able to carry out such an order if I knew the lives were innocent beforehand."

"Do you believe the empire as an entity, is innocent?"

Rhys frowned. "As a whole? No, I don't believe it is. Though there are innocent people amongst it. Everything I have learned here has shown me that the empire is rotten to the core, but there are still good, innocent people amongst them. Even some humans."

Amy didn't respond. She turned her back on Rhys and clasped her hand behind her back as she looked out over the river. Rhys wasn't sure if his answer had satisfied her or not, but he was scared to press for anything further. He felt a flutter of worry in his stomach as he thought about it. He had never thought too hard about what it was Amy was targeting with her movement, but her questions concerned him. He didn't know what he was getting himself into.

"How many innocents will die for this, Amy?" Rhys asked when it seemed likely that the starat wasn't going to answer.

Amy glanced back. "I don't want to kill innocents. We will target only those who are guilty, but that doesn't mean we will be able to shield everyone from harm. You're a soldier, Rhys. You have to be used to that by now."

Rhys nodded. "I am, yes. Never makes it any easier," he said. He paused for a moment. "We don't have the numbers for all-out war, unless you're able to bring the military to your way of thinking. Assassination? Is that what you're planning? Take down leaders? Replace them with people loyal to us?"

"That's part of the plan, at least. We have agents who can move like that," Amy said, snapping her fingers for emphasis. "While you were gone, Twitch has opened up a new avenue of possibility that we thought had been closed to us. But come here. Have a look at these."

Rhys stepped up by Amy's side and looked across the river as the starat pointed. The creatures on the far bank appeared to be similar to reptiles, thought Rhys couldn't tell whether they had scales or not. They were a dusty red in colour, and had six legs on their squat, but elongated, bodies. A long, prehensile tail whipped around behind them as they scuffled and fought each other. The middle two limbs were shorter than the other two, and were often held up above the creatures' foremost shoulders and used for grasping and grappling rather than locomotion.

"We call them dragons," Amy said, noticing the source of Rhys's attention.

Rhys tilted his head to one side and squinted. He supposed he could see a little resemblance to the creatures of mythology. "So long as they don't actually breathe fire."

Amy laughed. "Not that we've ever seen. I still wouldn't get too close to them though. They have a nasty bite."

"I'll keep that in mind," he said. He tucked his tail between his legs and shivered. Even from this distance he could see that their teeth and claws looked dangerous.

"They've got other abilities though. They seem to be quite sensitive to subspace. We think they even hunt using it. Some people have even been able to hold some sort of rudimentary control over them," Amy explained. She grinned widely and looked over the river. "No one knows quite why they have such abilities, but we're researching them to work it out."

"How could you control something like that?" Rhys asked. He stared across at the dragons. They looked almost like crocodiles, but seemed much faster and agile than the Terran creatures.

Amy shrugged her shoulders. "I don't know the specifics, but I'm told a strong enough psyker can throw down a subspace lure that they follow. I have no idea how it works. That's not my area of expertise. You'll have to ask Snow about that if you want to know more."

Rhys frowned and fell into a brief silence. The creatures across the river were strange, but at the same time bizarrely familiar. They still acting like typical Terra creatures as they fought and scrapped with each other. A few lay down, limbs sprawled out. One was eating something it had caught in the river. None of them had ever come within several light years of Terra, or even the Sol System. Life, no matter where it sprung from, had shared characteristics across two different star systems.

Amy placed her hand on his shoulder. She leaned in close to whisper into his ear. "You know we're giving you the chance to avenge Steph's death, right?"

The cool northern wind felt like nothing compared to the icy chill that swept through Rhys's body. He jerked back, almost losing his footing on the river bank as he tried to push Amy away with one hand. His other hand lifted up to point towards the warehouse. This time his fingers trembled in terror, not pain. "She's... just back there," he stammered, but he knew that wasn't who Amy was talking about. He had tried so hard for years not to think about her. He didn't know how Amy could possibly know.

Amy grabbed hold of Rhys's hand and pulled him away from the river bank before he toppled into the rapid current. "Don't forget about her," she hissed. Her eyes blazed with fury. "Use that injustice to prepare yourself for what you need to do."

Rhys's ears pinned right back as he shook his head. "But she wasn't killed. She died. It was an accident."

Some of the fire left Amy's eyes. "Even after all these years, you still believe that? Or do you just tell yourself that to ease the pain? Anger and revenge is a good motivator, Rhys. Use it to fuel you."

Her shoulders slumped slightly, and she placed her hand on Rhys's back, starting to push him towards the large warehouse again. "I'll send you some documents that we uncovered when digging into your past. You should read them."

Rhys bowed his head. He felt completely numb as a few memories trickled back into his mind. He thought he'd long forgotten that infectious laugh of hers, but it was as clear in his mind as though Amy was imitating it right there in front of him. He wriggled free of Amy's touch. "I'll catch up. I just need a moment."

Amy just raised her hand in farewell as she kept on walking, leaving Rhys alone with his thoughts and a memory he had thought had been left far behind in time and space. The starat looked up to the dark sky and sighed. It had been so long since he had allowed Stephanie into his thoughts. Her ghost had moved on. The surface of Centaura was not the place he had thought she would return.

Despite Prox's presence in the sky, there was enough darkness for a few other stars to twinkle in the twilight. The brightest of them all were the twin stars of Alpha Centauri, gleaming close to the crimson disc of Prox. Stephanie had often wondered just how many stars she would be able to see in her life. She had been so optimistic about the future of humanity, but whatever destiny lay before her was never fulfilled. She had seen one star in her life. Sol. Like almost every other human that had ever existed. She had been so much more special than that.

With tears in his eyes, he tightened his hands into fists and spoke up to the stars. "What would you think of me now? Would you be proud of me?"

A human woman with long blonde hair danced in Rhys's imagination. He wiped his eyes dry. She wouldn't even recognise him anymore.

chapter eleven

Rhys was surprised when he received a summons from Amy Jennings the following day. He was to travel back into the city with William so the other starat could meet Amy and be fitted with his new leg. There hadn't been a reason given, but Snow had given him no choice but to accept the invitation. The albino hadn't been the one to take them into the city though. Instead it had been the starat he had met on their first visit into the city; Mortimer. William and Mortimer were engaged in conversation for a large part of the journey. Neither of them ever involved Rhys. Mostly William talked about his excitement for his new limb, and Rhys didn't begrudge him that anticipation. He was glad the starat would be able to walk properly again, but it put him into a problematic situation for himself. He knew his hands weren't getting better. He had been trying. Doctor Sparks had tasked him with several exercises to rebuild his wasted muscles, but all they did was leave him in pain without any signs of progress. He had little choice but to accept Amy's offer, but he was too scared to commit himself to it.

Rhys's mind was also distracted by the notification that continued to flash on his tablet. He hadn't opened it yet. He didn't want to open the scars that he had thought long healed. Stephanie had once been so important to him, but now… He had thought she had long faded from his mind, but he had to keep wiping the occasional tear from his eye as his thoughts drifted back to her and the messages Amy had sent though.

Even when they reached the massive Jennings Tower in the middle of Caledonia, Rhys hung back from the other two, feeling almost like he wasn't truly wanted. He was only there for Amy to press him to make a decision, and he still wasn't sure he was ready to make it. He kept his head down as he walked through the main lobby, and he remained silent as they ascended up the elevator.

Amy wasn't in her office when they arrived, and Mortimer left the other two starats alone to fetch her. Rhys stood by the windows and looked out over the city, while William stretched out his leg as he sat down in front of Amy's desk.

Even at their great height, Rhys couldn't see far enough to spot the factory on the outskirts of the city. Almost everywhere was covered in buildings, with only the light green of the hydroponic farms in the distance breaking up the monotonous sprawl of suburbia. Everything was cast in the golden red glow of the slowly setting Prox as it neared the western horizon.

The doors soon opened again, and Mortimer and Amy came through together. They carried a large, heavy case between them, which they hauled up onto the large desk in the middle of the room. Rhys turned from the window and cautiously approached the desk as Amy smiled brightly at him.

"It's lovely to see you both again," Amy said, reaching out to shake William's hand. She didn't shake Rhys's hand, instead just patting him on the shoulder. Rhys was glad of it.

"If you could take your leg off please," Mortimer asked, turning to face William. The suited starat unbuckled the heavy case on the desk, but he didn't open it just yet.

William had to remove his trousers for that, but he didn't seem to show any shame as he stripped down to his underwear before removing his leg with a grateful sigh. "I will be so happy if I never have to see that thing again," he said in relief. He rubbed at his leg stump, just a few centimetres below his hip.

Mortimer crouched down in front of the starat to pick up the discarded leg. He staggered back as he stood back up, surprised by its weight. "We can discard it for you, don't worry," he said. He tucked the leg beneath the desk so it was out of sight as Amy worked on removing the metal ring around William's leg that the limb had been attached to. William whimpered and hissed in pain as it was removed, and Amy had to mop up a bit of blood before she was able to twist it free.

The metal ring fell to the floor as Mortimer pulled out a moulded silicone cast from within the case. He held it out to William to show him. Rhys could see the gleam of some metallic rings embedded within the silicone. "When I put this on, it will sting a little. It uses nanotech to connect to your leg, and it had to make lots of little nerve connections, but it will provide a much cleaner connection than that old thing," Mortimer said, kicking the old ring away.

"You're lucky that one never gave you any bad infections," Amy said tersely. She wrapped her hand in a cloth and picked the metal ring up. She placed it down beneath her desk, where it clanked against the remainder of William's old leg.

"It did. Thankfully I had one human ally on the ship," William growled. He glared pointedly at Rhys for a moment, but a smile flashed across his muzzle a moment later. His eyes softened before he looked back to Amy. "The ship's doctor always tried to find time for me. Unfortunately, he wasn't the one who treated my leg the first time."

"Well, this new cap will be much better for you," Amy said, laughing a little as she patted the starat on the shoulder. She handed the piece of silicone to Mortimer, who gently placed it over William's stump. It fitted perfectly around the truncated leg.

William clenched his teeth and hissed as it fitted into place, giving off a small whimper. His tail thrashed, but a few seconds later he took a deep breath and was able to relax again. "That felt strange," he said, grinning nervously at Amy.

Rhys approached the desk, curious to see what the process looked like. His tail flicked nervously. If he were to agree to accept Amy's help, would he have something similar to what William now had on his leg? Would his arms end in a small connector port enclosed in a soft silicone cap? Would they really remove his limbs? He looked down at his arms and tried to imagine it, but he just couldn't.

Amy didn't say anything to Rhys. Instead her focus was solely on William as she gently lifted a prosthetic leg out from the case. It looked so realistic that Rhys wasn't convinced at first that it was artificial. It perfectly matched the fur colour of William's other leg.

"We expect this will be your regular, day-to-day leg," Mortimer explained. He held it out for William, who took it into his hands. The starat ran his hands up and down the leg, his eyes wide in delight.

Amy crouched down to help William attach the leg into its socket. It connected with a twist and a small click. It hung limply down, and for a moment William's face showed concern.

"It will take a few minutes to properly sync up, don't worry," Amy said to reassure the starat. She rose to her feet as William started to stroke through the synthetic fur on his new leg. Tears formed in his eyes as he touched and prodded at the new leg.

A second leg was then pulled out from the case. This one lacked any of the artificial fur. Instead it was smooth and sleek, though it maintained the same colouring as the first. The claws of the second leg were wickedly sharp. Mortimer showed off that they possessed a retractable sheath for protection, something a starat did not normally possess. William cradled the leg lovingly over his lap as his toes began to wiggle for the first time.

"I could move them," William squeaked, clapping one hand up to his muzzle. His watery eyes were open wide as he stared down at his new foot. "I can feel it. Oh Essie, I can feel it!"

With both Amy and Mortimer to help him, William slowly rose up to both feet. He swayed slightly despite their support, leaning heavily on his right leg still. He took a couple of careful steps and almost fell over, caught at the last moment by Mortimer. The suited starat took the spare leg from William and propped it up next to Amy's desk.

"Take it slow," Mortimer warned. William tried again, and this time he didn't fall right away. He stayed standing even as Amy and Mortimer took a step away, letting him stand on his own two feet.

"Thank you both," William whispered. He embraced both Amy and Mortimer. He then limped past them both to stand in front of Rhys. For a moment he stood awkwardly, before pulling Rhys into a tight hug. "Thank you as well. For all the unpleasant things I said to you before, you did this for me."

"It may not undo all the things I did as a human..." Rhys said, but William silence him with a finger over his mouth.

"Nothing will undo the past. It happened. It was shit," William said. He barked out in laughter. "Everything you're doing now is repairing that. For my part, I'm sorry for doubting you."

Rhys couldn't help but laugh as well. "I don't blame you for doubting me. When I first met you, there was nothing I had done for you to have belief in me."

William stepped back and lifted his left foot from the ground. He wiggled his toes and beamed widely. "Well, I'll always have a reminder now. Thank you again. Just do one more thing for me. Don't let Twitch get his hands on it. I dread to think what he'll do."

"I can take you for a little walk if you'd like to get used to it," Mortimer offered. He held his arm out for William to take again. William nodded and took hold of the starat's hand.

The two starats slowly walked towards the wide double doors out towards the little reception outside. There was still a trace of William's limp as he walked, though Rhys was sure it would take him a while to get used to a proper leg again. That left Rhys alone with Amy, but she didn't say anything until the doors closed behind William and Mortimer. When Rhys turned around to face her, she was already sat behind her desk again, the big case that had carried William's prosthetics clipped closed.

"Have you made a decision yet?" she asked Rhys.

Rhys crouched down in front of her desk, pretending to be interested in William's alternate leg. He should have expected such a question would follow. It could only have been one of two things. He was glad she didn't bring up Stephanie, but he still didn't have an answer prepared for her. He lightly touched William's leg. It felt perfectly smooth beneath his trembling finger. His ears pinned down low. "What would it mean for me? What would you do?"

Rhys heard the scrape of Amy's chair as she got up, but he didn't look around. He could vaguely see her reflection in the windows, but he was still surprised when he felt her hands on his arms, just a few centimetres down from his shoulders. "We would remove your arms from here," she explained in a calm voice, as though she was talking about nothing more complicated than trimming claws. "We have two different types of prosthetics. Total replacement, or partial replacement. For you, it would be easier for the partial ones, as there's nothing wrong with your shoulders. You would then have arms just like William's leg. Only the most observant would actually realise they were artificial. They would be strong and capable. An improvement on anything you had before. But that wouldn't be all. We could also provide arms with a more military focus."

"What do you mean?" Rhys asked, glancing back at the other starat as a shiver ran down his tail.

"You would never need to carry a weapon again," the starat replied. Her hands moved up to rest on Rhys's shoulders. "Your hands could become a rifle, a pistol, a blade. Whatever you may need."

"You would turn me into a weapon?" Rhys asked. His ears flicked up in surprise.

"You're a soldier. A fighter. A weapon is what you need to be," Amy said. She turned away from the windows. "It would give you an advantage over anyone you came up against, allowing you to become one with your weapons. It's what you need, and what we need."

"And who am I to be aimed at?" Rhys asked, after a small silence. He spun around on his toes to watch Amy as she started to clear her desk up.

"Commit to this, and I'll tell you exactly who, and exactly when. Until then, I am not convinced you can be trusted, or that you will be able to help us until your abilities with subspace are improved," Amy said. She sat down on the edge of her desk, her legs crossed as she raised her brow. "As you are right now, you present a liability, even if you develop your abilities with subspace faster than expected. You would be a hindrance on any mission without specialised equipment, and with the knowledge you brought back from Charon, we are already preparing our next one. There's no doubting your mind and your beliefs, but it is your physical condition that worries me. If you wish to accompany us, then I will need an answer from you."

Rhys sighed and tucked his tail between his legs. He knew it would be nice to be rid of the constant ache and weakness in his hands, but he still wasn't sure if it was too big a price to pay. He twisted his muzzle, and he wondered if William would help make up his mind. If he could ask the other starat what the leg felt like, then perhaps he would be able to soothe some of his fears. "Do I have to answer right now?"

Amy clicked her tongue. Then she shook her head. She held one finger out to Rhys. "I can give you one week. No more than that. For now though, if we are not to be discussing your arms, why don't you wait outside for William? Help yourself to a biscuit."

Rhys didn't move right away. "I'm not a weapon. Not for you or for anyone else," he said with a small shake of the head.

"You were a weapon of the empire for many years. That's what a soldier is," Amy said, raising her brow slightly. She straightened her back as she looked over Rhys. "Us putting a pistol in your palm will not make you a monster.

"Then what will it make me?"

"Efficient, Captain Griffiths. It will make you efficient." Amy placed her hands down on her desk as she smiled at Rhys. "I do hope you will think hard about your decision. I look forward to hearing your answer."

Rhys knew he had been dismissed without any allowance to question her further, so he bowed his head to Amy and made his way outside. There was no sign of William or Mortimer out in the small reception, so he sat down on one of the chairs and reached for a biscuit while he waited for them. He closed his eyes. He had a lot to think about.

chapter twelve

Rhys kept his doubts and thoughts to himself. Though he knew he should ask the advice of William, he never gave himself the opportunity to approach the other starat. He constantly warred with himself over what to do with his arms. Every time he thought he made a decision, he was beset by further doubts and concerns. He had been given a week to come up with an answer for Amy. Five days had already passed, and he felt no closer to an answer.

Amy didn't press him for any answer, and Rhys kept his mouth shut on the rare occasions he saw her. She didn't come down to the factory every day. Instead, the other half of the starat group were being taught by a starat called Shira, who Rhys hadn't yet been introduced to.

Instead, most of Rhys's thoughts and dedication went towards Snow's lessons. The albino starat had been teaching her students mostly how to clear their mind to get into the right state to reach out for subspace. Everyone had been able to relax their minds in meditation, but little further progress had been made at all. Rhys still wasn't convinced that it was a real ability that could be learned, but he didn't want to lose face to Nick and stop. He wanted to prove to the starat that he had the dedication necessary, even when he knew he was never going to convince Nick of it.

The days were starting to all blend together. It had been a full week since his return to Centaura, and every day was almost the same. Rhys and his group of starats were taken to Amy's factory. When they got back to Appletree Estates Rhys often shared dinner

with the rest of his crew. Everything felt simple, and after the manic month Rhys had endured prior to his arrival on Centaura, and even compared to the Charon mission. He was quite glad for the chance to relax. His only worries were the back-and-forth in his mind about his arms, and the silence from Major-General Ulrich and Fleet-Admiral Bosler since his debrief after the Charon mission. He occasionally missed what he had left behind, and sometimes still questioned if he had made the right choice, but those concerns were quickly put to the side any time he heard a starat talk. They were happy in Caledonia, and that was all Rhys needed to know.

Of course, there was still one starat who wasn't happy with Rhys around. Nick hadn't spoken to him once since that first confrontation, but Rhys felt the starat's eyes burning into him every time they were close. Rhys tried to ignore him most of the time, but that was difficult to do when all he had to occupy himself was the back of his eyelids as he tried to clear his mind. As he sat in Snow's lesson and stared into the blackness, the face of Nick kept appearing in his mind, no matter how many times he shook his head and twitched his ears to try and clear it.

A door closed and Snow cleared her throat. Rhys opened his eyes to see she held up a number of items in her hands. The albino made her way around the room, placing two ear plugs and a blindfold down on each table in front of her students. "You've been passively seeking subspace for some time now. This clarity of mind you've been seeking is important, for you need to ensure that you do not bring errant thoughts into subspace when you try to manipulate it. We may not know what it is made of or why it works, but what we do know is that intention and purpose help us manipulate it. If your mind is clouded with troubled thoughts, then that will influence subspace in ways not intended."

"And just what is in subspace?" Rhys asked, his mind going back to the entities he had seen on the *Shield of Justice*. Whenever he had mentioned them to Snow in the past, she had just smiled and refused to answer.

Snow flashed a quick smile. "We do not know. Follow my lessons, and you will come to no danger. Stray from the path I set for you... Well. Stronger minds than yours have been lost to the void."

"Sometimes you speak like it is a conscious mind," Leandro said. Rhys noticed his tail was curled around his chair leg. He had not come to all the lessons, as he had spent time with the Silver Fox

during most of them. The former pirate had requested a day of rest, and he had encouraged Leandro to return to the factory for the day.

Snow shrugged her shoulders. "Sometimes it acts like a conscious mind. But these lessons are not about what subspace is, for no-one knows that answer. Other minds are researching what it is. We are here to learn how to use it, and for that, we have a more active task today to find it," she said. She swept her hand around the tables. "The senses are very important with reaching subspace, but one is more important than the others. You'll isolate this sense today. You each have a pair of ear plugs and a blindfold. When you put them on, you will try to detect my voice with your sense of smell."

"With our sense of smell?" Nick asked sceptically. "How does that work?"

Snow turned her sightless eyes to look towards the starat. "I can see you with my ears. Why can you not hear me with your nose?"

"That's not how it works," Nick replied with a frown. Rhys glanced back to see the starat scratch behind his ear. For a moment their eyes locked, before Rhys quickly turned away again. He could hear the little growl beneath Nick's breath. "I'll try it though."

"I'll place my hand on your shoulder when I want you to free your senses again," Snow said. She sat on the edge of a free table and crossed her legs. "I will keep talking throughout. Well, what are you waiting for? Begin."

Rhys put the ear plugs in first. They fit nicely into his ears, and were clearly designed for a starat. All sound was immediately cut out the moment they were both in place, rendering him completely deaf. He looked up to Snow and could see her mouth moving, but he couldn't hear a single word of it. With a silent sigh, he pulled up the blindfold and secured it around his eyes.

Rhys's sense of smell felt amplified almost immediately. The world seemed so different with just scent and touch left to experience it. He could feel the grain of the wooden table beneath his fingers and the gentle movement of air from the air-conditioning. His clothes felt particularly bothersome as they moved slightly in time with the rise and fall of his chest. The thump of his heartbeat in his ear was all he could hear. With effort, Rhys wrenched himself to the task at hand. He didn't know how he was meant to do it, but he put his focus into his sense of smell.

Beneath the blindfold, Rhys closed his eyes and focused on what he could smell. Fragrant floral shampoo that lingered on Twitch's fur; the crisp air from the air-conditioning; a touch of mint that wafted in front of his nose occasionally; a bit of mud that had been traipsed in from outside. Nothing out of the ordinary.

Time lost meaning to Rhys had he focused on his nose. He didn't know how long he had been sitting still before he felt Snow's touch on his shoulder. He tugged down on his blindfold and pulled out one ear plug as she moved on to Twitch. Leandro and Nick had already removed their blindfold and plugs. Once Twitch had likewise restored his senses, the albino turned to face the four.

"So what did you learn?"

Rhys tentatively raised his hand. "You use a minty mouthwash."

Snow clicked her tongue. The shadow of a smile came to her lips. "Yes. There's clearly nothing wrong with your nose, but I wanted you to go beyond scent. I wanted you to detect my words."

"Uh, were you talking about chocolate at all?" Nick asked, speaking uncertainly. "Thought I could smell that."

"Oh, no. That was me, sorry," Twitch said. He pulled out a half-eaten bar of chocolate from his pocket. "I was hungry."

"Damn, thought I was onto something there," Nick muttered. He rapped his hand against the table. "Can we try again?"

Snow nodded and sat back on the table. Once again, Rhys set himself to the task of cutting away his senses. He was slower than the other starats in getting everything ready. His hands trembled with the effort of replacing the blindfold. He was still clumsy with his shaking hands, but after a few seconds of struggle he managed to seal off his ears and pull the blindfold down.

Just as it had been before, Rhys was almost overpowered by his improved sense of smell. He turned his head to the side and forced himself not to focus on the various scents. He wanted something more than that, something beyond, though he didn't know how to do that. He tilted his head until he could pick up the slight minty smell he associated with Snow's breath. He tracked it back and forth as it moved through the air, obviously where Snow was moving her head as she spoke. She seemed to be pacing around the room as she talked.

Rhys thought he could detect slight variations in the strength of the scent. He focused on that, trying to work out what those variations might mean. He leaned forward in his chair to try and get closer. The fluctuations could have been related to Snow's mouth opening and closing. He wished he was able to open his eyes to match the scent with the motion, but he kept his hands on the table.

A new scent emerged beneath the layers of mint. To Rhys's nose, it seemed spicier than the cool fragrance of mint, almost a little like cinnamon. At first he thought it was Twitch's shampoo again, but this was different. This came from the same place as the mint. Rhys flared his nostrils and let the spice overwhelm his senses. He followed it, never once moving from his seat as his head slowly swayed from side to side. The spice grew stronger in Rhys's nose, feeling like a sneeze building deep in his throat. He followed it more and more.

"...carried him up the Stairs of Toliman so he could see the light of the twin stars one last time..." A whispered voice caressed around Rhys. He turned his head to find it, and then...

A bright white light burst across Rhys's blackened vision.

Someone screamed.

Rhys realised he was standing up, his chest heaving. He ripped the blindfold from his eyes and discovered he had pushed his table over onto its side, though his arms weren't hurting like they should have been. His chair had scraped back against the floor, and he was almost standing on Nick's foot as he had leaped backwards. It had been him screaming. His throat still felt raw.

The starat pushed him away, a snarl on his lips. "Essie's tail, what is the matter with you?" Nick growled. He had pulled his blindfold off in frustration.

Rhys slowly looked up towards Snow, who had stood up from the table. She placed her hands on Twitch and Leandro's shoulders, but her eyes were solely on him.

"What did you experience?" she asked.

"A voice," Rhys replied hesitantly. His throat felt tight as he tried to speak normally. "A voice talking about the Stairs of Toliman. Then everything went white. It was... it looked like subspace through my ship's viewscreens."

A smile broke across Snow's muzzle. "That's because it was. Do you think you could find it again?"

"I think so," Rhys said uncertainly. He shiver travelled down his spine and through his tail, which was tucked between his legs. He rubbed his nose, still feeling the urge to sneeze deep in his throat. He cautiously approached his upturned table and rested his hand against the back of his chair. A gentle ache was starting to spread through his arms, but he was still sure he could never have had the strength to push the table over. He coughed and tried to clear his dry throat. "It smelled a bit... I don't know. Almost spicy, I think. Like cinnamon. I focused more onto that, and suddenly everything changed."

Snow nodded. "Now you know what to find, it will become easier with practice. After a lot of practice, you will be able to enter subspace with just a thought. Eventually, you will always be aware of subspace, like I am. You will always be able to rely on the information it gives, but for now it is just a great achievement to reach it once."

"It felt... intense," Rhys panted. He closed his eyes for a moment. When he opened them again, he looked down at the fallen table. "Did I do that?"

Snow nodded once. "You did," she said tersely. "It was only your first time, so I can't blame you for accessing powers you could not be aware of, but I must impress on you not to try that again, until you are ready."

"Is it dangerous?" Rhys asked nervously. He crouched down to right his chair. His hands ached more than usual.

"More dangerous than you could realise. Telekinesis through subspace is an incredibly powerful tool, but one that should not be utilised without knowing the dangers," the albino starat said. She smiled and gestured to the door. "Why don't you go and get yourself a drink of water, and I can see if anyone else can find subspace today."

Rhys nodded. His legs shook as he walked across the room. He was aware of three pairs of eyes on him. Nick glared with hatred, while Twitch gazed with awe. Leandro just tilted his head to the side and watched on with curiosity. Rhys flashed a quick smile from the doorway before he pulled the door closed behind him.

Rhys stumbled through the corridor as he made his way down to the small canteen. His head spun as he slowly came to realise what he had done. He had sensed subspace with his own mind. He had somehow heard Snow's voice and understood what she had been saying using only his nose. There couldn't have been any other explanation. He had never heard of the place she had mentioned before. His head buzzed, and for a brief moment he felt like his mind was trapped within a body that was too small to contain it.

"Shit," Rhys muttered as he sat down in the canteen. A glass of cold water was already in his hand, though he couldn't even remember filling it. He felt like water wouldn't be enough to quench the confused daze he found himself in. His thoughts and memories were scrambled. He really wanted some wine, but there was nothing of the sort in the canteen. The water would have to do. At least it would soothe his burning throat.

It took a lot of effort not to close his eyes and try to reach out for subspace again. Rhys wasn't yet sure if he could trust it. The memory of the mysterious entities he had seen on the *Shield of Justice* still burned into his memory. There was so much more he didn't yet know about subspace, and he didn't want to do anything without Snow's supervision. Still the temptation lingered.

"Are you alright, Captain Rhys?"

Rhys looked up to see William standing in the doorway. The starat approached the table. Rhys still wasn't used to seeing him walk without a limp.

"Brain is a bit messed up," Rhys admitted. He pushed out the chair on the other side of the table with his foot for William to sit down. "I didn't think I could do it, but I touched subspace before. It was a bit surprising."

William gratefully took the offered seat and eased himself down onto it. "Sounds like a bit of a mindfuck from what Twitch was saying," he said.

Rhys slouched over the table. "You've got that right, and we haven't even gotten into the weird things Snow is able to do with it. You're the lucky one, I think. Everything must be much more normal with Amy and Shira."

William laughed. A bright light shone in his eyes as he leaned back in his chair. "Certainly nothing quite so bizarre, that's for sure.

With Aaron's help, they've been teaching us how to shoot. I'd never even held a gun before, but apparently I've got a good eye for it." He grinned as he lifted his prosthetic leg up to rest on a vacant chair. "There's a few cool things too. A few plans for the future. Things I didn't know about the empire."

"What sort of things?" Rhys asked in curiosity. He hadn't heard much coming from the other lessons, as his head often hurt too much after his classes with Snow to inquire.

"How the empire formed and who is really in charge, that sort of thing," William replied. He drummed his claws against the canteen table. "And how much Centaura has been able to infiltrate. There's no real war happening, but the Centauran government has agents throughout the empire. A few other smaller factions like Amy have their own spies too."

"And what are they wanting?"

William shrugged his shoulders. "Depends on who you ask. Some seek to eradicate the empire, some to vassalize them into Centaura," the starat said. "Amy has always said she doesn't want to kill innocents, but Shira said all starats will be free from the pain of slavery."

"Where are they all, anyway?" Rhys asked. No one else had come in from the corridors during their short conversation.

William waved his hand towards the window. "They took a break and went for a walk to look at the dragons. I forgot to charge my leg last night, so it's a bit low on power. I don't want to walk too far." He paused for a moment to bark out a laugh. "Imagine that. I forgot to charge my leg. It sounds absurd."

"Yeah, that sounds a bit weird," Rhys replied. His tail curled up at the tip. He rose to his feet so he could refill his glass of water. He struggled to turn to tap, whimpering in pain as he pulled it around. Eventually he was able to get the water flowing to fill his cup.

William leaned forward. "Why don't you speak to Amy and get something better? They haven't been improving," the starat said.

Rhys's ears dipped down. He shook his head. "I can't make that choice yet."

"When? You've been saying that for weeks now. You kept saying you were waiting for Doctor Sparks, but he's said they can't be cured. Then you said you were waiting to see what my leg was like, but you haven't even asked me about it. Seems like you've been avoiding me. You need to commit one way or the other," William replied. He tapped his claws against the table. "And if you choose not to, then you will be a hindrance to anything we try to do, no matter how much you're able to reach into that subspace."

Rhys leaned back against the wall and held onto his cup of water. It felt so heavy to his trembling hands. He knew William was right. If he could barely hold a cup of water, what hope did he have in holding a firearm? Even if he managed to learn how to manipulate subspace in time, he would never be proficient enough to be of much use. He couldn't rely on the power gloves all the time.

"Has Twitch tried to modify your legs yet?" Rhys asked nervously. He knew he was trying to divert the subject away from his arms, but his mind didn't want to linger there.

"Tried, yes. Succeeded, not yet," William replied. A smirk came onto his lips, but then the starat sighed. "You can't keep avoiding it, Captain Rhys. Sooner or later, Amy is going to demand an answer from you."

"I have two more days to decide," Rhys said quietly. He stared down at his hands. They trembled as he struggled to keep hold of the glass of water. His eyes slowly drifted across to William, and the foot that was resting up on the chair.

William noticed Rhys's attention. He hitched up his trousers a little to show off a bit more of his synthetic leg. There was barely anything to tell it apart from the starat's other leg. "You know there are thousands of starats with wounds as bad as mine – as yours too – who don't get what we're getting. I was lucky to get the leg I had before. Normally I'd have just been killed and replaced," the starat growled. He jabbed a finger in Rhys's direction. "We're in a better place now. Starats don't need to suffer as I did. As you are. Don't squander that."

Rhys bowed his head as he leaned back against the countertops. He sighed and nodded gently, before drinking the entire cup of water in several quick gulps. He imagined it was wine, but he didn't get the buzz he needed from the cool water.

Before Rhys could answer, a squeal of delight came from the doorway. Rhys looked up just in time to see Twitch barrelling towards him. He put the glass down on the counter behind him and braced for impact. The starat wrapped his arms around Rhys and laughed in delight.

"I did it, Captain Rhys. I did it," Twitch crowed gleefully. He bounced up and down, dragging Rhys with him as he danced around the canteen. "I found subspace."

Their feet tangled, and the two starats tumbled to the floor. Rhys winced as he landed beneath Twitch, but the other starat didn't seem perturbed at all. Instead, Twitch just kissed Rhys on the side of the muzzle and cackled in delight again.

"Proud of you," Rhys said weakly. He patted Twitch on the back and rested his head against the cool tiles.

Nick stepped over the two of them without even looking down, while Leandro stood by the table. "We all did," the older starat said. "Your explanation didn't make much sense at first, but then we worked it out. Nick was first, then Twitch. It's a bit more difficult to teach an old starat new tricks."

Snow stood behind Leandro, and she placed her hand on his shoulder. "You have all done exceptionally well," the albino said. She looked around the room with her sightless eyes. "There will be a rest day for most of you tomorrow, but try to reach subspace by yourself. Do nothing when you touch it, but I want to see if you can find easier ways to get there."

A shiver ran down Rhys's tail, but his look of concern wasn't shared by anyone else in the room. But then, no one else had seen the strange entities that seemed to exist in subspace. Their eyes still terrified him. Snow didn't warn of them though, so it was unlikely they would be an active threat. Rhys still knew that if ever he saw one of them again, he would do everything he could to rip himself out of subspace again.

Snow turned her pale eyes to Rhys. "For you, Captain Griffiths, it will not be a rest day. We have some excitement for you."

"Excitement?" Rhys asked. His toes curled in apprehension. His heart thudded in his chest. "I'm not sure I need any excitement after all of that in your lessons."

Snow bared her teeth in a smile. "There's someone who wants to meet you. Major-General Ulrich will be facilitating this meeting."

Rhys's tail swished. "And who is this person?"

"Major-General Ulrich will explain it all tomorrow, don't you worry," Snow said. She waved her hand at Rhys to stop any further questions. "He will help you understand what we're planning, and he'll persuade you to do something with your arms. You'll like him."

Rhys wasn't sure if he liked this mysterious person already, but he kept quiet and nodded his head. At least it would give him another chance to see the major-general. He felt like he was overdue another update from her. For that reason alone, Rhys agreed to go through with this plan from Amy and Snow. He was determined to find a way to help in this war. If the major-general wasn't going to give him a way forward, then he would have no choice but to agree to anything Amy offered him.

chapter thirteen

Major-General Ulrich was flanked by two guards as Rhys stepped into the familiar little room at the base of the space elevator. Just as Snow had promised the previous day, he had been summoned back to meet the major-general, though he had not yet been given an exact reason for the meeting. There had been no mention in the summons about meeting a third person She sat down behind the desk opposite Rhys, and she gestured for the two surly human guards to wait for her outside. They closed the door behind them.

"No improvement in the hands yet?" Major-General Ulrich asked. She nodded down to Rhys's arms as he rested them on the table between them.

"Nothing yet, no. I still haven't decided what to do with them, ma'am," Rhys replied. He turned his head to the side. He had hoped to avoid a conversation about his hands, as it only served to remind him how close the deadline on his decision was. He had little over twenty-four hours left before Amy expected an answer.

The major-general nodded her head. "And what of your living situation? You have little over a week left at Appletree before we will require you to move on."

Rhys grimaced. "I will admit, I have been too pre-occupied with my lessons with Snow," he admitted. He bowed his head and bit his lip.

"Everyone on guaranteed income is provided a house, Captain Griffiths. All you need to do is choose it," the major-general said.

The tip of her tail arched up from behind her chair. "We have also received word that your imperial funds have been transferred across. It was a stroke of luck, but we were able to access the bank information of your whole crew. With that money, you will have the choice of almost anything in Caledonia."

"I appreciate that, thank you, Major-General," Rhys said. He bowed his head slightly as he clasped his hands together on the desk. It cut into his wrists painfully, but he tried to keep that discomfort out of his face and ears.

The major-general held up her hand. "Don't thank me. We had a few people dedicated to extricating refugees' assets from Terra. It can be difficult for military refugees as everything is often locked down quickly, but in your case, it seems like no one was willing to touch you or your crew. Probably on account of your starat nature."

Rhys grimaced and nodded. He couldn't take the pain in his wrists anymore, and he held his hands to his chest in an attempt to soothe the surge of pain that spread through his arms. "I'm still grateful for all the efforts they made. It was more than I expected."

"All the same, you don't have long left before we will require you to move on. But that is not the purpose of this meeting," the major-general said. She leaned forward in her chair and rested her wrists on the table. "I know I said it would still be a few months at least before you were involved in any further military matters, but I have had a request from General Carson. Given what we learned from the prisoners we freed on Charon, he has requested a meeting with you. He wishes to meet you in Cambria today."

"Cambria? Is that far?"

"It's on the southern continent. Should take a couple of hours to get there. I'll be getting some clearance sorted for you, as you'll be visiting the barracks on the outskirts of the city. The general didn't say why he needed you, but he impressed on me that it was a matter of importance and urgency. I believe he intends to contravene the usual wait period before you can join the Stellar Guard."

Rhys rubbed his hands together nervously. He assumed that this meeting had been at least partially arranged by Amy and Snow, and Rhys wasn't sure what motives there were behind it. "So I'll be leaving now, ma'am?"

"As soon as we have a shuttle ready for you, and I've gotten confirmation of your temporary clearance," Major-General Ulrich replied. She rose up to her feet, and Rhys quickly followed suit. "If you'll come with me, I'll escort you to the shuttles."

With the two guards either side of them, Major-General Ulrich led Rhys through the wide corridors that wound their way through the mountain beneath the space elevator. Everyone they passed saluted the major-general, and a few curious looks were cast in Rhys's direction. He tried to ignore them, but he couldn't help but feel like it was a reaction to his injuries. His arms had been freed of their bandages, but his fur still hadn't fully grown back. The scars on his palms were still clearly visible, and the skeletal appearance of his arms beneath his elbows was obvious. He tried to tug down on his sleeves in a futile attempt to cover them even slightly.

The light from Prox was always weak enough that even in the middle of the day, artificial lighting was needed. Deeper inside the mountain, it would have been pitch black were it not for the strips of white light that shone down from the ceiling. Rhys quickly lost his bearings, unsure just how deep into the mountain they were going. The major-general didn't once lose her way though, never making a misstep as she navigated the nearly identical corridors.

Finally, after a long walk, windows appeared again in the distance. The dark sky was visible through them, though there was no sign of the familiar light pollution from the city. As they approached, Rhys could see long lines of light along the flat ground beyond. They stretched out all the way to the horizon in perfect parallel lines. Rhys paused by the window as he looked out at the view. He realised that the lines were hydroponics farms. There were even more than those that surrounded the city.

"These farms feed the whole system," Major-General Ulrich said. She stood behind Rhys's shoulder and pointed out a small prick of bright light on the horizon. "There are several distribution centres dotted around the continent, and they control where the food goes. They are incredibly well defended and restricted. Even I don't have clearance to visit one."

"The other planets don't grow their own food?" Rhys asked. He was surprised by that. In the empire, only the smallest colonies didn't produce their own food, like Ceres.

"Centaura is the only one with the right conditions, and even then, Prox makes it difficult, hence why everything is in greenhouses," the major-general explained. She placed her hand on Rhys's shoulder and gave him a small push. "The shuttles aren't far now. You will be on a civilian flight, but we've already got a seat sorted for you."

Rhys allowed himself to be shepherded down the next corridor. They passed through a security checkpoint, before emerging into a wide terminal that reminded Rhys of a Terran airport. They came out from a small side-entrance to the side of the rows of wide doors that opened out onto the main road. Hundreds of starats and humans all mingled and wandered around the terminal as they tried to work out where to go.

The major-general needed no such assistance as she strode across the terminal. Rhys and the two guards followed behind. The crowd parted around the starat, giving them an untroubled route across the wide, cavernous room. The major-general led Rhys to a small queue that led to another security checkpoint. A mixture of starats and humans stood in front of Rhys.

"This is where I leave you," Major-General Ulrich said. She held out a slip of paper for Rhys to take. "Here is your ticket. You'll be told where to go, and there will be someone to meet you at the other end. By the time you land your security clearance should have gone through."

"Most appreciated, thank you, Major-General," Rhys replied. He quickly saluted the starat, but she waved his hand down.

"We will see you on your return. I can't expect the general will need more than a few hours of your time. Safe trip," the major-general said. She turned on her toes and started to make her way back through the terminal.

Rhys took a deep breath as he was left alone. He turned to look down the small queue of starats and humans. Ahead there were two short humans processing the passengers, sending their belongings through a scanner. They were moving reasonably quickly, and it was only a few minutes before Rhys found himself next in line.

"Ticket," one of the humans asked.

Rhys quickly handed over his ticket. He hoped he didn't need to provide any identification, as all he had still was his old Terran military card, and that still showed his human face. The human behind the computer didn't ask for any, and the ticket was quickly handed back. Rhys was waved on to the body scanner, and he quickly passed through.

On the other side was another human monitoring the passengers as they collected their bags. She looked to Rhys for a moment, but he had no possessions to collect from the conveyor belt. He kept moving, not wanting to hold anyone up.

"Safe flight," the human said, before he walked past her.

"Thanks," Rhys replied quickly. She had already moved onto the next passenger behind him; a human who had set off the body scanners. Rhys ignored the beep of the alarm. Before him was a large sign pointing the way to the various terminals and shuttle gates. Rhys checked his ticket to find the right gate before he descended into the crowd.

***

True to the major-general's word, the shuttle flight took a few hours before it came in to land. That time was almost entirely uneventful, with just a screaming starat kit to bother Rhys during the flight. The journey itself was pleasant and smooth at least. Though the humans on Centaura were shorter due to the higher gravity, they were still a little larger than starats, and so Rhys had plenty of leg room to stretch out in.

Cambria was bathed in darkness. There was no moon to illuminate the night sky, but there was just enough starlight to dust the red land in illumination. Artificial light from the city gleamed off the sparkling water. The city was built on the edge of a wide estuary, though the mouth of the river as it flowed into the ocean was hidden from view beyond the horizon. There were no hydroponics like those that surrounded Caledonia. From the air, the red landscape looked almost like a desert, but then Rhys noticed there were individual trees that provided the red colour. It was not a sandy desert, but instead a patchwork of red-tinged forests and grasslands.

That all soon disappeared beyond buildings as the shuttle came to land in the outskirts of Cambria. Half an hour after grounding, Rhys was stood outside the terminal, looking around for the person who was meant to be meeting him. No one caught his attention, leaving Rhys to stand alone in the cold midnight outside the terminal.

Just as Rhys was beginning to wonder what to do, he heard someone calling his name. His ears perked up as he tried to find the source of the voice. He eventually saw a human going up to every starat waiting outside the terminal and asking them the same question. "Are you Rhys Griffiths?"

Rhys lifted his hand and waved towards the human. "Over here."

The human looked across to Rhys and rested his hand on his chest. "Oh thank goodness. I was running late and I thought I'd miss you, but I'm glad I found you." The human tapped at an electronic wristband, before holding out his hand for Rhys to shake. "The name's Santiago. I'm to be your escort while you're in Cambria."

Santiago's hand felt cold against Rhys's, lacking the usual warmth of organic flesh. Rhys tilted his head to the side, slightly thrown off by the strange feeling. He held onto Santiago's hand for a moment longer than necessary, despite the pain the contact caused him. The human's skin felt rubbery, nothing like the usual sensation he got when touching a human, or what he remembered of his old human body. "Your arms...?" Rhys asked hesitantly.

Santiago grinned as Rhys let go of the human's hand. He held both hands up, spreading his fingers. "Both artificial, right to the shoulder. Same as the legs. The only flesh I have left is this squishy bit in the middle."

Rhys winced and pulled back slightly as an involuntary shudder ran down his spine. "How did you get so badly injured?"

"Huh? Oh, no. This was entirely voluntary," Santiago replied with a laugh. He started to walk back the way he had come from, and Rhys hurried to stay by his side. "I chose to go through with this. Makes my work so much easier, and I can upgrade my hands and feet to do more and better things all the time."

Rhys flicked his ears, surprised by the human's frank admission. "Don't you worry about, I don't know, maintaining your humanity?"

Santiago scoffed. "My humanity? Nah, not at all. I know who I am, and I still stay as myself no matter how much I change. I've got nothing to worry about there, and anything you hear otherwise is just Vatican scaremongering. Nasty sods are becoming a little louder around here now."

Rhys kept his mouth closed. For so long he had been told that augmentations like that were wrong, and that to change the human form was tantamount to blasphemy. It had been the Vatican who had loudly preached that, but sometimes it had been difficult to tell apart their beliefs with those of the empire. Often they were one and the same. Rhys looked down at his hands again. He partially clenched his fists and sighed. It wouldn't quite be a necessity to have his arms replaced, but it wouldn't be the same as an entirely voluntary process. Knowing people willingly swapped their organic flesh for cybernetic alternatives was tougher to comprehend.

Santiago chuckled beneath his breath. "With injuries like yours, I don't expect it to be long before you decide to upgrade. Trust me, most of the people here have at least something artificial on them," the human said, swinging his arm around to gesture the passengers as they made their way out of the terminal.

Rhys wrinkled his muzzle and shook his head slightly, but he still didn't trust his tongue enough to speak his thoughts. He had so many questions about it all, but for now at least he didn't really want to know the answers. Instead he shielded his eyes and squinted up into the black sky, trying to find the twin stars of Alpha Centauri. They either weren't visible, or Rhys was looking in the wrong part of the sky. "Do you have the shields here too?"

Santiago glanced up. "Of course. It covers the whole planet, though it's certainly needed more this much closer to the equator than Caledonia is. That's why they put all the hydroponics closer to the poles. Even with the magnetic shields, non-native plants struggle around here. We think it was because the soil was damaged over the millennia before we arrived and started to change things."

"There's no danger to anyone here?" Rhys asked. He sidestepped a couple of humans who hadn't appeared to notice him. They had made their way out to a massive carpark that stretched almost as far as Rhys could see in the dull gloom. Even the regular street lamps couldn't fully dispel the twilight darkness.

"With the shield up, none at all. And don't worry, the shield can't be taken down. There are failsafes scattered over the entire planet," Santiago replied. His answer didn't soothe all of Rhys's worries, but they suppressed them for the time being. "We're as safe here as anywhere on Terra. But come, it's only a short drive from here to the barracks."

The human opened up the door of the nearest car, gesturing for Rhys to get in. Once Rhys slipped into the seat, having to lean forward as there was no hole for his tail in the back, Santiago got in on the other side. To Rhys's surprise, the human twisted and clicked off his right hand and slotted his arm into a port between the two seats.

"Gives me access to the navigation computer, so I can tell it where to go and get access to all the information it provides. If there's traffic ahead, it will tell me and I can redirect us," Santiago explained, noticing Rhys's surprised recoil. The human smiled widely. "Told you there were plenty of benefits to be had."

Rhys's ears curled up as he looked away from the human. He suppressed another shudder that threatened to trickle down his spine. He didn't like the idea of giving so much of himself away. If he was forced to lose his arms, then that would be all he would ever want to do. A like-for-like replacement was all he could ever be comfortable with. Amy's suggestions of becoming a living weapon worried him. Where would it end?

Santiago just shrugged his shoulders as Rhys didn't answer. The human kept his arm plugged into the car as it started to drive, though he didn't appear to be focused on actively driving it at all. Rhys's eyes occasionally flicked across to look at the human, but mostly he just stared out the window as the car slowly crept through the traffic as it filtered out of the terminal carparks. Once they reached the roads beyond, their pace picked up as they turned away from the city.

"You're certainly very uncomfortable with cybernetics, aren't you? Must be a Terran thing, I guess," Santiago said. The augmented human shook his head and chuckled. "Most people with arms like yours would have replaced them long ago."

Rhys nodded. He held up one hand and slowly clenched his trembling fingers. "I was tortured by the church back on Terra. Replacing them feels almost like giving up. They won. They made my arms so useless I needed to replace them with a machine," he said, before leaning his head back in his seat and sighing. "Everything is so different here. I didn't realise how restricted everything is in the empire. There's so many new things to get used to."

"I suppose being so close to Mars means the Vatican has a lot of sway on Terra," Santiago said. The human looked straight ahead out of the car. "But don't think of it as giving up. If anything, you're giving up now. You're letting their actions limit you."

"Oh you have no idea," Rhys replied with a grimace. He rubbed his fingers together, before holding his hands over his face. "I suppose things are better here. But there's so much I don't understand. My whole life I was told the human body was sacred and couldn't be altered, and yet here..."

"Would you want to go back?"

"If I could go back to before any of this started?" Rhys said, gesturing down to his body. He sighed. "No, I don't think I would. Being here has shown me so many of the flaws I'd never known I had. I wouldn't want to go back to a time when I was still unaware of them. There are too many friends I would lose because of it."

"Probably for the best that you don't want to go back," Santiago said. He leaned forward as the car started to slow. They were nearing a large cluster of buildings surrounded by a tall wall, with only one single gateway. "The general wouldn't like you sticking around if he thought you were going to be running away with our secrets."

Rhys shook his head. "I'm sure they know I don't have any future on Terra, whether I wanted it or not. I could hold the key to destroying Centaura, and they wouldn't listen to me in the empire. You could tell me how to shut off those shields or how to destroy the farms, and I would be ignored," he said. Some small part of him was still sad about that. He knew he was going to miss Terra, and yet accepting that there was no place for him there anymore was difficult to accept. But it was the truth.

Santiago slowly rolled towards the lone gate, where several armed humans stepped forward. Rhys suppressed a small shiver as they approached. A flash of red light shone at the car from the gate, and the vehicle shuddered to a complete halt.

"Santiago Cruz, escorting Rhys Griffiths to meet General Carson," Santiago said as he opened the window to speak to the guards.

"Griffiths?" the closest human grunted, looking in towards Rhys. "Yeah, his clearance came through an hour ago. He's still considered a civilian, so he's to remain supervised at all times until he meets the general. He's in the drill square right now."

"Understood," Santiago replied. At the guard's command, the car started to roll forward with a flash of green light coming from the road beneath the automated car. The gates opened and allowed them into the compound.

A small tarmac square was surrounded by the dark and imposing buildings. In the middle of the square was a statue. Rhys had to look twice to make sure what he was seeing was correct. The statue was of three starats. In one hand, the lead starat held an upraised sword, with a pistol in his other hand. The other two stood just behind the first, locked in the position of drawing their own pistols. Rhys stared at the statue as the car came to a halt beneath the building to the left of the gate. He slowly got out of the car and approached the statue as Santiago reattached his hand.

Beneath the statue was a small plaque. *'Commemorating the starats who gave their lives to save Centaura from the threat of invasion. They died so starats could be seen as equal to humans. Shown here: Second-lieutenant Ayo flanked by Cadet Sierra and Cadet Alisson.'*

"They really did help win the war, didn't they?" Rhys said quietly. He ran his hand over the plaque and looked up into the eyes of the starat statues. He wondered who they had really been, and what they had done before the Terran army had come. Even on Centaura they would have been treated poorly, but they had been given the opportunity to prove themselves worthy. The starats on Terra had never been given that chance. Given the strength of the Vatican, Rhys doubted they would ever be given the opportunity.

"They did, yes," Santiago said. He flashed a smile to Rhys, and gestured for the starat to follow. "Come on, I don't want to keep the general waiting. He should be finishing off his drills soon."

***

General Carson was a tall man, especially compared to every human Rhys had seen on Centaura. The general towered over everyone around him as he stood with his hands behind his back, overseeing a training exercise that was taking place in a large, open field contained within the compound walls. Rhys had yet to be introduced to him. He instead waited with Santiago at the base of the wall.

For most of the training, General Carson remained silent, but when he did open his mouth his voice bellowed out commands so loud they echoed off the far wall. The general wasn't just tall. He was powerful. Even from a distance, Rhys could see that his uniform bulged with muscle. Unlike all the other humans present, General Carson was not clean shaven. His face was covered by thick, almost overgrown black facial hair. Rhys almost felt like cowering, and the general hadn't even looked directly at him yet.

General Carson eventually brought the training session to an end with another thunderous roar of his voice. His troops marched off the field, all still perfectly in step with each other. It wasn't until they disappeared inside the building on the far side of the field that Rhys noticed any of them relax even slightly. Once the last of them had gone inside, General Carter turned to Rhys at last. From halfway across the field, Rhys quailed.

The general had a long, loping stride as he quickly covered the distance between them. If anything, he seemed even larger close up. His hands clasped around Rhys's. "Pleasure to meet you, Rhys Griffiths. I'm General Sam Carson," the general said. His voice was surprisingly soft compared to the thunderous roar that had bellowed around the training field moments earlier. "Care to come with me to my office? There is so much I want to talk about."

General Carson's ears wiggled slightly as he smiled. He let go of Rhys's hand and swept his arm around to the small building on the far side of the training field, nestled against the enclosing wall.

Despite the great strides General Carson was capable of, he walked slowly so Rhys could stay by his side as they crossed the field. Santiago didn't join them. The augmented human instead disappeared back into the building Rhys had first come through. The looming shadow of the general made Rhys a little nervous, and it took a lot of effort to keep his tail from tucking between his legs.

"May I ask what this is all about, General?" Rhys asked. He craned his neck to look up at General Carson. There was something strangely familiar about him in a way that he couldn't place.

The general waved his hand in Rhys's direction. "Please, don't feel you need to stand for formality with me now. It's always made me uncomfortable. Sam will be fine. Carson, if you must," the general said. His loping gait was unlike anything Rhys had seen before. The general seemed to favour walking on his toes, despite the heavy boots he wore.

"I'll try to keep that in mind, General. I mean, sir."

The general laughed softly. They had reached the far side of the field, just outside the small, square building. General Carson pushed open the door, revealing just a single room inside. Rhys stepped in, finding himself in a cluttered office. A desk and chair was squeezed into one corner, while a number of maps of the various planets in the system covered the walls. Cabinets and shelves filled what space wasn't taken by the maps. A number of framed photos were scattered around the room. Most were of General Carson with what looked like other military or government figures, but a couple confused him. They were blurred pictures of starats at work. They were out of focus, as though someone had taken a larger photo and cropped out anything that wasn't the starat that was now framed. He flicked his ears and turned to the desk as the general sat behind it. The human gestured to the chair in front of it, and Rhys quickly sat down. He tucked his tail through the hole in the back.

"Grey and Beaumont have given us some fascinating information," the general said. He leaned back in his chair as he watched over Rhys. "But they have also provided us with some worrying news that Terra is finally starting to utilise subspace tech. It's all highly classified at the moment and certainly isn't being mentioned around people of your old rank, but senior authorities are pushing hard for further research."

"Research into what?" Rhys said, mostly musing to himself. He frowned and tapped his toes on the floor nervously.

"We're not entirely sure," the general replied. He leaned forward and clasped his fingers together. "All we know is that they're planning to develop subspace weapons. What they are or how they work, we don't know. We're glad to get knowledge of this, but we still need more information."

"I can't think of anything that it could be," Rhys said nervously. He wasn't sure if that was why he had been summoned, to provide information on what the empire could be researching. He knew nothing about it.

The general waved his hand. "Don't worry, Captain. I'm not expecting you to spill all the empire's secrets, especially ones you had no right to know. Truth be told, I want to discuss a different matter first. I want to talk about you. I find myself fascinated by your history."

Rhys pinned his ears back. "It seems lots of people are, in some way or another," he said quietly.

"I have heard bits and pieces of your story," the general said. He leaned forward and rested his elbows on the desk so his chin rested on his hands. "But do you mind telling me what happened on the day you became a starat?"

Rhys's muzzle twitched. "I don't really remember much of it," he said with a small shake of the head. "I stepped into the teleporter, but the next thing I remember after that was waking up in the medical bay. I was told it was an electrical fault with the teleporter, but beyond that I was never given the full story. Not many people wanted to talk to me afterwards."

General Carson pursed his lips and nodded. "That sounds about right. The empire excels at hiding any information they don't want to let out. Frankly, those teleporters have so many issues it's remarkable there haven't been many more incidents with them," he said tersely. He shook his head and looked to the pictures on the shelves. "There's a fundamental flaw buried deep into the system they use, and it should never have become common use. We don't use them here for that very reason."

"So why does Terra use them if they're so dangerous?" Rhys mused.

"Convenience," General Carson replied. He snapped his fingers. "You can teleport in an instant. Shuttles take time, and can be intercepted. They can crash. To the uninformed eye, teleporters are a fool proof system, but there are some of us who have paid dearly for that misconception."

Rhys bowed his head. "I certainly have. I never want to use a teleporter again. The last two times have both been horrific experiences," he said. He clenched his teeth and suppressed a growl. "The first time I woke up like this, and the second time my first officer was killed as he tried to save me. They are a curse."

"I am sorry to hear about that. I wasn't aware of your first officer. He sounds like he was a good man," General Carson said. One of his large hands briefly held Rhys's, before it was withdrawn.

"He was. He was one of the only humans who immediately saw that I was unchanged in here," Rhys replied, tapping his hand against the side of his head. He ignored the brief contact from the general.

He sighed. "Edgar Scott saved my life more times than I realised. He saved me by treating me like a real person after my change, and then again when he rescued me from the Vatican. I will be forever grateful to him for that, but he shouldn't have paid for it with his life."

"I understand that. Sadly it happens any time the Vatican comes across anything it does not understand or approve. You say the teleporters are a curse, but to me, it is them. The Vatican. They are the curse that blights the empire," General Carson said. He wrinkled his nose and tapped his hand against his desk. "I know you are associated with Amy Jennings and her plan to help strip the Vatican of their power, but that isn't what I wanted to discuss with you yet. Instead I wanted to ask you a question that may seem strange at first. Are you familiar with Captain James Herschel?"

Rhys frowned and scratched the side of his muzzle as he thought. The name sounded familiar. "Doesn't he serve on the base on Pluto? I think I remember his name on some of the briefing sheets Major-General Ulrich gave me for the Charon mission."

General Carson nodded. "That's correct, yes. Can you recall ever meeting him, or seeing what he looked like?"

Rhys started to shake his head, but then he looked up to the general again. He squinted a little, and tried to imagine the general without the unruly facial hair. "That's... that's not possible. Captain Herschel is still on Pluto, as far as I know. How... how can you be him?"

The general smirked. "You are right. I have his face. I have his body. But I am not Captain Herschel. You were not the first person to lose their identity in a teleporter. I know of at least two dozen occasions where a human lost their identity to another human. Most are secreted away from the Vatican, but a few escaped to Centaura. However, then we get a case like yours. Human to starat? Unprecedented. Only once before was a starat involved in a cross-species teleporter incident."

"You?" Rhys whispered. His eyes were wide as the general nodded.

"Me. I was once a starat on Charon, when the teleporter failed. One moment I was Samantha, the next, I was James Herschel."

"Samantha?" Rhys asked in shock. "You were female?"

"I was. That was quite the shock to discover. But I was luckier than you. I was conscious as I came out of the teleporter, so I was able to act right away," the general explained. He again looked towards the pictures on the shelf. "I used my new identity to make a few necessary orders, and I was able to commandeer a ship to escape. I tried to free some of the starats, but they were naturally distrustful of me. I did what I could, but I was confused and scared. I ran, and I came to Centaura. Few here know my true history."

"I thought I was the only one," Rhys said. He looked up at the general. It was hard to believe the towering human had once been a starat. "Do you miss it? Being a starat?"

"Terribly, yes. The tail is the worst part. It's been fifteen years, and I still have to remind myself I don't have one," the general said. He shrugged his shoulders. "I'm mostly used to it though. I've gotten used to considering myself a human, and a male. But if I could go back... If I could go back to what I was, I'd take that opportunity in a moment."

"Can't you just get cybernetics?" Rhys asked, thinking of Santiago. The human had replaced most of his body with artificial parts.

The general shook his head. "It wouldn't be the same. Don't get me wrong, cybernetics here are wonderful and much more advanced than anything in the empire. It would be amazing to be covered in fur again, but it would just be a shadow of what I want. Almost a mockery. No, I'd rather not have anything at all compared to that."

"I think I understand," Rhys said. Behind the chair, his tail flicked back and forth. He had gotten used to the new appendage now, and it was rare that he forgot it was there. He could only imagine what it would be like to go the other way. He looked down at his fur-covered hands. Would he cope with being human again? With every day that passed by he grew less confident that he would.

"But this brings me onto an important matter," General Carson said. He got up from his chair and pulled the window closed and locked the door. Rhys remained seated, twisting around to keep his eye on the general. "Fleet-Admiral Bosler and I disagree on many things. I don't think she has the right methods when it comes to taking on the empire. She doesn't know what it's really like to live as a starat there. She's a Centauran human. How could she know? I do, of course, but she doesn't trust my opinion. I'm just an empire human to her."

"She doesn't know who you were?"

General Carson shook his head. "No. There are perhaps half a dozen people who know, and she is not one of them."

"I'm honoured you trusted me enough to tell then, thank you," Rhys said.

"That number will soon rise. Given the information we have gathered from your Charon mission, we know we must start acting quickly. There is a plan being developed that will require more to know who I once was. It is something that I need you for," the general said. He slowly paced around the room, one hand brushing against the maps on the wall. "I need anyone who has knowledge of the empire and especially the Pluto system. You have recently been there, so your knowledge and your presence will be crucial."

Rhys flicked his ears in confusion. "I don't understand what you're asking me to do."

"Charon and Pluto are more important to the empire than most people realise. There are systems run there that are critical to the Vatican, and there is important research and development being carried out in the labs. It is not just a prison. There's a research centre there too, where they are developing some of this disturbing new tech implicated by Grey and Beaumont. We are going to be going there," the general said. He turned to face Rhys, hands behind his back. "It will be a long-term mission for myself, but there are things which I think will be best carried out by yourself."

"Will I be permitted? I was told it would be three months after Charon before I'd be put into active duty with the Stellar Guard," Rhys said.

General Carson tapped on his chest. "I'm one of the three people who will decide if you can serve with us. Fleet-Admiral Bosler has already given her approval. General Campbell has also indicated his support. I won't lie. I had to pull in a few favours to get this approval. Everything I have seen about you indicates that should be worth it. Please don't prove otherwise."

Rhys let out a deep breath and twitched his tail. "Then I look forward to returning to active service," he said, bowing his head towards the general. "When will I be leaving?"

"It will take us about two weeks to get everything prepared. I would recommend fixing your arms in the meantime. It doesn't matter how you do it, but we can't risk you like this."

"I understand," Rhys said with a nod. The fingers of his right hand started to trace around the bones of his wrist that pressed up against his skin. "I assume I'll be briefed more fully on the mission details closer to the time?"

"Of course," General Carson replied, but he didn't get any further before someone hammered their fist against the outside of his office door.

"General, you're needed urgently," a frantic voice called out.

"Situation report," the general barked out immediately. His voice had lost the soft touch it had possessed in his conversation with Rhys.

"There's been an attack in Caledonia. Major-General Ulrich has been wounded."

The general snapped his fingers in Rhys's direction. "You come with me."

chapter fourteen

Any plans Rhys had for remaining in Cambria for any period of time were quickly scuppered. Whatever information he could have learned from General Carson had to wait. He was rushed out of the barracks with General Carson and a few other military personnel who all appeared to be of high rank. No one introduced themselves to Rhys, but from their conversations he could tell they were Colonel Jones, Lieutenant Calvers, and Captain Son. They all bowed their heads in close and spoke in hushed tones. Though he tried to listen in as much as he could, Rhys couldn't quite gather together a complete picture about what had happened in Caledonia. All he knew was that the major-general had been wounded, but he didn't know how severely.

The shuttle journey back was mostly quiet. This was not a civilian shuttle either, so it was only Rhys and the four humans on board. He sat by himself and stared out the window as they travelled north east over the great ocean that split the two continents. There was just inky darkness outside the small windows. He could see occasional flashes of light in the ocean, though Rhys could never be sure exactly what formed the lights. They could have been ships, or small islands. The murmur of conversation continued all around him, but never involved him. He heard only a few words here and there, but nothing painted a clear picture of what had happened. There hadn't been a large-scale attack, or else they wouldn't be going to Caledonia mostly unarmed, but Rhys was still nervous about what he would find.

The familiar lights of the space elevator lit up the night sky before the shuttle came in to dock at a military base Rhys had yet to visit. If his bearings were correct, then it was close to the civilian airport he had flown out of earlier in the day.

Rhys was shepherded out of the shuttle by General Carson. "Stay close to me until we know if the threat is neutralised," the general warned.

"Understood, sir," Rhys replied. For all the informality he had shared with the general earlier, he easily slipped back into formal speech that their surroundings required. General Carson's nose twitched as he followed after the other humans.

A starat ran out to meet the newcomers. "Glad you could make it so quickly, sirs. Follow me, I'll take you through to the major-general. She requested to meet you specifically."

"What happened, lieutenant?" Colonel Jones asked before any of his companions could ask the same question.

"I'm still not quite sure, Colonel. There were conflicting reports, and I haven't been given the latest briefings," the starat replied as they started to walk. "I believe there was a group of around a dozen. It's only rumour, but I heard they may be working for the Inquisition. They appeared to be here to liberate a male refugee we had taken into custody. It is my understanding that they all managed to escape."

"Worrying," General Carson said, which prompted a ripple of nodded agreement.

The starat quickly led them through to the medical ward. His eyes paused as they passed over Rhys as he waited to let everyone through the ward doors, but he didn't say anything that told Rhys he wasn't permitted to enter.

The medical staff within the ward barely reacted at the sudden influx of four humans and two starats. They appeared to be busy as they bustled between the beds. Rhys noticed it was mostly starats that they were treating. Most had only minor wounds, though there were a couple here and there who had suffered more serious injuries. Major-General Ulrich was one of the latter.

The major-general raised her hand in acknowledgement of her company. She was laid back in her bed, muzzle clenched in pain. The right side of her face was wrapped in bandages, as was most of her right arm as it lay on the thin sheets. Dried blood still clung to her fur around her muzzle and neck.

"How are you feeling, Nessie?" General Carson said. He knelt down by the side of the bed and gently took the major-general's uninjured hand into his own.

"I'll live, but that bastard certainly cut me up good," the major-general replied. She winced as she shifted in her bed. Her eye flicked around the humans around her, but she didn't look down to Rhys. "We'd taken a refugee from Terra under arrest as he flagged up in our system as a problem. Didn't get the chance to look up why before we were under attack. It was only a small strike team, but they hit hard and fast. By the time we'd scrambled our defences they were already on their way out. It was all planned."

"Who was the refugee?" Colonel Jones asked.

The major-general hissed softly as she sat up a little straighter in her bed. "Erik Aurealiusson. Does the name mean anything to you?"

Rhys couldn't stop the squeak of fear that escaped his mouth. He took a step back, bumping against the bed opposite the major-general. The eyes of all four humans and the major-general all turned to him. "It's him. It's the cardinal," Rhys said. His voice shook as his tail wrapped around his leg. "He's here for me."

"Are you sure it's him? You're light-years from Terra. Would he really come all this way for you?" General Carson asked.

Rhys nodded. He felt cold. "He gave me his name once. The first time I met him, when I was still human. When he wasn't trying to kill me," he said. His thoughts were frantic. "Do you know where he went? Does he know where I'm living?"

Major-General Ulrich's ears pinned down slightly. "It's possible. I was responding to a data breach just before I took him into custody. I don't know what information was lost or who accessed it, but if he was here for you, then it's possible his rescuers gained information on you and your whereabouts."

"I have to go," Rhys said. He took half a step away from the major-general's bed, before one of the other humans stepped to the side to get between him and the door. "Please, I need to go. My crew is in danger. I have to get to them."

General Carson rose to his feet. "I'll take him," he said to the rest of the gathered humans. No one offered any protests. "I'll be back as soon as I can. Keep me updated if possible."

"I'm sorry," Rhys said to the major-general, feeling that the blame for the attack had to fall on him. The cardinal had come all this way for him. She had just gotten in the way. He turned and fled from the ward before anyone could respond. General Carson was right on his tail.

This time it was difficult to keep up with the general, whose long legs gave great speed to his urgency. Rhys struggled to keep up as he followed behind. His chest burned as they raced through the wide corridors beneath the space elevator. No one stopped them, though Rhys did notice a few curious glances in their direction. There were more security guards than he had ever seen before, but given the recent attack from Cardinal Erik and the men who had rescued him, Rhys wasn't surprised.

General Carson led Rhys out into the familiar carpark perched on the plateau beneath the space elevator. The human pulled Rhys away to the right, where there was a small row of cars parked right up close to the entrance. The general slapped his ID against the side of the nearest car, and to Rhys's surprise the door opened.

"You have a car here?" Rhys asked as he got inside.

General Carson held up his ID as he closed the door behind him. "Perks of being a general. There's always a few cars reserved for our use at every base around the system," he explained. He pocketed his ID and switched the car's navigational systems on. "Now, where are we going?"

"Appletree Estates," Rhys said. Immediately there was a responsible beep from the car's dashboard as it understood the location. It began to roll back and pull away from the carpark. Rhys willed it to move faster, but despite his urgency the car stuck to the same, leisurely pace as it wound its way down the mountainside. Rhys could only hope they would make it in time. The cardinal had had a big head start on them, and Rhys didn't want to think about what could have happened in that time.

***

Everything appeared calm as they finally reached Appletree Estate. Rhys hurried out the car and unlocked the front gate, holding it open so General Carson could follow behind. His eyes scanned around the small street. He slowed at the unmarked white van parked on the side of the street. "I don't trust that," the starat said, pointing it out to the general. No one was inside the vehicle, and no one protested as the human approached it.

General Carson crouched down by the front of the van. He fumbled around beneath it for a few moments, before hurrying back across to Rhys. "Remote tracker with a built in EMP. Just in case," the human explained.

Rhys grimaced. He hoped it wouldn't come to that, for that would mean the cardinal would have made his escape. With his heart thudding in his chest, he approached his apartment block and pushed open the doors.

Cool air washed over his fur as he stepped inside. A few of his crew were sat in the cafe, and Rhys hurried over to meet them. Chekolin was the first to see him, and the ship's pilot raised his hand in greeting. "It's been a while, Captain. How is everything?"

"Cardinal Erik is here," Rhys said, cutting across any other greetings from his crew. A hushed silence immediately fell. "There was an attack up at the space elevator, and it's possible that he's coming here. I think he might already be. Has anyone seen him?"

A rumble of "No, Captain," spread through the dozen people present. No one sounded certain, and a prickle of worry trickled down Rhys's tail.

"We haven't really been looking for anyone," Chekolin admitted. He bit his lip and grimaced. "Sorry about that, Captain."

"Lock the building down. Make sure no one leaves without my permission," Rhys ordered. His crew quickly came to attention and got to work. Four of them stood by the front doors. They weren't armed, but Rhys knew they would hold back the cardinal if they could. The starat clicked his fingers and instantly regretted his choice as the instinctive action sent a sharp stab of pain all the way up his arm. "Chekolin. You come up with me and the general. Everyone else, be on alert. Notify anyone else you see. Do not let the cardinal reach any of the starats. He will kill them."

Rhys didn't wait for a confirmation from his crew. He knew they would get it done. He hurried to the stairs and leapt up them three at a time. The thundering footsteps of General Carson and Chekolin followed just behind.

The corridor at the top of the stairs was empty. There was no sign of the cardinal at all. He pointed towards the nearby elevator. "Chekolin, look into shutting that down. I don't want to sweep upstairs and have the cardinal slip down by us that way."

"Will do, Captain. I'll catch up to you," Chekolin said. The pilot ran towards the elevator, while Rhys turned back towards the stairs that rose up to the next level. General Carson followed right behind him. Again, everything was quiet with no sound of the cardinal, or of the starats. There wasn't even any movement around from Rhys's crew. His tail twitched in worry.

"How do we know we haven't gone past them already?" General Carson asked. He placed a hand on Rhys's shoulder as they moved up to the third floor.

Rhys shrugged his shoulders. "We don't, I guess. Though I would smell that man anywhere. I don't think we've gone past him yet."

"I sometimes forget how much I've lost in senses," General Carson said wistfully, but he didn't say anything to speak against Rhys's judgement. Footsteps followed up the stairs behind them, but Rhys didn't wait for them to catch up.

Rhys came to a stop on the fourth floor. A door slammed a little further down the corridor, but it was the whimper of pain in the other direction that caught his attention. He wrinkled his nose at the scent of blood on the air. Using that metallic tang, Rhys was able to find the room he wanted.

The door was ajar, with bits of broken scrap metal scattered across the floor. Rhys slowly pushed open the door, using his foot to push aside some of the metal. He heard another whimper from inside.

Rhys didn't hesitate. He burst through into the bedroom and stared in horror at the scene before him. Blood was splattered against the wall, and the bedsheets bundled up on the bed were stained crimson. A lamp had crashed to the ground in a struggle, and everything kept on the cupboards and shelves had been swept to the floor. Scared of what he was going to see, Rhys stepped over the scattered debris and looked around the other side of the bed.

David lay on the floor. He bled from several wounds on his arms and torso, and his right leg was held at an awkward angle. He seemed to be having difficulty focusing as he tried to sit up. Rhys hurried by David's side, trying not to wince as he knelt down in a pool of the starat's blood. He put his hand on David's shoulder to stop him moving. "What happened?" Rhys squeaked.

"Cardinal Erik," David whispered through gritted teeth. His head rocked back and forth as he struggled to keep it upright. "He has Twitch. He took Twitch. I couldn't stop him."

"How long ago?" Rhys asked. He placed his hand on David's shoulder, making sure that the injured starat didn't move too much.

"Not long. Minutes," David said, speaking through a tight grimace. He reached up and grabbed hold of Rhys's hand. He didn't relent, even as Rhys gasped in pain. "Get him. Get him back, please."

Rhys extricated his hand from David's grip. He glanced to the door, where General Carson and Chekolin were waiting. "He's not gone far. Chekolin. Get downstairs and warn everyone the cardinal is probably still in the building. Barricade the lobby and any other exit," he ordered. The ship's pilot saluted and turned on his heel, leaving almost before Rhys had finished his command. The starat then looked to the starat-turned-human who remained. "Can you help me take David to a medical centre?"

David whimpered in pain as General Carson gently picked him up. The human didn't seem to care that the starat was leaking blood onto his uniform. "I never thought I'd see something like this again," the general said softly. One hand rested gently on David's head to try and soothe him, but there was fury in the human's eyes as he looked to Rhys. "Kill the fucker if you can."

Rhys looked up to meet the general in the eye. He clenched his hands into fists and nodded, before standing out of the general's way. It hurt to see David in the human's arms, but he couldn't sit and dwell on that. He had to find Twitch before anything terrible happened to him. He took a couple of steps away from the bloodstained bed. His chest heaved in nausea and anger. He didn't care if he had no strength in his arms. He would find a way to strangle the life from the cardinal.

"If you hurt him," Rhys whispered beneath his breath. "If you fucking hurt him…"

Rhys left behind the bloodstained room and closed the door as he stepped back out into the corridor. He could feel little trickles of David's blood in the fur on his legs, but he forced himself not to think about that for now. He knew the cardinal was close by. He wasn't going to let this opportunity to slip through his fingers.

The scent of Cardinal Erik lingered around the corridor. Rhys glanced towards General Carson as he disappeared down the stairs. The starat hesitated, before turning in the other direction. The cardinal hadn't taken the main stairs, or else they would have run into him on the way up. He had to have taken the fire escape, given the elevators had been shut down. Sure enough, Rhys found that the cardinal's scent was strongest around the fire escape door.

Rhys barged the door open. It crashed against the concrete wall behind and echoed throughout the shaft that ran up the entire height of the building. Rhys's nose wrinkled in disgust. Cardinal Erik had definitely been here. The scent of other humans mingled together in a way that confused Rhys to their number. One starat had been with them. "I'm coming Twitch."

Rhys hurried down the winding stairs as quickly as he could. His shoulder bumped against the concrete wall on his left as he spiralled down. He began to feel a little dizzy as he descended, and his feet stumbled a few times as he landed on the flat areas between the floors. Down below he could hear voices and a door smash open.

Gunshots rang out.

Rhys's hand instinctively moved down to his hip, but he didn't carry a weapon at all. His tail puffed up in fear, but he didn't slow down at all. He barrelled down the stairs as more shouts echoed out from the ground floor.

He burst through the door at the bottom of the stairs. The first thing that caught his eye was the open doors at the far end of the lobby. Cardinal Erik was there, looking bizarre out of his usual religious robes. Twitch was held in his arms. A knife was to the starat's throat as the human backed away. He was flanked by four other humans, who had rifles aimed at Rhys's crew still inside.

Rhys lunged forward, but strong hands gripped around his chest to stop him from running across the lobby. "We'll get him back," Riley said. Rhys glanced up. The navigator had hold of him, but the human only had eyes for the cardinal outside. "We almost gave up on him once. We aren't doing that again."

"Again?" Rhys asked. He wriggled free from the navigator's grip, but it was too late to catch up to the cardinal. He had bundled Twitch into the van waiting outside. No sooner had the doors slammed did it start to drive away. The electric motors barely made as sound.

"On Terra," Riley said, dragging Rhys's attention back to the humans around him. "We'll get him, Twitch. We won't leave him."

Rhys's hand shook as he pointed towards the door. "That's Twitch. He took Twitch," he said, his voice as unsteady as his arm. His ears curled down. "Did the cardinal think he took me?"

"He said… he said he did," Riley said uncertainly. He started to salute Rhys, but the starat quickly waved him down.

Rhys was about to ask what had happened, before General Carson came down the stairs with David still in his arms. The human looked around and seemed to understand just what had gone on. "He still has Twitch?" he asked. He gripped David tighter as the starat tried to struggle free, even as he whimpered in pain.

Rhys nodded. He felt numb.

"He had a knife to Twitch's throat," Riley explained. "He thought he had Captain Griffiths though. Kept telling us to stay back or he'd kill our captain. We couldn't risk getting close, and his guards were better armed than us."

"Who can take David to the hospital?" General Carson asked. Riley volunteered himself right away, and he carefully took the bloodied starat from the general's arms. As soon as his hands were free, the general took the pistol from its holster at his hip. "Anyone else who has a weapon handy, follow me. We're going after the bastard."

Three humans were able to volunteer themselves. Chekolin, Briggs, and Dewson were ready to leave right away, and they followed the general as he ran outside. Rhys paused for a moment and looked around the remaining crew. They were scared, he could see that easily. This was a trouble that they should have left behind in the empire, but it had followed them all out here. Followed him. These were the humans and they were scared. He could only imagine the starats were terrified. Without a word, Rhys turned and fled. He needed to be there with General Carson when he caught up with the cardinal. Nothing was going to make him miss that.

General Carson wasn't difficult to catch up to. The humans had paused at the entrance to the small estate. The general had a tablet in his hand as he looked up and down the road. "Do you have a weapon, Captain Griffiths?" he asked as the starat approached.

Rhys shook his head.

"Then you should stay back here."

"Not a chance, sorry General."

The general pursed his lips, but didn't command Rhys to stay back at all, for which the starat was glad. General Carson was his superior, and he didn't want to deliberately disobey a commanding officer.

"I've disabled their van with the EMP. They won't get it running again without some serious work, so they'll probably call for backup," the general explained. He pointed to the right. "Our best bet it to catch them before their backup arrives. This way."

Rhys struggled to keep up with the four humans. They were all much taller than him, with longer strides. His chest burned, and his legs still ached occasionally from the wounds Cardinal Erik had inflicted on him back on Terra. The thought of saving Twitch from such pain gave him the energy he needed to stay close behind the humans.

"Thought he had you, Captain," Briggs said. The *Harvester's* service commander was the closest to Rhys, lagging a few strides behind Chekolin and Dewson, with General Carson leading the way. A couple of Centauran humans sidestepped out of the way as they sprinted past.

"I wish he had," Rhys replied. His voice was strained as he struggled to keep up. He had not been maintaining his usual work in the gym since arriving on Centaura, or indeed since his transformation into his new body. He was regretting that now, as he had lost much of his fitness from his human self.

Briggs grunted a non-verbal response. Rhys was surprised to see his services commander here. He had been surprised when Briggs had remained with the crew instead of remaining on the Star Hub, and this was something else entirely. Before, he had not cared about starats at all, even going so far as to abuse them behind Rhys's back, but now he was actively trying to save one.

Rhys flicked his ears as he stumbled slightly. Plenty of time to think about how his crew had changed after they had Twitch back. For now, nothing else mattered.

They didn't have much further to run. The van had been parked up on the side of the road, causing a small queue of cars behind it. A couple of humans and starats were trying to push the van off the road, but Rhys recognised none of them as the guards who had been with Cardinal Erik.

Beyond the discarded van was a park, filled with the strange native plants. Waxy red leaves appeared to wave in a wind that didn't exist. General Carson ignored the empty van and followed a trail Rhys didn't immediately see. It took him a few moments to notice the footprints in the soft muddy ground inside the park.

General Carson raised his hand to slow the group down. They came to a stop and the general turned to face them. Rhys hunched over and leaned against the nearest tree, finding it to be covered in a sticky resin that immediately gummed to his fur.

"We know they're armed, but we're in public here," the general said. He kept his pistol unholstered. "They can't risk a firefight, especially not with the military. If we show enough firepower, then they'll be forced to surrender."

"Cardinal Erik is monstrous, General. He won't think that logically," Rhys warned. He tried to brush off some of the sap that had stuck to his fur, but it only managed to gum up his fingers on his right hand.

"The cardinal isn't the dangerous one here," General Carson replied. "We need to worry about his guards, as they're the ones with weapons. They'll be trained too, but they're also Centauran. They know it will not be in their favour to open fire, no matter who is ordering them."

Rhys swallowed the immediate retort that came to mind. If General Carson wanted to focus on the guards, then that just meant he would need to deal with Cardinal Erik. It was not a situation Rhys was too upset with. He would have preferred a gun in his hands, but he would have to make do with what he had. His fingers had been declawed, but he had other ways of harming the cardinal.

General Carson led them forward again. This time they walked slowly as he pushed through the trees. More sticky sap dripped down onto Rhys's fur and clothes as he stayed close behind Briggs, letting the large human push most of the foliage aside. The wet mud was cold and slippery beneath his bare feet.

Voices came through the trees. "What do you mean it will take twenty minutes?" Cardinal Erik snarled.

"That's just how far away they are," a weary voice replied.

Cardinal Erik scoffed in disgust but didn't say anything.

Rhys pushed forward to walk alongside General Carson. They weren't far away now, and the human pushed aside some red-tendrilled leaves to reveal the cardinal on the other side of a small clearing in the park. The human was crouched down in front of a starat, while the four guards stood around the pair. Rifles were held ready in their hands.

The humans all had a small gold pin over their breast. From his distance, Rhys struggled to make out exactly what it was, but it looked like a golden cross.

"On my mark, we advance," General Carson said quietly, addressing the whole group. "Stay behind me and let me do the talking."

General Carson waited a few more seconds before signalling to advance with one hand. Rhys let the humans move ahead of him as they all raised their pistols.

"Drop your weapons," General Carson bellowed. "I am General Carson of the – shit!"

The general ducked as two of the guards opened fire. Sticky bark from the tree just behind them exploded as the bullets struck.

"Shit," General Carson said again. He kept crouched down and retreated a few steps. The other two guards raised their rifles. "Fall back and find cover."

"Kill them," Cardinal Erik ordered. He had his hand on Twitch's throat again.

General Carson kept retreating. His pistol remained raised, but he didn't fire a shot. The other humans followed back. Rhys turned to leave, but his foot slipped in the wet mud and he tumbled to the ground. His weak hands didn't save him from the fall, and he rolled a few times before coming to a halt in a small ditch. By the time he was able to lift his head, the guards were almost on top of him. None of them even looked down. Their attention was solely on the humans ahead.

"One of you stay back here," Cardinal Erik shouted, but none of the guards seemed to listen to him. They all advanced after General Carson and Rhys's crewmen.

Rhys barely dared to move until the guards had disappeared amongst the trees. His breath had caught in his throat, and he slowly sat up. He rustled as he moved. He looked down to find that the sticky sap from the trees had caused his body to be covered in leaves when he had fallen. The red ochre detritus had plastered over most of his body.

Slowly, Rhys rose to his feet again. None of the guards shouted or came back to him, and he was still obscured from Erik by the trees. The leaves that covered his fur gave him a little more camouflage. He crept forward until he could see the cardinal again. His heart thudded so loud he was sure the human had to hear him.

The cardinal was crouched over Twitch. The blade was still in his hand, but it wasn't pressed against Twitch's throat anymore. Rhys was about to move forward when he noticed something he had failed to see before. The cardinal was armed. There was a pistol at his hip. Rhys grimaced and cursed beneath his breath. He had no weapon he could use, and he didn't want to wait around in the hope that General Carson was able to subdue the guards. If he were to fail and the guards returned, then Rhys would lose his only opportunity. He had to do something now.

Rhys stared down at his hands. He knew he wouldn't be able to defeat the cardinal in a fight. Even if he had full strength in his arms, he would be at a disadvantage. But he had something else at his disposal. He didn't understand it, and he certainly didn't know how to fully control it, but he had subspace at his fingertips. Snow's most recent warning about it sent a prickle of worry down his tail, but he had no choice.

He retreated a couple of steps, making sure that the cardinal wouldn't see him should he look up. He closed his eyes and held out both arms, his palms facing up in the pose that had become so familiar in Snow's lessons. If the albino starat could see with her ears, then so could he.

Rhys tried to slow down his thoughts and his mind, but he couldn't block out his panic and fear. His breaths still came short and sharp, no matter how hard he tried to pace himself. He gritted his teeth and opened his eyes again. "Dammit," he muttered quietly to himself. He had managed to find subspace once again after his initial discovery, but he had been calm then.

"Come on Rhys, you can do this," he whispered. His ears pinned down as he blindly reached out to touch the nearest tree. Sap coated his fingers, but he wanted something physical close by to anchor him.

Rhys tried again. He slowed his breathing and tried to ignore everything else around him. Instead of trying to find that spicy smell of Snow's voice, Rhys strained his ears to hear the objects in his path. Energy crackled like heat around him, and this time the burst of white subspace came to him. He took a step back as his senses were overwhelmed by the sheer whiteness that encompassed everything around him. A surge of panic threatened to well up inside his chest, but he quickly restored his focus and tried to clear his mind. He couldn't think of anything but for his surroundings.

From out of the whiteness came a series of flashing shapes. They were not the entities that had swirled around the *Shield of Justice*. These were different. They were dark and static, forming columns all around Rhys. He moved his arm against the nearest tree and saw a flash of red burst out against the backdrop of black, before fading away again. He moved his hand away and the lingering red light diminished further, though the shadowy pillar remained. Rhys grinned savagely to himself. He didn't understand what he was doing or how, but he hoped he had enough of a grasp on this mysterious skill to fight Cardinal Erik. That was all that mattered now. As the cardinal came to his mind, two bursts of red light distracted him. They burned beyond the shadows around him, out in the endless expanse of white beyond. One was bright, while the other was dimmed slightly.

Shadows swirled around Rhys as he crept forward again, relying on subspace to safely guide him between the trees. He kept his mind clear, trying not to think about what he was going to do.

A scream tore through Rhys's ears and wrenched him out of subspace again. Twitch's agonised yell pierced through Rhys, and it was all he could do to stop himself launching towards the cardinal right there and then.

"They will not get you," the cardinal snarled. His back was still turned to Rhys, but the starat could see the syringe in his hand. Whatever contents had been inside it had been injected into Twitch's thigh. A second quickly followed, and Twitch threw his head back and clenched his jaw to suppress a second scream.

"It feels different this time, doesn't it?" the cardinal continued. He grinned savagely, and even from this distance, Rhys could see the anger in his eyes. "It was just a quarter dose then. This is the full thing, too strong for any antidote. There is no cure. There is no saving you."

"Or maybe you're full of shit," Twitch growled. There was so much pain in his voice, but he was still able to summon anger and rage.

"You ran all this way," the cardinal said, seeming to completely ignore Twitch. His fingers gently toyed with the blade of his knife. "But no further. You will not run. You can not run. There is nowhere you can go that the Vatican can't reach."

"Fuck you," Twitch spat. "My name is…"

The cardinal struck Twitch to silence him. "You have no name, animal."

"Captain Rhys Griffiths," Twitch said defiantly.

Rhys shivered in worry. How long would this charade last? Even the cardinal had to realise he had the wrong starat eventually. He doubted Twitch would be spared from his wrath. He had to do something before Twitch was hurt again. He dreaded to think how potent the poison in those syringes was, after what they had done to his arms.

The cardinal snapped forward and placed his hand around Twitch's throat. "I see you have descended further into blasphemy. This is a foul place. One that has been left to fester for too long," he snarled.

Twitch pushed back at him and slashed across the cardinal's face with his claws. "Yeah, because they're free from you," Twitch retorted. Rhys was impressed with how well the starat was changing his voice to sound more like himself. Though they shared the same body, Twitch's voice was usually a little lighter in tone, as well as the more clipped, neutral Cerian accent. That was all gone, and Rhys was almost convinced he was listening to a recording of his voice.

"Your claws..." the cardinal said uncertainly. He grabbed hold of Twitch's hands roughly. "There is no power that could have saved your hands."

"Miracles do happen," Twitch said. He was rewarded by another slap across the muzzle.

"I see the fire needs to be quenched again. This time I will not hesitate. Already a ship is prepared to take you directly to Mars. There is no escape this time," the cardinal said. He took a step back from Twitch. "This park will soon be swarming with my men. Your precious, misguided supporters will be captured, and we'll all be going right to Mars."

"We'll see about that," Twitch snarled, though all he had was vocal defiance. He seemed incapable of moving, and the cardinal was being wary of his claws after the first strike.

Rhys scanned the area as the starat and human bickered and traded insults. There wasn't much he could use as a weapon, but his eyes turned to the small bundle of bags just behind the cardinal. There were fallen branches amongst the foliage. They were barely weapons at all, but it was all he had. Rhys looked down at his hands. Snow could manipulate matter with subspace. He had accidentally managed it once, but he hadn't attempted it again. He didn't know how. The albino had warned him against trying. He had no choice but to try. There wasn't much else his hands were useful for.

Rhys extended his arm and closed his eyes as he sunk his mind back down into subspace. It was easier this time to keep his mind clear, and it took only a few seconds before he was plunged into senseless white. Again, he could sense the shadows of the trees around him. The red flare of Cardinal Erik and Twitch burned brightly in front of him. He could still pick up the words of their conversation, though it felt muffled as his focus was away from his realspace senses. He reached out with his extended arm, seeing the orange-red impression in subspace move with it. He tried to force it out further, but he just felt the tendons and muscles in his arm strain without any tangible effect in subspace.

His mind anguished. Dark spots appeared around him as he struggled and strained to do anything that he had seen Snow accomplish with absolute ease. He had done it once, but he didn't know how. Nothing worked.

"Help me!" His mind shrieked out to the void of subspace.

Something answered. It was not a word, or a thought. It didn't use any language, but it communicated nonetheless. It was an emotion. A feeling. Pride. Satisfaction. Usefulness. Help.

Light burst all around him. Colours he had never seen before swirled into existence. He felt hot. He was burning with the energy that suddenly flowed through him. His arm lifted almost out of his own control. It flared red amongst the dazzling array of colours that filled subspace all around him. It extended out further that he should have been able to reach, towards the bundle of bags beyond the cardinal. Then he pulled.

The bags pounded into the cardinal. Rhys's mind snapped back to realspace and severed the connection to the burning heat that had enveloped him. The pile of bags had all been flicked into the air, splitting and spilling their contents across the floor as they landed. The cardinal spun around and stared at the destruction. "Who's there? Show yourself," the human barked. In his hand was his pistol, and for a moment Rhys's confidence almost faded.

Before it could slip away entirely, Rhys reached out into subspace again. Some of the energy remained, but mostly there was just a sense of lingering satisfaction. He wrenched some of the fallen foliage towards the cardinal. His hand burned in pain, but the human was forced to shield his face as branches and sticky leaves were flung in his direction. It gave Rhys time to leap from the shadows and grab hold of the pistol. He couldn't get a good grip on the weapon, and he didn't pull the gun away in time before one of the cardinal's elbows swung back and caught Rhys in the face.

Rhys staggered back, but he refused to let go of the pistol. The cardinal had the advantage of size and strength, but Rhys had pulled the human's arms behind his back. The starat kicked hard into the back of the cardinal's knee. The human staggered, and the pistol slipped from both their hands and fell to the muddy ground between them.

"Captain Rhys!" Twitch crowed in joy.

Cardinal Erik whirled around, his eyes blazing with hatred and recognition. "You dare use the holy gifts against me?" Spit flicked from his lips with every word. "I see I took the wrong beast. You've kept the scars of my attempts to cleanse your sins. Perhaps you know you deserve them. There may be hope for your immortal soul after all, once you are held in safety beneath Olympus Mons."

"You think I'll go with you willingly?" Rhys asked. He kept the pistol in his sights at all times, but nor did he ever lose track of the cardinal's movements.

"You think I'll ask a beast like you for permission?" the cardinal retorted.

The human made a sudden move, and immediately Rhys lunged to the floor. His fingers closed around the gun before Cardinal Erik could reach it, and he quickly rolled to the side. Then he realised his error. The cardinal had not gone for the weapon. Instead he had Twitch, a blade held to the starat's throat once more.

Rhys's hands shook as he tried to raise the pistol up towards the cardinal's head. "Let him go," he growled.

"You would never," the cardinal said.

Rhys couldn't be confident in his aim. His arms screamed out in pain from the weight of the pistol, and his fingers could barely grip the weapon. If he fired, he would just as likely hit Twitch as he would the cardinal.

"Let him go," Rhys repeated. He tried to aim for the cardinal's head, but the pistol shook even more.

"You fucking animal," the cardinal snarled. His blade pressed a little firmer against Twitch's throat. The starat didn't make a sound as a line of red opened up. "Give that to me."

Rhys felt his heart pound in his chest. His fingers tensed around the trigger. He wanted so hard to just squeeze. He had the cardinal right where he wanted him, but he was too worried about his aim and the knife at Twitch's throat. He couldn't risk the starat's safety. The two glared at each other, while Twitch wiggled and squirmed by the cardinal's side, still moving even with the blade pricking at his skin.

A distant voice called Rhys's name. General Carson called out, searching for him.

For just a moment, Rhys's eyes slipped away from the cardinal. While he was distracted, Cardinal Erik acted quickly. He thrust his free hand out, and a prickly static spread up Rhys's arms. The gun burned in his hands, and with a yell he was forced to drop it. It fell to the ground. A moment later Rhys was pushed to the floor as Twitch was thrown at him. He wrapped his arms around the starat as they fell down together. He landed hard in the mud and felt his shoulder jar painfully.

"You deprive me of all the fun," the cardinal growled.

Two gunshots fired, and Rhys felt an explosion of pain in his right arm as Twitch squeaked in shock. He braced himself for something more, but instead he just heard the retreating footsteps as the cardinal fled the scene. Three more gunshots fired from through the trees. They were followed by frantic shouts that echoed into silence.

Rhys rubbed his muzzle with his left hand as he tried to clear some of the sticky leaves from his fur. His right arm was still wrapped around Twitch's body, which lay unmoving on top of him. He could feel the starat breathing, and the frantic beat of their hearts were in sync.

"Are you hurt?" Rhys asked. He held onto the other starat tightly.

"I don't think so. Are you?" Twitch replied. His voice was muffled as he spoke into Rhys's shoulder, making no attempt to move and free his muzzle.

"Injured, but I'll live," Rhys replied, before he looked down to his arm. "Ah shit, Amy's not going to give me a choice this time." His right hand had taken the full force of the cardinal's bullet. Only one had hit, but his hand was a mess of broken flesh and blood as it had opened up one of the scars on his palm. It didn't hurt, but Rhys could barely move anything below his right elbow.

Rhys kept his arm wrapped around Twitch's body, hand resting over the other starat's back. Twitch didn't appear to be bound in any way, but he wasn't moving at all.

Chekolin's voice called through the trees. "Captain Griffiths, are you down here?"

"Over here," Rhys called out in response.

Rhys grunted as he tried to sit up, but Twitch was too heavy a weight on his chest to move. His ears twitched as he heard several pairs of booted feet approaching. Cardinal Erik had fled before Rhys's allies were able to arrive. They wouldn't have long before the cardinal's summoned back-up got here.

"Hey Captain Rhys," Twitch said in a quiet, trembling voice. He spoke directly into Rhys's shoulder still, not lifting his head at all. "Is David alright?"

Rhys's ears flattened. "I don't know. He was hurt badly, but Riley is taking him to get help."

"That's good," Twitch replied weakly. "Captain Rhys, I think there's something stuck in my tail."

Rhys's hand slipped from Twitch's arms to touch against the top of the starat's tail. His fingers immediately touched something wet. Blood. "Oh shit. Twitch?" The other starat trembled. "Chekolin! Hurry!"

"I can't feel my legs," Twitch whimpered. Rhys felt the starat's hands clench tight against his arms. "Captain Rhys, I can't move them at all... help me, please."

Almost immediately the approaching footsteps arrived. Twitch's limp weight was gently removed from Rhys, who quickly got up to his knees as he looked down at the wounded starat. One bullet had found its mark, a few centimetres down his tail. There was so much blood already.

"Stay with us, Twitch."

Rhys looked up to see Doctor Sparks by his side. His hand was pressed down on Twitch's tail, just above the bullet wound. The doctor grimaced and turned aside for a moment. He rummaged through the medical bag by his side and pulled out an absorbent pad, which he stuck down over the wound. "We need to get him to hospital immediately. I can only hope they're able to fix the damage I'm about to do."

With that, Doctor Sparks put his arms beneath Twitch and lifted him up. The starat finally responded, giving a small whimper as he hung limply in the doctor's arms. Rhys jumped to his feet and placed his hand on Twitch's head.

"Captain Rhys," Twitch said in a voice that was barely a whisper. "Tell David I love him."

"You'll be able to tell him yourself..." Rhys said uncertainly. His hand slipped away as Doctor Sparks started to carry him away. He hurried after the doctor, trying to stay by his side. Twitch's eyes slowly closed.

"Twitch!"

chapter fifteen

The hospital was bright and clean. That was all that stuck on Rhys's mind as he paced back and forth around the waiting room. He had not been allowed to go and see Twitch or David, as they had both been admitted into emergency surgery. Instead he was forced to remain with Chekolin and General Carson by the reception while they waited for some news to come through. Briggs had returned to Appletree. He had been wounded in the fight with Cardinal Erik's guards, but nothing severe enough to need a visit to the hospital.

News had reached Rhys that the other starats on his crew were safe. Leandro had been out of the city with the Silver Fox. William, Richard, and Steph had all been together in the city centre, but they had not been caught up in any harm. It was a small relief to Rhys, but his attention had quickly returned to Twitch and David.

Rhys hugged his arm close to his chest. He had been treated again, with fresh bandages wrapped around his hand. The blood had been stemmed easily. His wounds would heal, but his fingers felt even weaker now. No one spoke to him, though a few of the patients waiting to be seen gave him some odd looks as he walked up and down.

He didn't know how long he waited for. He made an effort not to look up towards the clock above the reception area. The more time that passed meant that Twitch and David's injuries were worse and would be more difficult to repair. If he didn't know how many hours had gone by since they had been admitted, he could convince himself that there were really alright. It was all fallacy, but it was all Rhys had before he broke down into tears.

Finally, after a wait of several hours, Doctor Sparks emerged from beyond the wide double doors at the far end of the reception. Rhys immediately stopped pacing and froze still as the doctor approached. Chekolin and General Carson both rose from their seats.

"How are they?" Rhys asked in a strangled whisper. "Can I see them?"

Doctor Sparks raised both hands to forestall any further questions. "They're alive, I can tell you that much right away. Let's get somewhere more private and I can explain what's happened. You won't be allowed to see them now anyway."

Rhys wanted to know everything without having to wait, but he nodded his head. The doctor led him outside, with Chekolin and General Carson right behind. They took a short walk from the hospital. The streets were mostly dark and quiet as a few stars glimmered through the light pollution from the city. The hospital was in the outskirts of the city, close enough that the massive skyscrapers were visible, but far enough away that they didn't loom over the streets and obscure the sky.

Across the road from the hospital was a large park, and it was to there that he doctor led them. The park was filled with native plants, and their waxy red leaves waved softly in the gentle breeze that was gradually cooling the heat from the long day. Small tendrils extended out from the leaves, twisting and writhing around with independent movement. It looked like they sought something out with determination, but what powered the movement or what they were seeking was beyond Rhys. He just kept his distance from them and instead focused on the ochre grass beneath his feet.

A short way into the park was a small picnic area with several tables in close proximity to each other. No one was present, and Doctor Sparks took a seat on the nearest one. Though Chekolin and General Carson sat down as well, Rhys stayed standing. He bounced nervously on his toes.

"David will be fine. He fractured his leg, dislocated his hip, and lost a lot of blood from his cuts, but he will recover without any issues. He'll have a few scars, but that's it. He'll be walking again in a day or two," the doctor said. He paused and rubbed his hand over his eyes. "Twitch is another matter entirely. He'll live, there's no doubt about that. But his tailbone was shattered and there was significant damage to his hips as well. As for his legs... I honestly don't know what that bastard gave him. It's similar to what he gave you, Captain Griffiths, but so much more potent. The antidote I used on you appeared to do nothing. None of the staff here know how to treat it. They're trying to repair the damage, but it's probable that he'll be paralysed."

"Shit," Rhys muttered to himself. He wiped a couple of tears from his eyes. "This was my fault. If I'd have had a better plan... if I'd had better hands..."

"Your fault, Captain?" Chekolin said. "No. You saved his life, just as he saved yours. If you hadn't been there, that monster would probably have killed him. Either right there, or taken him off to Mars to be killed later."

"I know that, but I could have done better," Rhys said. He finally sat down at the table and drummed his fingers against the wood. He stared down at his hand as he did so. Clawless hands. Weak hands. Frail hands. Hands that could not aim the pistol when he had the cardinal right where Rhys wanted him. Twitch had saved him from Cardinal Erik, at the cost of his arms ever working right. Rhys had rescued Twitch from the same human, but the starat had lost the use of his legs. Both times it had been Cardinal Erik who had inflicted the wounds. Rhys clenched his hand into a fist and slammed it against the table with as much force as he could muster, not caring how much damage he did to himself.

Chekolin placed his hand on Rhys's shoulder. His touch was tentative at first, but became stronger when Rhys didn't shrug him away. "He surprised us, Captain. We know he's here now, so he won't slip past us again."

"Next time I kill him," Rhys snarled. He felt like slamming his fist down on the table again, but this time he held himself back. He took a deep breath to compose himself. When he next spoke, his voice was softer, more fragile. "I thought I was safe from him here. I'm as far from the Vatican as I can possibly be, but if they can still reach me then what else can I do? How could he get here?"

General Carson leaned forward. "There are ways people can move between here and the empire. Small civilian ships do slip through imperial defences with refugees for Centaura. Sometimes there is even movement the other way, though mostly through our spies and operatives."

"So you're saying he what, just bought a ticket and flew out here?" Rhys asked bitterly. He glared up at the general.

"Not without help, but essentially, yes," the general replied. He swirled his fingers around the wooden table. "There are plenty of organisations he could get in contact with who would be willing to help a man of the Vatican. He could even have posed as a legitimate refugee and not disclosed his affiliation with the church."

Rhys groaned and rubbed his muzzle in his hands. "What can we do to stop him? If he can find me here, then where can I go to be safe?"

"There is no such thing as safe, with someone like that hunting you." A new voice spoke up, though it was a familiar one. Rhys almost wasn't surprised to hear Snow. He turned to see the albino approaching, stepping confidently through the undergrowth despite her lack of vision.

Rhys growled softly beneath his breath. "Why are you here?" he asked the albino.

For the first time, Rhys saw uncertainty on Snow's face. "I felt something," she said. She sat down on the other side of Chekolin. "I have known the touch of subspace every day for many years now, but what I felt a few hours ago I have never felt before." Her sightless eyes turned to look directly at Rhys. "What did you do?"

Rhys tried to think back to what had happened down in the basement beneath Appletree. He spread his hands and shrugged his shoulders. "I don't know. Or, at least, I can't explain it. I was scared for Twitch, and I just called out for help. Someone, or something, answered me."

"You speak like it is conscious, Captain Griffiths," Chekolin said nervously. "Like subspace has thoughts. It's just a… nothingness."

"That's what I thought too," Rhys said, turning his head to Snow. "But then I saw those things when I was on the *Shield*. You must have seen them too, when we went to Charon. They were like eyes, watching us."

"I wish I could tell you what they were," Snow said softly. She clasped her hands together on the table. "We have never been able to communicate with them, if they even can be communicated with. All we know is that they appear to feel emotions, but that's all."

Rhys frowned. "The cardinal seemed to know something about subspace as well. I think he may have used it, even." His tail curled up in anger.

"We've long known the Vatican have been able to access these powers as well," General Carson said, speaking before Snow could answer. "How or why, we're not sure. Usually it's only starats who can slip into subspace. It's certainly biological. I can't do it, and I…"

"We think it might be why they torture starats so much," Snow said in a quiet voice. "That they're somehow able to draw power from us."

A small silence met her words. Rhys felt nausea building in his stomach. "That's sick. That's absolutely vile," he growled. He looked around the small group and clenched his weak fists. "How could we have let this happen?"

"It was never your fault, Captain Griffiths," Doctor Sparks said. He reached across the table to rest his hands gently on top of Rhys's, though the starat still had to pull back in pain.

"No, it was never my fault. But I still served for an empire who thought that behaviour was justified," Rhys said. He growled softly and looked to Snow, then to General Carson. "But you'll put an end to that, won't you?"

General Carson nodded. His voice was still gentle, but the fire burned behind his eyes again. "We will end it, once and for all. You commit to my plan, and we will see it done. You have my word, Captain Griffiths."

Rhys held his head in his hands. "And what is that plan? All I've ever been told since getting here is 'trust me' and some vague promise of action," he growled. He kept his eyes closed and didn't look up at anyone. He knew he shouldn't speak with such a tone to a superior officer, but he decided that unless they treated him as one of the Stellar Guard, then he didn't have a rank and didn't need to stick to decorum. "I'm sick of being treated like a child who can't be trusted. I want to know what the plan is, how we're doing it, and how it will help starats back on Terra."

General Carson didn't reprimand Rhys for his outburst. He just looked across to Snow, who nodded her head gently.

"We have located access to a newly developed weapon on Pluto," the general explained, keeping his voice low in case of any passers-by.

"We as in who?" Rhys asked. "The military? Government? Or just the Freedom Union?"

"The Union," General Carson said. "Using information passed on from the military after your raid on Charon."

Rhys wrinkled his nose and looked up at the general. "So, the military and government know nothing about this weapon?" A cold shiver ran down his tail. He was beginning to get an understanding for the depths of Amy's ambitions. "Will they get access to this weapon once we acquire it?"

"They do not understand the implications of the tech you helped uncover. Nor do they have access to some of the research Twitch did for us. But even if they did, they would do nothing with it," Snow said. She placed her hands on the table. Her sightless eyes gazed right into Rhys's. "You may not be familiar with them, but we are. We know what they will and won't do. If we want to end all this suffering on Terra, then we need to do it ourselves."

Chekolin cleared his throat. "What you are asking is treason," the pilot said. He stared around the small group with wide eyes. "I will do what my captain chooses. I trust his opinion, but this is no small choice. You ask us to act against the military and the government of Centaura. To strike the empire without their permission."

Snow slowly nodded her head as she turned her head to gaze sightlessly in Chekolin's direction. "Treason, yes. Some might consider it that. You have experience of it, of course."

"That was different," Doctor Sparks said. "We did it then because we had a choice, we had somewhere to go. What you're proposing here... it sounds like you're asking us to betray those who gave us refuge from the empire. Who will give us refuge if this fails? This isn't the Centaura that was sold to me."

"You don't have to do this," General Carson said, addressing Rhys once more. He smiled weakly. As Rhys looked up at him, he thought he could see the shadow of the starat he had once been in his eyes. "You can go to Fleet-Admiral Ulrich and let her know the situation. You can try and get the Stellar Guard or the government to act, but they're too tied up in their rules and regulations to strike quickly."

"And what is this weapon?" Rhys asked. His fingers dragged across the table, sending spikes of pain through his hands. If he'd still had his claws, they would have dug in to the wood.

"We don't fully understand it," General Carson said, but he was interrupted by Snow.

"It uses subspace in ways I'd only ever theorised before. It was only recently I realised it has legitimate potential. The empire seems to have realised this too. It's incredibly powerful, and incredibly dangerous in the wrong hands," she explained. She snapped her fingers and a small stick materialised on her palm. She spun it around her hand. "Our mission is to protect ourselves, as much as it is to strike them. We cannot give them the opportunity to turn this weapon on Centaura."

"What happens if they do?" Rhys asked. The shiver had returned to his spine, but this time it was at the thought of what the empire might wish to do to this planet.

Snow shrugged her shoulders. "I don't yet know the full extent of what they can do. All we know is that the Inquisition here have been making plans for what they're calling the end times. There's something being planned, but at this stage we don't know enough to say exactly what."

Rhys frowned and thought things over for a few moments. His eyes flicked to Chekolin and Doctor Sparks, but neither of them said anything. "I'll compromise with you," he said after giving himself a chance to think over everything. "We go to Pluto and we steal this tech. We bring it back to Centaura, but Amy does nothing with it without government and military approval. Does that sound fair?"

"I can agree to that," General Carson said quickly.

Snow was slower to speak. A small frown touched her brow. "I think we can accept that," she said. She tossed the small branch to the side. "It would mean you have to ignore Cardinal Erik though. There is not time for you to go after him before we must leave."

"So long as someone goes after him, I'll be happy," Rhys replied. A snarl came to his lips as he thought about the cardinal. He had never felt such a strong hatred for anyone as he did for Cardinal Erik. There was nothing he wanted more than to see the cardinal suffer for what he had inflicted on him. If he got the opportunity to tear down the institution that had allowed such a monster to exist, then that would be enough for him.

"Save the fury for what you can control," General Carson said. The general shook his head and looked up to the sky for a moment, before he looked down again and took hold of Rhys's hand in his own. "Revenge is not for us. We must think bigger than that. Cardinal Erik is a snake. Our target is the medusa's neck."

"I assure you, Cardinal Erik will come to justice," Snow said.

Rhys snarled and held out his hands. "Then give me a knife. Make me a weapon if you must. I'll cut off the head myself."

chapter sixteen

"Can't I at least visit him to say goodbye?"

Rhys knew the answer would be no, but he still had to ask. As he had expected, Snow shook her head. "We can't risk the delay. We need to get you back to Cambria to get you fully briefed with General Carson." They were sat together in Rhys's room in Appletree. It would have been the starat's last night at their provided accommodation, but it seemed now that Rhys wouldn't have the chance to enjoy his new home for a few days.

"But we still have another week, right?" Rhys asked. He had been counting down the days to his departure from Caledonia before journeying back out to Pluto, hoping through all that time that Twitch would wake up. The starat was still in his induced coma since the attack from Cardinal Erik six days earlier.

Again, Snow shook her head. "There have been new developments from Pluto that means we have to push our plans forward," the albino said. She flicked her ears and sighed, reaching one hand to rest on Rhys's knee. "I'm sorry, but it means that your arms won't be ready in time either. The surgery will take too long, and we had expected a few days for you to practice with them first. We have decided not to take the risk of sending you out there without any experience using them."

Rhys pinned his ears down. He stared at his hands. Another few days still hadn't done anything to his recovery. They were as weak as ever, especially after the fresh wounds he had received in the cardinal's attack. "You're sending me into a warzone and I can barely even hold a pistol?"

Snow raised her brow. "Would you rather be left behind?"

"No, absolutely not," Rhys hissed in horror. The last thing he wanted was to be left behind, and even the knowledge that he would have to suffer through his weakness wouldn't deter him.

"Then we need to get you on the next shuttle to Cambria. Everyone else is ready to go, so we're just waiting on you now. We leave in half an hour," Snow said. She rose to her feet and looked down at Rhys with her sightless eyes. "I know you want to see Twitch, but we just don't have the time. We will make sure we get regular updates on his condition when we leave."

Rhys sighed and nodded his head. He didn't have any choice in the matter. He couldn't remain behind, but nor would he be able to change Snow's mind. "Will all of my crew be coming with us?"

"Almost everyone, though most of your starats will be remaining behind," Snow replied. "We're filling your ship to capacity with anyone who can fight, as we only want to take the one ship. Of your starats, we feel only William will be able to play a role there."

"Can I at least say goodbye to the others first?" Rhys asked wryly.

Snow smirked and flicked her ears. "I'll send your starats down, so long as you keep it quick."

"Thank you. I'll meet you downstairs in half an hour," Rhys replied, nodding his head in Snow's direction. He still wasn't sure if she could actually see his small gestures, or whether she could only see the eerie silhouettes like he had seen. Though he had asked her many times how her vision worked, he had only ever been met with silence and a smirk.

After Snow left, Rhys slowly went about gathering all his things together. Almost everything was packed as he had been planning on moving to his new home the next day, but there were still a few things to gather, and his uniform to pull out from the cupboard. He quickly flattened out any of the creases, before he changed into it. It only took him a few minutes, and by the time he heard a knock on the door, everything was packed but for his tablet. He still held that in his hand as he went to open the door. Steph and Richard were both waiting for him, and Steph wrapped him in a gentle embrace as she came in.

"You'll be safe, won't you?" Steph asked as she released Rhys.

"I can try to be," Rhys replied with a smile. He placed his tablet down on the armrest of the sofa as Steph sat down on it. Richard settled down beside her, leaving Rhys with one of the dining chairs to sit on. "What will you be doing while I'm away?"

Steph shrugged her shoulders. "Not sure exactly what. Amy suggested we might end up interning for some government officials, but nothing is finalised yet. Someone called Minister Bakir, apparently."

"Amy's got her fingers in everything, but she's always wanting more," Richard added. He twitched his muzzle as he gently stroked his fingers through the thick fur on his tail. "She thinks there's a rot in the government here, and so she wants us to keep an eye on things in case it looks like it develops into something like on Terra."

"Well then perhaps I should be telling you both to be careful," Rhys said. He wasn't sure he liked the idea. It sounded too much like Amy was trying to control things on Centaura as well as on Terra. A chill ran down his spine, but there was not much he could do. He could only hope that the two starats wouldn't be put in any dangerous situation. It wasn't like they were going into a warzone like he was.

Steph glanced down to the tablet Rhys had placed down by her side. "Hey Captain Rhys, you've got a message to read," she said, pointing down to the little flashing green light above the screen.

Rhys's ears pinned down. He knew exactly what that was. For over two weeks he had been ignoring that message, and sometimes he had even managed to forget about its presence entirely. It had come from Amy, giving him information about the death of someone he had been able to long ago forget. Or so he had thought. His breath caught in his throat just thinking about it, but before he was able to protest or even say anything, Steph was holding the tablet out to him.

Rhys took hold of the tablet. His hands shook from the weight, but also the knowledge that he knew he needed to open the message. Some part of him deep down knew that he had to know what had really happened, but he was also terrifying of learning the truth.

"Is everything alright, Captain Rhys?" Richard asked. Rhys knew his fear had to be obvious.

Rhys swallowed. His throat felt dry and constricted. "A long time ago, I was engaged to be married," he said. His voice sounded so quiet to his ears. The words didn't sound like they belonged to him, like he was merely listening to someone else speak. "She was called Stephanie too. But she died in a shuttle accident. It took me a long time, but I moved on. I had barely even thought about her for years, until Amy mentioned her a couple of weeks ago. Said that she had information about Stephanie that I had never seen." He tapped his fingers on the tablet. "That's what this message is."

"And you haven't opened it?" Steph whispered. She held her hand out for the tablet. "I can put it away again, if you like."

Rhys shook his head and kept the tablet away from Steph. "No. I should have opened it before now, but I was scared. Scared to know what it would tell me. Then everything happened with Twitch, and I just forgot about it for a few days. I should probably open it."

Rhys's fingers didn't respond to his intentions. He stared down at the black screen of his tablet, with only his reflection visible on its surface. He took a deep breath and closed his eyes for a moment to build up his composure. Then he clicked on the notification and opened it. He felt his heart seize as he saw a few images pop up on the screen. He recognised most of them. They were news clippings of the shuttle crash that had claimed Stephanie's life. No new information was amongst them. A navigation error had occurred and had sent the shuttle slamming into the side of a mountain. Then he swiped his finger to move it to the next page.

He stared at a short military transcript of the same incident.

Suspected starat heretic terminated on Shuttle 005412a SH-DEL flight. Forty lives lost in collateral. Crash blamed on navigation computer error. Vatican notified of heretic death.

Rhys read the small paragraph several times before he looked up. There were several more pages of information to look over, but right now he didn't think he could read on. He didn't need to He could barely see through his tears. "They killed her," he whispered. He blinked a few times, but couldn't clear his eyes of all the tears. "They killed forty people because they thought one starat... one person was a heretic."

A hand touched on his shoulder, but he couldn't tell whether it was Richard or Steph. He had never known how low the empire had been willing to sink until his eyes had been opened to it. He wondered how much he had been complicit in, simply following orders and never realising the true meaning of his actions. How many innocent lives had he ended? Had Stephanie and the other forty people on that shuttle known what was happening in their final moments, or had they too believed what was to become the cover up story? Had they even known they were about to crash into a mountain?

"I never knew," Rhys said, his voice trembling. A second hand pressed against his cheek as he bared his teeth in anger. "For fifteen years I thought it was an accident. I grieved for her, but I never knew there was someone at fault. Someone I could blame. I swear if I find who did this, I will kill them."

"This would not be the only time." A new voice spoke. Rhys looked up through blurred eyes to see Leandro standing beside Richard. The grey-furred starat looked like he had been crying recently too.

Rhys held his hands against his muzzle. "I know," he said. If it had happened once, he was sure it had to have happened multiple times. He flicked his ears and looked down. Did Aaron know much about it? He knew he would have to ask his friend when he got a chance. Too many innocent people were dying, and Rhys was glad Amy and Snow were giving him the chance to help correct that. He could do nothing to bring back the lives that had been lost, but he hoped he would be able to save lives in the future. The empire was corrupt, he could see that now. But there were enough good people there that he could hope a good future for everyone in the empire could be won.

"Are you going to be alright, Captain Rhys?" Steph asked. She rested her hand on Rhys's knee.

Rhys nodded. He took a couple of deep breaths to clear his mind again, before turning off his tablet. He would go through the rest of the information on his way to Pluto, when he would have more time. "I'll be fine. Thank you for being here with me."

"Just promise us you'll be safe out there," Steph said. She pulled Rhys into another hug, resting her head against his chest. Rhys gently stroked his hands down her back.

"And look after Emile for me," Leandro added.

Rhys pushed out of Steph's embrace. His ears flattened down to his head and his tail drooped as low as Leandro's. "He's coming with me? Why? He should be here with you."

"He said it was his last chance to make a difference," Leandro said dully. There was little of the joy in his voice, and his eyes kept staring down to the floor. "He is right. His experience will make a big difference to you, but I'm scared…"

Rhys pulled Leandro into an embrace. It hurt his arms, but he knew the older starat needed it. Leandro's arms slowly rested against Rhys's back. "I promise you, I will bring him back safe."

Leandro tried to wriggle away from Rhys. "Do not make a promise you can't keep. If his story must end, then it must end. I just…"

Rhys allowed Leandro to pull back slightly, but he held the grey-furred starat's muzzle in his hands. He looked Leandro right in the eyes. "I promise you, Leandro. You look after everyone here, especially Twitch and David. You stay safe, and we'll see you again in little over a week."

Richard smiled. "We'll look after each other, Captain Rhys. Good luck."

***

Rhys tried not to think about Stephanie on the journey to Cambria. He wanted to talk to William about her, as he was the only other starat from his crew left, but he didn't want to talk about her in the presence of Snow. The wounds of her death felt like they had been opened up anew, after so many years of being closed and scarred over. He wondered if there had ever been a time he could have gotten justice for her death while he had still been in the empire. Or would he have been killed to prevent the truth from getting out? The thought sent a shiver down his tail.

At least Rhys knew that now he was being given a chance to help redeem himself. He still didn't know what Amy's final objective was, but he knew that she was planning to make life better for starats everywhere. If she was targeting bringing down the government of Terra and the Vatican, then Rhys knew that he would be fully behind that cause.

The Silver Fox passed most of the time telling one of his stories to William and Snow, though the albino didn't seem to be listening. Rhys's mind was too distracted to pay much attention to the human's story. From what little Rhys heard, the Silver Fox was telling William the story of one of his first raids with Leandro by his side. The old human spoke much like the grey-furred starat did. A small smile did reach Rhys's lips. He wondered who told stories first; Leandro or Emile. They both had a love for the craft, though the Silver Fox's telling was often punctuated by fits of coughing that left a little blood on his hand.

"Are you sure you're up for this?" Rhys asked the old human, after his story had been interrupted once again.

The Silver Fox swallowed distastefully and patted at his lips with a tissue. "My place is up there with you, Captain Griffiths."

"Your place is here with Leandro. You deserve that," Rhys replied. The human somehow looked older than when he had been first rescued from Charon, only a few weeks earlier.

"Deserve? The moment you start thinking like the universe owes you anything is the moment when you give up on fighting," the Silver Fox said. He held his hand to his sternum and suppressed another cough. "I have fought against the empire for my whole life. I am, and always will be, a pirate. I may be old now, but I know more about getting around imperial defences than anyone else alive. You need me, Captain Griffiths."

"I just don't want you getting hurt. It would break Leandro's heart," Rhys said quietly. He bowed his head, but the Silver Fox reached out to lift his chin again.

"Every second we have had together has been a miracle neither of us could have dreamed of. We both know this is borrowed time, and we have taken full advantage of that. If it must end here, then we are grateful for what we did have," the Silver Fox said. There was sadness in his eyes, but he was still smiling. "Though if it makes you feel better, I don't plan on leaving the shuttles. I can coordinate enough from there."

Rhys sighed and nodded. "That does make me feel a bit better. I still don't want to risk you. Leandro would kill me if anything happened to you."

The Silver Fox laughed, which descended into another short coughing fit. He quickly recovered and wiped his mouth again. "He knows the risks as much as me," the human wheezed. He closed his eyes and leaned his head back against the rest behind him.

"He'll be as safe as any of us," William said. The starat leaned forward and placed his hand on Rhys's knee. "But we all want to fight for this, Captain Rhys. Don't try to take that away from us."

Rhys nodded. "You're right, but that doesn't stop me from being worried about you. Being in combat, it's… the first time is always the hardest. Don't be ashamed if you're scared. Don't try to be brave when you're not, because that's when you make stupid mistakes."

"I'm not –"

Rhys held up his hand to interrupt William. "If you're not scared, then you're stupid. I'm scared, and I've trained for this sort of thing my whole life. War is always scary. Please don't try to convince yourself otherwise."

William bowed his head and clasped his hands together. He didn't try to speak out or argue, for which Rhys was glad. He knew William would have no idea what it was really like to be fighting for his life. The starat had always been in danger of being harmed in the empire, but this was different. This was a whole new set of skills that William would have to quickly learn. Even with training, new soldiers often froze in their first combat. Rhys knew he would have to keep an eye on William to make sure he came to no harm out there.

Rhys glanced back out the window of the car. They had arrived at the barracks. Rhys recognised a few of the humans who had come out to greet them. The towering General Carson loomed over Aaron, with the starat Nick standing between them. Four other humans stood in front of the statue commemorating the starats in the rebellion war with Terra, though Rhys didn't recognise any of them.

Rhys saluted General Carson after he stepped out of the car, standing right in a puddle as he did so. A small snicker emerged from the crowd as he wrinkled his nose in disgust, and Rhys could easily recognise that it was Nick who had laughed. He quickly stepped out of the puddle, trying to shake his feet dry as he approached the gathered group. His companions followed behind him, all able to avoid the scattered puddles that lingered from a recent rain shower.

"Sorry we've had to bring things forward, Captain," the general said. He gestured with one hand to the closest door. "We're ready for briefing now, so if you can come with us and we can begin. I'm sure you're all interested to know what we're going to be doing."

The general led the large group inside the building and through to a briefing room. The white walls were mostly bare, with a projector screen on one wall. A small gold ornament of two crossed swords hung on the side wall. Only the general remained standing, while everyone else filtered down into the seats. A few humans and starats had already been present. Rhys recognised some from his crew, but there were others who Rhys had never met before.

Rhys sat down by Aaron's side, despite the little growl that came from Nick, on his friend's other side. William took the other seat next to Rhys. The other starat nervously adjusted his prosthetic leg as he settled down. The Silver Fox leaned forward in his set, on the other side to William.

General Carson waited for everyone to take a seat before he started to speak. "You are all here because you have been chosen as the most suitable for this mission. Some of you are from the *Harvester's* original crew, but you have been supplemented by others who have ground combat training and experience," he said, looking around the room. His eyes lingered on Rhys for a moment, before passing on. "Some of you have access to information or knowledge that we can utilise, but every one of you has been chosen for a reason."

The general paused again. He smiled, his mouth barely visible through his thick beard. He clapped his hands together once. "Now, this is not a usual mission. We will be acting alone without the strength of the Stellar Guard. We will be without back-up. That being said, I have worked hard to ensure that there are as few dangers as possible, which is why we've had to move things forward."

"And why is that, General?" Rhys asked.

"The empire is moving defences around," the general replied, turning to look down at Rhys again. "Thanks to your raid, they have decided that more ships are needed to defend Pluto. They already have one in orbit, but they are planning for a three-ship garrison, which will be installed in just over a week, which is why we need to act now."

"And just what is it we're doing?"

The general smiled again. He tapped his fingers against his thigh as he paced around the front of the room. "I have told you individually who I am, and who I was. You also know who I look like, and where he happens to be. I'm sure most of you will have figured out where this is going."

"You're going to pose as Captain Herschel?" Nick asked.

General Carson pointed one thick finger towards the starat. "He's got it. But that's not the only purpose we will have there. The mission will be to capture Captain Herschel and bring him back to Centaura, with me remaining in place there to act as his decoy," the general explained. He looked around the room again. "It has also come to our attention that the empire has been developing some new technology in secret on Pluto, and we need to oversee it to ensure that it does not fall into the wrong hands."

"Who do you mean my 'we', sir?" one of the humans asked.

General Carson turned to the human. "We, as in Jennings and the Starat Freedom Union, Lieutenant Davids," he said, his hands resting behind his back.

"So this isn't organised by the government?" Davids asked. The human had risen from his seat, his hands still resting on the table in front of him.

General Carson rested one hand on his hip. "The Starat Freedom Union isn't controlled by President Shawn, or any affiliate of the government, no. You all know this. Amy Jennings works how she sees fit, and nothing she does is endorsed by the president or his party," he said. His ears twitched as his beard was pulled up by another hidden smile. "You were all told this the first time you met Amy, and you were reminded of this before being assigned to this crew."

Rhys shifted in his seat as Lieutenant Davids lowered himself back down and dropped the matter. He wasn't sure if the unpleasant sensation in his stomach was borne from the historic worry of doing anything against the government or the Vatican, or whether he had deeper misgivings for doing something without the authority of his new governing body, who had welcomed him to a new home. He had never met the president, and had heard little about him. Rhys had not pledged himself to President Shawn and his cause, but he still couldn't help but feel some degree of loyalty towards him now. He chose not to bring up any of his concerns. The Union was offering an immediate course of action, where the military and government were not. This was necessary.

The general waited in silence for a few moments again, as though waiting for someone else to bring up a dissenting point about working beyond the authority of the government. No one else spoke, so he continued again. "We will be striking hard and fast. We will disable or destroy the ship in orbit, and quickly move to raid the port. We expect a fierce defence, but that is why you were chosen. You are the ones we believe will crack their defences and overwhelm them."

Rhys raised his hand again to attract the general's attention. "Do we know yet which ship is already in place at Pluto, and which are planned to reinforce the garrison?"

"Not yet. We haven't been able to learn the name of the ship already in place, I don't think it's yet been decided exactly which ships will reinforce," General Carson replied with a small shake of his head. "We have our spies searching for information, but nothing has come through yet."

Rhys twitched his muzzle. He could only hope it wasn't someone he knew that had been chosen to garrison on Pluto. He knew he would never be recognised, but he didn't want to risk the moral dilemma of opening fire on those who had once been friends and allies. He wasn't yet sure if he was capable of it, though he knew it couldn't be long before that was put to the test.

"And what of you, sir?" Aaron asked. "What is it you plan on doing after we leave you behind?"

General Carson grinned and twitched his ears. "Directing their research to benefit us and attempt to sabotage their attempts to learn more that could harm us. What they have there could be incredibly useful, or incredibly dangerous. I need to make sure we can use it and they can't."

"And just what do they have?" the Silver Fox asked. The former pirate's brow was furrowed as he looked up to the general.

"The end to war." The general gazed around the room, his fierce eyes blazing. In that moment it was hard for Rhys to accept that he had ever once been a starat. He clapped his hands together again.

"We know what we have been tasked. I truly believe that if we do this right, there will be peace and prosperity for us all within months. That is what's at stake here, and you are the lucky chosen to finish this war."

Rhys leaned forward in his seat. He glanced to his sides and shook his head slightly. "And why us, may I ask?" He swept his hand to gesture the room. "Those who came to Centaura with me aren't even permitted to serve for the Stellar Guard yet. It doesn't make much sense to send us."

General Carson hesitated for a moment. "The fleet-admiral refused to authorise any other ship for the mission. Yours was the only one that could be spared, and I wanted a crew that was familiar with the ship."

Rhys tapped his fingers against the table and winced as the jolt sent a twinge of pain through his fingertips. He understood why a familiar crew would be important, but he didn't understand why no other ships would be available. His ears folded down as he frowned. There was some information that he wasn't getting, but he didn't know what to ask in order to learn it.

"Are there any other questions?" the general asked, clapping his hands together and looking around the room once more. Everyone remained silent. "No? Well I recommend getting some sleep while you can. You will be shown to some temporary quarters for tonight. Rest well. We will be departing in twelve hours. Information on where and when you need to be has already been sent out to your quarters. Good luck everyone."

Chairs scraped as everyone rose to their feet. The general was the first to depart the room. He didn't turn back to speak to anyone, and by the time Rhys made it outside he couldn't see the tall human at all. A few starats were waiting outside for them, and they led the group through the barracks until they reached the quarters.

There were no captain's privileges for Rhys, or for Aaron. They were both in the communal quarters with everyone else. Rows of bunk beds lined the large room, with communal toilets and a shared kitchen at opposite ends. It had been a long time since Rhys had bunked with his crew, not since before his promotion to first officer many years previously. He shared a quick glance and smirk with Aaron, who would likely have been in the same situation.

Rhys knew it wasn't a slight against him. He was not strictly a captain for this mission, as he had not been enrolled in the Stellar Guard. He couldn't expect to maintain his former rank and privileges just yet.

After the rush of bunk claiming died down, Rhys found himself sharing a bunk with William, tucked away in one corner of the room near the kitchen. The other starat took the top bunk, for which Rhys was grateful. He wasn't sure he would be able to haul himself up to the top with his weakened arms. Just as the general had indicated, there was a small envelope on every pillow, giving directions on where to go once they were rested, as well as a time. There were only ten hours before they had to be prepared to leave the barracks.

Rhys sat back on his hard mattress and stared down at his hands. His back leaned against the wall behind him and closed his eyes, only opening them again when he felt someone sit down beside him.

"Any improvement in them?" Aaron asked.

Beyond Aaron was Nick, who silently snarled at Rhys before clambering up to the top bunk opposite. Rhys tried to ignore the other starat. He turned to his friend and shook his head. "Nothing," he sighed. "I can barely even hold a pistol, let alone aim one. I'm hoping they have power gloves for me like last time, or else I'll be useless."

Aaron placed a hand on Rhys's shoulder. "You've still got a good mind. You can think on your feet, and I know you'll be useful to us," he said.

Rhys wrinkled his muzzle. "If I had such a good mind, I'd have seen what was really happening in the empire. The way they treat starats, how the Vatican holds everyone back," he said with a growl. He glanced up at Aaron, still caught off guard how much taller his friend was compared to him. "They murdered Stephanie. I only learned that a few hours ago."

Aaron froze completely. His fingers gripped tightly against Rhys's shoulder, and for a few seconds he didn't move at all. His mouth hung open as he slowly turned to look at Rhys. "Stephanie? Your fiancé? You haven't even mentioned her in years," he whispered quietly. His hands both dropped down to his lap. "Why did they do it?"

"Because one starat on that shuttle could do this," Rhys said. He reached out into subspace and tried to access the power he had used against the cardinal, trying to pull a pen across from Aaron's bed. Nothing moved. He grimaced. "Pretend I actually did something there. You've seen what Snow can do, right? One starat could do something they didn't understand. One starat could use subspace, and they killed forty humans for it. They didn't even say how many starats died."

"Shit."

Aaron didn't need to say anything else. It summed up Rhys's thoughts perfectly. He rested his head back against the wall again. "Did you ever suspect we were being lied to?"

"In the empire? No. Occasionally I thought something seemed a little odd, but even knowing what I did about starats, I never really questioned them too much," Aaron admitted. His hand returned to rest against Rhys, this time on his knee. "I would have thought we'd have heard more about it though. We were captains there. If the rot is as pervasive as we've been told, some of it had to come down to us, right?"

Rhys shrugged his shoulders. "I don't know. I never questioned it either. I received my orders and I followed them. Maybe that's why Admiral Garter thought I'd be a good replacement for him. I wouldn't question anything that seemed suspicious."

"You figured it out though, same as me," Aaron said.

Rhys spread his hands. "It took this to happen first. Were it not for that teleporter, I'd probably still be there," he said. He sighed again and picked the pen back up, making sure he had a proper grip on it this time. "I'd still be fighting ships that were from... I don't even know where. They're not from here."

"They're not, are they?" Aaron replied. The two dropped into an uncomfortable silence. It had been a thought that had occasionally crossed Rhys's mind. There had been no talk about the war anywhere on Centaura. It constantly dominated the media on Terra and through the empire. There was always talk of the latest Centauran raid and how they had been pushed back by the emperor's military and the divine will of the Vatican. None of that happened on Centaura. The war simply didn't exist. But if Centaura wasn't sending ships to fight in Terran space, then who was? Rhys didn't know if he wanted that answer.

Aaron patted his hand on Rhys's knee, before he rose up to his feet. "We should get some rest while we can. Anything you need from me before I go? Any jam jars that need opening?"

"Low blow, Aaron. Low blow," Rhys replied with a laugh. He threw a pillow at his friend, but it just bounced harmlessly off his chest. "No, there's nothing. Thanks for coming over though."

"Always a pleasure. I'll be your first officer again, so it will be nice having you around," Aaron said, firing off a quick salute to Rhys. He turned away and returned to his bed, where he had a quick, quiet conversation with Nick.

Rhys turned his head to the side, not wanting to catch the words exchanged between the two. He was still conflicted about Nick. He wanted to try and mend the damage he had caused, but he knew the other starat was not willing to even let him try. He owed nothing to Nick, but the starat was an important part of Aaron's life. He owed it to his friend to at least try.

Putting such thoughts to the back of his mind for now, Rhys started to prepare himself for rest. The lights would be shut off before long, giving them the opportunity to sleep for the last time before boarding the *Harvester*. Nerves were starting to make themselves known in Rhys's stomach. He closed his eyes and laid his head back on his pillow as he tried to ignore them, but they wouldn't go away. Not only was he worried about going into combat against his former allies, but the condition of his arms terrified him. He would barely be able to defend himself should the need arise. It wasn't the most comforting thought to circulate through his head as he tried to sleep.

Even after the lights switched out and the communal quarters were plunged into darkness, Rhys still couldn't sleep. The sounds of people moving all around kept him awake, and the fears of what could happen kept rotating through his thoughts. He stared up at the bottom of William's bunk and tried to keep quiet as tears wetted his cheeks.

chapter seventeen

Twitch knew he was dreaming, but he couldn't escape his nightmares. No matter how hard he tried, he couldn't wake. His subconscious had taken him from Ceres to open space and back. He always found himself returning there, resisting any attempts to escape it. All the starats were dead. They had all been killed, and Twitch was the last one left. He walked through the familiar port alone, with only faceless humans towering above him for company. When they didn't ignore him they taunted him. He was going to die, and there was nothing he could do to prevent his fate.

At some point the dream shifted. The corridors he walked down were no longer on Ceres, though sometimes they looked like they could be. Other times they reminded him of the *Harvester*, but most of the time they were just blank and featureless. But he was not alone. Someone stalked him.

The ever changing face of the human who chased him was sometimes Cardinal Erik. At other times, it was Captain Jacques Favre from Ceres. Sometimes it was even Captain Rhys, as the human Twitch only vaguely remembered. He was never sure what would happen if the shape-changing human ever caught him, but nor did he want to wait and find out. He kept on running, but more and more he felt like he wasn't moving anywhere. Even in his nightmares, he couldn't walk.

Panic set in as he felt the human right behind him. A distant scream echoed in his ears. He tried to thrash away, but his legs were dead and stiff beneath him. It was only the human's arm around his chest that kept him upright. Pain blossomed from the base of his tail and quickly spread through his whole body. This time he knew it was him screaming.

His eyes snapped open in a panic. He panted rapidly as his heart threatened to burst from his chest it was beating so fast. He quickly took in details from around the room. White walls and ceiling so bare that he was convinced it was still a part of his dream; a small window behind thin, almost transparent curtains; and an achingly familiar starat sitting in the corner, asleep on a chair.

"David," Twitch called out. He tried to reach out for his partner, but his arm was stopped by an IV drip connected to his wrist.

He didn't need to worry. The moment Twitch spoke, David's eyes flickered open. In an instant, he was by Twitch's side. "You're awake, I was so worried... How do you feel?"

"I thought I was dying... I don't think I like this afterlife. Too many needles in me. But you're here though," Twitch responded. His mind was struggling to catch up with everything. Flashes of his dreams mixed in with his memories, and he wasn't yet sure which was real and which had been imagined.

"You nearly did die," David replied. He sat on the edge of the bed and placed his hand on Twitch's, careful not to dislodge any of the needles. "But you're made of stronger stuff than anyone thought."

Twitch frowned. He stared down at his hand as he tensed his fingers. "So... I didn't?"

David laughed weakly. "No, not quite."

There was something David wasn't telling him. Twitch could already tell that. David's ears kept flicking up and down, like he was trying to hide the sadness he felt inside. Already, Twitch thought he knew what the matter was. He'd known even in the midst of his nightmares, but now he was awake the reality felt a little more manageable. Twitch rested his hand on the side of David's muzzle and pulled him down for a gentle kiss. "It's my legs, isn't it?"

David bowed his head, pressing his forehead against Twitch's. "There was too much damage there to fix."

Twitch gave David another gentle kiss before he looked down at his legs. They were still there. He could see their outline in the sheets, but he couldn't feel anything below his hips. It wasn't even a numb sensation, like he had been lying on his arm for too long. Both his legs and his tail were simply a void of feeling. He blinked as an urgent thought came to his mind. "What about my bits?"

With his brow raised, David cupped his hand over Twitch's crotch, and he leaned back and sighed. "Oh thank goodness," Twitch said in relief. "I can still feel that at least. That's not too bad then."

David chuckled and shook his head. "Glad to see you're still the same," he said. He carefully lay down and rested his head on Twitch's belly.

Twitch slowly stroked around David's ear, bringing out a small purr from his partner. "It'll take more than that to change me, don't worry," he said. He twitched his muzzle a little and lay back against his pillow. A smile spread across his face. "Am I going to be like William and get some cool new shiny legs?"

"I'm not sure. Amy came to visit you a couple of days ago, but she didn't say anything about it," David replied. His voice was taken over by the purr that rumbled through his throat.

"At least I won't be sold or killed for it," Twitch said. The smile lingered on his mouth, but his ears folded up. Even knowing they were safe from that on Centaura, the worry still plagued the back of Twitch's mind. It had been a constant fear on Ceres, and a lifetime of that didn't disappear so quickly.

David's fingers tensed against Twitch's belly. "No, not here. We're safe from that now."

Twitch sighed softly. "Do you think Captain Rhys will be coming to visit me soon? Usually it's me seeing him in a hospital bed."

David slowly pulled himself up to a sitting position again. He gently squeezed Twitch's hand in his own. "He's already gone back to Sol on that mission he was talking about. He left earlier today, just a few hours ago."

"Huh? I thought that was a couple of weeks away still," Twitch replied. He frowned and flicked his ears. His mind was still sluggish from waking up, but he knew that had been right.

"You've been asleep for a few days, but Captain Rhys sent on a message to say they had to leave early," David said, squeezing his hand a little tighter around Twitch's.

Twitch fell back into his pillow, shocked into stunned silence. His muzzle and ears twitched as his slow mind struggled to get up to pace with that new information. He drew his hand back from David's and tried to sit up a little straighter, having to drag his legs back up the bed. Useless weight now. He had once been forced to walk on a barely healed broken ankle in order to prove himself useful to his owners. This though, was so much worse. Even knowing he wasn't about to be sold off and killed for his injuries, he could always feel his thoughts teetering on the edge of a dark precipice.

Something of that must have shown on his face, as David leaned in to kiss him gently on the cheek. "Are you alright?"

Twitch wrenched the smile back onto his face. "Fine. Just trying to wake up a bit. Think I might need a coffee."

"Oh no, I'm not letting you have coffee. Not after last time," David warned, giving Twitch a gentle tap on the nose. He slid off the bed and stood by Twitch's side. "But I can go find a doctor to let them know you're awake. They might have something to help you perk up a bit. But no coffee."

"Spoilsport," Twitch replied, sticking his tongue out.

David replied in like, sticking his tongue out as he made his way across the small room. Twitch grinned at him for every step, but as soon as the door closed and he was alone, the smile vanished from his face in an instant. His ears folded inwards and his glum eyes were already starting to flow with tears.

Twitch's hand trembled as he pulled his bedsheets to the side. His legs looked perfectly normal as they stretched out down the bed, though held at a slightly awkward angle. He ran his hand through the fur, but it was like touching someone else. He could feel the living warmth and the gentle thump of blood flow, but that was all. There was no sensation from his legs at all; nothing beneath the hips. Even his tail was little more than useless meat and bone.

"Put me back to sleep please, I don't want this," he whispered. His voice was haggard and cold. He had no joy left to feel.

***

By the time David returned, Twitch's mask had been restored. He was bright and cheerful to the doctors who checked him over. They apologised that they had been unable to restore his legs. The cardinal had used a poison that was unknown to them, and it had attacked the nerves and muscles in his legs. They had prevented it from moving further through his body, but there had been no way to restore the damage. The broken bones in his tail had severed nerves there too. While that could be fixed, it would require further surgery to be scheduled.

The doctors gave Twitch some time to think through his options, which included the potential for prosthetic legs. They presented him with information on the possible options they could take, and the cost for them all. There was nothing more they could do for him until he made his choice, so they gave him permission to be discharged once they were sure he was stable enough to leave the hospital. He was sent home in a wheelchair that had been provided for him. It was hard for Twitch to maintain the smile as David wheeled him out the front of the hospital.

He was taken to an unfamiliar part of the city and eventually into a house Twitch had never seen before. It was tucked away in the corner of a secluded street, just far enough away from the centre of the city that the towering skyscrapers were just shadows on the horizon. The house was small, set on a single level. Inside was cosy, but not cramped. Carried in David's arms, he was given the brief tour of the kitchen, living room, and two little bedrooms. They were all fully furnished, and David soon lowered Twitch down onto the large double bed in the bigger of the two bedrooms.

The smile came to Twitch's muzzle with difficulty. "This is ours?" he asked.

David hugged Twitch gently. "All ours, yes. I would have loved to pick it out with you, but Captain Rhys helped choose it with me. When he gets back, he'll be just next door. We thought it would be a nice surprise for you," he replied.

Twitch's ears dropped slightly, and he smiled weakly. "That will be great," he said. He pulled himself up to sit upright, his back resting against the headboard of the bed. He looked out of the bedroom window, which overlooked a park. The red leaves of the trees still looked strange to his eyes, but he was used to grey and lifeless on Ceres. "It's a nice view here."

David stroked down Twitch's arm. "I thought you'd like it. It will be good here. Our friends are all close by, and it's a nice area. I've had a few walks around here, and it's pretty."

"I wish I could go with you," Twitch replied sombrely. He slowly turned his head to look towards his partner. His shoulders slumped and his lip quivered as he struggled to hold back tears. "I wish I could do so many things, but I can't now, can I?"

David pulled Twitch down into his arms. He cradled the starat close, hands brushing through Twitch's fur beneath his shirt. "You can still do as much as you set your mind to. This won't hold you back, I know it," David said, squeezing his partner close.

Despite the words of encouragement, Twitch couldn't hold back the tears. He started to sob in David's arms, unable to even conjure up any words in response. All that came from his mouth were cries of pain and sadness, a flood of emotion that had been held back for so long. The dam had been breached, and it felt like years of pain and humiliation were being unleashed at once. The memory of every cruel human returned to the surface of his mind, of any injury that had been inflicted on him by a cruel master.

David didn't say anything. There was nothing to be said. All he could do was hold Twitch close and gently stroke his hands through his fur. There was no comfort to be had for years of abuse, there could only be solidarity and support from someone who understood the terrible things from personal experience. David had gone through much of the same abuse.

"This was meant to be my escape," Twitch said between ragged breaths and choked sobs. He knew he was making a wet mess of David's chest, but neither starat cared too much about that. Twitch knew that he couldn't stop the tears, not now they had started. He would cry until he couldn't cry anymore, and then he would rebuild the mask he lived behind.

"I know," David replied, his voice hushed as he pressed his muzzle against the top of Twitch's head. "This isn't how I imagined it, either."

Twitch whimpered softly as he pressed his head into David's thick chest. His partner felt warm against him, as he always did. It felt comforting to just rest his head against the familiar, muscular chest. "I just wish..." Twitch said, before he descended into more sniffles. He didn't even know what he wished.

Everything that had happened since he had inadvertently given Captain Rhys his new body had been a frantic and chaotic experience, but Twitch knew that it had improved his life massively.

Right up until Cardinal Erik had gotten hold of him. There had been the brief thrill of impersonating Captain Rhys to confuse the human, but that had quickly faded into an explosion of pain. Pain was something he was familiar with. He had been kicked and punched countless times, and beaten many more times on top of that. But he had endured it with a smile on his face, even though he felt like screaming out his frustrations to the world. The smile had finally been broken, and Twitch didn't know what to do with himself.

David was the only company Twitch wanted, but they were only two starats. By themselves, they were powerless to help Twitch in the ways he needed. Even in a city like Caledonia, Twitch and David alone wouldn't be able to do what Twitch knew had to be done.

"How long will Captain Rhys be away for?" Twitch asked quietly. His sobs had almost quietened completely, though his cheeks and muzzle were sodden from tears.

"I don't know. A couple of weeks, I think. Same as last time," David replied.

Twitch whimpered softly. "I need him back here. He can help fix me. People listen to him."

"We'll get something sorted for you, don't worry," David encouraged. He squeezed his arms tight around his partner, and Twitch just leaned into David's chest. "Why don't you have a look through and see what options the hospital has given you?"

Twitch nodded sadly. David moved away to pick up his tablet, which had been left charging in the kitchen. He noticed his partner still moved with a little limp. His ears pinned down. He hadn't even asked David how badly he had been hurt. How badly he was still hurting. Tears threatened to come to his eyes again, but he wiped them away before David came back.

"Thank you," he muttered thickly as David passed him the tablet. His nose and throat felt blocked, and he coughed to try and clear it. Really, he just felt like crying again.

Instead, Twitch stared down at the tablet. He turned it on and flicked through all the pages that had downloaded. He saw all the pages, but he didn't read anything. Nothing stuck in his mind but the terror and fear of what was to come.

Twitch tried moving his tail, but all he got was a stab of pain in his spine. He tried moving his legs, but he didn't even get the gratification of any pain. There was just nothing there. They were dead weight. Flesh without function. Without purpose.

Just like him.

"I don't know if I can live like this." Twitch choked back another sob as the tablet fell from his hands.

David didn't say anything. There was nothing to be said. All he could was wrap his arms around Twitch and squeeze tight. Twitch returned the gesture, burying his head once more into David's shoulders as the tears began to flow anew. There were still so many left to cry, and Twitch didn't think he could stop until they were all done. It should have been the happiest day of his life. He owned his own house with David. It was something he could never have even dreamed of happening on Terra, but all he could think about was how he may never walk again.

The tears lasted long into the night, but not once did David leave his side.

***

By the time Twitch woke up the following morning, his eyes were dry. There was still a wet patch on the bed where his face had been resting, but no more tears were flowing. Though he quickly realised he was alone in the bed, he could hear the sounds of David in the next room. It sounded like he was cooking something in the kitchen, so Twitch stayed quiet and just looked out the window. He could see into the park, where there were a few kits playing beneath the floodlights that provided light in the dark days.

David soon returned, carrying with him a couple of plates of food. Twitch's nose immediately recognised one of his favourite breakfast: eggs and bacon. It had been a rare treat on Ceres to get anything more than just military gruel, but occasionally the starats had been able to get their hands on a 'missing' shipment of meat or fish. Those had been rare treats, and Twitch had enjoyed them all. Eating fish or bacon on a regular basis had not lost any of the thrill for him, and he found his smile was easy to maintain as he devoured every scrap on offer, even taking one of David's uneaten eggs.

They had just finished eating when someone knocked at their front door. The two starats exchanged a quick glance. Most of their friends had gone with Captain Rhys, and there were few humans or starats on the planet they knew well enough to consider friends. They certainly hadn't been expecting anyone.

David placed a hand on Twitch's knee as he got up from the bed. "I'll go see who that is."

"I'll wait here," Twitch said, giving a small giggle. His mask was back in place, and he would never let anyone but David know it had fallen. Or that he even wore a mask to begin with. He had worked so hard to keep it hidden from anyone else. He hoisted himself to sit upright against the headboard and made sure the fur around his eyes felt smooth. He licked a little sauce off his fingers, then grinned up at Amy as she came into the room by herself. She was dressed in her usual t-shirt and running shorts. A small sheen of sweat was visible on her fur.

"Good to see you awake again, Twitch. We were all worried about you," she said. David came into the room behind her, carrying a chair from the table in the dining area. He placed it down at the foot of the bed, and Amy sat down on it. She crossed her legs as she looked over at Twitch. "I am sorry to hear the extent of your injuries though, and that you missed Captain Griffiths before he left. I'm sure he would have liked you there with him."

Twitch shrugged his shoulders. "Would have been nice to go with Captain Rhys, but I'm not a fighter like he is. I wouldn't have been much good over there," he replied. He flashed a nervous smile and leaned into David's side as his partner sat down on the bed next to him. "And especially not now."

Amy leaned forward in her seat. "Well as luck would have it, there is something you can do here."

Twitch blinked and tilted his head to the right. He patted his hand down on his leg, hating the lack of sensation he got from the touch. "Even like this?"

A smile came to the corner of Amy's mouth. "If you agree to do this, we can fix you."

David's fingers tensed around Twitch's shoulder. "How?" he demanded. "I saw how much damage had been done to him. How hard they tried to repair it. If they couldn't fix his legs at the hospital, how could you do it?"

"I'm not talking about fixing what he has. We can give him something new," Amy replied. She clasped her hands together as she spoke, and the tip of her tail quivering.

Twitch's ears perked up, even as he felt David's fingers digging in deeper to his shoulder. "So I'd be like a robot?" he asked, a small squeak coming into his voice. The thought of being able to walk again shone like a sunbeam in his mind. A sunbeam from Sol, bright and clear. None of the weak, watery light from Prox.

"Not quite. We'd just be replacing your legs and tail. But you will be able to walk again," Amy said. She smiled warmly as she leaned back in her chair, her ears both perked up.

"And what is it he'd need to do," David asked, a small growl underneath his voice that slowly rose into a snarl. "And why would it be any better than what the hospital can offer him?"

Amy raised on finger. "It's better because we can do it faster and cheaper. Free, in fact, if you do this thing for me. It's something I think you'd both be interested in doing," she said, then paused for a moment. She rose to her feet and walked to the window. She looked out over the park. "The man who did this to you got away. No one was able to apprehend him, and in fact the law enforcement was quite reluctant to chase him. I fear he may have contacts that are loyal to the Vatican, even out here."

Twitch felt himself go cold, and for just a moment he glared down at the bed with a snarl on his lips. He quickly hid it, thankful Amy had been facing out the window. He reconstructed his face into one of shocked curiosity. "He got away? He's still out there?"

Amy turned back to face the bed. "He did, but we think we know where he is. There has been a couple of attacks on starats in Hadrian on the southern continent. We have no evidence to assume Cardinal Erik is behind it, but there is no known motive behind the attacks, so I'm considering it likely."

"And what are you expecting us to do about it?" David asked. His hand still gripped tight around Twitch's shoulder. "We just said, we're not fighters. We're not spies, or anything like that. We're just two starats who want to live our lives without any of your games."

"I don't want anything officially connected with my business getting involved in this. Even the Starat Freedom Union can't get involved. It's too risky, given the union is not meant to operate in subterfuge on Centaura, but I need this investigated," Amy explained. She slowly approached the bed and placed her hands on the headboard, close to David's.

"You want us to hunt him down?" David asked. The other starat nodded, and David snarled again. "That's absurd."

Amy held her hands up. "There's more to it than that. Information is coming out of Hadrian that worries me. Talk of a machine being built. It fits the description of a Denitchev Drive, but unlike any other," she said quickly. Her eyes turned to Twitch. "I need you to see this machine and confirm my suspicions. I may need you to sabotage it."

"It has to be me?" Twitch asked in a small voice. He looked up to David. His partner's nose and ears flicked in anger.

"It has to be you. You know these machines better than anyone else I know. I trust you will know how to break them as well as building them," Amy said quietly. She lowered her head. "I wish I could send anyone else, but it needs to be you."

"I don't –"

Twitch cut David off with a hand on his partner's wrist. "Can we talk about this privately?" Twitch asked Amy. A small shiver had run down his back at the thought of hunting down the cardinal. The thought of the Denitchev Drive confused Twitch, but it was the prospect of being able to get revenge on the cardinal that really attracted his attention. He perked up his ears and smiled brightly towards Amy. He could feel the squeeze of David's fingers get tighter still, claws digging in to his skin.

Amy bowed her head. "Of course. I'll take a walk in the park and come back in a while," she said. She smiled at the two starats again, before making her way outside. David rose to his feet to see her out, but he didn't leave the bedroom.

As soon as the front door closed, David whirled around to face Twitch. "You can't seriously be considering this?" he hissed beneath his breath.

"What choice do I have? I want to walk again, and I want to stop him," Twitch replied. He tugged on the bedsheets and pulled them up against his chest. His heart hammered hard in his chest.

"You have the choice to turn away and ignore him. He's already done too much to you," David pleaded. He knelt down on the edge of the bed and held Twitch's hands in his own. "It's too dangerous. What if next time you aren't so lucky and there's no one there to save you?"

Twitch tensed his jaw. "It's not just me he's hurt. His whole life has been hunting and killing starats, whenever he could. He's still doing it now. If I sit back and let him carry on..." Twitch pulled his hands away from David's, and he turned to look out the window. "I can't let him hurt any more starats. I can end this."

"Or he could kill you," David retorted. He sought out Twitch's hands again. "I know he hurt you, but please. This isn't sensible. And this other thing with the Drive? She's got this massive empire of informants, and you're the best one for the job? I don't buy it. Something else is going on here. It's too big for us. We can't risk it."

Twitch's ears folded down. "But I will be able to walk. That's worth the risk." He gripped hard on David's hand, bringing it up to his muzzle to gently kiss.

"The hospital can offer you that already," David said weakly.

"But how long will that take?" Twitch whimpered. He didn't let go of David's hand. "Weeks? Months? Amy is offering this now."

"And what is her price?"

Twitch tensed his hands, before he released David. His hands slumped down to his lap. "I would do almost anything to get my legs back right now. But. If you really didn't want me to do it, I won't."

David sighed and pressed his forehead against Twitch's. "Being able to walk means that much to you?"

"I don't know how I'd be able to cope if I couldn't," Twitch replied, his voice trembling. He pulled David close. He grinned nervously. "Besides, I'd still have you to look after me."

David pinned his ears back and grimaced. "I don't know if I'd be able to protect you from him or the church. He's a monster, and those around him are little better."

"What?" Twitch said in surprise. His hand brushed down David's chest. He stuck his tongue out. "My big, strong protector? Not able to look after me?"

David gently swatted Twitch over the ear. "Oh don't start with the flattery. It won't get you anywhere," he replied. A red tinge appeared on his cheeks as he tried to avoid Twitch's gaze. He mumbled beneath his breath. "Alright, it might get you somewhere."

"So you'll do this with me?" Twitch asked hopefully.

David's tail thumped against the bed. "I suppose so. But we do it my way, and carefully. I'm not going to risk losing you, not after I thought..." He trailed off into another awkward mumble, not meeting Twitch's eyes.

"You thought you lost me?" Twitch said. His right ear curled down as he squeezed David's hand. "I was worried I'd lost you too, when I was out there with him. That's why he can't be allowed to hurt any more of us. No starat should have to suffer because of him."

David pulled Twitch into a gentle kiss on the lips, then rested his forehead against his partner's. "I won't let him take you again."

"I won't give him the chance," Twitch replied quietly. His hands gently brushed down David's arms. His smile faltered as someone knocked at the door. "I didn't see Amy come back."

"Let me go have a look," David said. He slowly rose up from the bed and approached the door just outside the bedroom. Twitch tried to crane his neck to see who had come, but he couldn't quite see. He could just about see the tip of David's tail still, but nothing more. He heard the door open, and then a familiar voice over the top of David's gasp of surprise.

David stepped back and let the visitor in. Maxwell came into the bedroom, with David following right behind. Minister Bakir's assistant waved awkwardly to Twitch as he stood at the end of the bed. Twitch pulled himself up and leaned against the headboard.

"I'm sorry to hear about your injuries," Maxwell said quietly. The starat's eyes briefly flicked down to Twitch's legs, before he looked up again. He idly played with his wrist, his fingers pressing down on the synthetic flesh. "Minister Bakir sends her regards as well. She wishes you all the best in your recovery."

"Thank you," Twitch said. He felt a little uncomfortable, and his eyes flicked to David. "I'm sorry we didn't contact you again. We were... someone tried to attack us, after we saw Minister Bakir."

Maxwell's ears flicked up and he blinked in surprise. "You were?" he asked. He tensed his synthetic hand, while his other arm rested down by his side. "I'm sorry, I didn't know about that. I just thought you were… scared off by what was offered."

"They said they're watching her. I don't know who they are though," Twitch said. He tried moving his tail again, only to hiss in pain as a sharp twinge shot up his back. David jerked forward, but Twitch waved him off. He pulled himself up to sit more upright. He laughed bitterly. "We thought we'd be safer if we didn't get involved."

Maxwell took a couple of small steps closer. "The minister is still willing to offer you a deal. She can help you."

Twitch's eyes flicked between Maxwell and the window overlooking the park. He could see Amy making her way back again after her short walk. He grimaced. "I don't know. I think I've already accepted someone else's offer for help."

"You have?"

"We have?"

Both David and Maxwell spoke at the same time.

Twitch nodded and took a deep breath. "I can't risk it. I know this will allow me to walk again. I've seen it already with William. I have to do this."

David didn't say anything further. He just nodded. His tail curled up between his legs, but he otherwise managed to keep his worry from his expression.

Maxwell flicked his ear up in curiosity. "Who is helping you?"

Before Twitch had chance to answer, the front door opened again. Amy poked her head around the bedroom door. She smiled as Maxwell turned around to face her. "I thought I heard voices," she said brightly. "I didn't expect to see you here, Maxie. It's been a while. How have you been?"

"Miss Jennings?" Maxwell said. He took a step back in surprise. His tail curled up and tucked in close to his legs. "You're the one helping Twitch?"

"If he chooses to accept my offer, I will be," Amy said. She smiled and looked at Twitch over Maxwell's shoulder. Twitch just nodded once.

Maxwell turned his head to glance back at Twitch. The starat's eyes were wide, and his left hand kept touching against his augmented right wrist. "I... I see then. Well, I'd better not hold you up then," he said. He smiled nervously, but Twitch could see the smile never extended all the way up to his ears. "Got a few errands to run for the minister anyway."

Maxwell bowed awkwardly to Twitch and David, before backing out of the room. He stared at Amy for a moment longer, before bowing to her as well.

"Nice to see you again, Maxie," Amy called out after him as the augmented starat reached the front door. "Maybe we'll get to chat a bit longer next time."

Maxwell didn't say anything in reply. The front door closed behind him. Twitch frowned as he looked up at Amy, but she offered no explanation for the starat's abrupt departure.

Amy sat backwards on a chair, her arms resting on the back. She grinned at David, and her tail swished behind her. "We go well back, Maxie and I. But I take it you have made a decision?"

Twitch looked to David. His partner very slowly nodded. A nervous smile came to Twitch's muzzle as he nodded as well. "We're going to do it. We'll find this Drive and deal with it, and we'll hunt down Cardinal Erik too."

Amy grinned widely. "I'm glad to hear it. Let me get everything prepared, and we can start as soon as possible. Cardinal Erik will regret ever crossing paths with you."

chapter eighteen

The planet of Centaura gleamed beneath the great satellite that orbited over the north pole. Rhys could remember the first time he had been at Network Central, when he had been nervous and confused on his arrival in Alpha Centauri. Even with so long on the surface, he still felt nervous about what he was about to do. He had come up the space elevator that launched up from just outside the city of Hadrian, a short journey away from Cambria. From there, they had travelled on a couple of shuttles that passed between the different stations that made up the Network around Centaura.

Most of the people who had come up with Rhys were those who had been in the briefing with General Carson, though there were a few new faces amongst their number. They had all greeted the general with familiarity, and had looked around the gathered group with interest.

A familiar woman had been waiting for them above Hadrian. Fleet-Admiral Bosler had greeted General Carson and escorted them through the various different shuttles that followed. It wasn't until they reached Network Central that she made her way back to greet Rhys.

"I got word from the surface," the human said, after Rhys had saluted her. "Your friend, Twitch. He woke up yesterday, not long after you left Caledonia. I am sorry to hear about what happened to him."

Rhys's ears perked up, but the news was also met with frustration. He could easily have made his own way up to Network

Central, giving him the opportunity to be there for Twitch when he woke up. He kept his annoyance out of his voice and body language as he nodded his head in the fleet-admiral's direction. "Thank you for letting me know. Can you send a message back down to him?"

"Of course we can," the fleet-admiral replied. "I can have a messenger sent down right away, should you like."

"Just that... I'll be back as soon as I can, and that I miss him already. It won't be the same without him around," Rhys said. His ears curled in slightly, and he stared down at the floor beneath his feet as he walked alongside the fleet-admiral. It sounded silly, admitting such a thing, but the human didn't laugh. She just rested her hand on his shoulder.

"I'll make sure he knows, don't worry." Her grip on his shoulder tightened, and she slowed her pace to drop away from the back of the large group. Her voice dropped down to barely a whisper. "When you get back, I want you to report everything to me and me alone. I don't trust Jennings, and she and General Carson have kept the details of this mission hidden from me and the Stellar Guard. I don't know what they're planning, and it is without my authority. She has influence over President Shawn and Generals Campbell and Carson, but not over me. She's gone above me to get this done, and I don't know if I can trust her."

"And you trust me, ma'am?" Rhys replied, keeping his voice just as quiet.

"No," the fleet-admiral replied bluntly. "But you're honest. Which is more than I can say for some. Keep your nose clean and report back to me when you return so I can see if any damage needs to be undone."

"I understand, Fleet-Admiral," Rhys replied. A flutter of nerves ran through his chest. He wasn't sure if he should tell the human everything he knew about the planned mission, but she had already picked up her pace again to catch back up with everyone else. He kept his silence for now as they approached the ship they would be using for the journey to Pluto. A moment of confusion passed through him. He had thought they would be taking the *Harvester* on the mission, but the ship he saw through the windows was not the ship he recognised.

Another familiar face was waiting for them a little further ahead. Major-General Ulrich was stood outside the airlock that led onto the ship. Her right eye was hidden behind an eyepatch, and her cheek was still scarred. She saluted both General Carson and Fleet-Admiral Bosler as they approached. "Everything is good and ready to go. I've overseen it all myself," she said brightly.

"Most appreciated, Major-General," General Carson said. The human put his hands on his hips and looked back over the heads of those who would be joining him on the mission. "Some of you will know this ship, but not quite as she looks now. Captain Griffiths, I hope you won't mind. We took the liberty of retrofitting your ship and giving her a little makeover."

"We also changed the name," Major-General Ulrich added. She wrinkled her muzzle. "I already expressed my displeasure at the name, so I was quite eager to change it. She's registered as the *Freedom* now. I hope you agree the new name is much more fitting."

Rhys stared out the windows again. Now he knew what to look for, he did recognise his old ship. It looked less angular than before, like the edges had been smoothed out. It was no longer grey either, but instead a pearly white. A spaceship never looked beautiful, but the *Freedom* didn't look ugly. It shone in the red light from Prox.

"It looks wonderful," Rhys said. He turned back from the window. The ship may have a new name and a new identify, but it was still his ship. "Thank you for your efforts."

"I'm glad you like her. But for now, please say farewell to Centaura," General Carson said as he started to open the airlock hatch. "We'll be back in a couple of weeks. Come on through. We'll want to launch within the hour."

In small groups, everyone started to filter through the airlock, with the general and fleet-admiral going through first. Rhys remained right at the back, and before he could go through in the last group, Major-General Ulrich put her arm out to stop him going through. She waved on the rest of the group and closed the airlock behind them.

"I know you're working for the union," the major-general said, keeping her voice low despite there being no one around to overhear them. "I don't think they're the only one with influence in this mission."

"What do you mean? Who else could there be?" Rhys asked in surprise. He thought Amy and Snow had been the only ones behind the planning, with help from Major Carson. He believed them to be fully behind the Starat Freedom Union. Two of them had founded the union.

The major-general wrinkled her nose and looked down at the red-hued planet below. "There is an organisation called the Inquisition, a subsidiary of the Vatican. I believe they were the ones who assisted the cardinal who attacked us."

Rhys pinned his ears down flat against his head. "What reason would they have for getting involved here?"

Major-General Ulrich shook her head. "I don't know. To sabotage the mission, perhaps. Or to twist the result into something that benefits them. I can't be sure, but I thought you of all people ought to know. We've both felt their wrath, and I trust you know what to look out for if their treachery is true."

Rhys took a deep breath and nodded. The last thing he wanted was news of the Vatican again, especially reaching so far out to Alpha Centauri. "I'll keep my eye out. Cardinal Erik isn't amongst these people, at least."

"I'll have people trying to hunt them down here too," Major-General Ulrich replied. She smiled at Rhys. "Good luck out there, Captain. I look forward to seeing you on your return."

"Thank you, Major-General," Rhys said. He saluted the starat. At her gesture, he made his way through the airlock. As the doors closed, he looked back to see her turn away. Her shoulders were slumped and her tail drooped between her legs. Rhys felt like mimicking the expression, but he forced his shoulders and tail to remain up as the airlock opened at the other end, welcoming him onto the ship that would be his entire world for the next few days.

The familiar clean, crisp scent of artificially processed air hit his nose. For just a few moments, Rhys was able to forget about the worries that had just been placed on his shoulders. The *Freedom* had that rare new-ship smell to it. The air filters were all new, and the narrow corridors gleamed with fresh paint.

"What was that about?" Aaron asked, coming up to Rhys's side as he stepped onto the ship.

Rhys shrugged his shoulders. "Nothing much. Just letting me know how Twitch is doing," he said. He didn't know who he could trust with the information the major-general had given him. While he was certain Aaron couldn't be part of the Inquisition, he was less certain about the interested ears around them. He doubted he would have much chance to talk about it with anyone before they reached Pluto. It promised to be a troubling flight.

***

As General Carson had requested, the *Freedom* was ready to depart within the hour. Rhys barely recognised it. Everywhere looked clean and fresh, but nowhere looked so different as the bridge to the ship. It reminded him of the bridge on the fleet-admiral's ship. A narrow stairwell led up to a platform that overlooked the rest of the bridge.

General Carson met Rhys on the balcony. Though this was Rhys's ship, the general was the one in command of the overall mission. Rhys would oversee the organisation of his crew, but he would still need to follow the general's commands should anything deviate from the expected plan.

Below them, Rhys's crew worked together to get the ship prepared to leave. Everything was all in the same places as it had always been, but the equipment had been upgraded to superior models. In the middle of the bridge, where Rhys would usually be situated, was a new terminal that hadn't been on the old version of the ship. It didn't take him long to work out what it was for, as Snow and a couple of other starats converged around the terminal. It would be from there that they would protect the ship against the subspace entities.

Aaron was down on the bridge organising everything directly. He would be the first officer once again, but it wouldn't be long before he would be up with Rhys and General Carson on the balcony level. Once all the equipment was calibrated correctly, they would be ready to launch and there would be little need for direct supervision.

Everything went smoothly, and it wasn't long before Aaron ascended the stairs to the balcony to let Rhys know that the ship was prepared to depart. Rhys glanced aside to General Carter, who nodded his head in permission to continue. Rhys approached the balcony rails and addressed the operations crew, most of which was familiar to him.

"We're almost ready to depart," he called out. He had the attention of everyone below. His tail perked up. He liked this position, raised up above his crew. It allowed him to see everything at once, and it felt like his voice carried better. "Mr Riley, start preparing for the jump to subspace. Mr Chekolin get us to a safe point just outside Sirius. From there, we'll vent heat and reposition for an approach to Pluto. The *Harvester* – I mean, the *Freedom* will fight for Centaura again. You all know what to do. Launch when authorised by Network Central."

The viewscreens at the front of the bridge showed an image of Centaura below them. Directly beneath them was lit up in the weak light from Prox. The land looked rusty red and barren from so high up, with little evidence of the cities scattered across the planet.

"It almost feels like we're leaving home," Aaron said, looking over Rhys's shoulder. The human smiled as he looked down on Centaura.

Rhys offered up a non-committal grunt in reply. He wasn't yet sure if he wanted to call Centaura his home. It was certainly where he lived, but his heart still desired Terra. He knew he would never fit in there, not without a serious change in attitude in the empire. But he knew that if he was given the chance to return there and be welcomed back without prejudice, he would take that chance.

The ship's engines began to fire. Slowly at first, the *Freedom* began to disengage from Network Central. The planet in the viewscreens moved slowly out of view, until all that was left was the inky darkness of space with stars splashed across the void.

"Twenty-five minutes until jump point," Riley called out. He began to work with Chekolin to ensure that their speed was correct, and they were heading on the right course. They didn't want to get this journey wrong, and accidentally end up too close to Sirius. It was already risky enough how close they planned to jump to the binary system, but they didn't want to approach Pluto from the direction of Centaura. That would be where the empire would be looking, and especially now they were on a greater stage of alert after the Charon raid.

Rhys took a deep breath and gently rubbed his calloused hands. His clawless fingertips still felt tender to the touch, and he still had none of the strength he needed. Below him was all the usual activity from the bridge, but as he watched it, Rhys felt curiously detached from it all. It wasn't the unfamiliar position above it all that bothered him, but something deeper than that. There was tension and worry in his stomach that he rarely felt before a new mission. He didn't know if he was doing the right thing.

"Did you want me to take first command?" Aaron asked. The human placed his hand on Rhys's shoulder. He looked down at the starat with concern in his eyes.

Rhys exhaled slowly and nodded. "I think that would be for the best, thank you," he replied. He needed to sort out his thoughts. He patted Aaron on elbow as he walked past his friend. "I'll relieve you in a couple of hours. Give me a call if you need me."

Rhys saluted the general as he left the bridge. He hurried away before anyone else could call out to him. He made the familiar walk up to his quarters. That part at least hadn't changed with the work that had gone on around the ship. The corridors were shinier and cleaner, but they still followed the same route. His quarters had not changed either. They were identical to how they had always been. Even his wine cabinet had been untouched.

He threw himself down onto his bed and closed his eyes. While he had been stationed on Ceres, this little room had been most of his world. He had been dedicated to the ship and to the empire it protected. Now that very same ship was about to travel back to the empire to wage war with it. Though he had already been back to Charon once, this time it felt different. This time they knew there would be a fight. There would be an enemy ship there to disable or destroy. This time there would be no turning back. Rhys would truly be committed to Centaura, and more specifically, to the Starat Freedom Union.

Rhys wished he could be sure he was making the right decision.

***

Rhys was glad for a little time to be left alone. He was no closer to sorting his thoughts out, but it was nice to be alone in a familiar environment. Even the lighter gravity was nice again, as it didn't feel like he was being constantly pressed into the floor by the heavy Centauran gravity.

The warnings from Fleet-Admiral Bosler and Major-General Ulrich were both still fresh in his mind. He couldn't understand how the Inquisition could have any influence in this mission, like the major-general suspected. Everyone was either a part of his crew, or they had been hand-picked by General Carson. He doubted the religious group would be able to infiltrate his ship, but Rhys knew he would still have to be alert for any potential treachery. He also knew to keep a close watch on Snow, for the albino starat would be the one to give away any potential plans Amy had been keeping from him.

Without any answers to his questions, Rhys rose up to his feet just after the ship jumped into subspace. He had heard the small change in pitch from the engines, so he didn't need any external cameras to let him know they had passed out of realspace. Though they would be pushing through the white void faster than imperial ships risked, Rhys knew there would be no issues with the mysterious entities. There were three trained psykers on board.

Rhys was undisturbed as he slowly made his way back through his ship. He didn't return to the bridge. He knew Aaron would have everything covered there. If he was needed, his friend would be able to contact him quickly.

Instead, Rhys made his way down to the mess hall. There weren't many people down there, but he was glad to see William and the Silver Fox sitting together in the far corner. William had detached his prosthetic leg and had rested it on the table, while the Silver Fox prodded at some of the exposed cabling with a small screwdriver.

"So, you'll let the Silver Fox play with it, but not Twitch," Rhys joked as he approached the two.

William grinned bashfully and pinned his ears back. "I won't get any lasers or explosives added with Emile," he said nervously. He shuffled his chair across to give Rhys enough space to sit down by his side. He tilted his head to gesture up to the stairs. "Shouldn't you be up there at the moment?"

This time it was Rhys who pinned his ears back. "Captain Lee is overseeing the bridge. I just needed some time to think things through. Had to work some things out."

"And have you?" the Silver Fox asked. He didn't look up from what he was doing.

"I'm getting there," Rhys replied. He swished his tail as he looked around the mostly-deserted mess hall. "But what I really worked out was that I could do with something to eat. How about you two?"

William wrinkled his muzzle. "I tried a few minutes ago. Said I had to wait until dinner in a few hours."

Rhys smirked as he rose to his feet again. He padded across to the kitchen hatch and leaned inside. He could hear the two cooks moving around deeper in the kitchen, just out of sight. "Could I have three meals of anything you have prepared?" he called out.

He heard someone swear, before they seemed to realise who was speaking. "Right you are, Captain," came the reluctant follow-up response.

Just a minute later, the ship's cook provided a tray with three meals on it. The meals were just ship's rations and little better than frozen instant meals that had been heated up. There was little opportunity for fresh meals mid-flight. Rhys thanked the cook and took the tray, wincing as the weight settled down on his weakened arms. He almost dropped the tray twice, but he was able to get it back over to the table before his strength gave out.

William squeaked in surprise at the arrival of the food. His nose twitched as he gratefully took one of the meals. "How did you manage to do that?"

"Captain's privilege," Rhys replied with a smirk. He rubbed his wrists gingerly as he took his seat again. He peeled back the film wrapping his meal on the second attempt, but he was distracted from eating by movement coming from the stairs. He looked up again to see two starats emerging. Snow accompanied Nick into the mess hall.

Nick's tail was held out rigidly behind him. His ears were pressed firmly down to the back of his head, and his eyes were wide and almost as sightless as Snow's. His black-furred hands trembled as he took a seat next to Rhys.

"You've seen them before, haven't you?" Nick asked, his voice completely devoid of any of the usual hostility. Instead there was terror in his words. His eyes moved up to look at Snow for a moment, before his attention snapped back to Rhys. "The shapes in subspace?"

Rhys nodded slowly. A shiver ran down his tail. Nick had been one of the starats on the bridge with Snow. She let Rhys know she planned to teach both of them more about subspace manipulation on the journey to Pluto. "I have, but I don't know what they are." He looked over Nick's shoulder to look at Snow, who stood impassively behind the distressed starat. "No one knows what they are."

"Have you heard them?" Nick asked. He looked like he struggled to swallow a couple of times. His hands pulled at his ears, dragging them down even further.

"Heard them? No. I haven't even tried," Rhys replied. His eyes flicked up to Snow again. She had never mentioned anything about hearing the entities before. The only time he had seen them had been that first jump after arriving in Alpha Centauri. Back then he had known nothing about subspace and the abilities that could be derived from it, and certainly hadn't known he could hear them. "What happened?"

Nick shuddered. His hands clenched tight against the metallic band around his head. He took a couple of deep breaths, but his claws quickly tugged down on his ears again. "They're screaming. Anger. Hatred. Pain. It's all there in their voices," he said. He looked at Rhys through his fingers. His eyes appeared dull. "They screamed at me and I can't get their voices out of my head."

"Did they say anything?" Rhys asked. His tail curled up beneath the table, the tip resting across his lap.

Nick shook his head and choked on a sob. "Nothing. There were no words. There was just anger."

"What does it all mean?" Rhys asked. He looked up to Snow, but she didn't answer.

Nick was still sat stiffly as he looked up to Rhys. He locked eyes with the starat briefly, before he looked down to the table again. "They don't like us. They really don't like us."

"But what are they? And why don't they like us?" William asked. It was a question no one was able to answer.

"Would you like to hear them?" Snow asked, speaking at last. If she knew more about the entities, then she wasn't answering the question.

Rhys laughed. "Are you kidding? Of course I don't. I never want to hear that."

"Then I can shield you from their calls," Snow said calmly. She held her hands behind her back. "But I still have much to teach you before we reach Pluto. If you want to be prepared to use subspace there, you will need to work hard. Hurry, finish your food, and I can see what I can teach you before you relieve Captain Lee."

Rhys stared down at his untouched meal. With the thought of what was to come, he suddenly didn't feel too hungry at all. He pushed the meal across the table to Nick. "Here, you have it. I'd better get this over with."

Nick blinked a couple of times and looked up to Rhys. His tail slowly started to straighten out again. "Thank you, Captain," he said uncertainly. He pulled the meal closer to him as Rhys slipped past him. The black-furred starat grabbed hold of Rhys's wrist before he could leave. The panic was still in his eyes. "Be careful. They're angry. I don't know what they could do to us."

With that thought lingering in his mind, Rhys followed after Snow as she left the mess hall. At least he wasn't thinking about the dilemma of fighting for Centaura. Instead, he had much worse terrors to contend with. Every time he blinked, he had the eyes of the entities seared into his vision.

They were watching him.

chapter nineteen

Twitch didn't know if he had made the right decision. For a couple of days he had been forced to remain in his bed, only getting out to be pushed around in his wheelchair by David. The furthest they had travelled had been to the small park Twitch could see from his bed. Those had only been short excursions to give the starat the chance to get out into the open air. Even during the day, Prox didn't provide enough light to completely dim all the stars. Twitch was particularly fond of finding the other two stars in the Alpha Centauri system, which were often visible close to Prox.

Twitch liked to lie down on the grass and just stare up at the sky, watching the occasional star and the clouds pass by. Occasionally the electromagnetic shields burst into life as they protected the planet from the dangers of Prox. The starat liked to imagine the sounds they must surely be making up there. They had to sound like sparks of electricity crackling through the air, or the roar of a ship's engine, but sadly for Twitch none of those sounds reached the ground.

He didn't talk much to David, worried that his partner would try to convince him to back out of his promise to Amy. The larger starat never brought it up though, and Twitch didn't broach the conversation either. He was scared. His legs were numb and still, but they were his. Whenever he was alone, he would run his hands through the fur on his thighs, desperate to feel anything through them. Anything that would give him the excuse to back out and claim that his legs were beginning to recover, but they never did. They remained as lifeless as ever, and as the hours slowly ticked by,

Twitch knew that he would have few opportunities left before he would lose his natural legs forever.

They would be replaced, he knew that. But he doubted that it would feel the same. They would be cold and mechanical, not at all like the organic legs he had taken for granted.

If he wanted to walk again, Twitch knew that he had no other option. He had to go through with this so he could walk, and so he could go after Cardinal Erik and the Denitchev Drive the Inquisition had acquired. That didn't mean he was ready to go through with it. They would be leaving soon, and his heart hammered at the thought of it. Twitch felt a wave of terror threaten to overwhelm him.

David touched his hand against Twitch's shoulder, bringing him out of his reverie. "Are you ready?" he asked. His fur was still a little wet around his hands from cleaning up the dishes left over from the previous night. Twitch hadn't been allowed to eat in the morning leading up to his surgery, so they had enjoyed their breakfast before going to bed. It had been bacon and eggs again. Twitch was getting used to those. He hoped they would continue, even after he had recovered. Maybe he would have to cook at for David, if he could work out how to avoid getting eggshell through the scrambled eggs. No one liked crunchy scrambled eggs.

Twitch mentally affixed his mask and beamed from ear to ear. "Of course," he replied brightly, letting no trace of his inner turmoil come through. "I'm going to be Twitch: cyborg hunter! No, wait. That makes it sound like I'll hunt cyborgs. I'll need to work on that."

David ruffled his hand through Twitch's headfur. "Well, let's get you to the hospital then. Don't want to be late for your appointment." David had a smile on his muzzle as well, but Twitch could easily see through his partner's mask. It didn't extend up to the ears, which drooped in worry. David just didn't have as much experience in hiding his true emotions as Twitch.

Twitch tried to ignore David's worry, as he knew that it would bring his own concerns back up to the surface. Instead he let himself get lifted out of bed and into his wheelchair for what he hoped would be the last time. He managed to give David a quick kiss before he was settled into his chair. The kiss was returned with an unexpected passion, and broken off with a small whimper from David.

Twitch knew there were words that were not being spoken. It was an unfamiliar sensation, but neither of them had the courage to say they knew what the other was thinking. Instead, Twitch was only able to mutter a quiet, "I love you."

David quietly repeated the same words as he began to push Twitch outside. Neither commented on the tears in each other's eyes. Neither said another word as they got in the small car waiting outside for them. They remained silent as they travelled to Caledonia.

The hospital was not the same one Twitch had originally been treated in. This one was situated in the heart of the city, but it still didn't take long for the two starats to reach it. Amongst all the towering skyscrapers, the hospital looked quite small, though Twitch was sure it was bigger than the previous hospital. It took Twitch a few moments to realise that the building directly behind the hospital had the name Jennings emblazoned on the side. Amy's office was in there. He was sure it was no coincidence this was the hospital that had been chosen for him.

Once inside, Twitch was quickly shuttled up to a small room that would be his while he recovered from the upcoming operation. It was simple, with little more than a bed and bathroom, with a small TV suspended from the wall in the corner. There was a window though, which overlooked the city streets below. Through the buildings, Twitch could just about see Prox as it was gradually swallowed by the horizon. David was still with him, but they knew that would end soon.

David stood with his hands clasped behind his back as he looked out the window. His tail was tucked between his legs, and his ears pressed down flat against his head. His shoulders shook slightly as though he was crying, but when he eventually turned around, his eyes were dry. "You know you don't have to do this. I'd care for you no matter what. Even if you couldn't walk, I'd always be there for you."

"I know that," Twitch said. He beckoned for David to come closer, and pulled him down into a hug when he got close enough. He nuzzled and licked against David's neck, before kissing him on the lips. "I know you'll always be there for me, and me for you. But as scared as I am, I need to do this. I have to be brave and do what scares me. It's what Captain Rhys would do."

David held Twitch's muzzle in his hands. "Captain Rhys wasn't brave enough to do something like this with his hands."

Twitch flicked his ears and grinned nervously. "Then maybe Captain Rhys can be brave like me when he gets back."

"Just promise me you'll come back," David said. He pulled Twitch into another hug. "Promise me that you'll still be the same starat as you've always been."

"You're not getting rid of me that easy, don't worry," Twitch said. He returned the hug and rested his head on David's shoulder. Neither of them pulled back out of the embrace. They didn't want to. Twitch closed his eyes and just enjoyed the touch of David's body against his. Here he was comfortable and safe, and he didn't need to worry about anything at all.

The moment couldn't last though. The door to the small room opened, and the two starats parted from their embrace. A human had come into the room, and she looked between the starats before her eyes settled on Twitch.

"You must be Twitch?" she asked. She closed the door behind her and stood forward to stand by the side of the bed. "I'm Doctor Reynolds, and I'll be the one overseeing your procedure today. I just wanted to give you a quick visit before we start prepping everything, and to make sure you're fully aware of what we'll be doing. May I?"

Doctor Reynolds held her hands just above Twitch's hip. The starat nodded.

The human placed her gloved hands on Twitch, though he had to look down to see that she was touching him. "We'll be removing the legs and tail in their entirety," the doctor explained. Twitch had to suppress a shudder down his back, and David let out a small squeak. The human either ignored or didn't notice the reactions. "The hips will be left intact, as they will provide the anchor points for your new leg prosthetics. We will also be reinforcing the base of your spine to provide a stronger anchor for your prosthetic tail. This will allow for a full range of movement and sensory input, as well as data gathering and information storage, assuming you have compatible attachments. Does that all sound like what you expected?"

Twitch nodded. He struggled to keep the smile on his face. "What kind of legs will I be getting?"

"You won't be getting your legs installed right away," the doctor explained. She glanced down at the small tablet in her hands. "Ms Amy Jennings has already requested to see you as soon as you have recovered from the surgery. She will be providing the new limbs then. They are a private specification. Not the usual ones we would provide to patients undergoing your surgery. I'm afraid I can't tell you specific details, but according to the information I have here, they will be a variation on the standard model. Fine tuned features and senses, all of the fancy frills you get from private sponsors."

Twitch forced himself to keep breathing steadily. He wanted to curl his tail up, but it remained stubbornly between his legs, which also remained perfectly still. "I don't care about all the fancy features. I just want to walk, and I want them as soon as possible."

"You're lucky to have such a starat looking after you," the doctor said. She tucked away her tablet and looked over the two starats. "She's pushed you through to have this all done as soon as possible. Would normally have been waiting weeks for something like this, probably months even. We would normally custom build everything for you, but that takes time. Someone like Ms Jennings is able to speed the process up significantly."

"How long will the surgery take?" David asked. His hand rested on Twitch's shoulder, stroking him gently. Twitch could feel the trembles in his partner's hand.

"The procedure itself will take up to about five hours," the doctor said, her eyes turning to look to David. "We expect to keep him unconscious for twelve hours for monitoring, during which time we will use nanotech to accelerate the healing process. By the time he's awake, he should be ready to receive the prosthetics."

David's tail thumped against the side of the bed. "That's very quick. It would have taken months with what we had. Even the humans on Terra would have to wait weeks."

Doctor Reynolds smiled. "We aren't held back by their thinking. I am sorry patients suffer so much on Terra, when we have the technology here to help them." She held a hand to her chest as she looked back to Twitch. "I'll return shortly when everything in theatre is ready. It shouldn't take long."

"I'll be ready for you," Twitch said brightly. He waved goodbye to the doctor as she left, though his smile faltered slightly as he looked up to David when the door closed. "I guess this is it, isn't it?"

"Yeah, it is," David replied. He sat down on the bed and pulled Twitch into another tight embrace. Once more, they didn't want to let go, but Twitch leaned back away from the other starat before the human doctor returned. He sat with his hands resting in his lap as he tried to put on his brave face. He didn't want to leave David behind with terror in his heart. He had to be brave. He needed this. He would do something that even Captain Rhys had been too scared to do.

The doctor returned a few minutes later, flanked by a couple of nurses. Twitch squeezed his hand around David's. They only had a moment before Twitch was moved back into his wheelchair, but in that moment they exchanged a warm smile. In that smile was none of the fear Twitch knew they both felt. It was just love and trust. David had to trust in Twitch that this was the right thing to do, just as Twitch had to trust in himself. And the love was there, no matter what happened. They would always have that.

And then they were apart. David was left behind, and Twitch was taken through the unfamiliar corridors of the hospital by Doctor Reynolds and the nurses. He may as well have been alone. The three humans spoke amongst each other, but Twitch quickly tuned them out. All he could hear was the blood rushing through his ears. He felt a little nauseous, though he hadn't eaten anything all day. One last time, he pinched his legs, but still he felt nothing.

His fear was not helped when he was finally pushed through into the operating theatre. It felt cold and sterile to Twitch, and there was a sinister appearance to the bed in the middle of the room, with all the medical equipment around it. There were various monitors and sensors that would make sure he was kept alive through the operation, and all the different tools the surgeons would use to cut up open and remove a big part of him.

He wanted out.

He wanted to go back to David.

He couldn't speak. Terror had robbed him of his voice.

Twitch was gently laid out across the bed, and a couple of straps secured him in place. The doctor and the nurses all spoke kindly to him, but he couldn't recall anything they said, even moments after they had finished talking. He nodded in response to a few of their questions, but was never quite sure what they were asking.

A mask was placed over his muzzle.

A familiar voice cut through the chaos of sound and spoke deep within Twitch's mind. Doctor Anthony. "Just focus, Twitch. You can do this. You're brave. You're strong."

Beneath the breathing mask, Twitch smiled. "I can do this," he repeated.

"Alright Twitch, I want you to count down from ten."

He made it to eight.

***

"Seven!"

Twitch jerked awake from his dreamless sleep. He blinked in surprise as he found himself not in the operating theatre, but back in the small room he had last seen David. Outside his window he could see the busy streets of Caledonia, still lit by artificial lights with the darkening sky just about visible between a couple of buildings. Prox had almost set.

Slowly, Twitch's mind caught up with his surroundings. He was alone, but he could hear voices and movement just outside the door to his room. But he wasn't in the theatre, which meant that everything must have been done. He was lying down flat on his back on his bed, and he hauled himself up to sit upright against the headboard. He had gotten used to the deadweight of his legs and tail, but now he felt light as he moved himself.

The bedsheets were flat against the mattress below his hips. He whimpered softly to himself as he reached forward to pat where his thighs would have been. His hand grasped at nothing.

His breath caught in his throat. His mind was still trying to tell him that something should be there, but his hand brushed from side to side and felt nothing. There was nothing for it. He would have to pull away the sheets.

Even so, it took Twitch almost a full minute of grasping the sheet in trembling fingers before he was able to pull the sheets back. He let out a low whimper at what he saw. He was naked, but that didn't attract his attention. Instead of legs, he had two metal plates where they had once been. A number of divots and connectors ran around the metal, and Twitch stroked his fingers around the smooth surface. The touches sent a few tingles of electrical sensation into his hips.

His hands explored around to his back until he felt a third disc of metal, this one over where his tail had once emerged from his back. This was all he was now, and he quickly flicked the sheets back across to hide himself away. He leaned back against the headboard and rubbed his hands over his eyes.

"Fuck," he said quietly. He had known what was going to happen, but the reality of it felt like a punch to the chest.

His ears flicked as the door opened. "David?" he called out desperately.

"Afraid not."

It was not David who came into the room, or even Doctor Reynolds or Doctor Anthony. Instead, Amy appeared through the doorway, with Mortimer right behind her. The starats carried what appeared to be a massive briefcase between them, which was placed down on the edge of the bed. Twitch could feel its weight as it pressed down on the mattress.

"Where's David?" Twitch asked nervously.

"He's sleeping," Mortimer replied. "He tried to stay awake with you the whole time, but we chased him away about an hour ago to get some rest. We thought it would be a nice surprise for him if you were already walking when he woke up."

Twitch glanced down to the heavy case on the end of his bed. His ears perked up. "My legs are in there?"

Amy nodded. "We worked hard to get them ready so soon. Do you want to see them?" she asked, her hands resting on the clasps that held the case closed.

Twitch grinned widely. "Yes please!" He managed to hide his discomfort at the fact he tried to wag the tail that was no longer connected to him.

The case was slowly opened, and what was inside surprised Twitch. There were no sleek, metallic limbs. Instead, there were two legs and a tail that looked almost identical to what he had possessed before. For a moment, he was convinced they were simply the limbs that had been removed from his body, until he reached out and touched them. They felt cool, but not icy cold like he had expected.

"They look... normal," Twitch asked in confusion. His ears drooped slightly, almost disappointed by how they appeared.

270

Amy chuckled and picked one of them up. The limb hung limply in her hands. At the end of the limb was a silvery plate that looked just like the one attached to Twitch's hip. "These are just your basic limbs. Nothing fancy about them. They're designed to match your fur, and to the casual glance, they'll look perfectly normal," she said. She held the limb out to Twitch, who took it in both hands. It felt slightly heavier than he expected. "We already have a spare set ready that have some extra features, but we thought to get you used to these first."

Twitch wiggled his hips as he stroked his hands through the soft, synthetic fur of his new leg. It felt almost real, but there was a sense of the fur being too perfect to be genuine. There was none of the coarseness of natural fur, instead being completely silky smooth.

"Would you like me to show you how to attach it?" Mortimer offered.

Twitch nodded eagerly as the starat cautiously approached. "Yes please."

Mortimer took the leg from Twitch's hands. He lined the leg up with Twitch's hip, but didn't connect them just yet. Instead, he took hold of Twitch's hand and held it beneath his so he could guide Twitch through the process. "It's pretty simple to attach," Mortimer explained. "You see the raised bit in the middle? That connects directly into the opposing port on your hip."

"Every complete limb we produce uses the same connectors, so you never have to worry about compatibility," Amy added. She held up the tail, showing the same connector plate on the end. "Though you won't be able to use partial replacements like William's leg, for example. He didn't need the remainder of his leg removed, but we felt this would be better for you."

"So it just pushes on?" Twitch asked. He tried to push the limb in place, but Mortimer's hand held him back.

"Almost. There's a couple of notches just here," Mortimer said, pointing to a couple of the little divots in the connector. He then pointed to a matching set on Twitch's hip. "These need to line up, or they won't connect properly. It won't take long before you get used to it though. Why don't you try now?"

Twitch squeaked eagerly as Mortimer's hand came away from his. With his right hand, he traced around the two connectors to find the little notches, and with his left he slowly pushed the left leg into place. There was a moment of resistance as the two metallic plates came together, the ridges and ports lining up perfectly. Twitch almost pulled back, feeling like he was pushing too hard and was about to break it, but neither Amy nor Mortimer warned him to stop. He pushed a little harder still, and with a satisfying click the leg popped into place.

With a gasp of delight, Twitch ran his hands from his organic flesh to the new artificial limb. The fur colour perfectly matched his own, even if the feel of the artificial hairs were slightly off. It took him a few moments to realise something wasn't quite right though. His ears drooped. "I can't feel it at all."

"It'll take a little while for everything to connect up properly and sync," Amy explained as she passed the second leg over to Mortimer. "It won't be like that every time, don't worry. Give it a few minutes and you should have full sensation, or close to it."

Twitch nodded and breathed out a sigh of relief. He would have hated the thought of getting these new legs, only to still have no sensation from them. His hand kept stroking through the fur of his leg as he looked down to the splayed toes of his foot. Everything looked identical to what he had had before. He didn't know how they had done it, as he had not been aware of them getting any measurements from him. His ears flicked. He wondered if Captain Rhys had been involved at all. The thought sent a little tingle down his spine. The captain had his body, so they were still his legs, but it felt weird that they had come from Captain Rhys.

Mortimer clicked the second leg into place as Twitch was distracted by his thoughts. With both legs connected, Twitch felt a lot more like himself. Just the sight of them there soothed his worries a little, though some still lingered. He recognized that those would remain until he was able to move them.

With Amy and Mortimer's help, Twitch rolled over onto his belly for the last of the three limbs to be connected. His tail was probably the most important of the three. It wasn't just used for balance when walking, but it was crucial in conveying emotion as well. Without it, he felt like he was lacking in his physical vocabulary. He heard it click into place, and his body was whole once more.

Twitch rolled over onto his back again. He grinned up at the two starats. He wanted to twitch and thump his tail against the mattress, but it remained still against the bed. "Thank you both, they look amazing."

"You're more than welcome," Amy replied. She even bowed slightly to Twitch.

Mortimer's hand came to rest on Twitch's hip. He raised his brow and looked up at the other starat, a small blush coming to his cheeks. He was almost disappointed that Mortimer's attention was still on his artificial limbs.

"If you feel around here," Mortimer said, touching to a point on the inside of Twitch's thigh. He held one finger there, seemingly unaware of the reaction he had nearly caused. With his other hand, he held a finger directly opposite the first. "And here as well. There are a couple of small latches. Push them both in and you'll be able to detach the leg."

Amy sat down on the bed on the other side to Mortimer. "When you're skilled enough with using your legs, we'll be able to provide some that don't have physical latches, as they can be a hindrance and easily compromised. Eventually you'll be able to control their attachment directly with your thoughts. When you get more complex limbs you'll be able to control a lot of features directly."

Twitch tilted his head to the side. "Oh, that's pretty cool. What sort of stuff could I do?" he said. He pulled himself to a sitting position, pulling his tail to the side to keep it out of the way.

Amy placed her hand on his right ankle, and a small jolt of electrical energy pulsed through Twitch's body. "We'll be able to add all sorts of receptors and sensors that will be able to augment your senses, as well as providing more strength, speed, and dexterity compared to what you're used to."

Twitch grinned and nodded. "That sounds really cool," he said brightly. A couple of strange sensations rippled out from his hips, making him gasp and twitch his muzzle in concern. He held his hands down on his legs, tensing his fingers into his fur. His legs and tail had gone from a blank void to an exceptionally numb cacophony of conflicting sensation. It felt like a mixture of pain and pleasure, as though hands rubbed up his limbs while they were simultaneously being jabbed with tiny needles at every point together.

Mortimer placed his hand on Twitch's shoulder. "Try to relax. It's just the nerves connecting and calibrating. It will be over soon," he said, his voice soothing and soft.

Twitch scrunched up his muzzle as the sensations got worse. He clenched his fists and thumped his tail against the bed in distress, before it abruptly stopped. A burst of heat felt like it washed over his legs and tail, and suddenly it all felt normal again. The tip of his tail flicked against his leg, and he gasped in surprise as the movement and the sensation he felt from it.

His hands held tight around his tail and he pulled it close to his chest. He could feel it, and he could move it. He slowly flexed his toes, wiggling the digits. Hugging his tail close, he squeaked in delight at the movement. A dark weight on his mind was suddenly lifted, and the smile that spread across his muzzle was a genuine reflection of the brightness that was growing within him.

Mortimer stood up to give Twitch the space to swing around and lets his feet drop to the floor. The other starat placed his hand back on Twitch's shoulder to offer support.

Twitch took a deep breath as he felt the floor through his new feet. He could feel the roughness of the thin carpet with incredible distinction; every ridge and bump in the fabric making itself known to the pads on the bottom of his feet.

With Mortimer's support, Twitch slowly lifted himself up off the bed. He swayed slightly and leaned into the starat by his side as he struggled to find his balance. The weight of his legs and tail weren't quite the same, and he took a few moments to adjust. He moved his tail around as he found his centre of balance again, keeping his arm around Mortimer's side as he did so. The starat kept close, not once letting go as Twitch tentatively took his first couple of steps.

"This must be what Captain Rhys felt like," Twitch giggled as he fell sideways into Mortimer. The other starat was able to catch him as Twitch struggled to stand upright again. "He was so funny when I was teaching him how to walk."

"Once you get your balance right, it shouldn't be much different," Mortimer said with a smile. He provided support to keep Twitch from falling. When Twitch was standing upright again, the starat took a step back.

Holding his arms and tail out rigidly, Twitch's torso swayed on his new legs, but this time he didn't fall over. He shuffled his feet forward and slowly relaxed his arms to a more natural position. A few more steps followed, and Twitch's back slowly straightened up as he grew more confidence in his sense of balance.

"We made sure the limbs were as close to yours as possible," Amy said as Twitch cautiously walked past her. "With some of the older tech it would take days or even weeks to get used to walking again, but these allow you to bypass that process almost entirely. With some more... exotic prosthetics it may take a little longer, but these should feel natural pretty quickly."

"We'll show you some of the other features and how to keep them charged later," Mortimer added. "But for now, why don't you get something to wear and we can take you through to see David? I'm sure he won't mind being woken up if you can walk."

Twitch had entirely forgotten about his nakedness in the excitement of his new limbs. He grinned sheepishly and sunk down onto his bed. There was a folded set of his clothes on the table close by, and he quickly slipped them on. His synthetic fur bristled as his legs were partially covered up. It was a different sensation to normal. It felt sharper and clearer, like he could feel every individual hair as it moved. He shivered and tried to smooth down his fur beneath his shorts. Once he had his shirt on, he was ready to go.

Amy reached out to take his hand, and slowly they walked out of Twitch's small room. As they emerged outside, Twitch saw Doctor Reynolds behind a small desk with a couple of nurses. He couldn't see Doctor Anthony at all, and Twitch wondered if he had imagined the *Harvester's* doctor. The human looked and raised her hand in greeting to Twitch, but she didn't protest him being out of his bed or room. He took that as permission to follow after Amy as she tugged on his hand to lead him in the opposite direction. She was gentle but insistent as she led him through the hospital, with Mortimer in the lead just a few paces further ahead.

There were so many sights and smells through the hospital that Twitch wanted to investigate, but overarching over everything was a pervading scent of blood and fear. That alone made Twitch eager to just be on his way. He could sense there was a lot of suffering around him, and that no matter how hard the medical staff tried, they would never heal everyone who came through their doors. His ears drooped slightly. They had helped heal him, at least. They had provided him with the means for Amy and Mortimer to fix him, and for that he could be grateful.

It wasn't long before they were away from the wards, which eased some of the misgivings running through Twitch's mind. The unpleasant tang of blood was no longer in the air, and the bustle of the hospital was diminished. They had gone up a few stories in a small elevator, and had emerged into a more homely area. Gone were the wards and clinical, sterile corridors. Instead there was a large, open plaza with a ceiling of glass, letting in as much light as Prox could provide. A little cafe was situated on one side, and a large bookshelf took up most of the opposite wall. Tables and chairs were scattered through the open area, as well as a few large sofas.

A few humans and starats lingered around the open area, but there was one that caught Twitch's attention more than anyone else. Sprawled out on one of the sofas was David. His arm fell over the side, and he looked asleep.

Twitch pushed his way past Amy and Mortimer, but they held him back for a moment. Amy pointed out one of the corridors leading away from the open plaza. "When you're ready, head through there. You'll see signs to my office. Meet us there when you're done here, and we can discuss our plans for you. Both of you are welcome," she said. She smiled and shook Twitch's hand, but he pulled her into an embrace. Mortimer was given the same treatment, and Twitch beamed at the both as they left. His synthetic tail wagged behind his back as he turned to David.

Twitch knelt down beside the bed, automatically compensating for the little twinge he always felt in his left ankle, before realising he no longer felt that familiar pain. That ankle had been hurting for years, ever since he had been thrown down a flight of stairs by a disgruntled owner. His legs were perfect now, with no blemishes or faults within.

David looked tired, even as he slept. His fur was unkempt and rough, especially around his eyes and muzzle. His ears and fingers twitched as he dozed. Twitch didn't want to wake him.

A hand rested on his shoulder.

Twitch jerked backwards in shock and glanced up. One of the humans who had been working behind the cafe had approached. She held her hands up in apology. She held a cloth in one hand, and an empty glass in the other. "I didn't mean to scare you, sorry. You must be his husband," she said, a smile on her face as she nodded down towards David.

Twitch's ears flicked back. "Not my husband, no. We weren't allowed to marry or anything on Ceres, but he's my partner," he explained. He slowly rose up to his feet, carefully settling his weight down before letting go of the sofa.

"Well he's certainly been very worried about you. He's only just managed to get to sleep," the human said. She only then seemed to realise she had started to wipe clean the glass in her hand. She tucked the cloth into her belt, and she glanced back towards the cafe. "Can I get you a coffee or something while you wait?"

Twitch grimaced. "I don't have any money though. I didn't bring my wallet with these legs," he said, patting his hips. His wide grin faded when the human just looked blankly at him. He muttered a little more quietly, "These are new. All metal and stuff."

The human's eyes widened. "Both of them? Shit, that must have been pretty bad. Sorry to hear," she said, holding her free hand up to her chest. She then shook her head slightly. "But don't worry about the cost. They're free for patients and any visiting family."

Twitch tilted his head, unsure if she had just made that up or not. He shrugged his shoulders. If she was offering him a free drink, then he wasn't going to turn it down. He flashed a quick grin. "I'll tell you all about it if I can have a hot chocolate."

The human laughed quietly. "Come on. Take a seat over here so we don't disturb your partner, and you can tell me the story."

***

Twitch embellished everything. The story he told was barely recognisable compared to the facts that had happened, but he revelled in the admiration the human – whose name was Kellie, he had learned – gave him for his bravery. The steady supply of hot chocolate she provided was an added bonus, but it was the warmth of her praise that was the biggest reward. He even allowed her to touch his synthetic foot, allowing her to feel how it was constructed. She was impressed by it, though Twitch was surprised she didn't get the chance to feel prosthetics very often, given where she worked.

At the end of his story, the human just sat in silence for a few moments. She had grown less enthusiastic about the story when

Twitch had told her the true identity of his attacker, and she sat with her head in her hands.

"So it was the Vatican who did that to you?" she asked at the end of it all.

"Yeah. They didn't have the excuse to get hold of me back on Ceres, but they got their claws into me here," Twitch replied. He stuck his tongue out in disgust.

"My brother got taken by them," Kellie said. She kept her head bowed, and rested her hands on her knees.

Twitch almost dropped his hot chocolate. His ears drooped down. "They killed him?"

"Oh no, they didn't kill him. Sometimes I wish they had though," Kellie replied. She sighed softly. "I guess it's my turn to tell a story, isn't it?"

Twitch lifted up his cup. "Do you want a hot chocolate? They're really good to help storytelling," he suggested. He wasn't sure if he should joke when she had just told him about her brother, but she laughed and held out her hand to take Twitch's cup.

"Let me go get a couple of fresh ones then, and I can tell you about my brother," she said with a smile.

Twitch beamed in delight. He hadn't even expected a fresh cup out of his suggestion, but he happily drained the last dregs from his current drink and held the cup out for Kellie to take. He got another surge of elation when an exhausted starat sat down by his side. David leaned gently into Twitch to rest his head on the smaller starat's shoulder.

"Thought I could hear your voice," David mumbled sleepily. He wrapped his arm around Twitch's torso and yawned widely. "Your legs look good. How do they feel?"

Twitch slowly stroked down David's back, making the larger start rumble in appreciation. "They feel great," he replied. He lifted one foot up from the ground and wiggled his toes. "They work perfectly."

"That's good," David said. His head drooped against Twitch's shoulder, almost falling asleep again.

Kellie had clearly noticed David had mostly woken up again, as she brought three hot chocolates over. David perked up a little at the prospect of the drink, and he smiled up at Kellie as he took the offered cup from the human.

"Twitch was just telling me how he got the new legs," the human explained as she sat down in her chair opposite. "How he saved nearly a dozen people in doing so."

David blinked and looked up to Twitch. "A dozen?" he said with a tired smirk. Twitch worried that his story was about to be rumbled. "Don't be so modest. It was at least twenty."

Twitch beamed widely as David contributed to the admiration in Kellie's eyes. He squeezed his partner even tighter and gave him a quick kiss on the top of the head.

The sadness returned to Kellie's eyes after a few moments. "But I was going to tell you about my brother. We were never very close when growing up, and we almost always argued. What drove us apart though, was my ex-boyfriend. He was a starat, and my brother despised that."

"People here are still against that?" David asked. The larger starat had stopped leaning against Twitch, and was sat forward on the sofa with his hot chocolate held in both hands just beneath his muzzle. The steam from the hot drink drifted across his face, leaving drops of moisture clinging to the tips of his fur.

"I've heard stories of what it's like in Sol and Sirius, and it's not that bad for starats here in comparison. But there are still some people who think you're little more than animals, and deserve to be treated as such. My brother is one of those people," Kellie explained. She took a sip from her drink and licked her lips. "He attacked my boyfriend. Thankfully he survived, but we broke up not long after that. I think he was scared it would happen again. I never spoke to my brother again."

"What happened to your brother?" Twitch asked with a flick of his ear.

"Best I know, he went off to one of those weird religious communes that are starting to spring up on the southern continent. They're starting to get a little louder and more violent towards starats, but the government doesn't seem to be doing anything about them. They call themselves the Inquisition." Kellie sighed again and took another sip. "I hope they're not starting to come north, or else it could get dangerous for starats."

"Yeah, me too. I had enough of them already," Twitch said, growling softly into his hot chocolate. He twitched his muzzle and looked up at Kellie. "When did this all happen?"

Kellie brushed back a lock of brown hair that had fallen across her face. "Oh, about two years ago. Terran years, that is."

Twitch frowned. Amy had been explaining the rise in Vatican influence as a recent thing, but if it had been happening for far longer, then he doubted that Cardinal Erik was the person behind any of this. It may even be unrelated to the cardinal entirely. He kept his thoughts to himself, not wanting to share with Kellie the deal he had made to get his legs. It didn't seem fair to include her, especially if the Vatican were starting to gain strength on Centaura through the Inquisition. It would put her at risk, and she had been kind to him. She had given him lots of hot chocolate, and that made her his friend. He didn't want to do anything to endanger her. It was bad enough that his actions would potentially put David at risk.

After draining the last of his hot chocolate, Twitch rose up to his feet. "It's been lovely meeting you, Kellie, but we should move on. We're expected somewhere else soon," he said, reluctant to leave her. His tail swished happily as the human got up to her feet as well.

"Wait just one moment," she said. She took the empty cups from David and Twitch to take them back to the small cafe. She rummaged around behind the counter for a few moments before hurrying back. She held a small tablet in her hand when she returned. She switched it on and held up the screen for Twitch. "Do you have your contact details? I'd like to keep in touch if possible."

Twitch flicked his muzzle. He had been given a tablet on his arrival, everyone from Captain Rhys's crew had been, but he hadn't memorized any of his details for it yet and had simply kept all the information on the tablet itself. He patted at his hips. "I, uh. Left all of that on my other legs," he said with a wry grin.

David chuckled and produced his own tablet. "I have mine," he said. He quickly exchanged contact details with the human by pressing the tablets together screen-to-screen. They both beeped and a light flashed green.

"Thanks for that," Kellie said brightly. She tucked her tablet in her pocket before giving the two starats a quick hug. "Good luck with your new legs, Twitch. Stay safe, both of you."

"We will," Twitch replied happily. He swished his tail and hopped from foot to foot. "Thanks for the hot chocolate."

"You're welcome," Kellie said. She waved farewell to the two starats as they turned to leave, making their way in the direction Amy had previously indicated.

Twitch still leaned into David as they walked, though he didn't need the support. He was just happy to be able to walk by his partner's side again. There had been times over the last few days when he had been sure that would never happen again. He didn't have his own legs anymore, but the ones he had now seemed to be a huge improvement on his original, organic set. Everything felt more sensitive and, now that he'd sorted out his balance, he felt like he was able to walk with more grace. The little aches he had gotten used to over the years were gone as well. He felt as fit as a kit again.

"I wouldn't mention Kellie's brother to Amy," David said quietly, after they had moved well out of any human's earshot of the cafe.

Twitch flicked his ears and looked up at his partner. "Why not?"

David sighed softly and squeezed Twitch close. "I don't know. I just think we can't completely trust Amy yet. Or Snow."

"Captain Rhys trusts them both. And they've never done anything in our lessons with them," Twitch replied uncertainly. David hadn't ever been to any of those, as he had usually been too involved in his study with Doctor Anthony.

"I'm not sure. I just don't think they're telling us everything, and this thing with Kellie's brother," David said, before pausing for a moment as a couple of humans walked past them in the opposite direction. "I don't know. I think this thing runs deeper than Amy is telling us, so I don't know if we can trust her with everything we know. Just, until we know more, don't tell her everything, alright?"

A small shiver of trepidation ran down Twitch's spine and into his synthetic tail. He leaned a little closer to David. "I promise, yeah."

He could only hope there was nothing to worry about, but Twitch couldn't help but be worried. David was usually astute with who couldn't be trusted. It had been why he had been so happy when David had taken a liking to Captain Rhys. He would have to be on his guard.

***

Mortimer was waiting for them both outside Amy's office. He spread his arms wide and beamed at the two starats as they approached. "Lovely to see you walking so easily already," he said brightly. He opened the doors to Amy's office and led them through.

Sunlight streamed through the wide windows that ran around the office. The light was weak and gave everything a slight red tinge, but Twitch still needed to squint as he looked out towards the eastern horizon, where Prox was just rising. In the distant streets below, the city carried on as it always did. Night or day seemed to have little difference to the busy streets.

Amy was sat behind her desk, and she gestured to one of the seats in front of her. "Please take a seat, Twitch. Rest your feet up and we can show you a few important things," she said. She carried a bundle of wires and cables in one hand.

Twitch quickly did what she asked, taking care to keep his tail out of the way as he leaned back on the chair. He rested his feet on another chair and grinned up at David, who remained standing behind him. "Is this where you show me all the lasers and scanners you've put in me? That's how this usually works, isn't it?" he asked with a giggle. He heard David sigh softly behind him. Or it could have been a yawn; he didn't look back to see.

Ahead of him, Amy smirked. "Not exactly. I'm going to need you to take your trousers off again."

Twitch giggled and flicked his ears up. "Well, why didn't you say so in the first place?" he said, already starting to wriggle out of his clothes. "I didn't realise it was going to be that kind of meeting."

David swatted Twitch around the ears as Mortimer giggled. Amy just raised a brow.

"Not quite," Mortimer said, though Twitch did notice the starat's eyes flicked down to his legs for just a moment. Long enough for Twitch to smirk back at him. "We just need to show you how to keep your legs and tail working properly."

Twitch stuck his tongue out. "That's significantly less fun, but alright, I suppose." Mortimer grinned up at Twitch as he knelt down between his legs. Twitch's brow raised. "I thought you said it wasn't that kind of meeting."

Mortimer placed his hands on Twitch's thighs, close to where the release catches were on his legs, but this time a little further down. "Reach down here and feel this ridge," the starat instructed. Twitch did as he was ordered. He placed his hands down where Mortimer had indicated, and felt a strange bump running up his leg beneath his fur. It felt almost like a seam. "Press down on that firmly."

Again, Twitch did as Mortimer instructed. He pushed down on his leg, his eartips folded in curiosity. He felt something shift slightly, before a panel popped open where he had pressed. He gasped in surprise as he suddenly found himself staring at a small panel of switches and ports. Inside his leg. Inside the leg attached to his hip.

Everything around the small panel blurred. Twitch could focus on nothing else as his vision spun. He felt dizzy. His hand clutched onto his thigh, not daring to reach down at touch the exposed electronics.

A hand stroked down his cheek and a muffled voice reached through the haze in his mind. "Twitch. Are you alright?"

Twitch blinked and slowly looked up to see David above him. His partner's ears were curled down in concern. Twitch forced a smile to his muzzle. "Yeah, fine. Just a bit of a shock to see..." he said, gesturing down to his leg. "I mean, I knew what it was, but just to see it like that was..."

"It will take a while to get used to," Mortimer said, cutting across Twitch's confused explanation. "But in time you will come to see them as normal."

Twitch took a deep breath and nodded. He looked back down at Mortimer as the other starat's fingers moved closer to the open panel. He swallowed and tried to suppress the eerie sensations his mind was trying to convince him of. He wiggled his toes to try to remind himself that his leg was real, and the exposed electronics were a part of him now. It wasn't just some leg that was attached to him. It was his leg. The thought was difficult to quantify with what he could see.

"So what do I need to know?" Twitch asked. His fingers trembled as he reached down again, gently touching around the raised panel that had swung up. Even with it raised, he could still feel as his fingers brushed through the artificial fur.

"While these will get some energy from your own body, organic to synthetic energy transfer just isn't very efficient yet," Mortimer explained. He held up one of the cables Amy had passed down to him. "That means you need to manually charge them. There's a port like this on both legs, and one in your tail too. Normally they'll have enough charge for three to four days, but it's probably best to get in the habit of charging them up every night."

"And the others?" Twitch asked with a nervous giggle. He could see which port would plug into the cable in Mortimer's hand, but there were a few others as well.

"Most of these are just in emergencies, if there's a software fault. Diagnostics, that sort of thing," Mortimer said, his claw tapping each port in turn. His finger then stopped at the last one. "This one though is a universal connector. Once you get really advanced with working your legs, you can even connect up to other electronic devices. You can plug yourself in to something and control it as though it was an extension of yourself. But I wouldn't try anything like that just yet."

Twitch nodded quickly, his eyes wide at the thought. "And the little red button?" he asked pointing down at the button underneath the various ports. "I know how this goes. That makes them explode, right? Never touch the red button."

Mortimer grinned. "Not quite that dramatic, I'm afraid. That just turns on low-power mode. If you're stuck somewhere and don't expect to be able to charge them, put them into that mode. It will limit their abilities and sensitivity drastically, but you'll still be able to walk just fine. They'll last much longer that way."

Twitch nodded again as Mortimer pushed the panel closed. It clicked shut and appeared to vanish into his fur. He ran his fingers over it, only just feeling the seams that were raised up slightly from the rest of his leg.

"If a part ever breaks..." Amy started to say, but Twitch interrupted her with a smile.

"I was a mechanic on Ceres. I know my way around machines and electronics," he said. He flicked his ears. "But if I can't fix it, I'll come back to you."

Mortimer glanced up at Amy for a moment, before looking back to Twitch. "These are very complicated. If you're not familiar with them, they can be difficult to repair," he said. He patted Twitch on the leg as he rose back up to his feet. He took one look at Twitch's eager face and groaned. "I'll get you a manual."

Amy cleared her throat to get Twitch's attention. "While you are away, we will install a wireless charger in your home, and we'll have a spare pair of legs ready for your return," she said. She had sat down behind her desk again, with her hands clasped as she leaned forward. "Take care with those, for you will be in Hadrian and far from my help should you need it."

"When do we leave?" David asked. The larger starat rested his hand on Twitch's shoulder.

"As soon as your discharge from the hospital is complete. I promised Doctor Reynolds I wouldn't keep you for too long, so we should probably take you back soon," Amy replied. She smiled at the two starats. Mortimer took a couple of steps towards the office door. "We will transfer all the information we have on the Drive, and any last sightings of Cardinal Erik. Remember, as much as you will want to hunt down the cardinal, the Drive should be your first priority. They could be developing a weapon with it, and we need that disabled."

Twitch clenched his hands into fists as he stood. He could hear David's tablet beep as Mortimer transferred the information as Amy promised. "It gives us the chance to get Cardinal Erik and ruin his plans," he said with a growl. "I would do anything if it meant stopping him."

"I hope you do not have to give any more than you already have," Amy replied. She didn't stand, but she nodded her head to Twitch and David. "Be safe, both of you. I look forward to seeing you when you return. Mortimer will see to it that you get to Hadrian safely, and that you find your accommodation there. Good luck."

chapter twenty

The *Freedom* was almost ready to come out of subspace. But for a brief pause on the outskirts of the Sirius system, the ship had been in constant travel for just over four days. Rhys had spent most of that time with a horrific headache after Snow had pushed him hard with developing his subspace abilities. He had never heard the entities screaming like Nick had warned him, but he had occasionally seen a flash of darkness at the corner of his vision. Every time he had looked around, the flash had gone again. He could never be sure if it was the entities, but he could think of nothing else that it could have been.

Snow focused mostly on teaching Rhys how to manipulate realspace matter through subspace. It was already something he had managed to achieve by himself twice, though neither time he had been completely sure how he had done it. The albino starat taught him how to extend his influence through subspace, where it could interact with the shadowy imprints realspace left on the white void.

For the first two days, Rhys had struggled. He hadn't been able to make any progress at all, but for managing to give himself terrible headaches. The headaches never eased, but on the third day of travel he was able to finally move a pen around the briefing room where they had been practicing.

Snow hadn't let Rhys celebrate his achievement for long. She kept him hard at work, while impressing on him several important rules. He could never over-extend himself. Using subspace was like any muscle in his body. He had to work hard to develop his abilities, and to over-extend himself was to risk losing himself to the void. The second rule was to never interact directly with any living organic creature. The third rule was to ensure that he always dropped into subspace with a clear mind. Errant thoughts had a way of interacting with subspace in unexpected ways.

Rhys didn't dare to try breaking those rules. He didn't even want to imagine what the consequences could be. Instead he just focused on doing what he could, and gradually increasing his abilities in the safe environment of his ship.

Even when Rhys wasn't in his lessons with Snow, he tried to develop his abilities. When he was sat on the bridge, he kept a few pens close to hand, where he tried to move them around without having to sink too deep inside subspace. He didn't want to keep limiting his realspace senses, but he found that was an ability beyond him.

For four days, he had practiced hard. It had been a challenge mixing that in with meetings with General Carson as they prepared the tactics for their raid on Pluto, and by the time the newly-renamed *Freedom* was preparing to come out of subspace, Rhys felt exhausted. He sat back and looked down over the bridge with General Carson to his right. Aaron was down below, standing beside Chekolin as the pilot prepared to initiate the jump out of subspace.

Rhys knew his fur was a mess. He had been too busy and too tired to keep up with his grooming. He didn't have Twitch or Leandro around to help him when it got too much for his crippled hands, and he hadn't felt comfortable asking William for help.

Rhys called out to Deborah Simms, the weapons officer. "Miss Simms, ensure weapons and shields are prepared. We're expecting to jump out close to an enemy ship, and we need it disabled before they can open fire." Even his voice came across as tired. He wrinkled his muzzle and grimaced. He didn't want to have any stimulants just before a mission, but he felt like he needed a strong coffee.

"All active and ready," Simms called out.

Rhys took a deep breath and leaned forward in his seat. This was it. They were about to jump into realspace close to Pluto and open fire on an empire ship. A shiver ran down Rhys's tail. It all sounded so familiar to him, but this time he was on the other side. He glanced down to Aaron below. Last time it had been his friend jumping out of subspace too close to a dwarf planet than what should have been possible. Everything from that moment had led to this.

Chekolin called out a ten second warning.

Time seemed to slow for Rhys as the last few seconds ebbed by. The screens were white, with an angry red sphere of Pluto's shadow on subspace dominating the view. Rhys's hands tensed against his armrests. Every instinct was screaming at him. They were too close.

On the bridge, Snow and the other starat psyker by her side flung up their hands as they protected the ship. Then white turned to black, and the ship emerged into realspace once more.

Pluto and Charon hung ominously in the sky. Already, the *Freedom* was skirting the outer edges of the thin atmosphere surrounding the dwarf planet. He couldn't help but gasp in wonder. He had never jumped so close to a celestial body before. It shouldn't have been possible, but the ship had emerged without any reported damage. Rhys's eyes quickly scanned the viewscreens for any signs of the defending ship.

Simms was quicker to find it. "Locked on and opening fire. Enemy shields not raised."

Rhys had already given the weapons officer full authorisation to act however she saw fit. The priority was to disable the imperial ship. If that meant destroying it, then Rhys knew that had to be done.

The *Freedom* shook as the massive ionic cannons fired. Twin beams of light arced across the dark sky and converged on a small speck that was barely distinguishable from the surrounding stars. A burst of bright light briefly lit up the screens as the ionic beams struck their target.

"Target crippled. Picket guns enabled to defend against shrapnel," Simms confirmed a few moments later.

"Keep shields raised and stay on alert for counter attacks," Rhys called out. He knew that the enemy ship could still have active weapons, even if they had been crippled or compromised badly.

"Distress beacon launched from enemy ship," Pool called out. The sensory officer swiped across on her screen, sending some coordinates across to Simms's station.

"Shoot it down," Rhys warned. He didn't want the small, automated craft to make the jump to subspace. If it did that, then they would run the risk of any nearby ships jumping in to defend the port. Uranus was the closest major hub for military bases to Pluto, and that was several hours away even with the fastest imperial ships, but there was always the risk that there were other ships in the region, especially with the Pluto system under higher alert following the raid.

"Beacon destroyed," Simms called out.

A small sigh of relief passed around the bridge.

"Chekolin, get us in position above the Tombaugh Station," Rhys ordered. It was unlikely now that there would be any external threats to the mission.

"Ten minutes from destination, Captain," Chekolin confirmed.

Rhys exhaled slowly. "Then it's time for me to take my leave and get to the shuttles. Chekolin, you have the bridge. Simms, keep up with the suppression fire on that ship and any ground defences. Pool and Dewson, keep alert on those sensors. We do not want to be caught unawares by any other ships in the area. Good luck, everyone."

Rhys knew he didn't need to explain anything to his crew. They knew what their roles were, and he trusted them to keep the ship safe while he was on the surface. The *Freedom* would be waiting to take them back to Centaura when they were ready to depart.

The picket guns began to fire as Rhys turned from the bridge. Shrapnel and debris from the imperial ship had reached them. Rhys could feel the small vibrations beneath his feet as the guns fired. No alarms sounded, and no debris struck the ship. There was no return fire from the crippled enemy.

With General Carson following just behind, Rhys made his way down from the bridge. Snow joined up with them at the bottom of the stairs. The albino looked tired, and her ears drooped slightly. She would have been working hard, protecting the ship from subspace and the entities that lay within. Rhys was sure he looked as tired as she did, but he also knew that neither of them would complain or try to get out of the mission ahead. There would be plenty of time to rest after the mission. Now was the time for action.

***

Aaron was already in the armoury, along with most of the crew who would be descending to the surface. Only those necessary to keep the ship running would be remaining on the *Freedom*. The skeleton crew would maintain the ship's defences and keep watch on the sensors. There would be enough to get them back to Centaura in an emergency, but everyone with combat training was suiting up in preparation for the descent down to the surface.

The armoury was noisy as everyone worked quickly to get prepared, with just Rhys, General Carson, and Snow yet to suit up. Rhys found his suit by Aaron, who was helping Nick adjust his suit for a better fit.

"Almost ready to go?" Aaron asked Rhys as the starat approached.

"As ready as I'll ever be," Rhys replied. He glanced over the suit prepared for him, and his ears pinned back in distress. The suit was just the same as everyone else's, without anything to help him with his hands. "Wasn't I meant to have power gloves with these?"

"Briggs said he had everything ready for everyone," Aaron said, his voice hitching up in alarm. He stopped helping Nick for a moment as he turned to look around, but there were no power gloves in sight. "I reminded him to check for them a few hours ago."

"Shit," Rhys muttered under his breath.

"I'll go look for some," Aaron said.

"We don't have time," Rhys replied sharply. The words came out harsher than he had intended. He knew Aaron wasn't to blame, and he didn't want to take his anger out on his friend. He forced himself to suppress a growl. A sharp pain shot up his right arm as he struggled to get the suit on. "Can you just help me with this please?"

"Are you sure?" Aaron asked nervously.

"I'm sure, yes. I'll manage," Rhys replied. He wasn't convinced, but he knew he had little other choice. He would be needed on the surface. He wasn't going to volunteer to remain behind, just because there were no power gloves for him. There would be time to investigate why such a crucial part of his equipment had been forgotten when he returned.

If he returned.

Rhys knew he would be heavily compromised without the gloves, but he forced those bleak thoughts away. He had more than enough knowledge, and more than enough support, that he would be able to work around the issues with his hands.

Rhys clenched his teeth as both Aaron and Nick helped him into his spacesuit. The other starat didn't say anything to Rhys, but there was none of the usual hostility present in his eyes. Rhys knew the damage to their relationship was far from fixed, but he appreciated the temporary truce that appeared to have been called. Right now, he had far too much to worry about.

There were just a few minutes left until they needed to be in the shuttles. Nick handed Rhys his helmet. "Good luck, Captain," the starat said stiffly.

Before Rhys could answer, General Carson's powerful voice boomed around the armour. "Final checks for oxygen and ammunition. Two minutes until shuttles."

By the time the general had finished his commands, Nick had already turned away. Rhys slipped his helmet on and fumbled around the back of his head for the latches that secured it. His fingers couldn't manage it. It caused too much pain trying to maintain that level of fine control. Grimacing inside his visor, Rhys reached out to tap Aaron on the back.

"Can you get this, please?" Rhys asked, pointing to the back of his head.

Aaron didn't comment as he secured Rhys's helmet, for which the starat was glad. He didn't want attention being brought to his weakness. He stared down at his hands. Inside the thick spacesuit, there was little that gave away his injuries, but they were still there. He sighed softly and began to go through the final checks. His HUD displayed his oxygen levels at one hundred percent, and a quick couple of pats at his hips confirmed his ammunition was loaded with his pistols.

Rhys was about to approach General Carson when he noticed a small green light flashing in the corner of his HUD. A recorded message was waiting for him. Curious, Rhys activated it. A small video of Briggs popped up to the side of his HUD, leaving most of his vision still free.

"Sorry about the gloves, Captain. I found them broken earlier, and I haven't been able to fix them in time," the services commander said. The human held up one of the power gloves, which was missing most of the hand. "I don't know if it was accidental or not at this stage, but I did notice the auto-recording features with those new suits had been switched off as well. I've re-activated that, but the gloves need several more hours of work. I'm sorry I can't get them to you in time. If possible, I would like to speak with you when you get back. I'm worried about sabotage with these, so be on alert."

Rhys stood completely still as the video ended. The warnings from Major-General Ulrich came flooding back to him. Someone from the Inquisition had boarded his ship, and they were clearly trying to sabotage the mission. He growled quietly in the safety of his helmet. He considered contacting General Carson or Aaron to let them know of his suspicions, but he decided not to take the risk. He couldn't know if the spy was listening in to their communications. For now, he had to keep it to himself and stay on high alert for anything suspicious.

"Another desolate world." Aaron's voice cut across Rhys's thoughts.

"Can't be as bad as Ceres," Rhys replied. He tried to keep the worry from his voice. He smiled, even though he knew Aaron would not be able to see him.

"You really hated it there?"

Rhys didn't answer right away as his private channel with Aaron was cut off. General Carson overrode it as he addressed everyone. "Alright. To the shuttles. You know which one to take. A Team to shuttle A. B Team to shuttle B. Pluto awaits us. Let's go get her."

As Rhys and Aaron were both assigned as team leaders for the assaulting forces, they were designated to separate shuttles. They were still close enough together that they were in range to continue their private conversation.

"I really did," Rhys continued, as though their conversation hadn't been interrupted. He didn't look back to Aaron as they walked in opposite directions out of the armoury. "Had half a mind to tell you to bomb the place and just get it over with."

Aaron laughed at that. "You know I never would have done that, right?"

"I know. I called your bluff, but you got lucky with my shuttle."

"Lucky? Hah!" Aaron exclaimed. "You saw the jump we did. You could never have managed that back then, and he managed it without any psykers on board."

"One day I'll have to ask him how he did that," Rhys said, a little sorrow entering his voice. He walked into the shuttle behind a couple of humans. He wished one of them could have been Aaron.

"One day I hope he'll tell you," Aaron replied. "I wish you could have been friends."

Rhys bowed his head as he sat down by himself. "So do I, Aaron. I wish I could have been a better human than the one I was. Maybe I'll be a better starat than I ever was a human."

It took a while for Aaron to respond again. Rhys thought the connection may have been broken off. "Don't beat yourself up so much over it, Rhys," Aaron eventually said. "We all make mistakes, and you were hardly the only one to ignore Nick."

"But I was meant to be your friend as well, Aaron. I should never have done that to you both."

Aaron sighed. "How about I sit down with you and Nick when we get back to Centaura. All three of us can talk things through then. I think he should give you a second chance."

Rhys felt his eyes water for a moment. "Thank you, Aaron. I would love that."

"No problem. Hang on a bit though, got another message coming in." Aaron cut the connection between their helmets, and Rhys was left with silence again. He took a few deep breaths and looked up to the low ceiling of the shuttle. It took just a minute for everyone to board and take a seat. The airlock doors closed and the engines began to fire.

Rhys stared up at the ceiling and tried to clear his mind. This was not the time to be distracted by his concerns and worries. He needed to be a leader now. This was his mission, and he had two dozen humans and starats to command. He had to forget about everything but for what he would find on Pluto. Nick no longer mattered. His doubts about Amy and Snow couldn't matter. His fears for the Silver Fox, who sat just a few seats away, could no longer matter.

As the shuttle rumbled and shook, Rhys slowly rose to his feet and turned to face everyone. He looked around the two dozen starats and humans, all looking mostly identical in their spacesuits. They knew what was expected of them. They didn't need a rousing speech to lift their morale, and nor did they need to be told what to do. Almost without exception, they would have had experience of a ground raid before.

"Fight hard," Rhys said, keeping his voice quiet. He had no need to shout, for his voice would be projected through everyone's helmets anyway. "Fight brave. Look out for each other, and good luck."

Rhys turned to face the closed airlock door at the front of the shuttle. In less than a minute they would be docking with the Pluto station. They would know they were coming. There would be an armed response.

With a pained squeeze of his fist, Rhys activated the bullet shield on his right arm. He would be the first off the shuttle. He was ready.

chapter twenty-one

Hadrian wasn't as large as Caledonia, and it wasn't surrounded by masses of hydroponics farms like the capital. Instead the terrain was mostly natural, with crimson grasslands stretching out around the city until the distant foothills of a mountain range to the south east. It was from those mountains that the main river flowed. The Cambria River meandered through the city, before it arced to the east towards the nearby city that gave the river its name, before it flowed into the massive ocean that divided the two continents.

The buildings were smaller in Hadrian, not reaching as far up to the dark sky as they had in Caledonia. It was not the centre of commerce or trade on the planet, and most of the major businesses conducted their trade from the capital. The city reminded Twitch a little bit of Ceres, in some ways. It felt like the city had almost been forgotten in the minds of the rich and the powerful, and it had been neglected as it gradually fell into a state of disrepair.

Twitch had learned that the city had been initially settled because the region was rich in important metals and minerals in the ground. It was still a mining city, but the need for those supplies had dwindled somewhat. The same was true for the nearby cities of Cambria and Hibernia. Creone, the only other major settlement on the southern continent, was likewise sparsely populated as most of the workers flocked towards the larger cities on the northern continent.

That wasn't to say it was deserted. The mining operations were still crucial to the economy of Centaura and the system as a whole, and Hadrian was a hub of manufacturing. While Caledonia was the commercial core of the system, Hadrian was where everything was constructed. Factories were plentiful, and a constant stream of air-traffic flowed in and out of the three airports in the city's outskirts, and from the space elevator in the foothills of the nearby mountains to the south.

Twitch had only been in Hadrian a few hours, but already he found himself liking it more than Caledonia. The city itself was less chaotic, though the air felt hot and stifling. This far west, Prox still hung low in the sky, just touching the horizon. It helped that Amy had provided them with a fancy hotel room to act as a base of operations. The hotel was one of the tallest buildings in the city, and from their window Twitch could see almost all of Hadrian.

The starat grinned as he swished his tail, looking out of the window. David had sprawled out on the bed almost as soon as they had arrived, and he had still yet to move properly. He had barely slept through most of the last day as he had watched over his partner. Twitch didn't feel like he could sit down. He had spent long enough doing so on the shuttle across the ocean, and he felt like sitting or lying down would be a waste of his new legs. Instead he just stared out the window, admiring the view as his hands gently stroked through the synthetic fur covering his thighs.

"We should try the church first, I think," Twitch said. He didn't turn back to face David as he spoke, but the room was small enough that his voice would carry easily across to the bed.

"The church?" David replied. His voice was muffled as he didn't lift his head, speaking directly into the pillow.

"Yeah, I can see one from here. Looks very classical. Stone building, lots of spires," Twitch replied, pointing to a building on the far side of the city.

This time David did lift his head. Twitch could see the reflection moving in the windows. "It's not very subtle, is it? Do we just go there and ask directly for the cardinal?"

Twitch giggled a little and shook his head. He turned around on his toes to look towards David again. "No, of course not. But we can go there and listen around. Act interested in the church itself, and then see what information we can pick up on. See if we can find Kellie's brother, maybe."

David twitched his muzzle as he slowly sat up on the bed. "I suppose we can do that. I certainly don't have any better ideas at the moment," he said. He rubbed his hands over his eyes and groaned. "This Denitchev Drive had better be bloody important and something only you can fix. Or break. I'm grateful she got your legs, but why us?"

Twitch had no answer to that. He didn't have any idea why he had been chosen to hunt down Cardinal Erik and work out what the Inquisition were doing with a Denitchev Drive. He was just a starat from Ceres with no real experience beyond how to fix things. That's what he was good at. One of the best mechanics on the little dwarf planet, but this was all alien to him. He had no skills in espionage or finding hidden enemies. All he could do was turn around and look down over the city again, his hands clasped behind his back. Somewhere out there was Cardinal Erik. Twitch could only hope they found him before he found them.

***

As Twitch had expected, the church was a traditional design. He had never been into one of the holy buildings before, but he had seen images of them before, when some disgruntled Vatican official had tried to persuade the starats of Ceres that they were abominations and deserved their position of slavery in the empire.

The church was situated in the outer suburbs of the city, close enough to the outskirts that there were frequent wide expanses of crimson grass, rather than a dense network of buildings clustered on top of each other. The stone masonry of the church made it stand out easily from the rest of the buildings nearby. It was physically separated from everything around it by a small area of parkland, filled with imported plants from Terra. The splash of greenery felt strange amongst the red-tinged native plants beyond the park walls.

The front gate of the park was open, but neither of the two starats wanted to walk through just yet. There was something about the church that felt ominous and cold as it glowed in the last light from Prox. Instead, they sat on a bench opposite the park, just watching the people walk past. Few walked into the church, with most just walking past the park without even looking in.

Most of the people who passed them were humans, though there were a few starats amongst their number as well. They tended to cluster together in their species though, with little mingling between them. There were never starats on their own either, with all of them going by in groups of at least three. Twitch's ears flicked as he thought of the reports of starats being attacked in the region. Most starat tails were tucked low. They were all scared of something, but none of them even slowed down as their eyes passed over the two starats sitting on the bench opposite the park.

Of the few to go into the church grounds, all of them were human. Most were short, which appeared to be the norm amongst Centaurans because of the higher gravity of the planet. One though, was much taller. That grabbed Twitch's attention, and he squinted to look across the road at the human. It definitely wasn't Cardinal Erik, but the human was certainly from the empire.

Twitch nudged David in the ribs and gestured towards the church. "We should go in and see if anyone knows anything," he whispered. He grinned widely, trying to hide his nervousness. He doubted David would be fooled.

"Fine, but we need to be careful," David replied reluctantly.

Together, the two starats cautiously crossed the road and hung around the open gates for a few moments. The gates were mostly made of iron bars. Written across the top was a phrase in a language Twitch didn't know.

Twitch was the first to step across the threshold into the church grounds. The grass was green beneath his feet, and the oak trees swayed gently in the wind. He had barely experienced Terra, but he imagined that most of it had to feel like this. Green and vibrant, but also feeling somehow old. He brushed his hand over the wall, surprised to find that what he had thought was moss on the stone was in fact just painted on. A little residue came off on his fingers, and he brushed it through his fur.

The grass was springy beneath Twitch's bare feet, but there was something strange about it. He crouched down and tugged on a blade. It stretched, but it didn't snap. His ears flicked as he glanced up to David. "It's fake. Everything seems fake," he said with a frown. He placed his palm flat on the ground as he felt a miniscule vibration through his feet, but he couldn't detect it at all with his hand. "Can you feel that?"

"Feel what?" David asked. He crouched down and placed his hand by Twitch's, but he shook his head. "Can't feel anything."

Twitch kept his mouth shut as a human walked past them, leaving the church and heading back out to the street. The human looked down at them for just a moment, but he didn't say anything to them.

"Come on, let's have a look inside," Twitch muttered. He scampered across the fake grass of the lawn, before peering into the relative darkness of the church. The wide, wooden doors were wedged open with a couple of door-stops, and inside Twitch could hear the soft murmur of chanting voices.

The air inside the church was cool, and Twitch hugged his arms around his chest as he moved a little further inside. Small vents near the ceiling blasted out cold air, keeping everything frigid despite the open doors letting in some of the warmth from outside. The small foyer quickly opened out into the main chamber of the church. The high ceiling was dominated by several arches of stone, and the stained-glass windows threw incredible patterns of coloured light across the orderly rows of pews. Outside was too dark to throw such illumination through the church, so Twitch wasn't sure what was casting the light across the glass windows. He scratched his hand behind his ear as he looked around at them all. Light streamed in equally from both sides.

Four humans were sat down in the pews. They all had their heads bowed in muttered prayer and paid no attention to the two starats who had just joined them. There was no sign of the Terran human.

All around the walls were images of the human called Veritas. Though there were thousands of recorded images of the human, there wasn't a single photograph of the man on display. Everything was painted and hand-crafted. Twitch flicked his ears and turned away from them, his attention switching to two small doors, one on each side of the church. Both were open, leading into a tiny chamber that seemed only just large enough for two people to sit down. At the far end of the church was the altar. Behind it, he could see a couple of doors leading to another pair of rooms.

With a cautious eye on the humans praying, Twitch slowly made his way around the edge of the church. David followed just behind. Again, Twitch could feel a very slight vibration through the floor, but as he looked around nothing seemed to react to it. He tensed his toes mid-stride. How much more sensitive were his new legs?

As Twitch approached the altar, he was able to see through one of the archways beyond. A flight of stairs led down, but before he could investigate, one of the humans coughed and called out. "You can't go back there."

Twitch spun on his toes and tilted his head as he looked towards the human who had called out. "Why not?"

The woman who had spoken rose to her feet. She was elderly and her back hunched over, bringing her almost fully down to the height of a starat. She walked without a cane, though she did need to lean on the side of the pews as she approached the two starats. "You're not a priest. Only priests can go behind there. Were you wanting to see Father Nichols?"

Twitch pinned his ears back. He had been expecting the old woman to challenge them for being starats. This wasn't so bad. He grinned weakly. "Is he around?"

The old woman shook her head. "Not today. Not any day, it seems. I don't imagine he'll be here until after next sunset. He's often away these days," she said. She slowly started to turn around and return to a pew. "He's always away. No respect for his congregation anymore. For six months he's barely been here."

"Do you know where he goes?" Twitch asked.

One of the other humans tutted quietly to themselves, but the old lady turned back for a moment. "I wish I knew that. He just disappears entirely, and no one is able to contact him for days on end."

"Well, thank you for your help anyway," Twitch said, smiling a little wider at the old woman as she sat back down again. She returned the smile before bowing her head in prayer again. "We'll come back another time."

Twitch started to lead David back through the church, towards the open doors. Before they made it out, they were stopped by the human in the back row. The human appeared young, with blotchy skin and greasy black hair that hung down almost to his shoulders. He reached out and grabbed hold of Twitch's wrist. "She doesn't know what she's talking about," he said in a low whisper. He gripped even tighter around Twitch's hand when he tried to pull away. "Father Nichols never leaves. I live across the road, and I've never seen him walk out of these doors."

"Couldn't he just leave when you're not watching?" David asked, stepping up close to Twitch's side.

The human sneered. "I thought that at first too, but I found it strange. I've got sensors up now to watch everyone who comes in and out. Father Nichols is never one of them."

Twitch pulled his hand out of the human's grip. "So if he's not here, how does he leave?"

The human shrugged. "There no other doors out the back, and no way out of the gardens without leaping the walls. And Father Nichols is not a sprightly young man anymore."

"So he's still in the building?" Twitch asked.

"It would seem so. But there's nowhere here to hide for so long, and to block off all communication," the human replied gruffly. He held out his hand again, and Twitch recoiled, but this time it was just to shake hands rather than gripping onto his wrist again. "Name's Tyler, by the way."

"Well, thank you for the talk," David said, interrupting before Twitch could introduce himself. The larger starat held his arm around Twitch and started to pull him away from the human. Reluctantly, Twitch allowed himself to be led away.

"Couple of starats like yourself had better be careful around here," Tyler warned, speaking to the retreating backs of the two starats. "It's dangerous around here for your species. Especially if they're asking questions about the church. Trust me. I should know."

"Why do you say that?" Twitch asked nervously. David applied a little pressure on his shoulder, but Twitch stood his ground. His claws tug into the masonry beneath his feet.

"Starats being attacked. Stolen away. Never any witnesses for it, but rumours travel," Tyler said. He leaned back into his pew and faced the front of the church again. "Rumours come from somewhere. It's not safe for you. Soon it won't be safe for any of us."

Twitch suppressed a shudder and David guided him out of the church. He didn't look back at the human, and the human didn't say anything further that he could hear. David didn't let go of Twitch even after they had stepped back out onto the street. The larger starat walked quickly, at a pace Twitch would once have struggled with, but his new legs meant he was easily able to keep pace.

"I don't think he was safe," David said, after they had put the church far behind them. He still didn't let go of Twitch.

"He was a bit creepy," Twitch said in agreement. His ears folded down and he wrinkled his muzzle up in disgust. His wrist was still a little sore from where the human had grabbed hold of it so hard. "But I think we need to go back there."

"What? Why? We didn't learn anything," David protested.

Twitch slowed down and pulled David back. He paused for a moment and leaned against a nearby wall. "I felt something, both in the gardens and in the church. There was a vibration in the ground."

"I didn't feel that," David said, shaking his head.

"I know," Twitch replied. He lifted one leg up and flexed his toes. "I think these are much more sensitive than before, which is why I could feel it. There's something below the church, and I could see some stairs behind the altar. I think we need to go down there and have a look around."

David blinked and scratched behind his folded ear. "Isn't that just the... what do they call it? The presbytery? There's nothing interesting in there."

"There's definitely something unusual about it though, I'm sure," Twitch replied. He grabbed out at David's hand and held it against his chest. "Trust me on this, there's something interesting down there, and we might be able to learn something."

"We don't know that though," David replied with a sigh. He didn't pull his hand back though, letting Twitch gently stroke through his fur. "We don't know if the cardinal has been around here either. He's who we're looking for."

Twitch didn't reply at first. The gears were slowly turning in his head and he thought of something. He didn't like the thought, and it already scared him a little, but it was a possible lead. "That human. Tyler. He's been recording the church," he said slowly. David's eyes widened in fear, but he didn't interrupt. "I'm sure there's not too many Terran humans who go in. He might have seen Cardinal Erik."

David's tail curled up between his legs. "I don't know, Twitch. He seemed dangerous."

Twitch exhaled slowly, still rubbing his partner's hand in his own. "I don't see what other option we have at the moment. We'll look out for each other."

David sighed and leaned in close. He rested his forehead against Twitch's and gave him a gentle kiss. "Alright, we'll do it. Tomorrow though. I think he was right with one thing, and that's how we're not too safe around here. I don't want to stay for too long if I can help it."

"Sounds fair," Twitch replied with a quick nod. He gave David another quick kiss back, before wriggling free of his partner. He started to make his way along the street again, back towards the centre of the city and the towering hotel that was their temporary home. He grinned and spun around to walk backwards, facing David. "Say, maybe we should find a teleporter and break it like it did for Captain Rhys. If we're human, there won't be anything to worry about."

David stuck his tongue out in disgust. "Absolutely not. I'd much rather keep my fur, thank you very much."

"Yeah, me too," Twitch giggled in response. He didn't know how humans could manage without fur or tails. In that regard, Twitch knew Captain Rhys had been very lucky indeed.

It was just a shame most humans couldn't see things that way.

***

The western horizon still glowed with the last of Prox's illumination. It wasn't a bright light, but it was still fierce enough that Twitch wasn't able to properly look towards it without shielding his eyes first. Even as Prox gradually vanished from view, the electromagnetic shields that surrounded the planet provided a spectacular light show. They lit up brightly on regularly occasions as the planet was bombarded by more radiation from the fierce dwarf star.

Twitch could have sat for hours and just watched the slow descent of Prox. It barely seemed to move across the sky, a painful crawl that would take hours to just vanish beneath the horizon. It was so much slower than it had been on Ceres, which saw two sunrises in a Terran day. Even on Terra, the movement of Sol across the sky had seemed slow. Prox didn't seem to move at all. Though the starat lingered to watch the last rays disappear from the horizon, he reluctantly pulled himself away from the hotel windows at David's insistence. They had other things to do. Twitch's eyes lingered on the distant church spire for a moment, visible only as a shadow in the gloom. Soon they would be right outside it again.

The journey across the city was an easy one. In the middle of Hadrian, there was a healthy mixture of starats and humans, so much so that Twitch never once felt uncomfortable. But again, when they reached the outer regions of the city close to the church, the number of starats steadily decreased, and those that they did see walked with hunched shoulders and quick footsteps in large groups.

The church towered high over almost all of the buildings out of the city centre, and as such was visible from a great distance. Twitch tried not to look at the spires as he felt a sense of dread growing with each step closer.

Everything looked much the same, even in the early night darkness. The stained-glass windows twinkled with their own light, and a bell noisily chimed out the time from the top of the spire. Everything looked quaint, but Twitch could sense the malice behind it. Or maybe that was the lingering effects of the coffee he'd had in the morning. He couldn't be sure. David usually barred him from coffee, but he had woken up early so he could see Prox dip below the horizon, and he had needed something more to wake him up properly.

"Tyler said he lives opposite the church," Twitch said, bouncing excitedly on his toes. He stood outside the gates to the gardens with his hands resting on his hips. He looked across at the row of nearly identical houses opposite. "Do we just knock on the door of one of them and ask where he lives?"

David pointed to the house just left of opposite the church grounds. "Or we could try the house that has the cameras and sensors in the front garden," he said with a grin.

Twitch looked across the road and noticed the plethora of cameras installed across one of the houses, all pointing in their direction. He grinned up at David and tucked in his tail. "Yeah, that will probably be the one. Just making sure you were being observant."

"Sure you were," David replied, lightly swatting Twitch across the ears. "Come on. If we're going to get ourselves murdered, we might as well get it over with."

Twitch hurried across the road after David. He knew his partner had only been joking, but he couldn't help but feel worried. The human had definitely given off an uncomfortable aura the previous day, and Twitch knew they wouldn't be going back to him if they didn't need to know that Cardinal Erik had been here. He didn't believe he could trust a human who was so flagrantly spying upon the church opposite.

His tail twitched as the front door opened before David even reached it. Tyler looked down at them and swept some of his oily hair from off his face. "Saw you coming," the human said, tapping the camera perched above the door frame. He glanced up and down the road, before standing to one side. "Better come in quick before anyone sees you."

Twitch was reluctant to be welcomed so easily into the human's home, and he shivered in worry as he stepped inside after David. The door was closed behind them, and the two starats were shepherded through to a dirty living room. They sat down on a sofa, and Tyler swept aside a stack of books to sit on a chair opposite. "So," the human said, hands clasped across his lap. "Why have you returned?"

"How long have you been watching the church?" David asked. He looked out through the grimy windows, where the church was just about visible through the dirt smeared over the glass.

"Three months now. Two with the cameras. Why? You don't look like the sort to be protecting the priest," Tyler said, his eyes narrowing suspiciously.

"We're looking for someone who may have come here. We want to know if you've seen him," Twitch explained quickly.

Tyler leaned back in his seat and rested his head in his hands. "You want me to look through months of footage to try to find one person? Impossible," the human said. He clicked his tongue and shook his head. "I can only track for Father Nichols because I know what he looks like and can train the AI to search for him. Unless this person has some very distinctive features, it can't be done."

"He's Terran," Twitch said. He tapped his finger on his knee. "Well, Martian specifically."

That made Tyler lean forward again. "Martian? So you're searching for someone from the Vatican?" His face twisted in thought for a few moments. "I still don't know how I could find him. I doubt he'd be in his vestments."

"Height," David said with a sigh, having to point out the obvious connotation to the human. "He's from Mars, so he'll be taller than any other human from around here. There can't be that many Terrans going to church here, can there?"

"I didn't think of that," Tyler said, rubbing his hand over his unshaven chin. "I could probably reprogram the AI to go through its history and filter for anyone significantly above average height."

"Would you be able to do that for us, please?" Twitch asked.

The human rose to his feet, frantically gesturing for Twitch to sit back down as he started to rise as well. "Stay there. My set up is secret, alright?" Tyler said. He started to move across the room, before clicking his fingers and pointing towards the windows. "Close the curtains, if you would. I don't want someone to look in and see you."

Before Twitch had chance to ask anything, Tyler slipped out of the small room and closed the door behind him. The starat heard the snick of a key in a lock. They were locked inside. Twitch tried the handle, but he wasn't surprised when it didn't turn. He grimaced back towards David, who pulled closed the dusty curtains to hide them from the outside. He doubted anyone would be able to look through the filthy windows anyway.

"I hope this guy hasn't gone to get a gun," David said tersely. His tail was held rigidly behind him, stiff and almost entirely unmoving. "It wouldn't exactly be a glamorous way to go."

"He'll be fine, I hope. I think," Twitch replied. He couldn't feel certain about it though, and he looked nervously towards the door as something crashed loudly beyond it. They faced a nervous wait before Tyler returned, when they would learn whether or not the human could be trusted.

***

Just a few minutes passed by before the door slowly creaked open again. Twitch had jumped back up to his feet as soon as he had heard the door unlock. The human held his finger to his lips as the door opened, and he gestured for the starats to come out of the front room. He turned on his heel as soon as the two starats started to move.

Twitch wanted to ask Tyler what was going on, but instead he just reached back and grabbed hold of David's hand as the two starats followed the human down a dark corridor. Twitch's nose wrinkled at the unclean scents he picked up. Through an open door, he caught sight of a massive bank of computers, but that wasn't where Tyler took them. Instead he opened a small door in the wall opposite. Twitch could have sworn the wall had been smooth without any openings just a few moments earlier. Behind the hidden door a flight of wooden stairs descended into inky darkness.

"Down there, quickly," Tyler whispered. His eyes were so wide, Twitch could see the whites all the way around his pale grey irises.

Twitch's ear flicked. "Really? Why?" he asked, a flutter of fear spreading from his heart.

"The Inquisition is here," Tyler replied, still keeping his voice to a low hiss. He gave Twitch a slight push towards the stairs. "Go, quickly. Hide down there and don't make a sound."

"For how long?" David asked. His voice shook.

"Until I say it's safe, now go."

Twitch took a deep breath as he took the first steps down into the darkness. David followed right behind his tail, and soon the darkness was absolute as Tyler closed the door with the two starats inside. Not a single strip of light made its way past the door.

Holding his hands out against the walls either side of the narrow staircase, Twitch slowly made his way down, further into the darkness. He didn't know what was going to be at the bottom, but still he kept going. A few voices started to talk above their heads. Twitch could just about hear Tyler's nasally voice amongst them.

Twitch's leg jarred against concrete floor as the stairs suddenly came to an abrupt end. He found himself on solid, flat floor once more, but the walls didn't seem to open out at all. He took another couple of cautious steps forward and kicked against something hard. He suppressed a whimper of pain that was more from habit than his foot actually hurting, and slowly brought his hands around to feel over what was in front of him. His neck and shoulder fur fluffed up as David's hand on his shoulder surprised him.

A door was in front of him. Twitch's hands brushed over a handle, and he slowly opened the door. It slid open without a sound, and a few pinpricks of red light made themselves known to Twitch's eyes. Contrasted with the absolute darkness the light pierced through, they were almost blinding.

Twitch stepped beyond the door and closed it behind David when he felt his partner standing beside him, a brief silhouette blocking out a few of the red lights. The moment the door closed something clicked above their heads, and a couple of lights switched themselves on. Twitch threw a hand in front of his eyes to shield them from the sudden glare.

When his eyes adjusted to the light again, Twitch realised they were stood in what appeared to be a safety bunker. One side of the room was dedicated to shelves of tinned food, and there was a second door that the starat assumed led through to some sort of refrigerator. A small bed was tucked up in one corner, though it showed no signs of being used at all. A couple of computers had been the source of the red lights, and they had switched on with the lights.

David approached the computers and sat down in the chair in front of them. He wiggled the mouse as everything booted up. The first program to load was a live video feed. Twitch's fingers gripped on the back of the chair as he recognised the rooms upstairs. Tyler stepped across the screen, his hands wringing.

"Do you think they could see the lights?" Twitch asked nervously. He glanced back towards the door and noticed a couple of locks on it. Before David answered, he scampered across the room and locked them all. He didn't want to take any chances. Twitch paused as he looked at the door. There was something strange about it, and it took him a couple of moments to realise what it was. "It's an airlock. Why is there an airlock down here?"

David clicked around the video feed a few times, finding that he could change which cameras were on display. Eventually they were able to see who was the cause for Tyler's distress. Three other humans were inside the house with them. They all appeared to be Centauran, given their relative heights. Nothing seemed to stand out about them, but Twitch noticed that they were all wearing a gold pin on their collars, which appeared to be in the shape of a religious cross.

"Is there any sound?" Twitch asked.

David found the volume controls and slowly raised them. At first there was nothing to hear but the thud of heavy boots on the floorboards. Eventually an unfamiliar voice spoke. "Are you that mistrustful of everything, Brother Tyler?"

"I think I have every reason to doubt everyone," Tyler retorted. He stepped forward into view of one of the cameras. His eyes briefly looked up, but then they flicked back down to the humans in front of him. Twitch could only see the slightly-balding back of one of the other human's heads. "I supported your cause loyally and was given no support when I needed it most. I have no reason to believe you're in it for anything but your own personal gain."

The human with the balding head took a step forward, and Tyler recoiled back slightly. "My dear fallen angel, is that why you've taken to fraternising with starats?"

Twitch could see Tyler's eyes widen through the screens. "Fraternising with... I don't know what you mean."

"We have reports of you conversing with starats and even welcoming them into your home," the human said. Even though Twitch could only see the back of his head, he could tell the human was smiling widely. "What do you have to say for yourself?"

Tyler seemed to squirm beneath the gaze of the three humans. He brushed the hair away from his eyes, then held up one finger. "One, that's rubbish. I wouldn't do that." He held up a second finger. "Two, I'm not part of your order anymore, so I'm not bound by your rules. If I did have starats here, which I haven't, then you don't have authority to stop me."

The balding human laughed. "Oh my dear, do you know what the punishment for lying to the Inquisition is? Of course you do, and yet you still do it. You must be feeling brave today, or very stupid," the human said. He snapped his fingers, and the two humans either side of him darted forward to grab hold of Tyler, who wasn't able to get away in time. "We have confirmed reports that starats were in here three Prox cycles ago. And you may think we no longer have any authority over you, but you would be so, so wrong. You're going to be coming with us for further questions."

Tyler started to struggle, attempting to throw off the two humans who had a grip on him, but they didn't let him go anywhere. "No, please. It's not what you think," Tyler protested, but the balding human didn't appear to be listening.

"The end times are coming, Brother Tyler. It would do well to prepare for them with us," the bald human said.

"I am prepared," Tyler snapped back. He still tried to pull his arms free, but his captors weren't giving him any slack.

"Take him away," the human said, snapping his fingers again. The two others started to drag Tyler out of his home, easily able to overpower the smaller man. The balding human remained for a few seconds longer, and he turned around slowly so Twitch could finally see his face properly. The human's nose was wrinkled in disgust. "Stinks of starat in here too."

The human's hand brushed along the wall in the dirty corridor, and for a moment brushed against where the secret door was hidden away. Twitch's breath caught in his throat, but then the human turned away. He rubbed his fingers together, lip curled as he looked down at his hand. "Absolutely filthy."

Twitch watched the monitors carefully as the human left after the captive Tyler. The two starats watched through the cameras as Tyler was led across the road and into the church opposite.

"What happened there?" Twitch asked nervously. His hand moved from the back of the chair to rest on David's shoulder.

"It seems like the church has more power here than we realised," David replied. He reached up to rest his hand over Twitch's. "And we're not the first starats Tyler has had here. We were just unlucky that they came to see him now."

Twitch breathed out slowly. His shoulder fur still hadn't flattened down yet, and he nervously bounded on his toes. "We should wait down here for a little bit, I think. Just to make sure they're gone."

"That's a good idea. Then we should get as far away as possible from here, I think," David said. His tail thumped against the back of the chair, which had no hole for him to sit comfortably. "Tell Amy this is too big for us, and we get away quickly."

Twitch's ears flattened against his head. "And when she takes my legs and tail away for failing to complete our task?"

David sighed, his ears dropping down as well. He leaned back in the chair and rubbed his hands over his muzzle. "She's not going to do that."

"How do you know?" Twitch squeaked in fear. He stroked his hands down his thighs and shivered. "She might."

David groaned. "She's thrown us in too deep. But I guess we don't have a choice, do we?"

"I don't think so, no," Twitch said with a shake of his head. He grimaced and twitched his tail. It looked strange, to see that his tail fur hadn't puffed up despite his slight distress. Usually it would look even thicker than usual, but instead his fur was still smooth and tidy. He slowly stroked his hands through it, still not used to the feel of the synthetic strands against his fingers.

"There is something strange going on here, I'm sure," David said quietly. The starat tapped his fingers against the desk as he fell quiet with thought. "Why would he have an airlock down here? You're right, that doesn't make sense."

Twitch didn't disturb his partner's thoughts, instead turning away to idly look through the rest of the shelter. He had to wonder what sort of person Tyler was, to feel the need for this sort of thing hidden below his house, and with enough supplies to last quite some time. Based on how much food was stored, Twitch had to guess there was enough for several weeks at least. He didn't understand it. There was something about Tyler that didn't make sense. He shivered and flicked his tail. The balding human had called Tyler 'Brother'. Had Tyler once been a part of the religious order? How closely related were the Inquisition and the Vatican? He didn't know, and nor did he know where to find answers.

Twitch found a stack of papers on the desk behind the computer monitors. At first he was going to dismiss them as unimportant, but then he realised they all had the same golden cross symbol that he had seen on the collars of the Inquisition humans. Able to see the symbol a bit clearer, he was able to recognise that it was two golden swords crossed in the shape of the religious symbol. He quickly flicked through them. There all seemed to be letters of communication, back and forth between a few different people. Twitch recognised none of the names, though a few kept appearing regularly. Chief Inquisitor Richards was one, and Bjorn Olegsson was another of the frequent names, but there appeared to be no direct reference to what they did. The final name that regularly appeared was Tim Shawn. Based off the information Twitch could work out from the letters, they seemed to be high up in the Centauran government.

"Anything interesting in there?" David asked.

Twitch glanced up from the letters and shrugged his shoulders. "Not sure. I don't know who these people are, and there's nothing in here that we didn't already know really. They mention some plans for expanding towards Caledonia, but that's it," Twitch replied. There had been no reference to Cardinal Erik, or what role Tyler had once played within the Inquisition.

Twitch moved the stack of papers and managed to dislodge something else on the table. Something metallic crashed to the floor and shattered. Immediately, the two starats froze and stared at the computer monitors, but there didn't appear to be any movement from upstairs. Twitch's heart hammered as he carefully crouched down to see what he had broken.

"It's a shield emitter. That makes even less sense," Twitch said. He frowned and looked up to David. "Something this big would probably cover an area the size of this house. Perhaps a little larger."

David scratched behind his ear. "Well, they don't appear to be coming back, so I think it should be safe for us to go now," David said. He glanced back at the screens for a moment, flicking through the various cameras. Everything was still and quiet, both inside the house and out. "Take those papers. Amy might be able to make more sense of them than us."

Twitch slipped the small backpack off his shoulders and put the thick stack of papers inside. Something kept clicking at the back of his mind. There was something important about the information he had read, but he couldn't connect the dots just yet. He squared his shoulders as he prepared to leave the small bunker. David stood by his side, and together they unlocked the airlock. The moment the door unlatched, the lights switched off, leaving them in just the glow of the computer monitors. A few seconds later and they too switched off, plunging them back into near-total darkness.

Slowly, the two starats ascended up the staircase again. Twitch fumbled around for some way to open the door at the top, and cautiously they emerged back into the corridors of Tyler's home. There was no sound, and no one called out to them as they carefully closed the door behind them. David started to make straight for the front door, but Twitch hesitated. Tyler's computers were still on.

Twitch hissed to David to come back, then slipped into the room opposite the hidden door. The room was noticeably warmer from all the computers, all powered on and showing various clips of footage from inside and outside the house.

"What are you doing?" David said quietly, coming into the room with Twitch.

"We came here to see if Cardinal Erik had come here. We might as well see if Tyler had been able to work out if he had," Twitch replied. He flicked through some of the screens, trying to find evidence of Tyler's work, then gasped as he noticed a list of saved images, all dated within the last half hour. Twitch quickly searched through them. Most of them he didn't recognise, but then one face appeared. One that made him hiss in displeasure. Cardinal Erik. He kept searching through all the images. Cardinal Erik's face appeared several more times. In the past two weeks, Cardinal Erik had gone into the church half a dozen times, starting the day Twitch had been attacked. Not once did it appear like the cardinal had left the church through the same exit.

"Well we know he was here, but where did he go? When was the most recent one?" David asked.

Twitch flicked through the images again, finding the most recent one. His fur itched as he realised when it had been. "About an hour after we left yesterday."

"And you still want to go in there?" David asked, his voice descending into a small squeak.

Twitch nodded his head. He didn't want to. He wanted to flee as far as possible from the cardinal, but he felt a duty to go after him. Besides, he wanted to keep his legs, and was scared that Amy wouldn't let him keep them should he turn away now. He found a way to print off the images, then folded up the pieces of paper and slipped them into his pocket. He knew they may need to know when Cardinal Erik had gone into the church.

"Alright, let's get out of here before any of them come back," Twitch said nervously. He still couldn't hear anything from outside, but he didn't want to linger around any longer, just in case Tyler told the Inquisition about their presence. It had sounded like the human had been disillusioned with his time in the Inquisition and had tried to abandon them, but Twitch didn't want to take that risk.

Twitch led David outside. They quickly closed Tyler's door behind them and fled, not to the church, but around the corner where they couldn't be seen from the religious structure. They didn't want to risk anyone from the Inquisition still lingering and seeing them. There were no sounds of pursuit at all, so Twitch could only assume they had gotten away safely.

"We need to get into that church, and down the stairs at the back. There's something interesting down there, I know it," Twitch said. He leaned back against a stone wall and closed his eyes for a few moments. Again he could feel a slight vibration beneath his feet. His ears flicked slightly. He knew several humans had just gone into the church, likely straight out the back. Then there was the vibration. Was it some form of underground transport? Twitch flicked his nose. It would certainly explain why no one seemed to come back out of the church.

"What if Tyler isn't the only one watching the church though? What if the Inquisition are too?" David asked.

Twitch glanced across to his partner, having to look up as he always did. "If they were, then they would have been looking for us already. I don't think they know about us yet."

David breathed out slowly. "I can only hope you're right. We just need to get into the church when it's empty."

"I think I know what to do," Twitch said. His hand sought David's, and he squeezed gently around it. "Come on, we shouldn't waste any time."

Together, they hurried back inside the church. Just inside were two small chambers either side of the main doors. They were behind the rows of pews, and as Twitch had expected, none of the half a dozen human worshippers turned around as the two starats entered. No priest was stood by the altar to notice them, and they quickly slipped into the small chamber on the right of the church. They closed the door almost fully behind them, and then just needed to wait.

Peering through the crack between the door and its frame, Twitch and David were able to keep an eye on how many humans were in the church. They didn't know how long humans tended to stay in prayer, or how many of them would come to the church during the day, but they knew there had to be some time when it became empty. They would need to be prepared to hurry when that time came.

Twitch was glad they had thought to bring a little bit of food with them, as the minutes kept ticking by. There were always at least two humans in the main room of the church, preventing them from leaving. He had grown hungry, but David had been able to produce a few scraps of food they had kept from their dinner the previous day. It wasn't much, but it was enough to sate the hunger for the time being.

Finally, the last two humans stood up to leave. Twitch was on watch at the door, and he frantically gestured to David as the two humans left together. Though his vantage point was limited, Twitch could see all the pews were empty, and he slowly pushed open the door to make sure that his judgement was correct. No one was there, and though he could hear a couple of voices outside, the way to the altar was clear.

Without making a sound, Twitch and David scampered down the side of the church, keeping one wary eye back towards the main doors. No one called out to them, and Twitch's heart hammered in his chest as they quickly crept up to the great stone altar. He glanced back quickly. He couldn't see anyone outside near the doors, and the voices out there were receding. A crazy thought ran through his head, and he grabbed hold of David's hand before his partner could get too far away.

"What are you doing?" David hissed. He tried to tug his hand away, but Twitch's grip was too strong.

"Say I do," Twitch said, a grin slowly spreading across his muzzle.

"I do?" David replied. His right ear curled down in confusion.

"Hah! You just married me," Twitch giggled gleefully. He pulled David into an embrace and a kiss, and he was rewarded with a swat across the ears.

"That's not how that works, you idiot," David said, but Twitch noticed the swish of his partner's tail, and the wide grin on his face. David leaned in to kiss Twitch again. "Come on, before someone sees us."

This time, Twitch allowed himself to be pulled along. Once behind the altar, he doubted anyone would be able to see them. The two archways were clearly visible now. One stayed straight and level, going into a small room a few paces beyond. The other descended down a steep stairwell. That was the one that kept Twitch's attention. Before his courage could fail him, he hurried down the stairs, with David right behind. He didn't know what he expected to find at the bottom.

At the bottom of the stairs was a small room with stone walls. A single light flickered on the slightly sloped ceiling. There was nothing special about the room. It appeared to be just a changing room for the priests. A few robes were hung up on one wall, and there was a small sink with a dripping tap opposite the door. Three cups were stored next to the sink.

"This isn't right," Twitch said quietly. He paced around the room, but he could see nothing interesting or out of place. He brushed his hand over the robes. They were crimson in colour, with gold trim around the edges. Twitch was reminded of the robes Cardinal Erik wore on Ceres. His tail twitched and the fur on the back of his neck prickled at the thought of the cardinal.

"There's nothing down here," David said. He stood with his arms resting on his hips in the middle of the room.

Twitch slowly turned on his toes to face David, then paused when he noticed the gold symbol on the wall behind him. It was the same crossed swords again. The cross wasn't on the wall straight, and Twitch noticed a couple of scuff marks on the stone behind it. The cross had been moved. "Can you reach that?" Twitch asked, knowing that it was too far up the wall for him to reach without climbing on something.

David turned to look up at the cross. His ears flicked as he approached it. He stretched up as far as he could reach, just about able to grab hold of the bottom of the crossed swords. He yanked it to the side, and with a scrape of metal on stone, the cross moved. Something behind the wall clanked, and David pushed on the stone. It opened like a door.

Twitch bounced on his toes and hugged David from behind. "There we go, I knew there was something down here," he said happily, before being hushed by David. His smile didn't leave his muzzle, but he nodded and fell quiet. They didn't know who would be waiting down the secret passageway for them. They would have to be careful and quiet.

The corridor beyond the hidden door gently sloped down. The way was lit, but the lights were few and far between. The occasional rumble that passed through his feet felt a little stronger, and he could feel it through his hands down whenever they brushed against the rocky walls. Metal grating soon covered the stone floor, and a few small stairs followed. A light was growing at the end of the tunnel, more intense than anything that lit the way. Twitch's tail swished nervously behind him.

They turned a corner, and Twitch gasped in surprise at what he saw. Built underground, beneath the church, was a massive structure that looked familiar to Twitch, but he just couldn't place what it reminded him of. It was constructed in a massive cavern, though Twitch couldn't tell from a glance whether it was natural or artificial. Structures of metal rose up from the ground, a vast distance away from the walkway Twitch found himself on. The walkway snaked down the side of the cavern towards the distant floor. He could see a few humans on the floor, with flashlights moving this way and that as they walked between the buildings. There was no natural light, but several floodlights were built into the ceiling of stone, shining down on the facility below.

"Well, I knew there would be something down here," Twitch said beneath his breath.

"But what is it?" David replied, just as quietly.

The ground began to rumble again, and Twitch grabbed hold of the walkway railings. He looked down, just in time to see a few flashes of a vehicle rapidly decelerating. It followed some tracks that led almost directly beneath them, to come to a rest beside some of the structures nearly in the middle of the cavern. A couple of people got off the vehicle a few seconds later, and Twitch's grin widened. He was right. There was some sort of transport down here.

"This has to have something to do with the Vatican," Twitch whispered excitedly.

David placed his hand on Twitch's shoulder. His mouth hung open slightly. His fingers tensed. "What name did you say was on those papers again?"

Twitch frowned and racked his memory. "Uh, Richards was one. Bjorn Olegsson. And Shawn."

David's grip squeezed even tighter. "Shawn. Oh shit."

Twitch glanced up to see a look of pure dread etched into his partner. His ear flicked in confusion, before suddenly he realised. His throat constricted. "President Shawn."

"This is too big. We have to go," David urged.

Twitch didn't move right away. Instead he slowly looked back to the towering metal structures in the darkness of the cavern. A spotlight shone against the gleaming side walls. It all clicked in Twitch's mind. It had taken him a little while for his mind to catch up with what he was seeing, because it was impossible that such a thing could be so big.

"David…" Twitch said uncertainly. He pulled his partner back to the edge of the walkway. He pointed with one shaking hand to the towering machine. "I found the Denitchev Drive."

"We go now," David said, more urgently this time. "We tell Amy. Hell, we tell Maxwell. We tell everyone who will listen. But this is not something we can do."

Twitch bit his lip and glanced down towards the massive facility. He then nodded his head, but before they could go anywhere, voices reached Twitch's ears. They came from the tunnel they had just come through. He exchanged a quick, alarmed look with David. They only had one way to go. Down.

"Hurry," David said. He grabbed hold of Twitch's hand and together they fled down into the massive cave.

Twitch had never been more scared. He was running into the worst danger he could possibly imagine, but at least he had David by his side. Together they ran. Towards the Inquisition. Towards the Vatican.

chapter twenty-two

Rhys stood his ground as the shuttle descended to the surface of Pluto. Opposite the airlock door was the wide ramp that could be opened for a surface landing. Rhys stared at the hinged door, his feet resting on the seam of metal where the door would open up. He knew they would not be able to connect to the airlocks of the Tombaugh Station, so they would be landing on the surface just outside the outer perimeter. There were sensor screens located around the shuttle, but he chose not to use them at all. He didn't want to see the dwarf planet rushing closer, with the lone port lit up brightly.

The Silver Fox was sat by the sensors, where he would be located for the duration of the mission. He was still armed, just in case, but his role would be to stay with the shuttle's computers and try to coordinate any potential changes in plan from relative safety. It was his voice that called out their arrival time as it diminished down to the final few seconds. Almost everyone remained in their seats and braced for the landing, but Rhys remained standing.

The shuttle struck the ground with a bang and a shudder that almost threw Rhys off his feet. A stumbled, he but stayed upright as a loud alarm wailed through the shuttle. A low hiss filled the shuttle as air was vented out of the main chamber to fill the storage cannisters. It took just a few seconds for the shuttle to go from a breathable atmosphere to a total vacuum. Rhys's helmet HUD flashed red in warning to keep his helmet firmly secured.

A second alarm flared. A silent red light flashed on and off as the metal beneath Rhys's feet began to move. The back of the shuttle began to open, and a ramp descended to the rusty red rocks of Pluto's surface.

Holding his bullet shield up to protect his face, Rhys stepped down. He could hear nothing outside his helmet, but he could see the shadows in front of him as his assault team followed right behind.

The second shuttle had landed just a few metres to the right. Aaron led his assault team out a few seconds after Rhys emerged. The gleaming white walls of the Tombaugh Station loomed high. They curved away in both directions to back onto the red cliffs behind the station. The main airlock into Tombaugh Station was right in front of them, allowing access to the surface of the dwarf planet. There was no resistance just yet, but Rhys knew there would be some soon. They would likely be waiting for them just inside the airlock.

Two humans moved forward, one from each shuttle. They approached the airlock door, with their backs protected by the drawn weapons of the two assault teams. There was a control panel to the side of the airlock door, which would normally only be opened by authorised personnel within the port. They had to bypass that, but it didn't take too long before the doors began to open.

Bullet shields were raised as the massive metallic doors began to grind open. In the external vacuum, everything was silent as they moved. All Rhys could hear was the occasional chatter through his helmet as Aaron and General Carson ordered a few soldiers into position. Rhys glanced back briefly to the soldiers behind him. Everyone was in position and ready to fire.

Inside the doors was a large airlock shrouded almost entirely in darkness. No lights lit up to illuminate the metal-walled room. At the far end was the second set of doors that led into the station. There were no windows in the far doors, so Rhys couldn't tell if there was anyone waiting for them already.

"Captain Griffiths, take your team through first," General Carson said. There wasn't enough room in the airlock for everyone at once.

Rhys didn't need to vocally command his squad. They had all heard the general's order, and all he needed to do was raise his hand and gesture forward. Darkness swallowed him as he stepped inside the airlock. He flicked his comms over to speak to just his half of the assault force. "Last one in, seal the door," he commanded. He positioned himself in front of the control panel by the inner door, ready to open it when the outer door was fully sealed.

Light slowly started to bleed away as the door closed behind them. Rhys kept his right fist clenched, despite the pain that pulsed through his arm. He needed his bullet shield active.

As soon as the door closed, the control panel flashed up bright. Rhys started the process to open the inner door, and immediately pulled out his pistol. His fingers ached as they tightened around the gun. He could barely aim, but he had to be ready. Air hissed into the chamber, and gradually sounds began to reach Rhys's ears. He called out to his squad to prepare. Metal clanked and creaked, and occasional shouts emanated through the still-closed door.

Slowly, light pierced in as the doors began to open. Several shots immediately fired into his shield. The impacts jarred through his arm and made him wince, but he took a couple of steps closer to the opening door, wedging his shield in the gap to prevent any bullets from getting through. The doors kept opening and the gap got wider, but more shields were put in place by him as human and starat alike crouched down by his side.

Advancing forward, Rhys stepped over the metal door as it sunk down into the floor. His left hand trembled as he raised it, but for just a moment it was still enough for a shot to be taken. His finger squeezed the trigger. A sharp stab of pain ripped up his arm, but the human guard still crumpled and fell to the ground.

Rhys didn't want to delay. He needed to get Aaron through the airlock as quickly as possible. "Keep moving forward," he called out to his soldiers. There was only one way to go. They were at the end of a wide corridor of white walls. There was nowhere to retreat to but back inside the airlock. It also meant they could not be surprised by more defenders coming from behind.

The shield wall advanced. Gaps only opened up in it for a few moments as someone took a shot. A dozen guards had come to protect the airlock door, but that had not been enough. It took just a minute before the last of them was dead, or had fled.

Rhys called in Aaron as the airlock door closed behind them. "We're through. We'll hold guard until you get in."

"Understood, Captain," Aaron replied.

Rhys took a moment to compose himself. He gestured to a couple of humans standing close. Together, they advanced towards the end of the corridor, where there was a fork. One path led to the right, one to the left. In both directions, several doors led off the main path. Like the building itself did, the corridors had a gentle curve to them, making it impossible to see all the way down them.

Though Rhys's HUD informed him that the environment was breathable, he kept his helmet securely attached. Not only were his hands too weak to properly remove it, but he also wanted to maintain constant communication with Aaron and General Carson.

With no sign of any defending soldiers in either direction, Rhys returned his pistol to its holster at his hip. He flexed and tensed his fingers as he tried to work some sensation back into his hand. All he felt was a constant needling pain.

Rhys only had to wait a few minutes before the airlock doors opened again. Aaron and General Carson joined him at the head of the corridor.

"Captain Griffiths, you go around to the left. We'll take the right." General Carson said. "Fight through and defend the barracks if you reach it first. If we run into any trouble, we'll let you know."

"Understood, General," Rhys replied. They knew from their earlier surveys of the port plans that the entire facility was built in a ring. Inside the ring was mostly the research laboratories and study rooms. Half of the ring was exposed to the planet's surface, while the remainder disappeared beneath the sheer cliffs that were visible outside the windows. It was there, underground, where they expected to find most of the resistance. There was a small barracks there, near the staff and garrison quarters.

Rhys raised an arm to get the attention of his squad. "Follow me. Move out," he commanded. He took point position at the front as everyone else followed behind. Aaron and General Carson led the remaining half in the opposite direction.

The corridor slowly angled around to the right. Using the windows on his left, Rhys was able to partially see around the slope in the reflections. There was never any movement ahead. It was all still and quiet.

Rhys's eyes kept flicking up to the signs above each door and branching corridor as they passed them. The corridors all led deeper inside the ring and could be ignored. The starat knew that he only had to stay on his current course and he would reach the barracks. He remembered the maps he had seen on the *Freedom*, and the signs showed the way anyway.

Most of the signs named the research labs and some occasional training rooms. One sign almost made Rhys pause in confusion. His ears flicked inside his helmet as he looked up at it again. He wished he had time to investigate why there was a dragon cage on Pluto, but he knew he didn't want to keep General Carson waiting.

The shadow of a movement ahead caught Rhys's attention. He raised his bullet shield. "Be on guard," he called out to the squad behind him. He heard the movement of guns being raised.

A flash of brown fur streaked through the reflection in the windows. A door rattled and slammed.

Rhys held his hand up to call a halt to those behind him. His cautiously scampered forward. His bullet shield was still raised, but his gun was lowered. He opened the first door on his right and let it swing open. He quickly scanned through the room. Desks and chairs were lined up, all facing a projection screen on the far wall. He was about to back out again when he heard a small noise in the back corner. Crouching down, Rhys saw four starats huddled together beneath one of the tables.

"Hold fire. They're starats," Rhys said, ensuring that no one in his squad shot them. He knew they would be scared and defenceless. He holstered his pistol and held out his empty hand towards the nearest of the starats. They all recoiled. He swung his tail around so it would be visible to them.

Ears curled down in confusion and curiosity, but none of them moved any closer.

"I won't hurt you," Rhys said, switching over to broadcast his voice so they could hear him. "Is there somewhere safe you can go?"

One of the starats nodded vigorously. His bright green eyes stared at Rhys. For a moment it felt like those eyes could pierce right through him.

Rhys swallowed. "Good, then get there. Go, and do not get out until it's safe."

The starats needed no further encouragement. They all fled and sprinted left down the corridor. None of Rhys's squadron hindered them as they ran past. By the time Rhys made it back out into the corridor, all four had vanished around the curve. He took a deep breath and pulled out his pistol again. He had done all he could do for the port's starats.

"Let's keep moving," Rhys said. He took a deep breath and continued around the curving corridor.

A new voice came to Rhys's ear as he started to move again. The Silver Fox had patched him through to Rhys, Aaron, and General Carson. "I've been able to get read-only access to the port's computers," the human said, before having to pause for a moment to cough. "I don't think I can get any higher access than that."

"Can you see where their defences are?" Aaron asked. "We've ran into no resistance so far."

"Same here," Rhys confirmed. He didn't mention the starats. There was no need to do so.

The Silver Fox sucked in his breath and muttered quietly beneath his breath. "Ah, yes, I have the security footage. They're all gathered around the barracks. They have a strongly defensible position and are working quickly to reinforce it. I count… fifty humans. Captain Herschel is amongst them."

"Our entry points are still open?" General Carson asked.

"Yours is. Captain Griffiths, you may run into more trouble. I've just seen a detachment of twenty heading your way, leaving thirty defending the captain."

"Shit. Keep me updated if there's any change," Rhys said, before swapping his channel to speak with his squadron. "We have incoming. Defensive positions."

Rhys crouched down behind his bullet shield as he heard the first sounds of running footsteps up ahead. He briefly glanced to his right to see William by his side. The starat's tail thrashed around, but William seemed to be holding his nerve for now. Rhys wanted to share a quick word of encouragement with the starat, but he didn't want to further divide his comms.

His decision to keep comms open was justified, as a fresh warning came through from the Silver Fox. "They have heavy guns, Captain Griffiths."

Glad of the extra couple of seconds to prepare, Rhys was able to tuck himself in tight behind his shield. "Brace close together. Heavy guns," Rhys called out to his squadron. A little further down the corridor, Rhys heard a loud clunk and click.

Moments later, rapid-fire machine gun fire rained down on his shield. Bullets shattered against the shield with so much force that his feet were pushed back against the smoothly tiled floor, but his frame was slight enough that none reached his body.

A few around him weren't so lucky. The human to his left was struck. They recoiled instinctively, which in turn meant their shield was pulled out of position. Bullets ripped into their body, and they fell back against the shields behind them and did not move again.

The rain of bullets stopped as the guards ahead started to reload. It gave Rhys a second to think. They couldn't take much more of that, but they were too far away to rush the guards before they would be able to get the machine gun firing again. He tightened his grip on his bullet shield and closed his eyes.

Subspace came easily to him as he chased that elusive spice scent that he had familiarised himself with. He sunk down into the endless white with an ease that surprised even him. He forced himself to keep his eyes closed and mind clear. Not far ahead, he could see the imprint of the twenty soldiers and the heavy guns they had carried with them. The humans blazed orange against the backdrop of white.

Flashes of red burst out from the guns as the suppression fire began anew. With his senses dulled, Rhys couldn't tell if he was safe behind his shield. He gathered himself together and expanded his reach of influence within subspace. Using the techniques he had learned from Snow, the orange imprint of his arms reached out beyond what he should have been capable of, to wrap around the dark shadow of the machine gun turret.

Warmth spread up his arms. He could feel sweat on his brow and the constant thud of his bullet shield threatened to pull him out of subspace again. He clenched his jaw. Voices shouted in his ear, but he couldn't tell where they were coming from. Then, with a pained yell, Rhys pushed hard.

The starat rose to his feet. Still blind to realspace, he screamed in agony as the heat around his arms increased. It felt like he'd dipped his arms into molten metal. Pain he was used to, but this was something beyond even that. He pushed hard to spin the turret around on the spot. It continued to fire, and this time the bullets ripped through the defenders who had been trying to use it. They were not prepared, and most of them fell before they even realised what was happening. The red glows drifted apart like smoke torn apart by the wind until nothing remained.

Pain ripped Rhys from subspace. He staggered forward a couple of steps to witness the destruction he had caused. All twenty of the detachment had been killed. The mobile turret gun smoked. The metallic base it stood upon was twisted, and it looked ready to collapse.

Rhys slowly turned around. His pistol had fallen from his limp hand, and his bullet shield had returned back to its holster on his wrist. He felt faint and nauseous.

Almost half of his squad had been killed or wounded. He collapsed down to his knees as a starat hurried forward from the devastation.

"Are you alright, Captain Rhys?" William asked. The starat caught him before Rhys could topple over completely.

Rhys shook his head. A metallic taste burned at the back of his throat, and every movement in his hands and arms made him want to scream in agony. His comms were still open to his squad though, and he didn't want to show his weakness to them. He took a deep breath and spoke through gritted teeth. "Go and reinforce Captain Lee and General Carson. Anyone who can, keep moving. The dead can be recovered on our way back."

"You're in no condition to keep moving," William said. Rhys was glad the starat used a private channel. He wanted to protest, but he knew he had no grounds to argue. He couldn't even move his hands at the moment.

"You keep going," Rhys said, switching over to the private channel with William. With his voice no longer being broadcast to the rest of his squadron, he allowed some of the pain to leak into his voice. He whimpered quietly.

"Are you sure?"

Rhys nodded. "I'll go back to the shuttles. Go. Aaron and the general need all the help they can get." He took a deep breath and managed to haul himself up to his feet, with William providing a steadying hand on his hip. "Just... pass me my gun first, please."

William picked up Rhys's fallen pistol and held it out to the other starat. "Can you hold it?"

Rhys almost screamed in pain again as he tensed his fingers around the gun. His skin felt blistered after his subspace efforts. He took a couple of gasping breaths and tried to suppress his nausea. "Go," he croaked out to William.

The starat's hand came away from his hip. William hesitated for a couple of seconds, but then he turned around and chased after the remainder of Rhys's squad.

Rhys's right hand fumbled around the side of his helmet. Numbness was starting to spread beneath his elbows. It diminished the pain, but it made him clumsy as he struggled to patch himself through to the Silver Fox. "I'm hurt and coming back to the shuttles," he panted. He closed his eyes as he took a couple of stumbling steps around the bodies of the fallen. "Are there any enemy soldiers enroute?"

"None, Captain. They're all in the barracks now," came the swift reply from the Silver Fox. "Would you like my assistance in getting back?"

"No," Rhys replied sharply. "You stay there. I'll come to you. Just pass on the latest to Captain Lee and General Carson."

"Will do, Captain."

The line went silent as the Silver Fox cut off their comms. A wave of worry threatened to overwhelm Rhys. Though he had been assured that there were no enemy soldiers around, he still knew he was alone and compromised deep inside an enemy spaceport. He staggered forward, using his shoulder against the inner wall of the curving corridor for support. His vision swam, no matter how many times he closed his eyes and shook his head.

No one tried to communicate with Rhys, but he wasn't surprised by that. They would be fighting to secure entry into the barracks, and they would be too busy with fighting for their lives to worry about an injured starat. The silence inside his helmet was almost oppressive.

Rhys paused and looked up. He had reached the sign that had attracted his attention earlier. He had to squint to make sure he was reading it correctly, but he quickly confirmed that it was directing towards a dragon cage down a side corridor. Rhys quickly made up his mind. He had the chance to see what was going on here, and potentially answer a few of the mysteries surrounding the weapon Snow believed was being developed.

Rhys quickly found what he was looking for. Several of the rooms off the corridor appeared to be computer laboratories, though there was no one present in them. It looked like they had been abandoned in a hurry, probably with most of the workers fleeing to some safe location while the garrison tried to fight off the invading force.

The laboratories weren't what he was interested in though. He stopped outside a door that was different to all the others. This was reinforced with steel and several maglocks. There was a sign above the door. 'Dragon Cage'. Hazard symbols were plastered all over the door. With his hand shaking, Rhys aimed his pistol at the control panel and fired, hoping the destruction of the panel would cause the door to open. The panel exploded in a shower of sparks, but the door remained resolutely locked.

Muttering a curse beneath his breath, Rhys leaned forward against the door. His numb hands rested over the door, and he closed his eyes and followed the scent of spice into subspace. He poured all his focus into the door beneath his hands. Shadows of the wall sprung out of the white. Slowly, Rhys extended his influence down into the hinges of the door. Warmth prickled up his arms again, but it was nothing like the intense burning of before.

Rhys wrenched hard and the door was ripped from its hinges. Immediately a deafening roar emanated from within. Rhys managed to stand his ground, but only just resisted the urge to flee. Nothing charged at him, but the creature inside the large room looked like it wanted to.

The starat didn't know why there was a dragon on Pluto, but he would never fail to recognise the deep red, hexapod. All six legs were tied down with thick wire cables, and its head was held low to the ground by a steel collar that was secured in place with even more cables. The creature was also inside a cage, but that didn't stop it snarling and struggling against its bonds as it saw Rhys.

Up close, Rhys could see even more the resemblance and difference between a Terran crocodile. He could see that it didn't have scales, but instead a leathery type of thick skin. Its legs were short and squat, keeping the dragon's belly low to the ground. Each of the four claws on its front and rear feet were bigger than Rhys's fist, though the middle legs had five smaller digits, with one that looked akin to a grasping thumb. The long snout of the creature was filled with more sharp, razor-like teeth than Rhys cared to look at.

Rhys slowly approached the cage and placed his hand on one of the bars, far enough away from the creature's teeth that the dragon wouldn't be able to reach him. An idea started to form in his head.

Rhys called out to the Silver Fox. "Is there a third way into the barracks through the middle of the ring?"

"Uh, affirm. From your current position it's left, and then first left. Corridor runs straight to the barracks via a third entrance," the Silver Fox replied. Rhys could hear the questions biting at the human's tongue, but they remained unasked, and Rhys kept them unanswered.

Rhys slowly circled around the dragon's cage as he switched his comms to link up with Aaron. "Are you able to get somewhere safe? You may need to fall back a small way and barricade the doors to the barracks if possible."

"It's feasible, why?" Aaron replied shortly afterwards. He sounded nervous, and Rhys could hear gunshots come through the speakers.

"Because I'm about to do something very stupid and release a captive dragon," Rhys said.

A stunned silence came across the speakers for a few seconds. Aaron laughed nervously. "Well, I sure as shit don't have a better idea. They've got more than thirty men, that's for sure. Got any way to control it?"

"They're sensitive to subspace. I think I can point it in the right direction, but beyond that, no. Not really," Rhys replied. He could remember Amy talking about subspace lures being used to control the dragons. He closed his eyes for a moment and felt the warm flicker of subspace energy radiating out from the creature beside him. He could feel anger and rage like a monstrous storm that was waiting to be unleashed. Rhys just had to be careful it wasn't unleashed upon himself.

"I'll let the general and your team know," Aaron said, distracting Rhys from the anger emanating from the dragon for a moment. A small pause followed. "Don't get yourself killed, Rhys."

"Only if you don't, too," Rhys replied. He tried to laugh, but it only sounded like a pained whimper to his ears. "I'll let you know when I'm about to release it."

Rhys held his numbed hands out to press against the bars of the cage. The dragon snapped out at him, but its restraints meant it couldn't reach the starat. He couldn't smell the dragon inside his helmet, but as he closed his eyes he was overwhelmed by the sudden scent of spice. He didn't sink into subspace so much as it felt like he was dragged under. He was met by a powerful imprint of red and orange, blazing with a ferocious intensity. The dragon was watching him.

Staying in subspace, Rhys slowly moved his arms around. The dragon watched him intently. Its eyes watched him constantly. Eyes that reminded him of the entities. Rhys suppressed a shudder.

Rhys tried to remember what Amy had told him about the dragons. They hunted with subspace, and they reacted to lures cast. If that was how they hunted, then Rhys would need to give the creature something to chase. He pulled a ball of subspace energy towards him.

Through his distant ears, he heard the dragon thrash around in its cage.

Lifting the glowing ball of energy up, Rhys then pushed it away.

The dragon ripped so hard at its bonds that Rhys pulled himself from subspace in a panic. The creature had not escaped, but it had reacted violently at the summoned energy Rhys had been able to manipulate.

A nervous grin came to Rhys's lips. He now had a way he could point the dragon in the right direction. All he had to do now was free the dragon from its bonds.

The dragon was secured down with six metallic cuffs, one around each limb. The cuffs were secured to the side of the cage by thick bars of metal. At the anchor points was an electronic lock.

Keeping his eye on the dragon, Rhys slowly unlocked each of the cuffs. One by one, the cuffs fell from the dragon's limbs, but the creature remained perfectly still. One golden eye stared at Rhys the entire time. The bars of the cages suddenly felt very flimsy to Rhys.

"Are you safe?" Rhys asked Aaron. He didn't want to turn his back on the dragon, so he took a couple of steps back towards the computer terminals on the back wall of the small laboratory.

"About as safe as we can be," came the quick reply. "We're ready to bar the doors on your word."

"Alright. One dragon incoming," Rhys said. He took a deep breath and reached forward to pull open the locks on the cage. The front door opened with a creak of partially rusted hinges, and immediately Rhys plunged his mind into subspace. The radiance of the dragon almost blinded him again. Once more, he bundled up a ball of subspace, but this time he had to act quickly. He didn't want the creature to attack him. He pushed the lure away, aiming it towards the distant shadows of the humans in the barracks, making sure that the creature would follow down the empty middle path. He could see the dragon react to it with a burst of red emotion, and a low growl reached his ears.

Rhys ripped himself out of subspace in time to see the lithe movements of a predator start to prowl out of its cage. The sharp claws of its forelegs scraped across the floor as it moved slowly. At first Rhys didn't think the dragon had taken to the attempted lure. Its eyes tracked down towards the corridors, but it stayed tensed and still. Its nostrils flared as it took in the scents around it, before it suddenly exploded with motion. Its middle legs launched it from the cage, and it smashed through the open doorway.

The dragon appeared to ignore Rhys entirely, but the starat was not prepared for the long, thick tail as it smashed against his chest. He was thrown back, crashing helmet-first against the wall with so much force he could see the visor splinter and crack. His neck and shoulders immediately started to hurt as he sunk down to the ground, but he couldn't feel any serious damage done to his body. It was only another new pain to deal with, on top of everything else.

The same couldn't be said for his helmet. The HUD flickered across the cracked screen. Several error messages flashed up, warning him that the structural integrity had failed, and was no longer airtight to his surroundings.

"Dammit," Rhys muttered. He winced as he got up to his knees. His shoulders were in pain, and a deep ache had started to spread down his arms again, but he could still move them. Just. He tried to call in Aaron, hoping that his communicator was still working after the impact. "The dragon is incoming. Be careful."

"Is everything alright?" Aaron replied. His voice was slightly crackled and distorted through the damaged speaker, but otherwise the helmet still seemed to be communicated just fine. "You sound hurt."

"I'm fine. Just got hit by its tail. Helmet is damaged," Rhys replied. He gently patted his hand over the visor. He wasn't sure if it would hold for long. In the port, there were no problems. There was plenty of air inside, but he didn't know how he would be able to get across the small vacuum to the shuttle.

A small silence followed from Aaron, before his voice crackled through in awed tones. "Holy shit, that thing is fierce," the human said. "I'm glad you warned us before you released it. I don't think they were expecting it."

Rhys grinned weakly as he staggered to his feet. He was about to step out of the ruined door, before something caught his eye on the desk nearby. One of the computer terminals was still on, clearly where someone had been working before the attack had begun. Rhys frowned. On the screen was displayed a map of Alpha Centauri.

Rhys approached the terminal cautiously. In the corner of the screen was a symbol he had seen a few times over the last few months, but it didn't have anything to do with Terra or the empire. It was one he had seen on Centaura. A cross of golden swords. The fur prickled up his back as he clicked through a few of the images.

Nothing made sense. That was the symbol of the Inquisition, he was sure of it. Major-General Ulrich had warned him that they might try to infiltrate the mission somehow, but it seemed like they had already been here. His tail tucked in close to his body as he forced his aching arms to reach out and flick through some of the screens. He felt like he had been plunged in icy water.

Snow had been right. They were developing plans for a subspace weapon, but this was beyond his wildest nightmares. This was a technology that would destroy billions of lives. His vision blurred as he breathed quickly. How much did Snow and Amy know? He wasn't sure if he could trust them with this information, but Fleet-Admiral Bosler needed to be warned.

Rhys found a data stick beside the computer. His hands fumbled as he connected it to the computer. He searched for as much information as he could find, and he transferred it all to the data stick. He then tried to wipe everything from the network as he progressed, including all the back-ups he managed to discover. He could only hope that something critical was removed, and that it would take time for the Inquisition to recover it. When he was done, he slipped the data stick into one of the pockets of his suit. His heart hammered in his chest, no longer knowing what to believe. He felt like he was in a daze as he slowly approached the door.

He was quickly ripped from his mental daze as an alarm started to blare. A hissing sound started to permeate the room.

"Air... venting... hurry..." The Silver Fox's voice broke up as the human tried to speak across an open channel.

General Caron's voice followed just after. "They're... air... kill... dragon."

Rhys thumped the side of his helmet, trying to get the speakers to work again.

Aaron's voice came next, quieter and across a private channel. "Rhys... you safe with... helmet?"

Sudden urgency gave energy to Rhys's legs. He had no choice but to get to the shuttles and hope that his visor remained intact for long enough to get across the small vacuum. "No. No I'm not. Stay where you are. Finish the mission. Stay with General Carson. I'll do my best to get to safety." He didn't know how much of his message got through.

The first voice came across his speakers again. "I'm on... way, Captain Rhys."

"Stay where you are, Emile," Rhys barked back, but he got no response from the human.

Swearing beneath his breath, Rhys tried to remember exactly which way it was to the shuttles. He had to get out to the main corridor first. Once he got through to the airlock, he could sit in safety there until a replacement helmet was found for him. All the while he could hear the hissing of venting air, gradually getting quieter as there was less and less air left to carry the sound. Rhys's helmet continued to fill with air from the supply on his back as he breathed, but there was an ever-increasing flow of it leaking out through the cracks in his visor. And those cracks were starting to spread. His HUD warned him of the depleting air in his supply, and in the atmosphere around him.

As less air filled the void around him, the pressure difference between the inside of his helmet and the environment became more extreme. Small cracks threaded across his vision as his breathing became more and more difficult.

Rhys's vision swam, and he staggered to the side, his shoulder crashing against the wall. He squinted up to the signs on the walls, but he couldn't read them. They were blurred and hidden behind the lattice of cracks on his visor.

He wasn't going to be able to make it.

His lungs burned for air, but each time he tried to breathe in he couldn't get enough. Still he moved on, forcing his aching legs to carry him further.

The corridor never seemed to end. Rhys was half-convinced he had gone too far, and that he would run into Aaron and the general as they struggled to fight off the port's garrison. He recognised nothing he saw. Still, he staggered on. He knew it was hopeless. He knew he didn't have enough air.

Rhys dropped to his knees.

A shadow passed in front of him.

Brief pressure was applied around his neck, before his ruined helmet was removed entirely. For a short moment, Rhys's head was left entirely exposed to the near-vacuum. He choked and wheezed silently, his eyes squeezed closed.

Then there was air again. A new helmet had been clipped onto Rhys's suit, and he could breathe again. The first few lungfuls of air were beautiful, and Rhys drank them in with relish. Then he opened his eyes to see his saviour.

It took Rhys a few seconds for his vision to clear. Everything was still blurred, but he managed to make out the shape of the Silver Fox in front of him. The human smiled. He wore no helmet.

"No..." Rhys croaked. He struggled with the clasp on the back of his helmet, desperate to remove it again. If they shared the helmet, they might have enough air to get back to the shuttle...

Rhys's fingers couldn't undo the clasp. He was too weak even for that. Tears sprung to his eyes as the Silver Fox reached out to push Rhys's hands down. The human easily overpowered him, no matter how hard Rhys tried to struggle.

The human didn't say anything. He couldn't say anything. There was sadness in his eyes, but a soft smile on his lips. He swayed and slumped forward against the starat.

Rhys's vision had started to clear. He saw that he was just a couple of minutes from the airlock. He didn't know how he had stumbled so far. Rhys picked the Silver Fox up and staggered forward. Every muscle in his arms screamed in protest as he struggled to carry the human. The Silver Fox was thin and frail, and Pluto's light gravity helped, but Rhys's arms could still barely lift him. He couldn't feel the human moving at all, but he was damned if he was going to give up now. The broken helmet fell to the floor as it dropped from the Silver Fox's limp fingers.

The short walk through the airlock was agony for Rhys, mentally and physically. His mind screamed in anguish as he thought of the Silver Fox in his hands, the lifeless and still body sacrificed simply so he could have air. He thought of the promise he had made to Leandro, and how his carelessness had broken that.

By the time Rhys made it back to the shuttle, his vision was blurred with tears again. The airlock had been so slow, and the shuttle filled with air at a glacial pace. He could barely see anything as the little green light on his visor lit up. On Emile's visor. There was air again, and he carefully lowered the Silver Fox's body down to the floor. There was no rise and fall of the human's chest, and small drops of moisture had crystallised on his exposed skin.

Rhys frantically beat down on Emile's chest, desperately trying to perform some life-saving CPR, but without the ability to remove his helmet, Rhys lacked the chance to do the most crucial part. He couldn't provide Emile with any air. His hands felt like they were about to shatter, but still he tried even though he knew hope had faded. The human had been without air for too long.

"Why would you do that?" Rhys whimpered to himself. The human couldn't answer him, but Rhys thought he knew the answer anyway.

The pirate had been dying. He had been dying from the moment he had been rescued from Charon. Leandro had rescued him, but they could only have had a few last precious weeks together. The human had died on his terms, rather than waiting for the ravages of torture and age bring him down.

But Rhys still wept and held the lifeless body close. It all felt so pointless. His mind kept replaying everything over, trying to work out how he could have saved Leandro, but it all kept coming back to his hands. If he had been able to remove his helmet and share their air, they might have made it.

Dejected, Rhys let the shuttle vent air again. He knew he needed to keep the ramp open so the rest of the soldiers could return quickly. He watched as the barren vista of Pluto began to emerge once more. He still held Emile's hand in his own, but the human's fingers were slack and loose. His head thumped back against the metallic wall. He had lost lives before. People had sacrificed their lives for him before. Scott had died for him less than two months earlier. But Rhys had been in too much pain then for the agony of loss to overwhelm him. Now, he felt it all.

A loud, urgent voice spoke desperately in his ear.

"Rhys? Emile? Are either of you there?"

Rhys groaned and held his helmet in his hands. He didn't want to speak with Aaron, or anyone else, but he knew he had to. He sniffed and tried to bring an end to the tears that trickled through his fur.

"I'm here, Aaron."

"Oh, thank goodness. I was worried... you're coming through on Emile's channel?"

Rhys nodded, automatically responding with a gesture even though Aaron couldn't see him. "Yeah. He... he gave it to me."

"Is he alright?" Aaron asked. Rhys didn't respond. He couldn't respond. He didn't trust his voice at all, as though saying the words might somehow make it more real than the still body lying beside him. The silence was all Aaron seemed to need. "Shit, I'm sorry Rhys. We'll be back shortly, just as soon as we collect the fallen. We have what we need here. Your dragon did a lot of damage, but we were able to get Captain Herschel. Don't know where the beast went though."

Rhys still didn't reply. Instead he bowed his head and draped his hands across his lap. The dragon had done a lot of damage, but most importantly it had been what had cracked Rhys's visor. He sighed and shook his head. Hindsight was a wonderful thing, but it couldn't change any of his actions now.

Aaron was true to his word. Only a few minutes passed before the station's airlock doors opened. Aaron was the first to come through. The human crouched down next to Rhys and didn't say anything at all, just resting his hand on Rhys's shoulder. It was all Rhys needed. He didn't want any words, as he knew they wouldn't make things better.

The time couldn't last though. "We should hurry. You don't want to be alone though. Come up with me, and we can talk things through," Aaron said. He held out his hand to help Rhys up to his feet.

Rhys nodded, suppressing a whimper as Aaron's hand tightened around his. "Have you let Chekolin know we're coming back?"

"He's already expecting us," Aaron said. He pulled on Rhys's hand to get him to move away from the first shuttle. "Go an take a seat. I'll look after things and run a head count. Don't want to leave anyone behind."

Rhys nodded. "Thanks, Aaron."

Aaron patted Rhys on the back before the starat stepped back down onto the surface of the dwarf planet. He stood back out in the cold vacuum with little more than the glimmer of starlight to illuminate their surroundings. A few torches swung back and forth between the two shuttles.

There was a starat waiting for him before he reached the second shuttle. Snow held out her hand to take hold of Rhys's.

"I'm sorry to hear about the old one," Snow said. She walked beside Rhys as they approached the other shuttle. "He lived a good life."

"He definitely did. I'm glad he got a few more weeks of freedom," Rhys replied sombrely. He sighed softly and looked up to the glorious sight of the stars arcing across the sky, with only Charon to block them out. His ears twitched inside the tight confines of his helmet. There was still something that bothered him about the entire situation. He glanced across to Snow. "Who runs this place? I saw a few things that don't make sense."

"Terra, of course. Why else would we be here?" Snow replied quickly. She didn't look across to Rhys.

"Then why was there a dragon here? Why did I see a symbol on their computers that I'd only ever seen on Centaura? I'm sure it belongs to the Inquisition," Rhys said, pressing her a little further. He normally wouldn't have asked such questions, but the grief he felt meant he had to understand what the Silver Fox's death had been in aid of.

This time Snow did look across to Rhys, only for a moment. She didn't answer at first as they reached the shuttle. The ramp was already down, and the two starats stepped up onto it. Snow held out her hand to stop Rhys going inside the shuttle and taking a seat. Almost all the seats were already taken, with just half a dozen left empty. One human had his arms and legs bound as he was pushed down into one of the seats. That had to be Captain Herschel. By his side was a starat, which Rhys soon recognised as William.

Rhys could see Snow's shoulders drop slightly. "You are right about the Inquisition," the starat said. She kept her hand on Rhys's chest and pushed him back slightly, so he had nowhere to back up to without falling out of the shuttle. "They run this place, with the Vatican. The government on Centaura doesn't strictly condone the Inquisition, but nor do they do enough to condemn them."

"I saw what they were planning on doing," Rhys said. He suppressed a shiver of fear at the thought. "They were researching how to use subspace as a weapon in ways that go beyond anything you've taught me. They could wipe out millions in an instant if they perfected it. That's the weapon you were after, wasn't it?"

"You think that's not needed?" Snow asked. Her voice took on a harsh tone that Rhys had never heard before.

"Of course not. They would wipe out innocent lives indiscriminately," Rhys retorted. He raised his voice a little, but no one else around would be able to hear their conversation. Their words were locked inside their helmets, with only the private connection between them allowing the two starats to speak.

"Terra is a disease, and it needs to be cleansed. I thought you understood that, Rhys," Snow said softly. Her hand pressed firmer against Rhys's chest, and his attempts to push her away failed.

Rhys fell silent for a moment as the remaining humans came on board. Aaron paused for a moment as he looked down to Rhys, but he continued on to take a seat. The one next to him remained empty, but Snow again prevented Rhys from getting on to the shuttle. He looked back up to Snow. "You think Emile deserved to die? He was innocent in all of this. Millions of lives like his would be snuffed out without any chance to fight back. That isn't fair or just."

"Life isn't fair or just, let alone war," Snow growled. She finally released Rhys and turned around.

"But it doesn't matter anyway, does it? That's what we came here to do, wasn't it? To stop them developing and using this tech? Amy isn't going to use this, is she? General Carson stayed behind so they can't use it either?" Rhys asked. There was a rumble as the shuttle's engines were ignited, but the access ramp remained open. A hazard light flashed by Rhys's foot as the door tried to close, but the proximity sensors kept it open.

Snow slowly turned around again. She shook her head slightly. "No, Rhys. That wasn't why we were here. We were here because they refused to share or use that tech. We plan on using it."

Rhys felt numb, and he took half a step back so he stood over the hinge between the shuttle floor and the ramp, which remained lowered even as the craft started to rise. At the front of the shuttle, Rhys could just about make out Aaron standing up, and his voice just about managed to cut through the haze of his thoughts.

"Get that door closed and sit down," the human barked.

Rhys numbly nodded his head as he twisted his back so he could press the buttons to manually close the ramp. He almost fell back as the shuttle started to accelerate, but he was able to grab hold of a support handle in time. Beneath his feet, he could feel the floor start to move as the ramp began to close.

"Do you really feel there are innocent people in the empire, Rhys?" Snow asked.

"I do, yes. There are starats who need to be freed, and humans there who are willing to help," Rhys replied, shifting his feet to move off the closing ramp.

"You're wrong. They're all corrupted, every last one of them. The poison of the Vatican has seeped into their every thought. They must be eradicated, for the good of all of us in Centaura," Snow said. Her voice remained calm, even as her hand continued to press at Rhys's chest.

Rhys tried to step forward, but as he did so he felt something slam against his chest. Nothing was there, but it winded him as thoroughly as the dragon's tail. He doubled over, before a second concussive blast pushed him backwards. Before he had chance to brace himself, he found himself rolling back.

The gap between ramp and shuttle still looked so big, and Rhys couldn't stop his slide down towards it.

Someone cried out in fear. Aware that something was happening, both William and Aaron jumped up from their seats. Snow flung out one hand towards Rhys again, but she was distracted as William barrelled into her.

With a desperate lunge, Rhys managed to grab hold of the ramp as he slipped past it. His weak fingers clung on desperately. His legs were buffeted by wind as the shuttle started to speed through the thin atmosphere of Pluto.

Rhys desperately tried to haul himself up, but the ramp was still rising, ready to seal tight and close off the inside of the shuttle from the growing vacuum around the craft. He had seconds left...

Through the narrow gap left, Rhys could see Aaron and William wrestle with Snow. For a brief moment he could see into the albino's helmet. Her eyes burned red as another shockwave rippled through subspace.

The shuttle rattled and shook. Aaron and William slumped to the side. Rhys's fingers slipped.

With a scream of anguish that only he could hear, Rhys fell.